**PRAISE FOR THI**

IN

"Brilliantly plotted original
combining the historical with the futuristic. It's a real edge-of-the-seat read, genuinely hard to put down." – Sue Cook

CARINA

"This is a fabulous thriller that cracks along at a great pace and just doesn't let up from start to finish." – Discovering Diamonds Reviews

PERFIDITAS

"Alison Morton has built a fascinating, exotic world! Carina's a bright, sassy detective with a winning dry sense of humour. The plot is pretty snappy too!" – Simon Scarrow

SUCCESSIO

"I thoroughly enjoyed this classy thriller, the third in Morton's epic series set in Roma Nova." – Caroline Sanderson in The Bookseller

AURELIA

"AURELIA explores a 1960s that is at once familiar and utterly different – a brilliant page turner that will keep you gripped from first page to last. Highly recommended." – Russell Whitfield

INSURRECTIO

"INSURRECTIO – a taut, fast-paced thriller. I enjoyed it enormously. Rome, guns and rebellion. Darkly gripping stuff." – Conn Iggulden

RETALIO

"RETALIO is a terrific concept engendering passion, love and loyalty. I actually cheered aloud." – J J Marsh

ROMA NOVA EXTRA

"One of the reasons I am enthralled with the Roma Nova series is the concept of the whole thing." – Helen Hollick, Vine Voice

**THE ROMA NOVA THRILLERS**

The Carina Mitela adventures
INCEPTIO
CARINA (novella)
PERFIDITAS
SUCCESSIO

The Aurelia Mitela adventures
AURELIA
INSURRECTIO
RETALIO

ROMA NOVA EXTRA (Short stories)

---

**ABOUT THE AUTHOR**

A 'Roman nut' since age 11, Alison Morton has clambered over much of Roman Europe; she continues to be fascinated by that complex, powerful and value driven civilisation.

Armed with an MA in history, six years' military service and a love of thrillers, she explores via her Roma Nova novels the 'what if' idea of a modern Roman society run by strong women.

Alison lives in France with her husband, cultivates a Roman herb garden and drinks wine.

Find out more at alison-morton.com, follow her on Twitter @alison_morton and Facebook (AlisonMortonAuthor)

# · AURELIA ·

ALISON MORTON

Published in 2018 by Pulcheria Press


ISBN 9791097310165

## DRAMATIS PERSONAE

**Family**
Aurelia Mitela – Major, Praetorian Guard Special Forces (PGSF)
Felicia Mitela – Aurelia's mother, head of the Mitela family
Marina Mitela – Aurelia's young daughter

**Household**
Milo – Steward of Domus Mitelarum

**Tella family**
Domitia Tella – Head of the Tella family
Caius Tellus – Domitia's great nephew
Quintus Tellus – Caius's brother

**Military**
Numerus – Senior Centurion, PGSF
Volusenia – Lieutenant, PGSF
Fabia – Optio, PGSF, Berlin
Licinia – Captain, PGSF, Vienna
Mercuria – Guard, PGSF

**Government**
Tertullius Plico – Imperial Secretary, External Security Affairs

**Palace**
Justina Apulia – Imperatrix, ruler of Roma Nova
Severina Apulia – Justina's daughter, mother of Julian
Julianus Apulius – 'Julian', Severina's son
Aemilia – Nursery maid

**Berlin**
Joachim von und zu der Havel/Huber – 'Achim', Aurelia's cousin and Germanic Federal Police inspector
Scholz – Detective working for Joachim
Hahn – Detective working for Joachim
Manfred Grosschenk – A businessman
Fischer – One of Grosschenk's employees
Ernst Beck – One of Grosschenk's employees
Galba – Roma Nova legation lawyer
Magda – Prisoner 'boss'
Charlotte Halversen – Prison social worker

**Vienna**
Valeria Festa – Local manager of the Argentaria Prima bank
David Soane – Local manager of Soane's, an English private bank

**Other**
Miklós Farkas – A suspected smuggler
Prisca Monticola – Head of a silver extraction and processing company

# PART I

# DUTY

# 1

I left my side arm in the safe box in the vestibule and walked on past the marble and plaster *imagines*, the painted statues and busts of Mitela ancestors from the gods knew how many hundreds of years. Only the under-steward was allowed to dust them; I'd never been permitted to touch them as a child.

My all-terrain boots made soft squelching sounds as I crossed the marble floor. This was the last private time I'd share with my mother and daughter for three weeks. A glance at my watch confirmed I had a precious hour.

Through the double doors, the atrium rose up for three storeys. Light from the late spring sun beat down through the central glass roof onto luxuriant green planting at the centre of the room like rays from an intense spotlight. My mother disliked the vastness of the atrium and had partitioned a part of it off with tall bookcases, to make a cosier area, she said. Unfortunately, because of the almost complete square of tall units with only a body-width entrance at the far corner, and the way the shelving inside was arranged, you couldn't see who was there until you were on top of them. I'd been trapped by some of my mother's tea-drinking cronies more than once.

My mother, sitting on her favourite chintz sofa facing the entrance, looked up as I appeared in the gap. Two tiny creases on her forehead vanished when she stood and walked towards me with her arms extended. She greeted me with an over-bright smile.

'Aurelia, darling.'

I bent and kissed her cheek in a formal salute then looked over her shoulder to where my daughter, Marina, was sitting quietly on the sofa. She was twisting her hands together and glancing in as many different directions as she could.

'Marina, whatever is the matter, sweetheart?' I strode over and crouched down by her. She stretched her hand out to grab mine and pointed at the chair in the far corner.

Caius Tellus.

Hades in Pluto.

'Aurelia, how lovely to see you,' he said in a warm, urbane voice.

Taller than his brother Quintus who nearly topped two metres, Caius was well built without being overweight. Sitting at his ease, one leg crossed over the other, he ran his eyes over my face and body. His hazel eyes shone and his smile was wide, showing a glimpse of over-white teeth through generous lips. Nothing in his tanned face with classic cheekbones would repel you on the surface. Others considered him very good-looking with almost film star glamour and charm. I knew better what kind of creature lay underneath.

Even as a kid he'd had a vicious streak; I'd never forget his hand clamping my neck, forcing my face down into the scullery drain, him saying he'd drown me in filth. I'd retched and retched at the smell of animal blood, the grease and dirty water. In the end, the cook had found us and hauled Caius off. I'd crouched there sweating and trembling; only horseplay, Caius said and laughed. The cook had given him a hard look, but the other servants were won over by Caius's boyish smile. But when he'd stuck his hand up my skirt and tried to force me at Aquilia's emancipation party, I'd kneed him in the groin so hard he couldn't stand up for hours. I'd been in the military cadets for a year by then. But the others, woozy from wine and good spirits, gave him more sympathy as he writhed around on the terrace, playing to the audience.

After I joined the Guard at eighteen, I hardly saw him except at formal Twelve Families events and even there, he'd smarm his way to the head of the food queues or make a beeline for the most vulnerable in the room, be it male or female. He was a taker in life, a callous one. I loathed him with all my heart and soul.

I stood up, shielding Marina behind me.

'Dear me,' he said, 'are you off playing soldiers again?'

I should have been given top marks for not slapping the smirk off his face.

'Caius,' I said, keeping my voice as cool as possible. 'We're having a private family lunch before I go on an extended operation, so I hope you'll excuse us.'

My mother cast a pleading look at me. I closed my eyes for a second. She'd invited him to join us. How could she have?

I chewed my food slowly to try to reduce my tension. I was irritated Mama had chosen the breakfast room – a private family place – to eat in rather than the formal dining room. The servants flitted in and out with the food, and I said very little except to Marina, who ate very little.

'Aurelia, you're quieter than usual. I hope nothing's wrong?' my mother said too cheerfully.

Before I could answer, Caius intervened. 'She does look a little pale. Don't you worry, Felicia, that she takes on too much sometimes?' He tilted his head sideways and pasted a concerned expression onto his face.

I speared a piece of pork and sawed through it like a barbarian, scraping the plate glaze below. I knew Caius was trying to make me rise to his bait, but I refused to play. At least my work as a Praetorian soldier was serving the state. He served himself with his gambling and whoring. He put in just enough hours at the charity committees he nominally sat on to appear to be contributing to Roma Novan life.

My mother smiled at him. 'Yes, I do wonder. She was so exhausted after that last exercise abroad. You really understand, don't you, Caius?'

He extended his hand and grasped hers and smiled. I was nearly sick.

'"She" wasn't exhausted,' I cut across. 'It was food poisoning, as you know very well, Mama. And it was all over within thirty-six hours.'

Caius smiled at me this time, but it didn't reach his eyes. 'Your mother's right, you know. You have a duty to look after your rather, er, small family.'

I stood up and threw my napkin on the table.

'The day I need you to teach me my duty doesn't exist, Caius. Keep your nose out of my family affairs.' I held my hand out to Marina, but fixed my gaze on my mother's face. 'I'm sure Nonna will allow you to leave the table now, Marina. We're going for a walk outside in the fresh air.'

My mother gave a brief nod. I caught Caius's second smirk out of the corner of my eye. One of these days…

Marina and I crossed the terrace and wound through the formal parterres and reached the swings at the side.

'Nonna wants me to be friends with Caius Tellus,' she said, 'but I don't like him. He makes me feel funny.' I hugged her to me. She was so fragile; fine red-brown hair and a delicate face, light brown eyes like a frightened rabbit, not the bright Mitela blue like mine and my mother's. Never robust, Marina had coughed and wheezed her way through infancy, floored by the least infection.

My heart constricted as I recalled yet again that terrible day when she was just two. I'd rushed back, heart pounding, from the training ground. Still in my dusty green and brown combats, I'd stared down at my daughter; white, inanimate. I'd dropped to my knees and touched her forehead. Damp, cold, sweating. Her hand was equally chill. The nurse had wrapped her in light wool blankets and bonnet to prevent body heat loss and a drip line ran from her nostril up to a suspended plastic bag on a steel stand. I was a major in the Praetorian Guard and commanded some of the toughest soldiers in Roma Nova with the most modern weaponry on the entire planet, but I'd never felt more powerless.

Now I had to protect her against a subtler virus.

'You don't have to be friends with anybody you don't want to, whatever anybody says – me and Nonna included.'

'But Nonna said it was important. I have to get used to it for when he comes to live in our house.'

I stared at Marina. What in Hades was my mother hatching up now? All I could hear was an angry buzz in my head, soaring to deafening levels. Marina's face tightened. She dropped my hand and shrank back.

'It's all right, darling. I'm sorry, I didn't mean to scare you.' I swallowed hard. 'I was a bit surprised, that's all.' I delayed, struggling to keep my temper and not frighten my soft child. 'When did Nonna say that?'

'Before lunch.' She dropped her gaze to the ground.

I crouched down in front of her and touched her cheek.

'Look at me, Marina. I promise you here and now that I will never be friends with Caius Tellus. He will not come and live with me. If Nonna invites him, you and I will go and live on the farm together.'

She lifted her head, two tiny wet streaks on her cheeks.

'Cross your heart?'

'And hope to die in the arena.'

Caius was drinking coffee with my mother when I returned alone to the atrium. He gave a knowing little smile when I requested an urgent private word with my mother. We walked in silence to an unused office at the back of the house. Its virtue was that it was part of the ancient building and had very thick walls.

'What the hell are you playing at?' I said. 'And how in Hades do you think you have the right to pressure my five-year-old child to cosy up to that slimy bastard Caius?'

I stood a body-length away from my mother, further than my fists could reach.

'Don't use your rough soldier's language with me, my girl. I've dropped enough hints over the past year, but you've been ignoring them. You need another child. As insurance.'

'I hope you're not serious, Mama.'

'You have responsibilities. House Mitela needs heirs and Marina isn't strong.'

I stared at her for a full minute.

'I'm twenty-eight – not exactly past it,' I said. 'And I have two male cousins in the first degree.'

'Neither of whom could inherit except by imperial decree. That hasn't happened to the Mitelae yet. And Imperatrix Justina would be hard to persuade on this. Take my word for it.'

'She can't insist.'

'No, but she'd speak about duty and history and make you feel like a shirker.'

'For Juno's sake, it's the nineteen sixties. I'm not a breeding filly.'

'No, but you are the heir to the senior of the Twelve Families whose sworn duty is to support the Apulian imperatrix and the continued existence of Roma Nova. Caius is an ideal prospect, personable and intelligent. He belongs to a good family that has been allied to ours for over fifteen hundred years.'

'Don't hide behind history, Mama. I know what you're up to and the answer's no. Not a hope. Ever.'

'What's wrong with him? I know you didn't get on very well with him as children, but you've grown out that awkward stage. You're an adult now. Old Countess Tella would be pleased for an alliance with our family.'

No doubt Caius's great-aunt would be thrilled. I was the bait for every other one of the Twelve. But I would choose my partner myself, not submit to some old girls' cosy arrangement. I'd already had the dubious pleasure of one unsatisfactory companion in Marina's father; I didn't want a second one.

'If you don't get it, Mama, I don't know where to start. Can't you see how manipulative Caius is? He's flashed his teeth at you, said a few smarmy phrases to lure you onto his side. Now he has you trying to finesse Marina.' I snorted. 'Look at his eyes sometime when he's not trying to charm you. He's mean and cruel. Ask his brother Quintus.' I glanced at my watch. 'I have to go now.'

'Won't you even talk to him?'

'No. My mind's made up. There is no more discussion.'

'Well, have a think about it while you're away.'

She made it sound like a holiday. We'd be freezing our arses off on a snow-covered mountain, grabbing three to four hours' sleep, either bored out of our minds or targeted by tough criminals and snipers.

'We'll talk properly when I'm back, if you insist. But I don't want Caius Tellus within fifty metres of Marina while I'm away. A hundred, preferably. Promise me that.'

Her eyes dropped under my intense stare.

'Do you promise?'

'Don't be so angry, Aurelia. I'll do as you ask. But try to calm down and think logically. You need more heirs.'

For a clever woman, my mother was sometimes so simple. I tamped down the heat of anger rushing through my body.

'Let me assure you, Mama, that even if Caius was the last man on earth, I'd rather kill myself than let him touch me.'

# 2

'One more run should do it,' I said. 'Get the troops formed up, Senior Centurion Numerus, if you please.' I squeezed my gloved hands together hard and released them in the hope of stimulating some warmth in my fingers. And I felt the first touches of sleet on my face as I looked round the grey walls of the mountain valley. At least we'd been warm overnight in the winter hut and had stomachs full of hot field rations. But despite our mountain gear with fur-lined hoods and dark goggles protecting against the high-altitude sunlight, the icy wind found exposed skin and froze it numb.

Thank the gods this was our only permeable frontier, but curse them it was this high and cold. We were nominally at peace with all other nations around us, although the Reds in the East continually attempted to infiltrate. As a tiny country wedged in between the Italian Federation to the south-west and New Austria to the north, we were vulnerable. Our vigilance and electronic barriers were our joint protection. For my money, I would have kept a watchful eye on the Prussians to the north, but I was a mere soldier.

Numerus saluted and beckoned his NCOs over to receive their orders and assemble the patrol groups. Gamma Troop had set off straight after breakfast back to base with a truckload of prisoners, mainly smugglers, but also a couple of Balkanites looking for a better life. Minutes later, thirty-six soldiers stood in three groups of four by three deep in the lee of the hut. None of them showed any reaction to the cruel weather. Numerus's runner, Mercuria, a petite young woman lost in the folds of her winter uniform parka, handed me the deployment list.

We moved out at 09.00 with full backpacks, forty-eight more hours on the mountainside in front of us. Beta and Delta were west and east respectively of my Alpha Troop. An hour later, with snow falling lightly, we were creeping along behind the ridge overlooking the track we'd patrolled five days ago when I heard a thud below.

*'Scheiß Schnee!'*

*'Halt's Maul,'* hissed another voice.

Germanic, standard, a faint Prussian twang. I hadn't heard it for years.

I brought my hand across in an abrupt cut-off gesture. We stopped dead. What in Hades were they were doing up here on one of the highest, and most treacherous passes?

I signalled Numerus to take four troops to head them off. The senior *optio* I signalled to take her group up to the high point above the mountain pass the two were heading for. I would spring the trap from behind. Motionless, we listened to their heavy footsteps, smashing down on the crisp snow as they approached. When we saw the plumes from their breath, we pounced.

In the end, it was ridiculously easy. At my challenge, they ran straight into a grim-faced Numerus. Dropping instantly into a crouch, the two men drew black combat knives. The snowlight reflected the thread of silver along the cutting edges. The taller one, his arm bent back ready to force his blade into Numerus, ran towards the Roma Novan at full tilt. Numerus launched his fist like a battering ram into the Prussian's face before his opponent could make the thrust.

The other one slashed Mercuria's arm, but was overpowered by a charge from the other two Praetorians. Metallic clicks from above as the *optio*'s detail readied their rifles and aimed down at the Prussians' heads finished off any idea of escape.

We stood motionless for a few moments, legs braced, eyes darting around checking for others. The only sound breaking the silence was our breath. Then came a whoosh, a rustle, a half-sound so faint it could only have been a wild animal scampering away. But there wasn't any wildlife up here in the falling snow. I signalled silence. One of Numerus's troops stuffed his gloved fist in the conscious Prussian's mouth to stop him shouting a warning.

Shouldering my rifle, I beckoned two troops to follow me. Crouching down, and walking like ruptured crabs, we eased along the back of the ridge. I heard it again. A soft crushing sound on the snow, then another. I peeped over the edge, holding my breath so it wouldn't show. My pocket scope showed nothing, but as I went to withdraw below the edge of the ridge, I spotted a figure slinking away. I signalled my two troops to spread out ready to make a pincer movement.

'On my mark,' I whispered into my radio, hoping our quarry couldn't hear through the snow. I unslung my rifle, counted to three and stood up.

*'Halt!'* I shouted in Germanic. 'Stay exactly where you are. You have precisely three seconds to show yourself and surrender. Or we'll shoot.'

The only answer I got was a laugh, a full-throated, rich, masculine laugh. I couldn't believe it. What idiot laughed surrounded by an armed patrol authorised to terminate? Then I heard gunfire and a muffled curse in Latin. Mars, he'd shot one of my troops. I climbed over the ridge and advanced at full speed towards the point of origin of the laugh. Bastard. I'd laugh at him when we caught him.

A shot and a burst of pain in my ear. Hades, that stung. But I grabbed my breath along with my rifle and ran on, zigzagging to break his aim. Then I saw his figure outlined against the snow, legs pumping as he sprinted toward the next ridge. I pushed myself to my limit, freezing air dragging in and out of my lungs, but he was gaining space between us. I was going to lose him.

I stopped, steadied my breath, aimed at his upper body and fired. I saw him fall, then nothing. The snow was in full blizzard now. I trotted in the direction of the ridge, searched for the body, but found nothing. I looked down the slope in front of me and through the thickening curtain of snow saw a figure moving impossibly fast and swaying.

Skiing.

*Merda.*

. . .

Numerus had searched and cuffed the prisoners, as I held a pad to my ear to staunch the blood. I'd waved the medic off to see to the other soldier first, the one who'd been shot by the fugitive. He'd taken a round in his upper arm but luckily, it hadn't hit the bone or artery. The second shot had only winged my earlobe. The sound of my ripping flesh was still echoing in my head, though. Despite the cold and the morphine, my ear was throbbing as if Neptune was jabbing his trident at it with no trace of pity.

The prisoners wouldn't say a word, even after I spoke to them in Germanic. They stood there cool and collected. The one that hadn't tasted Numerus's iron fist even had the nerve to smirk. Their kit was standard survival equipment plus a metal-cased radio set and a bunched-up length of antenna wire. Clandestine obviously, spies probably. They had no papers, their outer clothes no labels. Whatever they were, it was political, which would give our interrogation service people something interesting to do. And if we could persuade the *vigiles'* forensic scientists to get off their backsides for once, they would be able to investigate in excruciating detail until they could tell what factory everything had been made in. It wouldn't surprise me if they could tell which sheep the wool came from.

I detailed Delta Troop to take the prisoners and our wounded people back, but to radio me through to confirm their arrival. Nothing further occurred and we made camp on the side of a cirque, protected at least from the wind. I wrote up my notes slowly with my numb fingers, cursing that we hadn't caught the last one. That would be an embarrassing note in my file. Only another thirty-six hours in these gods-forsaken mountains, thank Mars.

'Wake up, ma'am.'

My shoulder was being roughly jostled, relentlessly even. Then pain pinched my ear. That woke me up.

I glanced at my watch. Three hours since I'd rolled myself up in my sleeping bag and survival pod.

'What?'

'Flash message via company securenet. With an imperial code.'

I stared up at him, but saw no clue. I shook myself and sat up still cocooned in my sleeping bag. My face burned in the cold let in through the pod flap. It had to be several degrees below freezing. My stiff fingers tapped the code into the radio handset to release the message.

PERSONAL AURELIA MITELA. RETURN IMMEDIATELY. REPORT TO JUSTINA APULIA IMP.

At first light, even before the sun had crept over the horizon, we tabbed down to the vehicle park. As our personnel carrier bumped down the tracks through conifers then alpine pastures and eventually on to the tarmacked valley road back to the city, I scoured my mind to try to find a reason for such an imperative and imperial command.

Justina was traditional, and to be honest, more than a little frightening. She wore her authority naturally and intimidated her daughter Severina, frowning whenever the girl tried to express a different opinion but more so when she gave way. Severina had been my childhood friend and I'd thought she would grow out of her timidity, but she didn't. I was sure the imperatrix would have been happier if Severina had shown a touch of truculence or rebellion on occasion.

Still, Justina had approved of Severina's choice of partner, one of my second cousins, Fabianus Mitelus. They'd produced a son, a sweet child named Julian after the fourth century Julian the Philosopher, the so-called 'apostate' emperor.

I'd always kept it very formal if Justina was present, even when I was visiting Severina at the palace as a friend. Like the imperatrix, my mother was old school and had dinned respect into me for the imperial Apulians as soon as I could walk and talk. As a Praetorian officer, I could hide behind that formality even more.

But this emergency message was marked personal. If I was being called in to discuss my family situation, or lack of it, it wouldn't have been urgent. If it were anything else, surely my mother would deal with it; she was the head of the Mitelae.

On the edge of the city two hours later, we skirted the hill rising steeply to the old castle ruin perched at the top of a cliff; it commanded the whole river valley. Halfway up was the Golden Palace, a beautiful stone house built in the late seventeenth century around a much older villa and which served as the imperial home as well as housing government offices. With long single-storey wings running out from each side, it looked as if it were a bird poised for take-off.

The transport dropped me off at the palace staff entrance, where I hurried through the security post, waving my gold-crowned eagle ID at the guard. Praetorians had twenty-four hour access, thank the gods. It was too cold for me to sweat, but I was nervous. The steward took me through the atrium of the palace and instead of one of the drawing rooms, we went on to the old wing to the private family rooms.

As I was announced, I removed my field cap, bowed and waited. The imperatrix stood up from her bureau immediately and came over to me. A slightly stocky figure, her wavy hair was already streaked with grey, but contained in an elegant, swept-back style. She wore a dark wool dress with an enormous silver and diamond brooch which dug into my chest as she embraced me. She was rarely so demonstrative; I was too stunned to say anything. She led me to a chair then sat on its twin opposite me and looked straight at me.

'What on earth happened to your ear?'

'A smuggler took a shot at me, *domina*.'

'I presume he's in custody?'

'Unfortunately not, but I think I at least wounded him.'

'Gods, they're such a nuisance.'

She looked at the far wall for a few moments, then drew her gaze back and focused on my face.

'Aurelia, my dear, I've called you back for some bad news.'

Not Marina. Please, not my child. No, my mother would have told me. Where was she? As head of family, she would normally have been present at such a meeting.

'It's Felicia, your mother. She's had an accident. A bad one.'

I suppressed a guilty wave of relief it wasn't Marina.

'What do you mean, *domina*? What's happened to her?'

'She was injured in a road accident. A direct hit from the side. Nobody saw who the other driver was.' She looked away for a second. 'Of course the *vigiles* are investigating. I spoke to their prefect myself.'

'Is she— Is she alive? Where is she?'

'She's alive, in the Central Valetudinarium, but her injuries are very serious.'

She twisted her fingers around each other and looked uncertain. She lifted her right hand and brushed the skin under her eye.

I sat on the blue velvet chair and didn't move. People like my mother and the imperatrix were indestructible. They never suffered illness, never complained, worked impossible hours. Driven by duty themselves, neither gave any quarter to anybody else. Perhaps this resilience was forced into them by the stress of the Great War when they were younger women, or bred into them by the values held for the last fifteen hundred years. Whatever it was, it was terrifying.

It was equally terrifying to see the imperatrix visibly upset for another person outside her immediate family. She normally kept a tight rein on displaying her emotions to the point of coldness.

I was working out a way to escape and go to my mother when a steward brought Justina her hat and coat.

'Now you're back, we'll go and see her.'

I rode by her side in the armoured saloon, armed guard at the front, motorcycle outriders in front and behind. At the hospital, the director hovered nervously on the steps. After she greeted Justina, she glanced at me, then away and didn't look me in the face again. At the end of the corridor, a nurse frowned at the fraying field bandage on my ear and fussed around, covering my combats with a gown. I could see her point.

My mother lay in a nest of tubes and white sheets, green beeping machines framing her bed, all encased in a large plastic bubble. Her mouth was held open by a plastic support and several teeth were missing. The rest of her face was crushed and her head swathed in bandages. She lay as still as if she were on her bier.

A hand touched my arm. I looked up at a stranger in a white coat. After a few seconds, I refocused my mind. The doctor.

'Please,' he said and indicated one of the easy chairs on the other side of the room. I glanced at the imperatrix, but she was sitting by the bed, her back to me, her hand holding my mother's through a glove tube in the plastic bubble.

'Your mother has suffered multiple injuries and we think there is considerable brain damage. She's in a coma at the moment.'

'Will she recover?' I heard myself say.

'I don't really know. She has a strong heart and her medical history is excellent, but—' He opened his hands in a little gesture. 'I'm sorry, it's very likely she'll lose a significant proportion of her mental faculties.'

I covered my mouth with my hand and turned away, cold creeping through me, but not from the weather.

'Will Nonna come home soon?' Marina asked. She sat in my mother's favourite chair in the atrium as if guarding it for her.

'She has to stay in hospital where they'll look after her properly.'

'Shall we go and see her tomorrow?'

I took her hand between mine. 'She's too poorly to have visitors at the moment, so we'll have to wait, but you could send her a drawing, or write her a card.' Not that my mother would be able to read it.

She nodded. 'If she's not here, does that mean Uncle Caius won't be coming here as usual?'

I stopped rubbing her hand. A sour taste filled my mouth, but I fought to remain calm.

'What do you mean, Marina?'

'He comes and sees us nearly every day. And he brings me honey cakes and toys. Sometimes he sits on the sofa with me and plays games with me. I don't mind now.' I let her babble on about 'Uncle Caius', not believing what she was saying. I felt a deep anger against my mother, followed by an immense wave of guilt.

'Ow, Mama! You're squashing me.' She looked puzzled and hurt. I looked down. My fingers had made red marks on the sides of her fragile hand. I pulled her gently to me, folding the little body into the protection of my arms.

Pacing up and down in my study after I'd put Marina to bed, I eventually settled at my desk. The thought of writing direct to Caius to express my feelings and ban him made my hands tremble so violently I couldn't hold a pen firmly enough. Half an hour later, after creating a pile of torn-up drafts, I wrote Countess Tella a formal letter, informing her of my mother's illness and cancelling all visits from her household. It would have to do.

# 3

Within a week, Justina issued an imperial edict naming me *de facto* head of the Mitela family until further notice. She and my mother had been close friends since childhood, in some ways as bonded as sisters would be. I'd seen how upset she had been at my mother's bedside. I suppose it was the pragmatic thing to do; she must have taken the view that my mother wouldn't recover in the foreseeable future.

I wrote a letter resigning my military commission the same day, saying farewell to ten years of my life. I knocked on the legate's door to hand her the letter before my courage failed, but to my frustration her admin officer told me she wouldn't be back from a meeting in the Defence Ministry until the afternoon. So I went down to the mess bar and downed a double brandy. Navigating the shocked faces of my fellow officers and their commiserations over lunch was hard enough, but dealing with my inner resentment was worse. When the legate called me in that afternoon to give me feedback about the two Prussians we'd caught, I was in a morose mood and I hadn't even handed her my letter.

'Sit down, major.' She fiddled with the papers on her desk, pushed the bridge of her spectacles up her nose. 'I'm afraid it's not good news. They've claimed diplomatic immunity.'

'Impossible!'

'I'm afraid not. One is the younger son of some court official and the other is his friend.'

'But they were caught *in actu* – the transceiver, antenna wire, combat knives, ration packs,' I said. 'Hardly innocent hiker stuff, especially creeping across a guarded frontier.'

'I agree, but I had some snotty-nose kid from the Foreign Ministry with a signed order in my office the day after you brought them in.'

Why did we bother?

The legate gave me a bitter little smile. 'It's a bugger, isn't it? I've had the same, years ago, though. I thought that sort of thing had stopped. Obviously not. Until these cosy little arrangements are done away with, I'm afraid we have to swallow it.' She snapped her file closed, then glanced at me. 'Don't worry, I'm pushing this one all the way up the chain to the Defence Minister. He's no big reformer, but the *magister militum* is a hundred per cent on our side.'

Perhaps having the country's top soldier on his heels would spur the damned politico into action to push the legislation through. I wasn't optimistic. I stayed in my seat.

'Something else, major?'

I swallowed hard and drew the resignation letter from my pocket. I rubbed the envelope between my fingers. Hades. I shot my hand forward and laid it on the legate's desk before I lost my nerve.

She raised her eyebrow as she opened and read it.

'I see. I'm very sorry to see this, Aurelia. You are one of the few I can trust not only to carry out a task but to take it further, if necessary, without overdoing it. I realise you have to take over while your mother is unwell, but your resignation is refused. You're on indefinite leave. I want you back afterwards.'

Imperatrix Justina called me in to a full imperial council meeting to take the oath of loyalty. I wore the gold collar and myrtle-leaf insignia over formal robes and *palla,* but as I walked from the threshold of the double doors across the soft purple carpet and passed the measuring eyes of the twenty-odd councillors seated round the long table, I felt a sham. I was the understudy and would be found lacking and thrown out.

I felt less of a fraud when the matter of diplomatic immunity came up for foreigners caught in undiplomatic activity. The council members listened in silence as I outlined exactly what had happened on the top of the cold mountain with the Prussians. They nodded in agreement with the *magister militum*'s recommendations read out by the Defence Minister. But when they voted to shelve it to the Foreign Ministry for further investigation, I slumped in despair. Justina took one glance at me and then told them to implement the recommendations with immediate effect. The tiny triumph won me a frown from the foreign minister and a hard but not unfriendly stare from Defence.

The *vigiles* prefect came to the house the next day wearing an impeccable maroon uniform and a solemn expression, as any policeman would when delivering bad news. The gods knew why, but he walked across the atrium marble floor carefully and slowly as if it was into the pit of Tartarus itself.

'Countess,' he said and gave me a brief nod. A middle-aged man, dour and pasty-faced from being indoors too much. He stood stiffly, tapping his peaked hat against the side of his leg until I looked at it, then he stopped. He glanced over my shoulder when he spoke rather than look at me. I felt immediately antagonistic to him. It was illogical; we were colleagues in a way, dedicated to catching the ungodly, but instinctively I knew he didn't like me. I decided not to invite him to sit.

'I regret to inform you that despite several appeals, no witnesses to your mother's accident have come forward. We took statements from three people who'd looked out of their windows to find out what had happened to cause the noise,' he droned as if he'd rehearsed a set speech. 'Forensics have picked the accident site apart but found nothing significant. They were tyre marks on the street, some headlight glass shards and paint scratches on the wreck of your mother's car. These all matched the standard patterns of an imported BMW. These new Bavarian cars are becoming very popular,' he added, and shrugged while spreading his hands in a brief open gesture. 'The CCTV cameras on the main road showed a dark BMW 1500 saloon turning into the side street but then it disappears. Can't have CCTV everywhere, you know. No number plate, but the definition wasn't good enough to make a pastefit of the driver's face. Sorry.'

'That's it?'

'Yes, we can't do any more. We can't find evidence if it's not there.' He looked almost truculent. I knew he was delivering a difficult message, but there was an edge to his manner that confirmed my first impression. He shifted from one foot to another.

'However, I can't understand why there was a collision there,' he continued. 'It's a road with light traffic, only the back of a factory with infrequent deliveries, otherwise, the end of a row of those experimental red-brick two up, two downs. From the deposits on the road from the wheel arches, forensics conclude that your mother's car was parked when it was hit.' He looked away. 'We've put it down to an idiot boy racer. But I can't imagine why your mother was there in the first place.'

'Don't you find that peculiar in itself?' I said.

'Well, I don't know what her personal habits were.'

I gasped. How dared he?

'Would you care to rephrase that?' I said in my coldest voice.

'I didn't mean any offence, I'm sure.'

'Have you questioned my steward and my mother's business manager about her movements?'

'I'm sure my inspector covered that.'

'Wait here,' I ordered. I lifted the house intercom handset and summoned both of them to the atrium.

An awkward silence was relieved after two minutes when the steward marched in, carrying his housebook in his hand, followed a minute later by the business manager with his diary.

Suited and smiling, the business manager was a grey-haired and spare figure. His organiser, packed with high-level contacts, stretched back through his thirty-year career in running corporations. Working for my mother was his pre-retirement job, but she counted herself lucky to have secured such a competent manager.

Milo, the steward, knew everything about everybody connected with the house, including me since I was a young child. His upright figure almost stood to attention when he came to a halt. He was an ex-centurion my mother had found through the services redeployment scheme. Although he was dressed in slacks, shirt and tie, the short haircut and self-confidence made me imagine the silver vine stick rank badges on his collar points.

I waved towards the prefect, but spoke to the two other men. 'Please look in your records for the day of my mother's accident and tell me what appointments she had and any meetings she went to or hosted here. Everything she did.'

'We had the usual weekly investments review in the morning and she was due at a Senate committee meeting that afternoon,' the business manager said.

'She had lunch with your daughter, *domina*,' Milo added. 'I remember because Marina knocked her glass of juice off the table and, er, cried. We had to send the rug to the specialist cleaners.' He frowned and flicked the pages of his housebook. 'The countess left the house shortly after that, driving her own car.'

'No chauffeur? That's odd.' My mother only drove herself in the country on the farm. Going to the Senate, she used the journey time to check her paperwork and left it to the chauffeur to negotiate the traffic.

'Did you tell the *vigiles* inspector all this?'

'She didn't ask,' Milo replied. His face was empty of any emotion.

'What?' Grilling the household was basic procedure. I turned to the prefect. 'What are your people playing at? Can't they conduct a straightforward investigation?'

'My officers know their job. They might not be as glamorous as the Praetorians, but they carry out solid procedure methodically. If they didn't ask, they didn't think it necessary.' His eyes tightened and his face took on a red flush. 'I don't think there's any more to be said or done. We'll be in touch if there are any developments. I bid you good day.' He turned on his heel and strutted out. Anger and surprise robbed me of the ability to reply.

Frankly, I didn't expect to hear anything further and I didn't. The *vigiles* were more interested in tidying up paperwork and submitting high clear-up statistics than actually solving cases.

But the prefect's strange attitude from the beginning worried me. I managed to speak to the justice minister for five minutes after the council meeting the following week. She frowned when I told her about the prefect's manner, but said she was sure they had investigated thoroughly. I asked if she would let me see the file – I had the required security clearance – but she refused on confidentiality and personnel grounds. Faced with the steely, direct look, I had nothing else I could say, but as she strode off to her ministry car, I was left with the feeling something wasn't as it should be.

• • •

In a self-delusion that I could solve the mystery around my mother's accident I carved out two hours from my workload to visit the site. Most of my skills were military, but reconnaissance and intelligence training had taught me that nothing was ever as it appeared. But Juno, I was no expert. After walking up and down the narrow road, crouching down to search the gutter for any traces of I didn't know what, I stood up and panned around to take in the closed factory gates and the houses running in perpendicular lines from them. What on earth was my mother doing here, parked as if waiting?

The red-brick flat-faced terrace rows were well cared for, gates and woodwork all trim and painted. I nodded to an older woman clipping plants and weeding in one of the little gardens.

'Morning,' I said. 'Very peaceful around here.'

'Are you selling something?' She frowned at me, pushed a stray strand of hair back with her gloved hand and left a smear of earth on her forehead.

'No, absolutely not.'

'What do you want then?'

'I came to see where the accident was a few weeks ago.'

'That!' She looked down the street. 'Never seen so many *vigiles* around here before. You get no traffic through here for hours, then five police cars and an ambulance fall on us. They cut the poor woman out, but she looked in a bad way.' She turned round to face me. 'You're not a reporter, are you, or one of those ghouls who come to rubberneck?'

'No, that poor woman is my mother.'

She had nothing material to add as we drank a cup of tea in her small, but immaculate, reception room full of dark, polished-to-death traditional furniture. Although my mother owned some of them for rental, I'd never been in one of these strange houses, built as an experiment by an eccentric English architect in the 1800s. He'd gone bankrupt as few Romans then wanted a house with such a small hallway and closed rooms.

'I didn't see the accident,' the woman continued, 'but I rushed out when I heard the noise. The *vigiles* took my statement, then pushed off. I haven't heard anything more.'

• • •

It took me nearly a month to grasp the extent of my mother's work, let alone accomplish any of it. Not only did she lead an extended family of nearly a thousand, if you counted cousins to the third degree; her business and industrial interests were legion. I knew her business manager, but not the whole accounts team, and I had no idea her interests were so international. I slogged like a sixteenth-century indentured worker for the next few weeks, hoping I could remember all the new faces.

Then the family recorder presented me with a list of hearings I had to adjudicate. Unlike the business group who were happy to work in a direct way, giving me succinct non-partisan advice and accepting my decisions, the family affairs were a nightmare. I had to judge disputes, real or imagined, between people forty years older than me who frequently reminded me how they had wiped the snot from my nose as a baby.

I did away with the daily petitioning where a horde of 'clients', read indigent hangers-on, haunted the vestibule each morning. This old Roman custom had revived itself during the Great War in times of hardship and uncertainty, but that had ended in 1935 and we were in the 1960s, for goodness' sake. I told the under-steward to deal with them as he saw fit. He could offer them jobs in the house or on the farm at Castra Lucilla. No more free handouts.

I squeezed in quick visits to the hospital most days, but these reduced to once or twice a week by the second month. My mother's ruined face showed no sign of life, let alone animation. Only the green lines wobbling up and down on the screen showed she was technically still alive. They'd cut her beautiful hair short; it was now more grey than tawny. The nursing staff murmured polite comments that she was as well as could be expected, but hurried off as soon as they'd given me their brief report. I sat by my mother's bed each time, telling her everything I was doing, hoping somehow she would sit up, jump out of bed and come home.

Although disquiet still crawled around like a tiny worm in the back of my mind, I had to accept that the investigation into my mother's accident was closed and nobody had a clue why she had been there.

As a last throw attempt, I tried to contact the investigating inspector, but she'd been moved to a different department and was away on a course. Another coincidence or was I being paranoid? I wandered up to my mother's room, touching the brushes on her dressing table, opening the drawers, looking through the books, magazines and notepad full of jottings by her bedside. I even rifled through her study desk, feeling as if I were a barbarian invader, but couldn't find anything that hinted at what she was doing in that backstreet.

She regained consciousness three months after the accident and recovered enough to come home. Propped up in her wheelchair, she would stare out of the window onto the garden and parkland. On warmer days, the nurse wheeled her outside where she would raise her face to the sun and close her eyes as if sunbathing. But when she opened them again, the stare was empty. I wept to see my so able mother bound into a world of silence, miscomprehension and utter dependency. She smiled vaguely at me and patted Marina's head, but we couldn't be sure she knew us.

I was distracted by the workload I strove to undertake for my mother's sake. Attempting to rationalise it, I felt as if I were standing on a muddy battlefield with weapons firing at me from all directions with no quarter given, and making no progress in any direction. My social life had collapsed but Severina, Justina's daughter, came to see me now and again with her little boy, Julian. I was pleased to see them. Julian was a sunny, smiling child, happy to be entertained by Marina, but Severina started to get on my nerves after a while with her chatter and dithering. My only real relief was precious time alone with Marina after her tutor had left for the day.

# 4

One afternoon, not quite a year after my mother's accident, I was pinioned to my desk by a mountain of paper. I was finalising a commentary on the efficiency of the law enforcement system. The ineffectiveness, almost obstruction, of the *vigiles* after my mother's accident had made me determined to do something about the whole system; its operating organisation had hardly changed since the grand reforms in the 1700s.

Fingerprinting, forensics and other techniques had been integrated on the technical side, and their forensics service was excellent, if bureaucratic. But in their heads, the *vigiles* operated like a field gendarmerie. They were efficient at containing people and traffic, but responded with a hard thump more often than not. They couldn't think things through, nor were they fired by a passion to pursue cases. Consequently their investigative branch was badly trained and poorly regarded. The public called them scarabs, or dung beetles; my legate had called them jumped-up firefighters; that's what they'd been in ancient Rome and that's what she reckoned they still were. I smiled at the memory of her forthright opinion.

I'd amassed my suggestions for reform and was herding them together into some kind of order for my secretary to type up when my mother's nurse burst into my study.

'*Domina*, come now. The countess.'

I was still fast enough to reach my mother's room before him. She was still, her head braced by the headrest, tilted up towards the sunlight, her mouth open and jaw sunk back. Sightless eyes stared at nothing. I laid two fingers across her carotid artery, searching for a pulse in her still warm neck.

'I've pressed the alarm. The doctor will be here in ten minutes, but—'

We exchanged glances.

'Tell me,' I said.

'She gave a long moan, then silence.'

I clamped my lips together, and stared down at the tiled floor. The gods and we knew she would never recover from her accident, but my insides still tore apart at her sudden departure. I swallowed hard, blinking back sudden tears.

'*Vale* Felicia Mitela,' I whispered, and bent and kissed her lips.

Hundreds of the great and the good came to her funeral. Justina led the official mourning, which was just as well as I could scarcely finish the *laudatio*, my public speech, in front of the crowd in the forum. My throat ached when I'd finished and Justina led me back to my seat where I slumped, hardly hearing the secondary tributes.

The evening was falling as we processed by torchlight to the burning ground, following the self-important *praeco*, strutting along inviting every passer-by to attend the funeral. It was traditional, of course, and expected, but Justina's two Praetorians in full ceremonial dress shot glares in his direction as if they wanted to slit his throat and dump him in the river. Having all and sundry tag along would be a security nightmare for them, especially in the failing light.

In front of him four pipers, a trumpeter and two *cornicines* were churning out minor key dirges. Behind came the *praeficae*, the professional mourners, wailing and lamenting, pulling at their hair, a little excessively, I thought, but the *dominus funeris* had respectfully assured me they were the best when he'd presented his plans for the funeral a week ago. The ancestral images were carried by our household staff under Milo's strict supervision. He fretted around them as if he were walking on hot coals.

At last, the unnaturally calm *dominus funeris* and his lictors all in black led the bier with my mother lying on a blue velvet cloth and surrounded by myrtle leaves. Immediately in front of me two young cousins walked in that stilted way that came from constant supervised rehearsal. One carried a palm and basket, the other a traditional slim spade. They glanced repeatedly at each other for reassurance. Poor things. They, or their mother, probably considered it a high honour. I felt sorry for them. I'd refused to let Marina be cajoled into participating in the mummery and grasped her hand firmly in mine as she stumbled along.

At the burning ground, I walked around the pyre three times. Justina followed with Marina. I put the torch to the pyre and turned away as the flames erupted, and not merely to escape the sudden heat. People stepped forward when the flames began to rise, throwing on branches, oils, wine and scarves. One threw a ceremonial scroll with polished wood rollers decorated with gold finials. Thus we had burned and saluted our dead for hundreds of years. Now we used modern technology to accelerate the process, but the flames still roared, drawing our eyes in some kind of primordial fascination.

Hours later, the pyre doused down, the priest sprinkled the remains with wine and words of blessing.

Marina had fallen asleep in my arms well before the flames had finished their work. When we reached home in the early hours after consigning my mother's remains to the priest, I put my child to bed as she was, smuts on her face and her hair smelling of ash. I couldn't bear to disturb her further.

Nine days later on the Novendiale, we held a brief ceremony at the family crypt where a few cousins joined us. We made sacrifice, passed round wine and savouries, toasted my mother and wished her a safe journey to the underworld.

I drove back to the house in a mix of sadness and relief, but as the car stopped in the courtyard, I took a deep breath and braced myself for the next few hours. As I trudged up the steps, I caught the steward's sympathetic look followed by a nod. We were expecting nearly three hundred for the funeral feast: cousins, Mother's friends and senatorial and business colleagues descended on us. Some had visited her during her semi-existence, but most had drifted away to get on with their own busy lives. But they all turned up for the feast.

My life dragged on as before; no reprieve from business meetings, estate supervision, dull senatorial meetings. Perhaps I was imagining it, but I was sure people were watching me to see if I was going to live up to my mother. I drove myself to keep up with every aspect of everything, even giving up my daily run as I found I had no time. People stopped cracking jokes with me, or inviting me for a drink. Perhaps I refused too many times. Some days I didn't know where to start with the work.

When Milo suggested I could leave the household management and the estate to him and his team, I snapped his head off. My mother had left this all in trust to me for the future. I couldn't take my eye off any of the balls. But it was exhausting. How in Hades did people make time for a weekend off, let alone a holiday? I became more and more aware of my failure to keep a grip on things. It was all so boring as well as difficult. One morning, I lay in bed staring at the ceiling for I didn't know how long until I closed my eyes to shut everything out.

I woke to see the doctor's face frowning at me.

'So there is somebody still in there,' she said. 'Well, you certainly frightened your steward. He found you unconscious.'

Something pinched the back of my hand; a drip line snaked up to a plastic bag on a stand.

'What,' I croaked, 'what's happened?' My whole body felt as if it were made of soggy rubber.

'You've been out three days.' She placed her index and middle fingers on the inside of my wrist and pressed lightly. As soon as she released me, I went to wriggle myself upright. But my muscles didn't work. A wave of heat ran through my body and I broke out in a sweat. I licked my top lip and tasted salt. Did I have a fever?

'You're overdoing it, Aurelia. You've driven yourself into a state of stress and now your body is rebelling.'

'It's tiredness, that's all,' I mumbled.

'I'm prescribing bed rest for another two days and medication; then you can get up and do some gentle exercise. Take Marina out for a walk in the garden, but that's it for the rest of the week. A therapist will be in every day after that and you will walk and talk with her. No excuses.'

Hades. She was one of my mother's friends, but she didn't understand.

'And don't look at me like the Furies on a bad day.' She took my hand. 'You want so badly to do the right thing, but your mother would be the first to tell you not to destroy yourself in the attempt.'

Asclepius curse her, she was right. I slept, ate and walked. I even started reading books again, light, often silly stories, and writing my journal, not that I had anything scintillating to put in it. The doctor must have ambushed my household. Milo didn't come to see me until the fifth day after her visit. He gave me a few headlines of his steward's report and withdrew after ten minutes. Ditto the business manager. Strangely, I didn't fret; perhaps it was the medication.

I recovered my energy levels, but fitness took longer. Marina trotted beside me sometimes, her face becoming anxious if I stopped to catch my breath for too long. My heart squeezed when I saw her eyes widen with concern. If for nobody else, I owed it to this beloved child to regain my balance.

In two months, I had adapted to this leisurely life and realised what an idiot I'd been before. Milo and the business manager were perfectly capable, more capable and expert than I could ever be. I apologised to them for trying to micromanage their areas. Both were very gracious, murmuring polite things, Milo shorter in words than the more diplomatic business manager, but I'd keep to my consultative role in the future and let them get on with theirs.

My life developed into an undemanding cycle padded with Senate and occasional imperial council meetings, lunches, theatre, charity meetings and children's events with Marina. I loved watching her gain confidence and laugh, and I rejoiced as she glowed with pride when her tutor praised her studies.

But in the few quiet moments I allowed myself, I realised I wasn't very happy. Apart from having no male companion, I mourned the purposeful and active life of my earlier years. I was searching for Marina's medical card when I found a photo taken three years ago; me, Numerus and my Active Response Team. Back from an exercise in the north near the Hungarian border, we'd checked our weapons into the armoury, dumped our kit in the field room and headed for the mess bar. Caught in the photo raising our glasses, toasting our success after the tense fortnight, our eyes sparkled with laughter. Numerus was giving one of the younger ones a comradely thump on the back with his other hand and everybody was looking at him and laughing. I stared at it for a few moments, desperate with longing. I brought my hands up to my face and gave a big sigh which turned into a sob.

# PART II

# DECEPTION

# 5

'What are you doing here, my girl, sitting on your backside?' a strident voice rang out. I jumped, tipping my magazine onto the terrace. I twisted round ready to shout back, but stopped, my mouth open.

Justina.

Hades.

I struggled up from the sunlounger and the shade of the patio awning. Still dozy and squinting from the strong sunlight, I made a half-coordinated bow.

'Better. Wonderful you haven't got piles from all this sitting around.'

'I—'

She put her hand up and I collapsed into silence.

'You looked half asleep at the last council meeting. I know your reform proposal for the *vigiles* got dumped in the bin, but don't tell me you're moping about that.' She glanced indoors and I saw the two Praetorians exchanging remarks with Milo, who was nodding every now and then.

'If you would come indoors, imperatrix, we can be more comfortable,' I gestured her to precede me towards the cooler interior. The atrium was a fair few degrees cooler, ventilated from the shuttered louvre windows and the now open bull's eye in the roof. We passed the old *impluvium* set in the marble floor directly beneath it. The square depression had collected rainwater centuries ago but like the bull's eye had been glazed over. Maybe we could uncover it and fill it with water to add natural cooling as they used to do. Anything to help. I felt a tiny runnel of sweat run down my neck, perhaps from the heat, but more from nerves.

Justina was wearing a concentrated look of determination. She glanced around, but there were only her two Praetorians.

'Please, sit, *domina,*' I invited. 'It's always a pleasure to see you but I'm afraid we're poorly prepared for—'

'Don't give me your party manners, Aurelia. I'm here on a double errand.'

I hoped my mouth didn't gape open. I'd never associated this formidable descendant of a hundred generations of warriors with somebody who ran errands. Something critical or ultra classified had happened. And why had she come to see me about it? Of course, I was the head of the senior of the Twelve Families, but otherwise a middle-grade ex-soldier, living a run-of-the-mill life.

'Obviously, I've come to see how you're getting on and to see my foster sister's grandchild.' She looked round. 'Where is Marina, anyway?'

'She's upstairs in the nursery, painting, with a friend. I'll get them to clean her up and bring her down.'

'No, leave her. We'll go up later, if there's time. I need to talk to you, confidentially.' She fixed me with her unblinking stare. 'Severina tells me you're drifting between one thing and another and haven't been out in months. Is that true?'

'I live a calm life, I go to my meetings and business lunches, I work on my papers—'

'Juno,' she retorted. 'You sound fifty-nine not twenty-nine. Don't you ever go out and have fun?'

Fun? The last fun I'd had was chasing smugglers on top of an icy mountain a year and a bit ago. Not something most people would enjoy, but I missed it sorely. I'd die in the arena before I'd admit that to Justina; she'd think I was pathetic.

'Well, you can come and do something a little exciting for me. Knowing you, you'd enjoy it.'

'*Domina*? What exactly did you have in mind?'

'I'm having you recalled to the Guard. Your legate tells me she refused your resignation. Astute woman!'

'But I have my duties here.'

'Rubbish! You have people for most of that.'

'But Marina— I can't leave her.'

'Marina can join the nursery at the palace with my grandson Julian. Severina tells me they get on well.'

'But—'

'Stop bleating "but".'

I swallowed hard.

'Of course, I am at your service, *domina,*' I said, feeling truculent. She had a palace-full running around after her. But I couldn't ignore the centuries-old ties of duty. Nor could I contain my curiosity about why she was going to all this trouble. 'Why are you doing this now? Have I been neglectful in some way?'

'For Juno's sake, you're starting to sound as feeble as Severina.' She sat up straight. 'Look at me, Aurelia.' She'd lost some of the fire in her eyes and her shoulders relaxed. 'Felicia was my friend. She was fostered with me from six. We were as sisters. I cannot let her daughter fritter away her life, however much she thinks she wants to. '

I couldn't think of anything to say.

'You look bored out of your mind and, besides, you're perfect for the job we have in mind.'

'What would you want me to do?'

She glanced at her watch and stood up. I jumped up a moment afterwards, still trying to puzzle out what she meant. 'I'm afraid I haven't time to see Marina now, but I'll have many more opportunities when she moves into the palace.' She beckoned to one of the Praetorians who handed her an envelope. 'Here's your posting order. Report to Tertullius Plico – he's my external security affairs secretary – tomorrow morning at the palace. And, for Juno's sake, go for a run this evening and get some fresh air.'

'How's your Germanic? Know much about Prussia?'

Plico sounded irritated. I was his late afternoon interview. Never a good time. He was a second tier secretary, a high level functionary and one who reported direct to Justina, not via any minister. I'd never met him before, although I remember our legate mentioning him at the briefing meeting before my last mission.

I'd been on a round of activity since eight that morning. First there was a two-hour remobilisation session at the Praetorian barracks, including a full physical and mental check with medical prodding; I was embarrassed I'd gained several kilos and lost muscle tone. Once I'd been reissued with my Praetorian ID and crowned eagle badge, I made my way back to the Foreign Ministry; an hour of form-filling and then interviews testing my European diplomatic and commercial knowledge.

I knew the basics. Roma Nova was a part-producer, part-technological economy with considerable resources devoted to research and development. The strategy had ensured our technical development outstripped that of every other country, including the Eastern United States. And we had silver and fine glass sand, both of which were in high demand by the new technology giants like the United Kingdom in the north. Commercial transactions with the rest of Europe were important and thus well regulated, especially the silver.

As I sat afterwards in the bland but air-conditioned refectory munching on salad, olives and fruit, I thanked Mercury for the weekly briefings with my business manager. But still nobody had told me what this mystery job was.

Now I was sitting in a paper-festooned office that obviously hadn't seen a cleaner in aeons in front of a grumpy functionary firing questions about something I hadn't been near for years. And my chair creaked as if it were about to collapse every time I moved.

'My Germanic's reasonably good, I'd say. I spent several summers in Brandenburg with my father's cousins when I was younger and then a year at the university in Berlin before I came back here to join the military.'

'Why did you leave?' His dark eyes stared at me from deep sockets.

I shrugged. 'Didn't see myself spending three years in a classroom.'

He looked at his file. My file. 'No. A bit of a fidget. So, these Prussian cousins of yours—'

'They're more Brandenburgers,' I interrupted.

'Oh, excuse *me.*' He leant back, semi-sprawling against the chair rest. 'I didn't realise there were sensitivities. Not a word normally associated with our northern friends.'

He didn't quite sneer, but I'd had enough. I stood and picked up my jacket.

'If you're going to sit there and insult my relations, then I'll leave you to it. I have better things to do.'

'Sit down.'

I stayed where I was.

'Please,' he said with a false smile.

Why was he trying so hard?

'Look, we need somebody to go and do a little investigation work up there. It's only for a few weeks. The imperatrix suggested you as you have the connections and language. And you have military training.'

'You want me to go and spy on my cousins?'

'No, of course not. But they'd get you in where we want to look.'

I was assigned to the Foreign Ministry on detached duty, even given a desk and a title – Special Trade Delegate – but I reported exclusively to Tertullius Plico. He sent me to a place near Aquae Caesaris which appeared to be an elegant nineteenth-century villa with granaries and outbuildings attached, but turned out to be a spy training school. I'd never heard of it. He replied in a sarcastic voice that that was the whole point.

The tutors were happy with my physical and fighting skills – I thought I was sloppy. Evidently, the Praetorians had higher standards than the Foreign Ministry operatives. I'd led covert and intelligence-gathering missions in my military role but in the following two weeks I learnt about working solo and using the vast range of technological backup, particularly surveillance and recording equipment. By the time I returned to the city, I was a little fitter and lighter. I'd even been issued with my personal lock pick set disguised as a bank card holder.

'It's only a sketchy introduction but you won't need any of this if you stick to your brief,' Plico said when I saw him on my first day back.

'What exactly is my brief?'

He waved his hand around vaguely. 'A bit of economic

investigation. I'll give you more details before you go to Berlin. In the meantime, bring yourself up to speed on what a real trade delegate does, particularly in accompanying missions.' He handed me a paper slip. 'Report to the Germanic desk secretary tomorrow morning. You can have the rest of the day off.'

I glanced out of the taxi window at the dust, tourists and tree-lined streets. As we climbed up the road to the palace, I wondered how Plico could be so powerful that he commanded the resources he did. He was one of Justina's confidential imperial secretaries, so stood close to her. Close enough to order me back into service. These secretaries ran the imperial system, working mostly with the ministers who made up the imperial council, but sometimes not. Apart from his rudeness and untidiness, Plico must have other qualities to have people respect him so much. Perhaps he knew their secrets.

I pushed that thought aside as we drove up the plane-tree-lined drive into the palace forecourt. I paid off the driver and trotted up the steps to the entrance. Two young Praetorians, shiny and efficient, whom I didn't know, barred my way.

'At ease,' I said and flashed my gold eagle badge at them. They stood to immediately and saluted. A warm glow of familiarity settled on me. I had slotted back into my world.

Upstairs, I opened the nursery door carefully. Two heads looked up from the rug and pile of toys. Julian gurgled, but Marina leapt up and ran into my arms. As I crushed her to me, tiny bubbles of tears sprang from my eyes. I sniffed and released her from my body grip, but held her hands and searched her face.

'Hello, Mama,' she said in a formal, almost quaint way. Then she hugged me again. She took my hand and showed me round the nursery; their day room with a low table and children-sized benches, a drawing wall, easels, bookshelves and a huge pile of cushions plus the obligatory scattering of bricks and toys over the floors. She solemnly lifted and replaced pans and spoons from the play kitchen, and plastic work tools from the miniaturised workbench. There were even a couple of wooden play *gladii* and grey plastic sectional armour in the corner.

After we'd inspected her bedroom, she took my hand. 'Come and help me with the jigsaw?' She pointed to another table.

'Of course, darling.'

We sat companionably, finding and assembling wooden pieces in a dismembered picture of medieval Romans at the castle on the cliff above us. I watched my self-possessed daughter, calm and composed and intent on her game. She'd been here under two weeks and had already slipped into the routine. Marina had a compliant nature; perhaps she would be happy and safe here after all.

# 6

Four days later, I was on a plane to Berlin. We banked as we approached the city, turning from the south to an east–west axis to approach Tempelhof Airport. The original building had opened only two years before the outbreak of the Great War in 1925 but had been completely destroyed in the fighting.

The modernist terminal perched at one arc of the almost circular airfield had been built with League of Nations' support in 1937, over thirty years ago, as part of their aid programme. Planes looked crammed in at the north-east end. My brief mentioned the Prussian government had authorised a large extension. Not before time, I thought, as our plane squashed in between two others to park; the wing tips were barely metres apart.

I sailed through immigration on a diplomatic passport under the stern eyes of the black-helmeted Royal Prussian Police. Their eyes roved over my luggage, but however much they longed to, they couldn't touch it. I murmured a '*Vielen Dank*' and made my way to the arrivals concourse. I spotted the driver because he was flanked by a woman, calm, wearing a dark purple suit and scanning everybody and everything. Praetorian, of course.

At the legation in the old part of the city, they processed me with perfect politeness, giving me a ground floor room on the outside wall with a convenient separate entrance along the corridor into the city.

'We always put the temp spies here,' the steward said.

'I'm not a spy,' I protested.

'If you say so, Special Delegate.'

The administration clerk bobbed about nervously as I sat in his office completing my diplomatic card application.

'I'll take it over to the Prussian foreign ministry this afternoon, *domina*.'

'Major, please, or Delegate. Here, I'm just another servant of the state.' I gave him a stern look. Plico warned me that people would react to my civil rank, either subservient or sceptical that I could actually do the job. To most I was a high-profile presence demonstrating how important the visiting trade delegation was. My civil title had never been a problem for me in the military; there you had the rank granted you on merit alone and you were only as good as your last operation. Hopefully, the staff here would get used to me and adopt the same attitude.

Berlin-Brandenburg, to give it its proper title, was a gracious city, even if over-regulated. People actually obeyed the red man/green man pedestrian traffic signals. I awarded myself a couple of hours to stretch my legs and get a feel of the city that must have changed since I was here as a student.

I walked around the charming old streets with medieval gates and admired the few Renaissance houses within the old city walls that had survived. Berlin had escaped relatively lightly in the Great War; it had been declared an open city at the end as the Allies closed in. It was the religious wars in the 1600s that had devastated the city, but a Baroque building boom had exploded afterwards and the extravagant curlicues on practically every building looked fairy tale in the soft evening light.

In a bar overlooking the Spree, *Am Goldenen Ufer*, I found a table near the window away from the smoke. Eventually, the barman shuffled over and took my order; few single respectable women frequented bars in ultra conservative Prussia. Apparently satisfied I wasn't a streetwalker, he deposited a glass of Berliner Weisse in front of me. Gods, I'd forgotten how tart it was. I ordered a raspberry syrup to soften it. Maybe I could take a bottle of the syrup back and force-feed it to Plico to see if it worked with him.

His orders had been succinct; eyes and ears open and mouth shut.

Apart from contacting my cousins, who had connections throughout the country, my cover was accompanying a visiting delegation from our silver industry. I was to investigate and report on any whiff of rogue trading or smuggling. High-grade silver was one of our core products and had been since earliest times. Now we had a whole complex industrial sector based on it, especially for scientific and electrical appliances, photovoltaics, and medical uses. We worked on joint projects with other countries, sometimes providing the unrefined metal, if required, sometimes importing lower grade ores for less precise applications. It was a horribly complex sector, but a very carefully regulated one. Apparently, there'd been one or two rumours about the levels of Prussia's output which could impact on the balance of our trade with them.

Plico suggested that if I came across any documents or records concerning silver extraction or trading, especially marked 'confidential', I could photograph them with the tiny camera I'd been issued. Not if it compromised my diplomatic status or my personal safety, of course, he'd added a little too suavely. I'd crossed my arms and given him a look that I'd seen Justina use in council when demolishing a pointless remark. Plico should have been a pile of dust after that, but he'd just smiled down at his desk blotter.

I'd been chosen for my connections and language ability, but this clean, proper country was still a mystery to me. It swung from genius to savagery, high culture to crude vulgarity and from duty to reckless abandon. Romans knew a thing or two about these, but never hid them behind a prim facade.

Berlin had reverted to Prussia when the Allies split Greater Germany back into its provinces after the peace treaty in 1935. Some even had their monarchs restored. The plan had worked; despite a loose federation for certain strictly defined functions, the little dukedoms, princedoms and mini-republics argued about everything between themselves and didn't have time or motivation to threaten the rest of Europe again.

Fed up with the clouds of smoke and the continual tinny sound of English pop songs, I finished my beer, left a mark and some *groschen* by my empty glass and stood up. Out of the corner of my eye, I saw a man, brown hair, medium height, hurriedly finish his drink, stub out his cigarette and pull his jacket on. I smiled to myself. He'd been following me from at least the Nikolaiviertel, probably from the moment I'd stepped out of the front gate of the legation. I'd expected no less, but he wasn't very good. I nodded to the barman, left and wandered around for another half an hour before making my way back to the legation, followed by my incompetent shadow.

The silver trade delegation members arrived two days later at Tempelhof, a dozen of them. My driver and I were waiting in the business arrivals lounge to meet them but a fussy boots called Grindel from the Prussian Commerce Ministry hovered with two assistants clucking around him. They were the official welcoming committee, he said, there to help process entry visas and customs formalities. He nodded vaguely as I introduced myself as the third trade delegate, and then ignored me.

Seated by a window looking out airside, I watched the group disembark from the Air Roma Nova plane; seven women and five men, most clutching briefcases, and all smartly dressed. When they entered the lounge, Grindel gushed up to them. I stood back and let him get on with it. Once he'd finished flapping pieces of paper and card around and supervised stamping passports, I moved forward to greet the visitors. Grindel looked down his nose at me.

'The Commerce Ministry will look after our visitors' needs. You may run along and make sure the taxis are there,' he said, dismissing me as if I were one of his junior clerks.

The chairman of the Silver Guild gasped, the whole delegation fell silent and my driver, a Praetorian, moved half a step nearer me. I looked directly into Grindel's eyes, but said nothing. A good half-minute passed in awkward silence. The Prussian stared around, harrumphed and looked at the Silver Guild chairman for help, but the latter said nothing, merely looked at me. I nodded and gestured for him to speak.

'You mistake the situation, *Herr* Grindel,' the chairman said, his voice cold as if straight off the top of the Geminae peaks in northern Roma Nova. 'Countess Mitela is the head of one of our leading families and has graciously consented to introduce us to vital contacts. We will need not any further help from you.' He turned to his colleagues, nodded to them, picked up his bag and smiled at me.

In the legation minibus, he couldn't stop apologising. His tough mine owner's exterior evidently hid a sensitive core.

'Please don't worry,' I shouted above the engine and traffic noise, 'such attitudes are endemic here. And we *will* need to deal with the ministry, you know.'

'Well, I'm not having that pompous jerk anywhere near us. I'll request a female liaison officer.'

Privately, I wished him the best of luck with that.

At the legation, I handed the group over to the first trade delegate. Portly and on the far side of fifty, she came from one of Roma Nova's leading merchant families and definitely spoke their language. Sitting at the back while she outlined their programme, I learnt a lot more about the practical side of business networking and the subtle channels that interconnected that world than I did in all the time I'd struggled with my mother's business interests.

The full day trip to the Rammelsberg mine in Goslar, south-west of Berlin, was exciting for the miners and traders, but not so much for me. But I got to know individual members of the group better and it passed agreeably. The mine had been an incredibly important resource for nearly a thousand years and was a 'prize of war' that Prussia had somehow held on to in 1935. Plico had heard rumours the silver lodes were running out. Somehow he expected me to investigate this extremely confidential situation without getting caught. I broached it with Prisca Monticola, one of our leading silver mining and processing plant owners.

'Well, the price of silver has risen steadily here over the past three years – that's not abnormal – but you'd expect to see some fluctuation during that time. Silver often tracks gold and that's been all over the place on the Frankfurt Metal Exchange recently. They ran a huge feasibility study here four years ago.' She glanced towards the Commerce Ministry representative at the front of the bus, a female one, complete with formal suit and lacquered beehive hairdo. Goodness knows where they'd found her, but I was sure from her reserved manner and youth she was newly promoted purely for this job.

'We're not supposed to know about the study,' Prisca whispered, 'but these things leak out. Putting that together with the price rise which seems very controlled, and the eager way they invited this trade delegation all expenses paid, I'd say it was a good bet it's true.'

'You'd make a good intelligence officer, Prisca Monticola.'

She shrugged, but gave a little smile. 'It's called keeping at least one step ahead of the competition.'

'So are they vulnerable?'

'A technological country like Prussia needs constant and assured supplies of minerals, both rare and common. Let's say if I was the head of their minerals mining industry or the minister, I'd be making procurement plans and regulating the futures market better.'

As the silver group had a free morning the next day, I arranged to meet up with my cousin several times removed, Joachim *Freiherr* von und zu der Havel, at *Am Goldenen Ufer*, the bar where I'd enjoyed a beer a few evenings ago. I arrived early, and sipped my coffee, watching flower-covered green, red and blue barges chugging along the much engineered Spree past the sightseeing boats still moored. It looked pretty and peaceful enough.

He approached with an efficient but graceful stride along the cobbled pavement towards the tables shaded with maroon umbrellas where I waited. Although he had inherited his father's cumbersome name, he had his mother Sabine's tall, slim build and Viennese elegance. He still wore the same friendly smile and curly dark blond hair from our university days. Now, if I could have persuaded him to come back to Roma Nova, I would have been a happy woman, but he sought different company.

'*Hallo*, Aurelia! *Wie geht's Dir?*' He bent and kissed my cheek.

'Hello, Achim.'

He gestured a waiter for a coffee and soon we were reminiscing and laughing about ourselves, our fellow students, but mainly about a freer time.

'I'm sorry you left when you did, Aurelia. Our group was never the same.'

'I had itchy feet and although I loved my time here, I wanted to get back to Roma Nova and get on with my career.'

'You went straight into the military? Nothing else first?'

'Why do you ask?'

'Just curiosity.'

'What did you do?' I asked. 'Your mother sent mine a card each December saying you were doing well although she didn't understand why you had to choose law.'

He laughed. 'A legal career usually follows a law degree.' He waved his hand vaguely. 'We still have the estates, but like you, I wanted something different from my inherited role.'

After we'd run through the remainder of our more congenial friends, I asked about the class joke. 'Whatever happened to Grosschenk?'

A flicker in Achim's eyes. 'Why do you ask?'

'No special reason. I expect he went off to be a pompous little mayor in a chocolate box town,' I replied and laughed. 'Or did he end up in jail?'

'He set up one small business after another which turned into larger ones. He's done very well. Lives in some bourgeois merchant's house out in the Grunewald and dines regularly with the *Oberbürgermeister.*' He snorted.

'What's that for?'

'He's still a slimy little toad.'

I laughed, remembering Grosschenk's over-conciliatory manner with lecturers coupled with his bullying way with younger students. Achim had given Grosschenk a thrashing once when he'd attacked a new kid. Grosschenk had been wary after that, but never lost any opportunity to knock Achim in front of others if he could, but in an underhand, faux-innocent way.

'Come across him at all these days?'

Achim didn't answer, and kept his gaze on the green-grey surface of the river. He brought his gaze back and shifted in his seat.

'What are you doing here, Aurelia? Really?'

I made a moue of surprise at his serious face. 'As I said, I'm on a trade mission of prominent business people with important silver industry interests. They don't know Berlin and none of them speaks Germanic. And my presence is supposed to show everybody how important the Roma Novan government thinks the mission is.' I shrugged. 'I'm not so sure of that, but that's what they tell me.'

'Trade mission? Not some other kind of mission?'

'What's that supposed to mean?'

'When one of the highest ranking women in Roma Nova with special forces training claims she's babysitting a load of silver traders, I worry.'

'They're mining company and processing plant owners, not only traders. And why should it worry you? You're nothing more than a farmer with a law degree.' That was cruel. He was a significant landowner, but he was starting to annoy me. 'Anyway, my life in the military is behind me now, since my mother's death. Now I have a new career with the Foreign Ministry. And I have to start somewhere.'

He murmured some standard words about my loss, then glanced across at me. He said nothing for a few seconds and looked into the distance.

'Where are you taking them?' he asked.

'To meet business people, see factories and mines and so on.'

'Which ones?'

'The exact itinerary is commercially confidential, as I'm sure you can understand. Why do you want to know?'

'No particular reason.'

I didn't believe him. 'I thought we were having a friendly drink,' I said, 'catching up and so on. Why are you asking me all these questions?'

He didn't reply.

I glanced at my watch. 'I'd better be getting along. There are a series of meetings this afternoon, then a reception this evening with the *Oberbürgermeister*. I'll let you know if I have any other free time while I'm here, but I doubt it. Give my best to Aunt Sabine.'

He put his hand out, but I ignored it and walked off down the street.

I fumed my way back to the legation. Not a good start to my career. Why had Achim closed up like that? And those questions. Had I missed something in my research? Grosschenk was one of my possible leads and I'd only dropped him into the conversation on the off-chance. But Achim had reacted as if I'd mentioned a bucket of poisonous serpents.

# 7

Fuelled by my irritation partly at my cousin, partly at myself, I decided to deal with whoever it was tailing me. He was about five seconds behind me. Although it was mid morning when most people were at work, there were plenty wandering the old streets; a few tourists with maps and backpacks, but the majority peering aimlessly into shop windows. Any disturbance would rouse them out of their retail torpor and panic them.

Cutting through the old Nikolaiviertel down Propstraße, I walked briskly across the front of the St Nicholas church. At the corner, I dodged sharp left into the recess made by the lady chapel, slid across the brick and stone end wall and down the side into the shelter of the arched doorway. On an exact slow count to five, the brown-haired man appeared round the corner.

I held my breath, not daring to move, only hearing my heart pumping. The man stopped, panned around searching for me in the empty open space in front of him. Mild panic on his face, he glanced down the side of the chapel, not seeing me hidden within the deep door arch. He narrowed his eyes, then took a few cautious steps. I remained rock-still until he came level with me. Jumping out, I slammed into him, stuck my foot out and overbalanced him so he fell into the trees by the chapel door. I grabbed his wrists, secured them with nylon looped cord from my pocket. A few choice Germanic swear words were muffled by his face being pushed into the grass. Kneeling on his back, I glanced around, anxious to check we hadn't acquired an audience. Nobody was looking. Cars puttered along the main street, words and laughter from further up the road floated in snatches, but no shouts or alarms.

I bent down and put my mouth to his ear.

'Now, this can be easy or hard – your choice.'

He grunted.

'Who are you and why are you following me?'

'*Verpiss Dich, blöde Sau.*'

I smacked him round the head.

'Language! Let's try again and speak nicely if you don't want to lose an ear.' I jabbed his lobe with my pen.

He wriggled, trying to get up, but I lifted my knee a few centimetres and brought it down hard on his lower back, right on the kidneys.

'Who are you working for and why are you following me?'

Another grunt but no words.

I fished in my inside jacket pocket for my new transceiver. Highly secret, and we were actively discouraged from using them in public, but I was well hidden.

Eight minutes later, a mushroom-coloured VW Beetle drew up by the chapel door. Two casually-dressed women jumped out, left the engine running, nodded at me and hauled the brown-haired man to his feet between them. Without pausing, they pushed him into the back of the car, face down on the back seat and drove off.

'Would you care to explain why I have a Prussian national in my secure room?' The Praetorian commander growled at me and jerked her head towards the observation panel in the door. She'd called me through to her room in the military office downstairs as soon as I'd finished preliminary checks on the brown-haired man.

'I apologise for the inconvenience, major,' I said, 'but he's been tailing me ever since I arrived. He was being a hard case when I confronted him and I worried about causing a public scene.' This military commander was definitely old school and very starchy. I stood my ground and waited.

'Very laudable, but if we get stuck with a charge of kidnapping, we'll be in the shit up to our hairlines.'

'Believe me, I wouldn't have called in for a security detail unless I had my concerns.'

'What do you think he is?'

I glanced through the observation panel at the man now shoeless, tieless and coatless. 'He can't be police or security services. He's not precise enough in his technique. And he'd be shrieking blue murder by now, insisting on calling his department. And he's unprofessional enough to carry ID with him. Name of Ernst Beck.' I'd found his driving licence in a not very well concealed pocket in his coat.

Her eyes looked me up and down. 'Well, maybe you're more familiar with that side of things.'

'Do we have any worthwhile contacts in the local police?'

She looked away. 'Sadly not. Ever since that stupid bastard Melitus went on a drunken spree and smashed up three Prussian police squad cars, the best we've achieved is frosty – a vast improvement on glacial at the time of the incident.'

'What happened?'

'Melitus was my number two and when his promotion didn't come through, he went on a bender.' She gave a wry smile. 'We have bi-monthly liaison meetings as before with a well-mannered inspector who makes copious notes but now stuff-all gets achieved. Even after we paid for all the damage.'

'That's a bit childish, isn't it?'

'Come on, you know with your background how they get huffy if you affront their sense of correctness.'

I pressed my lips together biting back my reply. I couldn't help my paternal ancestry any more than she could, and the Prussian connection was two generations back, but the last thing I needed was her antagonism.

'You can have the use of the room to interrogate him,' she said. 'But whatever happens, he has to be out of here within twenty-four hours.'

I nodded at the medic. She unclipped the lid of a plastic box she'd set down on the table and selected a disposable syringe. She stripped the cellophane packet off and picked out an ampoule. Our prisoner watched as she drew the pale yellow liquid into the syringe body. He strained against the handcuffs securing him to the chair. The fear shone out of his eyes, he opened his mouth, but said nothing. She depressed the plunger a millimetre and a tiny bubble of liquid escaped from the end of the needle. She glanced at me. I gave a tiny shake of my head.

'Whoever sent you to follow me obviously doesn't care what happens to you,' I said to the man. 'You've been here several hours and nobody's come knocking. That makes you a freelancer or criminal.' I scribbled some odd words on a printed sheet pinned to my clipboard as if making notes. It was a standard visa information request form, but he didn't know that. 'You have no backup or perhaps you've been abandoned.' I leant towards him. 'So why should you protect them?'

He shook his head and looked down.

'Is it really worth it?'

He glanced at the syringe and swallowed.

'Why don't you start at the beginning when I went for that walk on my first evening here?'

He looked up, surprised.

'Oh, yes, I know you've been following me all the time, but I became a little bored after a while and decided to end it.' I snapped my fingers a centimetre in front of his eyes. He jerked his head back.

'In the olden days, a Roman punishment officer would have beaten you to a mass of bloody flesh, drawn a few teeth and fingernails, lashed you and anything else he could think of. Some of them were quite creative. This is the twentieth century so we're more civilised, but not that much more.'

I leant back in my chair. 'I'm going to give you five minutes. After that, my colleague will inject you with a chemical which will not only make you talk but also make you feel sick as a pig for a week and destroy all possibility of successful romantic encounters for a month, even two after that. Think about it.'

I bent over the desk and pretended to write more notes, and ignored him. Glimpsing through my eyelashes from time to time, I watched. His eyes darted around the room and after a couple of minutes, he started to tremble. Small beads of perspiration appeared on his forehead. After four and a half minutes, I glanced at my watch and yawned theatrically.

'Right, twenty-five seconds to go.' I stood up and pulled my chair back. 'You will excuse me, Ernst, if I step back. I don't want to be covered in your vomit.' I nodded again to the medic. She pulled his sleeve up, wiped it with a sterile gauze pad and laid the needle on his arm ready to inject him.

'No,' he croaked and struggled, pulling his arm back as far as he could.

'No?'

He glared at me, then looked away.

'I don't know who they are,' he muttered to the floor.

I signalled to the medic to proceed.

'No. Wait! They post me a letter with a docket for the key to a box at the Anhalter Bahnhof. I pick up the key and my instructions there. I've done other stuff for them before. Deliveries, escorting, you know.'

I nodded my head. People as well as drugs and numbers, no doubt. Charming.

'When I've made the delivery, the money's waiting in the box a day later. I put the key in an envelope and hand it in to the left luggage for a docket and post that to a postbox address.' He glanced at me. 'All I found for you was a photo, a name and instructions to follow you and make a note of where you went and who you met.'

'And how do you report back to them?'

'I leave my notes in the box at the station.'

'Never been tempted to see who picks them up?'

'I did once.' He shuddered. It was then I saw the ridge on his nose wasn't a natural shape. I walked over to the table and picked up a buff-coloured notebook, read the jottings.

'When are you due to report on me?'

He jammed his lips together, then glanced down at the needle still resting on his inner forearm. 'This evening.'

Disguised as a respectable Prussian woman in a two-piece green Loden suit embroidered with formal black swirls at the neck, I drank my *Kaffee* as if I were a *bona fide* traveller. Clusters of tables and chairs lined the edges of the grandiose cream and brown marble booking hall of the Anhalter Bahnhof. Apart from the discreet advertisements, it didn't look as if it had changed since the 1880s. The interior had been damaged in the Great War, but with characteristic Prussian thoroughness, the new government had restored it to its original appearance.

The heavy brogues I was wearing were making my feet ache, and I wasn't altogether sure I'd be able to run after anybody in them. I'd passed under the portico at the entrance which looked like one from home, but it was fake; the building was in the pseudo Renaissance style they'd all loved in the previous century, with Prussian iron girders holding the classic facade together.

I raised my cup again and glanced at the block of private boxes. Ernst Beck had left his notebook in his allotted box and scurried off to the platforms clutching the ticket I'd given him for Munich along with a wallet stuffed with the new intra-German marks. He kept glancing round like a frightened rabbit convinced a fox was going to snatch him and bite his head off.

I'd been there two hours and fifty-three minutes and I'd read every word of the *Berliner Tageblatt* including the stock market reports – it was that tedious – when I caught a movement by the bank of boxes. I eased my knees from under the table, ready to stand without making a fuss but carried on as if I was absorbed in the newspaper. A sturdily built man, probably in his forties, wearing a dark casual jacket and slacks over a roll-neck top, slipped a key out of his pocket and opened the door of the box in one smooth movement. He slid the notebook out, slipped the key into an envelope, stepped over to the left luggage counter and queued behind a student complaining about having to unpack the whole of his rucksack on the counter. My target slicked his hand over his thin hair that shone with grease and shifted his weight from one foot to the other while he waited.

I stood, grasped my small travel bag full of old clothes and crossed to the information kiosk where I intended to check the time of a fictitious train. From that angle, I'd keep my target in view while appearing to act normally.

The man's turn came and he handed over the envelope containing the key to the clerk in exchange for a paper docket. He nodded to the clerk and moved away. I tracked him with my eyes as he headed for the front exit fifteen metres away. His pace was steady, easy to follow, but I didn't want to risk him climbing into a taxi and me losing him. If I set off smartly, I'd get to the front at the same time. He might even hold the door open for me.

That thought making me smile, I turned and bumped straight into another human body.

'*Entschuldigung*,' I said, and stepped to the left. He mirrored my movement. I went the other way and he did the same. He smiled and shrugged. I glanced at the front exit. My quarry was nearly there. I took a wide step to my right to get round the idiot in front of me, almost too wide and nearly lost my step in my brogues. He put his hand out to steady me.

'Oh, for heaven's sake, get out of my way,' I pushed past him and almost ran towards the tall glass door. As I grasped the thick brass handle and heaved the door open, I spotted my target slipping into the back of a private car. I waved my hand frantically for a taxi, but the last one was vanishing into the Berlin traffic. Hades, there was no other form of transport, private car, or trader's van. Nothing. Not even a bloody bicycle. And my quarry's car had disappeared.

'If you hadn't done so well with the silver people, I'd have you recalled and chucked out. You're acting like a bloody idiot. Mind you, what did I expect from a thick squaddie?'

Plico's face on the video-conferencing terminal was turning an interesting shade of dark grey. A vein running up the side of his round head wriggled as if it were a worm trying to surface.

'One, why in Hades didn't you report the tail to me? We would have assessed it and mounted a proper surveillance operation. Two, you had no right to use the Praetorians in the legation. I suppose you pulled some old girls' act with the commander. Three, detaining a Prussian national illegally – need I explain? Four, taking no backup and no vehicle on the last leg was beyond stupid and, of course, you lost him.'

'I only lost him because of some clumsy oaf not getting out of my way.'

'Not good enough. Backup would have tailed him.'

'Look, I'm sorry, but when you've stopped shouting at me and hold your breath for a minute or two, I'll give you my side.'

He flicked his hand. 'It's done, let's move on.'

'But—'

'Send me your report tomorrow and I'll see if I can salvage something.'

I kept my hands under the table so he couldn't see me pressing them together so hard they were nearly turning white. He was right, I should have taken backup and had a car ready. But I had to swallow it. You were only as good as your last mission. Mine was unofficial and I'd fouled up imperially. Never again.

'At least we know he wasn't official Prussian,' I said to show him I wasn't completely incompetent. 'So who do you think was following me?'

'The gods know but I don't happen to have their telephone number.'

# 8

After Plico's shredding, I stared at the blank screen in the legation communications room and took some deep breaths to calm down. At least the terminal was in a private booth and I'd been using headphones. But it hurt all the same, especially as he was right.

The reception that evening at the Rotes Rathaus was sumptuous, generous and boring. At least half the *Magistrat* – the city council – were there as well as a crowd of trade officials. The austere columns, encircled three-quarters of the way up with bands of gold oak leaves and soaring towards the red vaulted roof, and the peppering of classical statues in the hall reminded me of home. And then of Marina.

'Going well, I think,' murmured a voice behind me.

I turned to find the first trade delegate, a glass of bubbling *Sekt* in her hand and a hint of a smile on her face.

'Thank you, First Delegate, but it's really due to the trade secretariat getting the right people along. I'm merely here to ease things along for my group in making those contacts.'

'You underestimate yourself, Aurelia Mitela. A lot of them have come to see you. The Germanics all love a royal and you're very close to the imperatrix.'

'That's nothing to do with me carrying out my job.'

'I know that and you know that, but,' and she nodded towards the *Oberbürgermeister,* 'his calendar's full for eighteen months, but curiously, he's found a slot for tonight.'

Luckily, one of the Prussian commerce minister's assistants came over to take us off for the official photos. After we dispersed from that set piece, I blinked hard as my eyes hurt from the flashbulbs. I checked with the silver mine owners and refiners that they had found those people they'd wanted to meet. The Prussians were polite and smiling, even a little deferential, when I made the introductions, as the first delegate had hinted. Unnecessary, really; I was simply doing my job. I was trying to explain exactly that to a beautifully groomed and suited man in his thirties who gave me a lazy smile and shrug; he declared he didn't need to work, so why should he? He gave me a puzzled look when I explained that unlike ancient imperial times, there were few free rides for anybody in Roma Nova. The patricians in particular had a duty to work and contribute to the state. But trying to get that through to him became the work of Sisyphus.

Prisca Monticola rescued me. 'Ah, Third Delegate, could you help me with some introductions?' She eyed up the exquisite creature talking to me and gave him a brilliant smile. 'If you'll excuse us, *Herr Baron*?'

She clasped my arm in a surprisingly strong grip.

'He's not really a baron, Prisca,' I whispered.

'I know, but he'll be flattered. You looked desperate.'

'He didn't seem to understand the basic concept of work. Never mind that, how are you doing?' People were drifting off politely bending over the first delegate's hand and smiling their farewells. 'Do you really want any more introductions?'

'Mercury, no! If I have to try to convince another Prussian industrialist that a "sweet little thing" like me can run a multimillion-*solidi* company, I'll burst. Gods, they're so blinkered.'

I gave her a grin. She was in her late thirties, but looked younger with glossy dark brown hair cut in a gamine style. Her high voice made her sound fifteen.

'Par for the course, I'm afraid,' I said.

'Why on earth do their women put up with it?'

'All Germanics are like that, and so is much of the rest of the world. Don't forget it's mostly because founder Apulius had four daughters with a fighting Celt for a mother that we are as we are. In those days, they just had to get on with it.'

'Maybe.' She sounded dubious. 'But the old legions reported the women in Germania fought like demons.'

'That was then, Prisca. Now they're all good little hausfraus.' I looked around at the faces of the few women present. 'But I think there's going to be a change.'

'Why do you say that?'

'Not sure, but half this year's uni registrations here are from young women.' I laughed. 'Another exciting fact from my briefing.'

She laughed back, her tension released. She glanced around the hall. 'How do you feel about changing into our casuals and finding somewhere quiet to eat?'

Berlin had over twenty thousand eateries, but we settled on one in Savignyplatz. The ornamental lanterns on the terrace were glowing brightly against the dark of the almost moonless night by the time we were sipping the last of our wine.

'Gone half ten,' I said, 'so I think we should start back. I think you have a couple of meetings tomorrow then a trip to a science park?'

'The meetings should be routine – sort of a "hello and nice to meet you". I've been in contact with both of them over the past year by mail. But the factory visit should be interesting. I want to see their super-cold coating process.'

I had to admit, the part of my brain that dealt with the silver industry shut down at that point. I glanced around to check for hostiles. Damn, it was a reflex. I shouldn't need it here, but it was hard to switch off after nearly ten years in the special forces. As Prisca was explaining exactly how the superfine Roman silver was perfectly suited to scientific manufacture, I was running my eyes over the possible places the ungodly could hide.

'Sorry, Aurelia, I didn't mean to be boring.'

I felt the red flush of embarrassment. 'No, I'm the one being rude. Sorry.'

She smiled, picked up her bag and we stepped out onto the square. I raised my hand for a taxi. The first one ignored us, but the following one stopped and the driver got out and opened the door for us. I should have realised how wrong that was, but Prussians *did* have polite, if patronising, manners towards women so it wasn't entirely unexpected.

I gave the legation address, but as I caught his cold satisfied smile in the rear-view mirror and heard the thunk of a central locking device, I realised we had made a colossal mistake.

'Stop,' I said. 'I've left my coat behind.'

But he carried on driving and in the opposite direction to the legation. The street lights became sparser and we turned into a side street full of parked cars. But no people.

'This is the wrong direction. Please turn round,' I said.

He ignored me. I exchanged glances with Prisca, signalling her to stay quiet and tried again. 'Please stop this vehicle and open the door. Now.'

He smirked at us in his mirror.

Hades.

Seizing the top edge of the passenger seat, I launched myself over it. His head jerked back as I thrust my hand against his neck under the jaw. I brought my right hand down to chop his nose and found a revolver barrel in my face aiming for my eye. Too late, I ducked, avoiding most of the impact, but pain exploded as the barrel hit my head millimetres above the eye socket.

Dazed, I shook my head to clear it. The gods knew where he intended taking us, but I had to finish it and soon. I brought my hand up, fingers clamped in parallel and jabbed them hard into the soft stomach area below his ribcage. He grunted, crunched forward. The taxi veered and crashed into parked vehicles, juddering to a halt and flinging me against the far window.

As I recoiled from the window, he shouted, '*Halt*'. His revolver was two centimetres away from Prisca's head. I froze. She was still as a rock, but her hands trembled.

'Hands on the dashboard where I can see them.'

A car alarm was sounding outside, but nobody came out into the dark night to investigate.

He jabbed Prisca's forehead with the barrel. Her head jerked back with the impact and she slumped over. I grabbed his outstretched wrist with both hands, twisted hard, forcing him to drop the weapon, then jerked his arm up hard to dislocate his shoulder.

He shrieked and swore, but drove his other fist towards my face but I ducked. I brought my own down on his nose and heard the bones crunch. I followed through with a punch to the angle of his jaw. Jupiter, it was solid as rock, but he screamed as his mouth dropped open, then he choked on the blood flowing from his nose. After a few seconds, he gave a moan and passed out. I fiddled under the dashboard and found the hidden central locking switch.

'Call the police,' I shouted at Prisca. 'One one zero. Find a phone box. Now.' She stumbled out of the rear door and away from the car. I heaved the belt from my jeans and tied our would-be kidnapper's wrists to the steering wheel. Through the windscreen, I saw Prisca speaking into a public phone a few metres away, nodding her head, but shifting from foot to foot and tugging on the phone cord.

I pulled out my precious transceiver and radioed the legation for a security detail. I spotted an apartment block with a bar on the ground floor called 'Studio 16', according to its flashing sign, and gave it as our location. Prisca tottered back to the car and flopped back on the rear passenger seat. The dim street lights were reflected in her anxious eyes as we sat waiting in the damaged taxi.

'What now?' she asked.

'Don't worry, it'll be some fussing and a little paperwork.' I reached over and pressed her hand. 'Depends who gets here first. I'd put my money on our people.'

I won my imaginary bet. A Praetorian *optio* and two guards, all in civvies, got to us six minutes before the police.

'Protocol?' I asked the *optio*.

He scanned us, the car, the thug tied up and the damaged car while one of the detail took photos. 'Civilian police – *Schupo*,' he said. 'You go with them. Maximum cooperation, but no admissions, no background. I'll roust out the legal *consultor*'s department to get somebody to dig you out.' He jerked his head towards Prisca in the back seat. 'Will she be okay with that?'

Prisca was pale, but sitting up straight now. She clasped one hand with the other, but she wasn't trembling. I nodded.

He glanced along the road. 'Here they come.' He and the other two guards melted away into the dark as the green and silver patrol car arrived.

• • •

At the main police station, the Landeskriminalamt Berlin, Prisca and I gave our names and a brief outline, but didn't answer questions until the legal *consultor* from the legation arrived. She breezed in, sharp suit, sharp haircut and sharp nose. Her Germanic rattled out at the detectives, almost cowing them. She gave Prisca a half-smile and me none. It was all routine, except they were curious about my willingness to attack our kidnapper.

'Our government forbids paying ransoms,' I said. 'It's up to the citizen to provide their own security against such situations when abroad.' I shrugged. 'We merely defended ourselves. But it's a shock to be attacked in a friendly, supposedly civilised, country.'

Sharp Nose gave me a warning look.

'So who is the thug?' I asked.

The detective studied the pen on the table for a few seconds then raised his eyes to me. 'We don't know yet, but we're looking through our files as a start. We'll let you know if there are any developments. When he comes out of hospital, that is.'

As Prisca and I were being herded by the lawyer towards the entrance, the interviewing detective hurried up to me. 'One moment, please, Delegate Mitela.'

Sharp Nose drew herself up ready to bat away any subsidiary questions, but the detective ignored her, directing his look at me.

'Could you help me with an administrative matter?'

What in Hades did that mean? I nodded to Sharp Nose to carry on; Prisca looked exhausted and needed to get back to the legation and her bed. I gave her an encouraging smile and promised to catch up with her tomorrow morning.

The detective led me into a different room, more a standard office with files piled neatly on the desk, a chipped filing cabinet and a smell of stale coffee, smoke and sweat. The nameplate said 'Huber' but behind the desk sat my cousin Joachim.

'Sit down, please,' he said addressing me in a formal voice. He nodded to the detective who promptly vanished out of the door.

'What's all this?' I said, waving my hand around. 'Why are you sitting in some policeman's scruffy office?'

'This is *my* office, Aurelia, and for the moment, you're my guest.'

'What's that supposed to mean?' The police medic's painkillers were wearing off and my face was beginning to throb. I glanced down at the nameplate then looked back at him. 'Your name's "von und zu der Havel", not "Huber".'

'I would have thought that you of all people would understand.'

'You're using your mother's name?'

'Yes, it makes things easier, but that's beside the point. I asked you before what you were doing here. You flounced off. Now I need a proper answer. And we're both staying here until I get it.'

Gone was my jokey cousin. In his place sat a completely serious *Kriminalpolizei* officer with a grim expression. He fished in his pocket for a pack of cigarettes and lit up. He inhaled and blew smoke to the side.

'Surely it's far more important to get out there and find the people behind our attempted kidnapping than sitting here discussing my babysitting duties,' I said. 'Anyway, who are you to ask these questions?'

He handed me his card. 'Kriminalpolizeikommissar Huber – GDKA/OK.' Juno, he was one of the German Federated States organised crime investigators. We were in the big time here. I glanced up at him, but he looked even grimmer, if it was possible. I decided to play safe.

'I refuse to answer questions without a lawyer from my legation present. And anyway, accredited diplomats are not subject to interrogation by foreign police officials.'

He snorted. 'Accredited diplomats, my arse. You're here on a spying trip, probably organised by that old bastard Tertullius Plico.'

I tried my hardest not to blush, but felt heat rising up my neck. 'Nothing of the kind. I'm here with a trade delegation. You saw me accompanying Prisca Monticola.'

'Right. And I'm the queen of Peru.' He smirked, then blew smoke out.

I wafted it away with my hand. 'Your personal habits are no concern of mine. And how is dear Hasi, by the way?'

Joachim flushed at his partner's name and made an angry backhand gesture.

'All right, Aurelia, let's stop posturing. Why does Plico want to know about Grosschenk?'

The more important question in my mind was why was the federal organised crime directorate so interested in a shady businessman who might or might not be a silver smuggler. We took it very seriously, but the German Federated States had never become involved; it was a local problem that concerned the individual countries on our border, such as Bavaria. I was only supposed to find out if Grosschenk had any connections within the group of people on my trade mission. I'd taken a flyer by asking Joachim about our former classmate. Now I was about to get burned.

'I really don't know what you're talking about,' I said. 'I only asked about him when we were catching up on the rest of our class.'

'You're not a good liar, Aurelia. You should practise more.'

'Will you stop accusing me of something I haven't done, or don't know.' I stood up. 'I have a sore face and hand from preventing one of your nationals kidnapping me and a prominent Roma Novan businesswoman, a guest of the Prussian government. I haven't committed any crime. I'm leaving now. If you lay a finger on me as I go out of this door, I'll invoke the diplomatic treaty.'

After him staring at me, and me refusing to look away he said, 'Very well, Aurelia. I can't stop you.' He stubbed out his cigarette. 'But I'm warning you. If I find you one centimetre out of line with your diplomatic mission, I'll have you arrested and PNG'd out on the first flight with an indefinite ban.'

# 9

'What a cock-up!'

Tertullius Plico's face stared out of the video screen. I was in the legation secure comms room in a private booth with headphones on again, but I was sure everybody else could hear.

'Well, I didn't know my cousin was some kind of federal super-cop. Or that he was using his mother's name.'

'Ironic, isn't it? An upright scion from a patriarchal Prussian, oh, sorry, Brandenburg, family following a matriarchal Roma Novan custom. Excuse me while I try and drag out some humour from it.'

'One positive is that we know they're really worried about Grosschenk,' I said. 'Perhaps they're running some kind of operation?'

'Hm. Leave it with me. I'll look into it. In the meantime, do nothing but babysit your silver miners. Out.'

'Your poor face!' Prisca stared at my forehead.

The legation medic had applied compresses and slathered it in cold gel which was taking the swelling down, but I'd need concealer for a week to disguise the round imprint of the barrel. Worse was the fuss around the attempted kidnapping. I'd typed up my report for the local security section despite the bandaging on my right hand covering the bruising. After a short debrief I thought that was the end of it. The trade delegation members had other plans. They couldn't be dissuaded from making a presentation after dinner the next evening.

'I thought it didn't show,' I whispered across the table to Prisca.

'Well, I can see it.'

We were interrupted by the portly chairman of the Silver Guild standing and calling for quiet. He blathered on about heroic deeds, Roman strength and traditional virtues and decisive action for a good ten minutes. Prisca tapped my foot with hers under the table at the end of the speech and nodded towards him. As I walked across the dining room, I flushed at the applause. The chairman presented me with a scroll of thanks and an exquisite silver statue around ten centimetres high of Diana in full hunting dress, her arm pulling back a bow strung with a thread-like string. Reflections from the lights and chairman's hand shone in distorted patterns from the swirls of the tiny athletic figure's contours. What a beautiful gift for a few minutes' action.

The normal babble resumed after I had escaped back to my table. I was raising my glass to salute Prisca and her colleagues when I saw the door at the back of the dining room open to reveal a Praetorian scanning the room. She stopped when she spotted me and beckoned me over. Standing beside her with a face like thunder was Joachim.

'Who in Hades let you in?' I hissed at him, closing the dining room door behind me. The guard handed me a sealed envelope. She stood back but stayed within a few metres, watching Joachim.

'Yeah, and I'm delighted to see you as well.' He tipped his head to the right. 'Read your message.'

I was about to retort, when I saw the 'Flash – Eyes Only' marking and cipher officer signature across the closed flap. I tore it open.

URGENT IMMEDIATE COOPERATION WITH GDKA/OK HUBER STOP CALL ME STAT T. PLICO

Tertullius Plico could be affable when he chose and now was one of those times. He apologised to Joachim for the secrecy, hoped I hadn't upset him too much and smiled one of those man-to-man smug smiles. I kept my mouth in a straight line and made no comment.

Joachim and I crouched around the video screen as Plico updated us.

'A new lead's come up.' He looked at Joachim direct. 'Your director's agreed this is the time to pool resources. What do you know about our silver industry?'

He shrugged. 'Much as anybody else does. You don't give out production figures, but I know silver's strategically and economically important.'

An understatement. Without it, and its power to trade and bribe, the Roma Novan founders wouldn't have survived past a few winters holed up in their mountains. Nor throughout the intervening fifteen hundred years.

'The mines produce a very high-grade ore which commands a premium,' Plico said. 'And not only the physical product. Shares in the extraction and refining companies are sought after not only on our stock exchange but worldwide. Because of its importance, a copy of any share transfer is always sent to the Oversight Commission at the Trade Ministry. Some eagle-eyed clerk found a transfer that wasn't.'

'How?' I asked.

'She was doing a random control check at one of the companies on the past month's transactions and found one that didn't tally with her register. We've traced it to the Berlin area, to a holding company with its HQ in a garage block on the outskirts.'

I glanced across at Joachim, but his face was set. The skin was tight across his cheekbones and his eyes made slits in his face. No, he wasn't happy at all.

'As Aurelia's in place, she'll work with you as your consultant. Her trade mission's finished tomorrow when the miners get back on their plane.'

'But—' I started.

'Yes?' Plico interrupted.

'You said I could go home after three weeks. I need to see my daughter.'

'Call her on the videophone. Your country requires your service.'

What a bastard. I was tempted to call Justina, but that would have been childish. She would have backed Plico and said service to the state overrode any personal wishes. Neither of us said a thing as I escorted Joachim back to the legation reception hall. Once through the security doors into the public area, the guard went back to join her colleague sitting at the small side desk. The main reception desk was deserted – it was nearly midnight. Bright street lights and orange floodlights on the ancient ramparts streamed through the floor-to-ceiling glass frontage. A dark car waited outside watched by two of our guards patrolling the driveway between the building and street.

Joachim turned to me. 'I don't like it either, but we're stuck with it. Report to me at the station after you've seen your people off.'

'Let's get one thing straight, Achim. I'm not one of your footsloggers. We work as a team. Clear?'

'*Glasklar*.'

In his office the next afternoon I was drinking revolting synthetic coffee. I'd been waiting over twenty minutes and had read the five pages of background notes twice. The door opened eventually and Joachim and two other men entered.

Joachim nodded to me as he slid into his chair. One man, slim, brown hair barely half a centimetre long and an expression as welcoming as a nightclub bouncer on the early shift, leant against a filing cabinet and crossed his arms. The other, obviously fond of eating, lowered himself into the remaining chair and gave me a friendly smile, but his attention quickly returned to his chief.

'This is my team – Scholz,' he said pointing to the standing one, 'and Hahn.'

'This is Major Aurelia Mitela of the Praetorian Guard Special Forces who will be our consultant. We are to cooperate on all levels.' His voice was neutral, but his two men exchanged glances which contained a world of meaning. I was not welcome.

'We've found the garage Plico mentioned,' Joachim continued. 'It's a derelict warehouse off the Landsberger Allee, a road called Am Wasserwerk. Post is held at the local sorting office. Hahn, you and Scholz go and have a word with the shift supervisor. See who's been collecting it. Check the register for frequency and any pattern.'

After they'd gone, he stood up. 'You're coming to the trauma hospital with me to see if that kidnapper of yours is capable of talking yet.' He flipped open his notebook. 'Fingerprints show he's a Karl-

Heinz Fischer, two petty larcenies, joyriding as a youth, assault with intent three years ago. Since then nothing.'

'Thanks,' I said. 'I mean, for taking time out for this investigation. I expected it to be left to the normal *Kripo*.'

'Kidnapping a foreign government delegate with diplomatic status and the head of one of their leading silver companies isn't exactly an everyday occurrence. And only a halfwit would think it's unconnected.'

I blushed in a half-witted way.

'What were you two doing out by yourselves? With no security?'

'Eating a quiet meal away from all the diplo-hassle. And I can take care of anybody trying to mug us.'

'True,' he conceded.

The *Unfallkrankenhaus* was a huge glass and brick building on the eastern side of Berlin. We crossed the wide, glazed hallway running along the whole front of the hospital and arrived at the reception, where Joachim flashed his badge. As we waited while the receptionist called to check exactly what number room Fischer was in, I heard the laugh. A full-throated, rich laugh that sent a tingle from my neck, down my spine and through my legs. That laugh I'd last heard on the top of a mountain in a blizzard, mocking me as I strove to capture its owner. I jerked my head round and stared in the direction of the sound. Nobody.

'Back in five,' I called as I sprinted in the direction of the sound.

'Aurelia! Come back here.'

I flicked a hand gesture backwards at him as I swerved round startled people, some in outdoor clothes, others in white coats or dressing gowns. I stopped and scanned the concourse, searching each face, looking for the remnants of humour. The skier had been tall and must have been super-fit. Nobody I saw in the concourse looked remotely like that. I glanced up at the main staircase. Only a couple of women and a female nurse.

One of twin lift panels pinged and the left set of doors opened. A tall figure suddenly appeared from behind my field of vision, sprinted across the concourse to the lift and jumped it. I ran after him, but the doors had shut before I reached them. I stabbed at the 'open doors' button, but the car had gone.

Pluto in Tartarus.

I glanced at the lift panels. The left one had reached the third floor and stopped. Just as I was running for the stairs, the right lift doors opened. A porter pushed an elderly man in a wheelchair out. I spun round and jumped into the car ahead of two people waiting, mouthed *Entschuldigung,* and stabbed the button for the third floor.

I barrelled out as the doors swished open. The wide corridor was deserted. A door swung at the end and I ran towards it. The emergency stairs. I pushed through and stood still, hearing only my pulse thudding through my body and the faint sound of running footsteps below. I shot down the stairs, jumping several at a time, missed once and bashed my bruised hand on the rail.

Hades.

I picked myself up and cupped my throbbing fingers in my other hand, but I had no time to do anything about the oozing blood. I ran on down the steps. At the bottom of the last flight, the door opened into a garage. A motorcycle sped past me, and the last thing I heard was that bloody laugh again.

'Plico said you go off on a hair trigger and he wasn't joking. What the hell was that all about?' Achim jabbed the lift button.

'Just a hunch. Nothing to do with this case.'

'So you're working another case here? Do tell me about it if you have a moment between your Hollywood stunts.'

I winced at his sarcastic tone. 'No, not another active case, but I thought I heard a voice from an operation I was leading against smugglers a couple or so years ago. We couldn't catch the last one. I shot him, but he escaped. But the bastard laughed at me. I've never forgotten it. I swore I'd get him. Whoever that was in the concourse sounded exactly like him.' I glanced at Joachim. 'You see why I had to go after him?'

'Fair enough,' he said, nodding his head, one law enforcer to another. 'It's bloody annoying when that happens, but try not to cause too much mayhem next time you go after somebody. I've just spent the last ten minutes apologising to the administrator for the disturbance.'

On the fifth floor, we marched along a side passageway, me still annoyed with myself and Joachim silent. Two armed, greenjumpsuited police officers were guarding a door with a nervous doctor hovering between them.

'So, doctor, can we talk to him?' Joachim said.

'Only for a few minutes. Although we've manoeuvred the shoulder back using closed reduction, he's suffered severe contusion to his face and jaw. Whoever attacked him wanted to inflict maximum damage without causing a fracture and knew what he was doing.'

I shuffled my bandaged hand to the side, out of the doctor's view, as we entered the room.

Half lying, half sitting in the metal hospital bed, the kidnapper's nose was covered in gauze, but wary eyes stared out of sockets surrounded by purple flesh. More purple centred on the jawline below his ear and his whole face was swollen and red. Tough luck.

'Fischer,' Joachim said, looming over the bed.

The injured man made no reply.

'Huber, GDKA/OK. Let's not mess around. Who are you working for and who told you to kidnap this woman and the silver delegate?'

'Piff off,' Fischer replied through his bandages.

'You have a choice,' Joachim said. 'If you don't cooperate, you'll be extradited to Roma Nova for interrogation.' He waved his hand in my direction, but kept his gaze on Fischer's face. 'Their methods are much more, let's call it, robust. They're not full signatories to the Vienna Convention – you'd have no rights or consular protection.'

Juno, he could twist the truth. Implying we were brutal torturers was not how I'd seen the conversation developing. And as a federal officer, Achim knew perfectly well that we had signed the Convention. The injured man's face tightened over the bruising and his hands gripped the bedclothes. I crossed my arms over my chest and stared down at him.

'My lawyer – stop you,' he gasped.

'He doesn't have the power to,' I said. I produced a trifold paper from the inside of my jacket, printed in Latin, and let him see the letterhead with *Roma Nova – Quaestiones perpetuae*. 'I have the extradition order here. Unless your own police is satisfied with your answers and you submit to their authority, I have the power to arrest you and take you back with me.'

Joachim shot a fierce look at me, but I ignored him. I'd given him some ammunition. Up to him to use it.

'So, Fischer, you heard it. Now who gave you your orders?' Joachim's eyes narrowed under his frown.

'Can't,' came his voice, low and muffled by the bandages. He turned his head away.

I leant over him. 'Won't, more like. Don't worry, inspector, we'll sweat it out of him.'

Fischer's hand shot out so fast for an injured man that I nearly didn't have time to pull back. As it was, he managed to grab my jacket collar. I grabbed his wrist with my left hand and prised it off with my right. Unfortunately, the doctor chose to come in at that moment.

'What are you doing to him? Let him go immediately.'

I looked at Joachim, who nodded. I dropped Fischer's hand, but noticed a tiny tattoo on the inner face of his elbow joint, revealed when his gown sleeve fell back. I couldn't get a second peek as the doctor came between us, but it looked like a Gothic G.

# 10

'Where the hell did you get an extradition order from? It's normally over two weeks before we get them.'

I smiled to myself as we crossed the hospital car park.

'Well?' he said.

'How's your Latin?'

'Reasonable.'

'Read that properly.' I thrust the paper at my cousin.

He stopped, ignoring a car trying to drive around him. After several seconds' frowning, he handed it back.

'That's not a warrant.'

'No, it's a vacancies notice in the justice service, but Fischer wasn't to know that.'

'Ha!' He grinned at me, breaking the tension between us.

As he looked left out of the car window before accelerating to join the link road, Achim said over his shoulder, 'He's obviously torn between threats – one from you and the other from his boss. We'll have to do it the old-fashioned way – circulate his details and get some foot sloggers out on the street, but whatever happens, he'll go down for trying to kidnap you.'

He guided his Audi smoothly into the midday traffic flowing into the urban clearway. Going round a square a kilometre further on, I saw a group of young men clustered around motorbikes, their figures weaving in and out of each other, some pushing and shoving, but nothing serious. I also saw the spray cans of paint.

'How bad are the gang problems here? I don't mean those kids over there but coordinated, purposeful crime groups?'

'Why do you think I'm based here?' he said and snorted.

'I'm not a cop, Achim, give me some slack.'

'Okay, there are three groups that operate here. They're so professional, the heads all belong to country clubs. One even dines regularly with the interior minister. Ironic, isn't it?'

'Crime *per se* or other things such as political stuff, economic terrorism?'

'Depends what you call terrorism.'

'You know what I mean – silver smuggling, rogue trading.' I wasn't going to mention the other half of my briefing from Plico about strategic reserves of silver unless he said something first.

'No,' he conceded. 'I don't know of any involved in that. But after talking to Plico I got the impression he thinks it's organised. What we need to find out is how large-scale it is.'

While Joachim tapped up his notes on a manual typewriter, I scribbled in my notebook, trying to reconstruct the tattoo I'd glimpsed on Fischer's arm; a three-quarter-full curve, dissected by a short vertical line and topped with an almost playful horizontal tail.

'What do you make of this?' I said as I pushed my open notebook across his desk.

He glanced down at my sketch. His fingers stopped mid movement. After a few moments, he touched the page with his index finger, below the drawing.

'Where did you see this?'

'What does it mean?'

'Answer my question.'

I shrugged. 'On the inside of Fischer's elbow.'

'*Du lieber Gott!*' He stabbed his intercom button. 'Hahn, Scholz. In here.'

He told them of my discovery. You could almost have heard the dust drop on the stacks of curled-edged files.

'Somebody tell me?' I looked at all three faces.

'That's Grosschenk's mob.'

• • •

Back at the legation, I reported to Plico.

'Excellent progress.'

At last, I had evidence Plico was capable of smiling.

'Is it?' I said. 'I mean, I can hardly walk into his house and accuse him of kidnapping me.'

'That's exactly what I want you to do.'

Grosschenk lived in a rural palace. Every big-shot criminal did, Achim assured me. Lying to the south-west of Berlin, the Grunewald wasn't popular only with walkers and riders, it was the exclusive district for the rich, famous and aspiring to live. A group of velvet-jacket-clad riders passed by on sleek mounts as I signalled my driver to press the gate entry phone. Dressed in dark purple uniform and traditional peak hat, he looked the ideal servant. He was, of course, one of the PGSF guards from the legation detail, with both assault group and hostage recovery experience. My other companion, posing as my assistant, was an *optio* called Fabia; the legation posting was her last before she took up promotion to centurion. Neat but not chic, in a chain store washable suit and with her hair drawn back in a ponytail, she looked harmless.

Beyond the ornate bars of gates overlooked by a static CCTV camera, the drive wound through wide lawns scattered with oaks and mature birches. What had started as a gracious merchant's house from the 1700s had been bolstered either side by two-storey wings of weathered sandstone set at right angles to the original building to form a courtyard. At the end of each wing an octagonal tower cleared the rest of the house by several metres – perfect for isolating a troublesome guest.

The gate swung open.

'Ready, Fabia?'

'Ready, major.' She nodded without smiling.

'No, remember to call me "countess" or "*domina*". We have to keep this civil in all senses.'

The sound of our heels clacking on the polished stone floor echoed round the entrance hall. We followed the middle-aged, equally polished man who had greeted us. He hadn't said a word, merely opened doors.

'Aurelia! *Wie schön!* So good to see you.'

Something shrank in my stomach. He still had a greasy face and an oily smile.

'Hello, Grosschenk.' I made myself smile back. 'Or should I say Manfred now we're all mature adults?'

He chuckled. 'Still the same sharpness, I see.' He waved his hand towards a Biedermeier-style sofa with a gold-and-ochre-striped silk seat almost too immaculate to sit on. As I settled myself on it, he glanced at Fabia who hung back by the door.

'Perhaps your friend would care to join you?'

'No, she's a servant. She can stay there.' I nodded her towards a plain chair by the door.

'You've become very proper since we last met.'

I shrugged. 'I have to think of my position now.' I cringed at how snobbish I sounded.

The silent man brought in a gold inlaid tray with two bone-thin porcelain cups and served us coffee.

'I heard your mother died,' said Grosschenk. 'My condolences.' He settled into his chair, crossed his knees and waited.

'Thank you.' He obviously followed, or at least had found out all about me. 'Yes, I had to leave my military career. To be honest, it was getting annoying, all that saluting and shouting. And mixing with all kinds of persons, some of them quite rough.' I secretly apologised to all my comrades-in-arms.

'But you must have some good memories from that time? And skills you could use elsewhere?'

'I made some social contacts among the officers that may come in useful at some time, I suppose, and I kept fit.'

He stopped smiling and shifted his gaze to my hand. 'Have you had an accident since you've returned to our lovely city?'

'Oh, that. Some petty criminal with ambition tried to kidnap me and one of the silver bigwigs I've been babysitting. I don't suppose the police will catch him. He probably belongs to some gang.' I looked at Grosschenk. 'Seems to be a bit of a problem here. Can't you do something about it? Lean on the city authorities or do you think they're in bed with the criminals?'

'I'm a private businessman. Why do you imagine I would have any influence?'

I waved my bandaged hand around the room with its silk hangings, crystal chandeliers and Fragonard paintings. 'You've obviously done very well for yourself. I'd have thought you could bring some pressure to bear, even if it was only a few words in the *Oberbürgermeister*'s ear.'

'You overestimate me, my dear Aurelia.'

'I don't think so.'

His face tightened and silence grew for a few long seconds. All I could hear was my own heart thumping. Had I pushed him too far?

'Well, you'll be going home soon,' he said and looked steadily at me. 'Much safer for you there.'

He stood and crossed the room to a side table where he picked up a large leather-bound visitors' book. Before he turned, I saw it. Out of place amongst all the fussy gold, stood an exquisite silver figure of Mercury, messenger of the gods. And protector of liars and thieves.

'Mercury? Are you sure?' Prisca asked when I was back at the legation.

'Yes, I'm sure. And he had the smallest caduceus I'd ever seen.' I smirked at her.

'You military are always so smutty,' she said. 'Describe it properly.'

'Two wings at the top, twin snakes curving round. They made a circle at the top and I swear there was a crossbar as well.'

'A crossbar? Like the old Greek symbol?'

'Yes, why?'

She paused, then said, 'A figurine with exactly that same caduceus was made as a one-off for a special presentation.'

'Who for?'

'Countess Tella.'

'Look, Plico, Prisca Monticola is neither slow nor stupid. I'd put money on it that she carries every design her guild ever made in her head. And this was a special piece. I only noticed it because it reminded me of the Diana they gave me the other night. Countess

Tella is one of their significant shareholders, over fourteen per cent, so they had a party and a praise-fest. That was three months ago. Prisca's sent a message to the manufacturer's museum to transmit a photo of it to you ASAP. And to me.'

'Hm. How did you leave it with Grosschenk?'

'He smarmed on a bit saying I must come to dinner, etc. etc.'

'I suggest you accept.'

'What? You *are* joking!'

'I'm not waltzing into Domus Tellarum accusing the most frightening old bat I know of silver smuggling and illegal metal trading until we've got something better to go on.'

'If Grosschenk's so bloody clever, then he's hardly going to leave clues lying around for me to find.'

'Scared?'

I said a rude word that involved the theoretical rearranging of Plico's anatomy.

He flicked his hand impatiently.

'Take the usual equipment with you plus backup detail this time.'

The military commander assigned Fabia and two others to me, plus an authorisation to draw on whatever field equipment I needed. As I'd be wearing a cocktail dress, there wasn't much scope for concealing bulky equipment. I could wind a length of thin, high-tensile rope around my middle – standard practice – but I needed to carry recording and transmitting equipment somehow. The usual body wire and transmitter would be too bulky.

'The tech people have come up with this evening bag.' Fabia handed me a sequin-festooned rectangle with a shoulder strap. 'The aerial's in the strap, so try not to bend or fold it or the wire may snap.'

'Won't the metal sequins corrupt the transmission signal?'

'They're plastic.' She grinned. 'A bit showy, I know, but Grosschenk won't even notice it. We'll be listening in, as will the legation signals office. Secretary Plico has authorised us to send a recording to Inspector Huber afterwards.'

She glanced at me and I nodded. We didn't want the local police blundering around in the middle of a live operation.

She handed me another strap, about a metre long with an

adjustable clip. It was covered in chiffon with sequin flowers. 'Under the decoration, it's reinforced steel mesh. It's fully flexible and you can use it for various things, even fold and twist it together as a cosh if you need to defend yourself.'

Fabia's detail took up position in a dark blue BMW not quite opposite the Schlosshotel Bon Souvenir entrance. It would be a long and boring evening for them, the only relief listening over the radio to Grosschenk and me exchanging banalities. Whatever Plico said, Grosschenk wasn't going to tell me all about his criminal empire over veal with truffle sauce. I briefed Fabia to listen only and not to intervene, whatever they thought was happening, unless I spoke the code word '*arx*'.

I took a taxi from the legation and met Grosschenk promptly at seven in the bar, as arranged. Originally a private mansion, the rococo building had been sympathetically converted. However, the high ceiling decorated with laughing, uncaring cherubs didn't help my mood.

'Shall we?' he invited as he stood after we'd finished our drinks.

'Where are we going?'

'A surprise for you.'

Hades.

He held my evening coat as I shrugged it on. The hotel doorman opened the door of Grosschenk's Mercedes and nodded to the chauffeur. I settled back in the seat – I had no choice. We drove south-west to the Grunewald. Were we going back to his place?

We pulled off the main road and drove along the tarmac lane leading to his house. It bordered on the forest itself and the tall conifers turned the evening light several shades darker. Suddenly, the car braked hard. It shuddered and I grabbed the armrest but I was thrown forward and nearly fell against the back of the chauffeur's seat. Grosschenk swore. At first I couldn't see what had happened as the chauffeur was blocking my view. I twisted my head round, but I needn't have bothered. An enormous deep brown horse and its rider stepped into my view. They stopped right in the middle of the road and blocked it. The rider, totally relaxed, his black curly hair waving in the evening breeze, looked down into the car with a haughty expression as if we had trespassed on his private property.

Grosschenk's chauffeur stabbed the window button. As soon as the glass had retracted enough, he stuck his head out and told the rider to clear out of the way. The rider smirked. The chauffeur swore at him, but neither animal nor man moved.

'Bloody gypsies!' Grosschenk said.

'What does he want?' I asked

'God knows. They lurk around the forest, annoying everybody and stealing anything not bolted down. Probably stole that horse.'

The rider patted the horse's neck, and ambled towards my side of the car. If I thought the horse was impressive, the rider was no less so; a tall figure, and supple as he moved with the horse, his strong-featured face was without expression but his whole person exuded confidence. He would move out of the way when he wanted to and not before. I craned up at him, but he would only have seen my outline through the smoked glass passenger window. But I felt he was staring right at me as if it wasn't there. I had an urgent need to see beyond the barrier of the window and stabbed at the window button. As the glass retracted, I found the horse rider looking at me, no, studying me. His eyes were half closed in concentration, but I couldn't break away. He seemed familiar, but I'd never met him before in my life. I vaguely registered a touch on my forearm. Grosschenk.

Then the horse rider broke his stare and nodded, but not in a friendly way. It was more an expression of satisfaction, as if he'd accomplished a task. I didn't stop to analyse it; my heart was beating at twice its normal rate and I almost forgot to breathe.

The Mercedes continued up the lane to the gates of Grosschenk's house after the horseman had moved. I barely registered the metal gates opening; my whole body was tingling. It was ridiculous, like one of the romantic films that Justina's daughter Severina loved watching. She would no doubt have used words such as 'powerful thighs', 'broad chest', 'strong arms' and 'come-to-bed eyes'. Juno, she was such a dimwit.

But I urgently wanted to explore what lay under the horse rider's open shirt neck, how it would be to touch his lips, to be encircled by those arms. A wave of hot sensation rolled through me right down to my toes.

Gods.

Batting away the attack of lust, I tried to pull my brain together. I had to concentrate on Grosschenk. Saying his name to myself and glancing at his oily face and squat figure shut down my aroused body. Eventually.

The car came to a stop alongside the left wing of his house, a few metres from the tower at the end. By dead reckoning, this had to be north-facing. I glanced up. It had to be at least four floors high. Grosschenk produced a key and unlocked the door to the tower and ushered me into a tiled octagonal hall. At the far side, an open stairwell curled upwards, the treads hugging the dressed stone walls. A light metal rail with occasional uprights and two parallel rows of steel wire strung between them gave no real sense of safety.

'I had the railing added a few years ago. I wouldn't want to lose any of my guests by accident.'

His slight emphasis on the word 'accident' was unnerving, but I turned and smiled at him as if agreeing. Grosschenk gestured we should go up. I paused on the second floor as the latticed window looked out on the drive and front gate. Apart from the light shed by the courtyard lanterns, it was completely dark. Fabia and the backup detail would have no trouble hiding nearby on such a dark night.

On the fourth storey, the last step opened onto a semi-circular landing interspersed with a door in the centre and recessed mullioned windows at each end. I looked back down and shivered. The safety rail had ended below the top step. One false step and I could plunge through the stairwell onto the red tiled floor.

'Yes, very wise not to tread too near the edge,' Grosschenk said and smiled. He tapped a four-figure combination into the small panel by the frame and pulled the door open. Immediately in front of us was a damask covered table with silver cutlery and crystal glasses, and two chairs. Normal enough, but the whole room was open to the sky, protected only by a dome of octagonal glass panels. Grosschenk flicked a switch on the back wall and the lights in the courtyard died. White, red and orange light from the city glowed along the horizon to the north-east.

'What a beautiful room,' I couldn't help saying as he took my coat. 'You must love it up here.'

'Indeed, many people admire it. However, few dare step out on the balcony. A pity, as you can get a nearly three-hundred-and-sixty-degree view from there.'

He opened a glazed door at the far end of the glass wall. A narrow ledge protected by a thigh-high glass wall with a curled edge metal top rail extended out about a metre from the wall. He was right; the view was spectacular. The sky glittered like a net of white diamonds on navy velvet. At times like this, you wondered if there really were gods on Olympus who could have created such beauty. I stretched my hand out towards Grosschenk, about to compliment him.

Before I could say anything, I heard the door click behind us. Grosschenk's smile didn't change, but his eyes tightened. He fished in his pocket, drew out a cigarette and lit it.

'What are you doing, Manfred? It's cold out here.' I shivered, not entirely acting. The handkerchief hem of my halter dress fluttered around my calves. 'Let's go back in.'

'No, I want to clarify a few things first. I don't know exactly what you're up to, Aurelia, but I tried to give you a warning. You should have gone home then.'

'What on earth are you talking about?'

He looked out over the view. 'I know you're working with the organised crime people, with Huber. My business associate advised me to keep an eye on you, but that amateur who tracked you at first was total shit. God knows where he's pissed off to.' He flicked ash from his cigarette over the parapet. 'One less for me to dispose of.'

I shivered again. Putting that 'amateur' on the train to Bavaria had been the correct thing to do – for his sake.

'I thought you'd be warned off after Fischer took you and your silver refining friend for a little tour.'

'So that *was* you.'

He turned back, his eyes cold and hard. 'I can't have you bumbling around upsetting my trading, especially with the biggest deal of my life coming up.'

'You mean manipulating the silver contracts? Or are you running the smuggling, too?'

'My, my, you have been busy sticking your nose in unwanted

places. A little forward buying here and a touch of shorting the market there. I'll net a good sum and my associate will also achieve his goals.'

'Who's your associate?'

He laughed. 'You've been watching too many movies, Aurelia. I'm not telling you all my little secrets. Even now.'

'What do you mean? Is this a final warning?'

'Sadly not, I'm afraid this is dismissal.'

He didn't move, he just stared at me. In the next split second, the impact of his words reached my brain. He was going to kill me. Cold washed through me, but I felt sweat dribble down my back.

'You can't. They'd come after you. You'd never escape them.'

'A tragic accident, obviously.' He sighed. 'Really, Aurelia, give me some credit. You know, I don't know why Plico sent such a beginner – you should have stuck to playing soldiers.'

He shrugged, fished something out of his pocket. I searched around, desperate for some way out, but he stood between me and the door. I glanced down. We had to be a good fifteen metres above ground level.

'Please, Manfred. I have a daughter, she's only just five.'

'We have to hope she'll mourn you for a few months, but Caius says she'll manage with the palace to support her.'

I stopped breathing. Marina would be lost. She'd be surrounded by friends and cousins, but she'd be lost. I gulped down a sob as I felt my strength and will seep out of me. Then I registered what he said.

Caius? How in Hades was he involved?

'You're working with Caius?'

He shrugged. 'I suppose there's no real harm telling you now. Yes, of course. How do you think I could do this without a partner from Roma Nova? He's been invaluable.'

Gods! Living at Domus Tellarum, Caius would have been able to access all his great-aunt's records and dealings, and her valuables like the Mercury statuette. He'd have got round any safe combination she'd set – she was bound to have written it down. I shook my head, but it didn't wake me up from this nightmare.

'But why? Why is he doing this?' I glanced up at Grosschenk's face.

'That's not important.' He flicked open the cardboard packet he'd taken from his pocket and withdrew a hypodermic needle. The barrel was fully loaded with a colourless liquid. He placed it on the top rail of the glass barrier.

I shivered as a breeze touched the tower. Even if I called now, Fabia and her detail would never get to me in time.

'We can do this the easy way where you accept your fate and fall on the needle as a good Roman would or I can choke you to unconsciousness first. Either way, you're going to end up dead in the courtyard.'

# 11

Any soldier will tell you: if you don't get home, then you pray for a quick battlefield death. A high-gauge stainless steel needle was not the way I thought I would die. It glinted in the moonlight. Out of my reach.

'Caius tells me your daughter's a fetching little thing and should mature well.' He leered at me, his eyes warm with perverted desire. 'He seems to have quite a yen for her. Perhaps he'll share.'

A sour wave rolled up from my stomach and revulsion spread through me. I feinted a lunge to the right. He grabbed the syringe and launched himself at me. Before he could touch me, I'd brought my hand up, fingers hard, and shoved them into his right eye. He screamed, then fell back, collapsing to the floor.

'Door combination. Now, or I'll put the other one out.'

Although he was sobbing in pain, he brought his hand towards me, jabbing the hypodermic in the air. I ducked and dodged, not risking even being touched by the tip of the needle. He rolled over, attempted to stand up. I kicked him hard in the ribs, but I was wearing light evening shoes. He grunted but staggered on. If I didn't stop him, he still might succeed in killing me.

Then I saw the interior door from the inner landing open.

Caius. His eyes gleamed as he strode across the room. His hand reached for the door to the ledge, but it didn't budge. Grosschenk had locked it. I expelled the air in my lungs.

Fingers clamped my ankle. I twisted round and stamped on Grosschenk's right wrist with my other foot. His fingers slackened their grip and I stamped again. He grunted. The syringe fell out of his right hand and rolled away.

Caius was smashing his fists on the glass wall, but the panes held under the impact.

I glanced down over the balcony edge. It was cantilevered from the tower itself. Tugging to unwind the ultra thin rope concealed around my waist, I prayed it wouldn't snag. Fabia's steel reinforced braided band unclipped easily. I looped it round the top rail as an anchor for the rope and threw the loose end over the edge into the darkness.

Glass crashed behind me. Jupiter's balls. Bloody Caius had smashed the bloody wall in. There was no way back for me. I ripped panels from my dress to protect my hands. I grabbed my bag, slung the strap diagonally across my shoulder. I took a deep breath and climbed over the rail.

Clinging on, I scrabbled down the rope, hand over hand. Sweat dripped down my arms. Must go faster. Then there was no more rope.

*Merda*. I was dangling a good five metres short.

'Aurelia, you bitch!' I looked up and saw Caius's face distorted with anger. A shot rang out and the bullet flew past my head. Swinging the rope to spoil his aim, I let go of it as I touched the tower wall and dropped to the ground into the worst ever parachute roll. I heard a crunch as my foot bent awkwardly. I sprang up and pain shot through my foot.

Hades!

My toes flopped at the end of my left foot. They were broken. No doubt of it.

Another shot. I flinched, and I pressed myself against the wall under the balcony out of his line of fire. But unless I moved – now – they'd come for me and slaughter me like a trapped animal.

I snatched off the remnants of my temporary gloves and fumbled around binding up my foot so tightly it felt numb. I prayed to Fortuna to protect me.

The first time I put my weight on my broken foot, pain shot up through it as if I'd been bitten by Cerberus. I was never going to make it to the gate. Was this my fate? To be slaughtered and disappear in the middle of a north German forest as happened to Varus's legions in ancient times?

To Hades with that.

I stretched my stride to minimise the times my broken foot had to touch the ground. Tears washed down my face each time. No tools left out or branches uncleared in this tidy garden to use for support. I crawled the last few metres on my hands and knees.

At the gate, I collapsed against the pillar, leaning back, and heaved in some breaths. My throat ached like Hades. I dragged the evening bag round to my front and shouted, '*Arx, arx*.' Nothing. Of course not, it was only transmitting. My brains had been jumbled by the pain. Had Fabia heard it? No sound from outside, but nothing from the house. Yet.

I glanced up at the walls. No grip or holds. I had to climb the damned gate. Dragging myself to the horizontal bar halfway up, I took a second to catch my breath. Blood was seeping from my foot bandages so much I slipped on the metal, nearly falling off. I couldn't feel my leg below the knee.

My muscles trembled with the effort as I reached up and grasped two of the rising uprights of the metal gate. When I touched the fleur-de-lys finials at the top, blood wept from my fingers. Razor sharp. Gods, if I pulled myself over them, I'd tear my flesh off.

Doors slamming in the house, running footsteps.

I shuffled along to the old stone pillar, nearly losing my grip as my broken foot slipped. Straining with the last strength my arm muscles had left, I hoisted myself up onto the top of the wall. Sobbing to get my breath back, I squatted there for a few seconds. I looked down. It wasn't that high, but I'd have to jump. No, I couldn't. Not in a million years. I turned onto my stomach and slithered down, scraping the skin on my thighs and arms, falling the last metre onto the grass verge.

I dragged myself up. In the silence of the night came the burst of a car engine starting back near the house. As I hobbled along the road, every step brought a new and intense jab of pure agony. I heard dogs barking. I limped along and looked round desperately. Speed sign pole. Grabbed it. Hung on to it. Dizzy, shook head to clear it, but the world wobbled even more in front of me.

There was nothing. No sign of the backup vehicle. Where in Hades was Fabia? I dropped to my knees and fell into the ditch by the road. Bliss. No longer standing on my foot.

I fought against closing my eyes. If I did, I'd pass out. Caius would drive through those gates any minute now and kill me. Mars help me now, if ever you were going to! I started shivering and my foot throbbed so painfully, I gasped at each pulse. Just a few seconds' rest to gather my strength. I took a deep breath and closed my eyes.

The smell was the first thing that hit me: antiseptic, thin, drenching. The dull ache in the back of my hand followed. A catheter and drip line led up to a bag of transparent liquid. I was in a hospital room, blind down over the window, but daylight fighting its way in. A weight around my foot; it pulled my ankle sideways. The bedding around it resembled a small igloo, lifted by a cage in the bed. But no pain.

The sound of a page flipping over. A figure in a dark purple suit was sitting on a chair by my bed and flicking through a magazine.

'Fabia.'

She leapt up and brought me a drink. 'How do you feel, major?'

'Pretty well.'

She smiled to herself.

'Where are we?' I said.

'At the *Unfallkrankenhaus*.'

'What happened?'

'We heard nothing after Grosschenk made that dirty comment about your daughter. Neither did the legation signals office when I checked with them, so we broke out from our cover position.'

'Disobeying my orders, Fabia?' But I smiled at her.

She returned it.

'The next thing we heard were two shots from the house. I was about to order the detail over the wall to come in after you when I saw you fall down by the gate and roll into the ditch. You were unconscious by the time I reached you. I was checking you over when two men ran out of the gates and started shooting at us. We returned warning fire. They, er, retreated.'

I could imagine Grosschenk running away panicking like the

Furies were after him as the rounds flew over his head, and Caius, cursing at him for a coward, following him.

'Then we brought you here.'

'Thank you, Fabia.'

She frowned. 'Something odd, though...'

'What?'

'As we drove away, I spotted a tall man on a horse among the trees. Getting you medical attention was the priority, but I looked back and he watched us until I could no longer see him.'

The rider. The same mysterious rider who had stopped Grosschenk's car, the one who had looked into my soul. Who the hell was he? I knew one thing – I had to find him again.

'Odd indeed,' I said, attempting to sound more composed than I was. I cleared my throat. 'Must have been the rider who stopped us. Never mind that, get Huber in here.'

Joachim strode into the room an hour later and came to a halt by my bed. He bent over and kissed my forehead, then flopped down on the chair Fabia vacated. She withdrew to the wall by the door.

'You have no idea how pleased I am you're okay,' Joachim said. 'The best thing is I won't have Plico breathing down my neck every half-hour.' He smiled at me. 'He's a grumpy old sod, but seems to have some kind of heart under all that toughness.'

'Grosschenk?' I said. 'Caius Tellus? Any chance you've got them?'

I wasn't optimistic. As soon as they realised I'd disappeared, they must have known their game was finished and fled.

'We've got Tellus, but no sign of Grosschenk.'

'That's odd. What was Caius up to, hanging around Grosschenk's house? What was he doing when you caught him?'

'Shredding paper. Looked like a load of transaction records for international trading. We recouped a stack he hadn't started on. Scholz and Hahn are going through it all at the moment. So, plenty of good circumstantial evidence to go with what was on your recording.'

'Have you listened to it all?'

'Plico had the tape sent round this morning. What kind of transmitter were you using?'

I asked Fabia to fetch my purse. Half the sequins were torn off, but the reinforced canvas underneath was intact. I opened it and showed him the silver and black plastic recorder, encased in protective rubber. Six by four centimetres and multi-band, it recorded and transmitted up to eight kilometres. The end of the long thin aerial that ran up through the strap had snapped when the bag and I had hit the ground. It had cut the transmission, but the recording had carried on.

'*Himmel!* Is that what was transmitting? It's tiny.' He stretched his hand out, an acquisitive look in his eyes. 'I'll have to take it as evidence.'

'No. It's imperial state property. You have your recording.'

He bent his fingers, beckoning impatiently.

'Sorry, no.' I glanced up at him. 'Anyway,' I said, trying not to sound smug, 'you don't have the hardware to transcribe it.'

For all their famous technological expertise, the Prussians weren't a patch on us. We kept our secrets to ourselves. As a tiny country, we had to use every advantage and our technology was one of the most important. Possibly more than the silver.

For a moment, I thought he was going to pounce. I shoved the recorder under the bedclothes, regretting I'd showed it to him. He looked as disappointed as if he'd thrown a dog at knucklebones.

'Your people will have to surrender their weapons for forensic examination,' he said. 'They will then be confiscated. We do not allow discharge of firearms by foreign powers within the Germanic Federation.'

'For Mars' sake, don't be so prissy, Achim. They were used in defence only.'

'They shouldn't have been carrying,' he grumped.

'Well, perhaps they could use a *gladius* and *scutum* shield next time. We've used them very effectively against Germanic aggressors in the past.'

'Apart from Varus,' he retorted.

'Never mind that,' I said. 'I've got something far more important to discuss. Well, two things. First, that evening Prisca and I were snatched by Grosschenk's thug. How did he know who we were? Nobody knew I was anything but a junior diplomat. Prisca was a more likely target. But criminals at Grosschenk's level know we don't pay ransoms, so there was no point. And you only had vague suspicions about me.' I looked at him, square in the face. 'Unless you shared those suspicions with anybody?'

'No, of course not.'

'Not even Scholz and Hahn?'

'Even if I did, my team doesn't gossip. They're rigorously selected for incorruptibility, before you ask.'

'Everybody's incorruptible until you find their price, Achim.'

He looked around the room. Apart from the door to the shower room, there was nothing to see but a chocolate-box picture on the wall, an over-bed table pushed against the beige wall, a bedside cabinet and another plastic padded chair. He glanced over at Fabia.

'Don't worry about her – she's paid to be incorruptible.' Apart from knowing they were the military elite, Praetorians had an advanced sense of duty, as well as the pay and good perks.

'Secondly, how did Grosschenk know I was investigating the silver smuggling?' I pulled him back to our conversation. 'After the kidnap, only you, Tertullius Plico and your director knew. Oh, and your incorruptibles. And none of them would leak, would they?'

'Of course not.'

The muscles on his face didn't move, but he blinked. That was enough for me.

'Talk to anyone at home about your day at work?'

I didn't like Joachim's partner, Hasi Wolff, cruelly named Hartiman by his parents at birth. He'd latched on to Joachim in the second semester at university and hadn't let go. He hadn't liked me either. Jealousy, I supposed, but there was nothing to be jealous about.

'Don't be ridiculous.'

'So what are the other possibilities? Your Director of Organised Crime?'

'I—'

'Thought so.'

'Christ, Aurelia, Hasi and I have been together since uni. He wouldn't.'

I said nothing. Joachim's shoulders didn't slump, he didn't wave his hands around in protest. He sat rock still. But the flesh under his eyes sagged and his cheeks sank as if the bones underneath had turned to wet paper.

He stood up, nodded at me and left.

• • •

I stayed in the hospital for three days then moved back to the legation. The first afternoon, I insisted on booking a call on the videolink. I had to speak to my daughter, to make sure she was well and safe. The logical half of my brain said of course she was – she was in the imperial home with her cousins, and guarded by Praetorians. The other half of my head couldn't forget Grosschenk's revolting remarks. I'd seen Caius's eyes linger on Marina before I'd left. He wasn't the only pervert.

Marina smiled at me, then told me in a very serious voice about the new *palla* and *stola* she had sewn for her best doll, and the honey cakes she had been making and eating in the nursery kitchen. I nearly choked with pleasure. I spoke to Aemilia, the nursery maid, who hefted Marina onto her knee while she gave me her report. Marina smiled up at the girl, and put her hand in hers. Envy ripped through me. I wanted to be in that soft protected world with my daughter. The problem was I knew I couldn't live in it and not go insane.

Fabia tried to find out who the horse rider was, but neither the police nor any public service knew him. She went round stables and riding schools throughout Berlin and Brandenburg with a zero result.

For the next week I lay on the sofa, frustrated by my broken toes, hardly able to totter to the bathroom even with a walking frame. Joachim hadn't been in contact. Plico had sent a terse acknowledgement of my report and told me to wait for the Berlin court to take my deposition. I passed my time writing letters to my business manager, to Milo and the farm steward and expanding my to-do list to a ridiculous length. I sent Marina cards and some toys Fabia bought on my behalf, including one of the bears from Steiff am Kurfürstendamm. Even my annoyance at losing one of my antique sapphire earrings at Grosschenk's during my flight had faded.

Bored out of my mind and almost dozing off from the painkillers, I woke abruptly one afternoon at the sound of a knock on the door. A steward opened it and admitted Scholz from Joachim's police team. He was frowning as he entered the room, his spare frame tense. The bristle cut of his hair still reminded me of a nightclub bouncer, but as he stood there he shifted the weight from one foot to the other and glanced around the room. His expression tightened as he spotted my bandaged foot.

'The chief's on suspension. I've been tasked to come to take your statement. I've only got an hour, so we need to hurry up.'

'You're not the only one with a to-do list, Scholz. I'll check if a lawyer is available,' I said and flicked the switch on the intercom to call the *consultor*'s department. I wasn't going to make any statement to Scholz without a lawyer present. If it had been anybody else, I might not have hesitated, but I didn't trust him.

'What happened?' I asked, after I'd had confirmation a lawyer was on her way. He looked down at the floor, then back at me.

'We still haven't found Grosschenk. Before he was suspended, the chief said he thought he'd done a runner – the Helvetian Confederation, possibly the EUS. His passport's still in his drawer, though. But Forensics have started taking the whole house apart.' He crossed his arms and stuck his hands firmly under the opposite armpits.

'For Juno's sake, grab a chair and sit down.' I was fed up with him fidgeting around in front of me.

'He told us to pull his "friend" in for questioning and eventually Wolff admitted he'd been taking payments from Grosschenk for nearly two years.' He looked away for a few seconds. 'The chief was watching from the obs room. The worst was when I popped out for a moment from the interrogation while Hahn continued. I had to clear a point with the chief. I was there watching through the window with him when that little turd said he was fed up with the chief's self-righteousness and fancied taking up with that effing Roman we've got in the next cell. I didn't know whether Huber was going to break down or smash his way through the two-way mirror. He turned pale, didn't move but seemed to shake on the spot. Then he turned to me, far too calm, and told me to process him.'

Joachim would be so hurt, bleeding inside with that Brandenburg uprightness holding it all in. In truth, I was desperately sorry he'd been betrayed by Hasi, whatever I thought of the little rat.

'I have to go to him,' I said.

'You can't do anything for him. You're a woman and the one who triggered the worst loss of his life.'

# 12

Scholz was right – Joachim refused to see me. I wrote him a long letter that wasn't returned. I saw him across the courtroom when Caius Tellus and Hasi Wolff were arraigned, but he didn't or wouldn't look in my direction. I learned via Plico that he had been suspended, pending reassignment elsewhere. In the meantime, neither the local *Kripo* nor the national German Federated States organised crime bureau could trace Grosschenk. He'd vanished into thin air.

I was able to walk with a stick after another week, hobbling around the legation garden but ending up with an aching foot each night. After another week, it was merely stiff and I ventured out one day to the Tiergarten Park, near the zoo. The paths were full of nice, ordinary people, strolling along with their children or on the lookout for friends, students bantering, lovers hand in hand, grandmothers exchanging secrets. A typical picture postcard idea the Berlin Tourist Board loved to project.

Only I overdid it, and was limping back to the main road, desperately regretting I'd been too proud to take a stick with me. At the kiosk about twenty metres from the gate, I clutched one of the ribbed metal posts supporting the narrow roof overhang. I was debating whether to call the legation to send a car or try to hail a taxi on the main road when I saw a movement at the edge of my vision. A figure riding a chocolate brown horse was heading for me.

He moved with his horse as if the animal was a part of him,

swaying in perfect rhythm to the horse's clip-clop walk. Neither horse nor rider seemed to be making any kind of strenuous effort, but they were closing in on me at a rapid pace. It was the mystery rider who had stopped Grosschenk's car.

They stopped so close to me that I had to take a step back, nearly stumbling off balance. The horse's muscles were smooth under the glossy coat. I put my hand out and patted its shoulder and was a little surprised when it turned its head to me, ears alert. Grosschenk had called the rider a gypsy but the horse was no feather-legged cob. I didn't know a great deal about horse breeding, but I recognised Arab and Hungarian when I saw it. Our estate manager would have paid a lot of *solidi* to secure an animal like this.

I looked up at the rider. He bent forward, gave me a half-bow. His black curly hair touched the collar of his beige shirt, but not the neck of the leather waistcoat he wore over it. Dark, slightly worn moleskin breeches were tucked into black scuffed boots. As I stared at him, warmth rushed up my neck. He smiled, knowingly. Pluto, was I so obvious? The warmth spread into my face. The only time I'd had anything near this sensation since I'd met Marina's father was two weeks ago when this same man had looked down from this same horse at me in Grosschenk's car. This was ridiculous; for all his self-assurance, he could only have been twenty-three or -four, my junior by at least five years.

I looked away, embarrassed. He swung his leg over the saddle and was standing in front of me in a second's fluid movement.

*'Wie geht's, gnädige Frau?'*

'Well, thank you,' I replied in Germanic. 'But, you, where have you come from? Are you allowed in here with your horse?' I gabbled.

I didn't poke his chest with my finger, but I wanted to. Why? He didn't have to account to me. But somehow I felt proprietorial. I swallowed. 'Why did you and your friend here stop Grosschenk's car? Wasn't that dangerous? The chauffeur might have been armed for all you knew.' I waved in the direction of his horse. To my complete surprise, the rider caught my hand and kissed the back of my fingers. I snatched my hand back at the shock of it. What cheek!

'Do you care about what happens to me?' he said, and grinned.

'No, of course not,' I retorted.

He glanced down at my foot.

'Would you like a lift back to the legation?'

'How do you know I live there?'

'I heard that a girl with a Latin accent had been asking round for me—'

Fabia.

'—so I made some enquiries of my own.' He paused. 'I knew it wasn't you – your Germanic is nearly perfect. I had to go away on some business of my own, but tracked her down when I came back. She's careful, but not quite careful enough. And she led me to you.'

'And who are you to say that? Some kind of policeman or security?'

He flicked the tip of my nose with his index finger and grinned.

I jerked my head back, but not before I had felt a tingle run through my cheeks. He said nothing, but grabbed me by the waist and lifted me onto the back of his horse. The animal fidgeted as I settled on him.

'Don't wriggle or you'll fall off,' he said.

He looped the reins over the front of the horse's head and led me back to the legation without saying another word. He lifted me down at the front gate and rang the bell. I caught my breath at his touch and looked up at his face. But before I could thank him, he'd mounted his horse and gave me a final wave. I didn't even know his name.

I captured his image from the legation CCTV camera feed. Nothing on our system, but the New Austrians had him pegged as a smuggler operating in the Hungarian Outlands, but no concrete evidence. His name was Niklaus Farkas, known as Miklós, twenty-three, son of a small farmer from north-west Hungary. The Prussians wanted to talk to him – he was marked on their system as a 'person of interest'.

Of course, we couldn't find an address in Berlin for him. He was one of those people who lived below the radar of normal life. But his horse had to be housed somewhere, so he must be near stables or on a farm. I couldn't explain why I was so drawn to him; it was more than a mere attack of lust. Something inside me had leapt up in recognition, a sense of a long wait over.

Before I could pursue it, a large envelope stuffed with questions arrived from the Berlin Court. I worked through them for the next two days and asked Sharp Nose, the lawyer, to check my answers. She tutted and redrafted them all.

Caius's trial for smuggling was set for two weeks after I sent the questions back. Plico wouldn't let me go home even for a visit. In the meantime, I had nothing to do, no assigned role – I wasn't a trained diplomat. My search for the horse rider had ground to a standstill. My thirst to find out more about him was threatening to invade and possess my mind. In desperation, I offered to do some analysis work for the military office. The centurion in charge looked over her glasses and said it was well below my competence; a little boring, in fact, but if I was sure?

I was fascinated by a new satellite surveillance tool they were trialling. You could see people eating their sandwiches in the park, but not quite what filling was between the bread slices. The feed was relayed from Roma Nova, and all overseas legations had been allocated the task of surveying their own countries in their downtime. I suppose it saved the Defence Ministry at home some of its budget.

I used it to scan the 'sites of interest' on the list the supervisor had allocated me, checking principally for changes and signs of vehicle movements or new buildings at strategic sites against the latest editions of large-scale maps and still photos we had of the same areas. Perhaps in the future these systems would scan this automatically; it would save a lot of muscle and eye strain. I was finishing the section in eastern Brandenburg when I spotted an entirely new building on the edge of the woods about two hundred metres from the gate of a Prussian army base. Rectangular and open on two sides, hay stacked up at one end, it must have been a small barn. Not significant, I told myself and batted down the curl of excitement beginning to open inside me. I noted it in the file and decided to take a mid-morning break. I stretched my arms and shoulders, relishing the thought of a cup of strong coffee.

'Most useful for tracking troop movements, especially when they run their exercises,' a voice startled me. The military attaché was standing behind me. His breath was warm and full of onions. His stomach bulging over his belt testified to too many rich meals and a lack of exercise. From the green T-shirt showing at the neck of his beige uniform shirt he was a regular infantryman. He'd bagged a plum, safe posting at the end of his career and neglected to keep up his fitness. He pushed right up against my chair. I shifted a little further forward, but he followed. Hades.

'Shame you won't be here to see the next one,' he said. 'You could have come out with me on observation.' He leant forward. 'I don't suppose you'd—'

'Excuse me, ma'am,' Fabia cut in with a file in her hand and slapped some papers down in front of me. 'Could you sign these off? The signals captain needs them urgently and there's no other field rank around.'

The attaché scowled at her, saw the sheets were marked 'Eyes Only' and had no choice but to move off.

'Thank you, Fabia,' I breathed, not even a whisper.

She bent over as if explaining something to me. 'A pleasure,' she whispered. 'He's a real pain.'

'You're telling me. That's the second time he's cornered me. I have to get out of here for a few hours or I'll go insane.' I gave her what I hoped was an innocent look. 'Tell me how the car pool works.'

I drove east out of the city on the Frankfurter Chaussee, attempting to convince myself it was coincidence. But that building I'd spotted on the overhead had to be a small barn, ideal for keeping a horse discreetly. The minor road leading to the army camp was tarmac, but halfway along, a narrow unmade track led through trees. I hesitated, then turned onto it and pushed down on the accelerator, bumping along between tall trees as if I were a rally driver. What an idiot! I hit the brake a few metres further on as the track widened out to a small farmyard complete with chicken run and vegetable garden.

I cut the engine and looked round. Everything was quiet; no sign of life except chickens scratching the hard ground, and clucking. Stacked on one open side of the barn were oblong bales of hay. In the covered corner, the roof soaring over it, stood a prefabricated building, an industrial unit but with windows. Troughs of straggly plants stretching for the sun hung from the window frames. To the side was a stall and tack area. For one horse.

After another glance round, I walked over to the building and peered through a window. Two chairs, an old-fashioned table with pieces of horse bridle, a pot of polish and a rag; a bureau piled with papers; bookshelves stuffed full. Two intricate patterned rugs with long fringes covered most of the floor. A leather jacket embraced the back of one of the chairs.

'Had a good look?'

I nearly fell over as I whipped round. There he was – tall, imposing, electrifying. I swallowed hard. 'Niklaus, no, Miklós Farkas, I believe.'

'Very good!' He clapped his hands slowly.

I flushed under his scrutiny.

'Your recognition software really does exist then – it's not merely a rumour.'

I frowned at him. It was supposed to be a secret.

'I may be a wanderer but I'm not ignorant or stupid.'

'I didn't think you were.'

'What are you doing here, Aurelia?'

'How do you know my name?'

'I know many things about you.'

'Why? Are you spying on me?'

He smiled, a knowing, sexy smile. I had the uncomfortable feeling of being outmanoeuvred. 'Now tell me, what are you really doing here, spying on *me*?' he said.

'I'm leaving Berlin soon and I didn't want to go without seeing you again.' I couldn't believe I'd said that. Just like an angst-ridden sixteen-year-old on her first date.

He came over to me and touched my hair with his fingers. He brought his hand down the side of my neck, then to my lips. I closed my eyes for a second, relishing the electric sensation rolling through me. When I opened them, I found his dark ones full of passion. He kissed me gently, then more urgently. Desire spread through me and intensified. He pulled back for a moment and looked at me as if he wanted to devour me. His arm gripped my waist and pulled me to him.

'Neither did I.'

I lay afterwards, my body stretched over the length of his, my hand on his chest gliding slowly over the fine curling hair covering his soft skin. A sense of completeness filled me, of relief that I hadn't imagined the message his smile carried. But the miracle had happened.

I was dying to ask him why he had stopped Grosschenk's car that evening and if he was the horseman watching Fabia collect me from the ditch. And what was he doing in the Tiergarten Park the day I was there? Coincidence? Had he been following me? But I didn't want to break the delicate, lazy mood of complete relaxation. He stirred. I felt his lips brush my forehead and he murmured something in a language I didn't understand.

'Miklós, can I ask you something?'

'Mm?'

'How did you—?'

'I've been looking for you,' he murmured, half answering my question. 'But here in Berlin you've always been holed up in your legation. I thought I'd have to burgle it to get to you.'

I traced the ridge of his collarbone with my finger, and laughed.

'You could have rung the bell.'

I felt the answering chuckle within him through his ribcage.

'Imagine it, me rolling up to the front door; "Please may I see the spy I met in Grunewald? You know, the one with the broken foot who was nearly shot by the silver smugglers?"'

I pulled myself up onto my forearms.

'How do you know about the silver?'

'I may be in the informal import–export business, but there are some areas you really don't go into. Roma Novan silver is one of those. But we all know about it.'

'"We all?"'

'Nothing doing.' He laughed and pulled me down to him.

When I next woke, I lay with my head in the hollow of his shoulder. His hand ran lazily down my spine, causing such ripples of pleasure that if I died tomorrow I would count my life as complete.

When he stopped and dozed, my brain came out of the soup of satisfaction. He still hadn't said why he had been tracking me. He'd near as Hades admitted to being a smuggler, a criminal, although he'd never been charged, let alone convicted. Why was he interested in me? Cynical as he seemed to be, he wasn't stupid enough to think he'd get information out of me, or any favours such as looking the other way. Apart from my personal convictions, that kind of betrayal earned a long sentence in a hard prison, or worse, in the silver mines at Truscium.

Should I even be in bed with him? My head told me rationally I was an intelligence agent, not a police officer, so it wasn't my concern. My heart told me I'd never love anybody in this way ever again.

I raised my head to say something jokey but caught sight of a puckered indentation in his shoulder, about twenty millimetres, the size of a *solidus* coin. A gunshot scar. I touched it. He blinked and caught my hand.

'No.'

'No, what?'

'Don't ask.'

When anybody said 'don't' the immediate impulse was to do the thing forbidden.

'Too late. Tell me.' I fixed my eyes on his, silently trying to command him. He looked at me out of the depths of those dark eyes for a full minute. 'You won't like the answer and you definitely won't like me if I tell you.'

I gave him a little shake, then looked away. 'I don't know how to say this any other way, but I think I can take it. Whatever it is, I'll forgive you. It can't be that bad. And I'm not some sweet innocent.' I smiled at him to encourage him.

'Very well.' He half sat up and pulled me to him. He kissed the top of my head then took a deep breath. 'What were you doing a year and a bit ago?'

'What do you mean?'

'Up on a very cold mountain.'

I tensed. 'I was hunting smugglers, if you must know.' I couldn't look at him, but babbled on. 'One of them wounded one of my troops in the arm and winged my ear. I think I shot him, but he bloody well skied off down the mountain. He had the nerve to laugh at me.'

He leant over and kissed the scar on my lobe. 'I'm so sorry about your ear. I only wanted to fire a warning shot over your head.'

# 13

He let me hit him until my temper wore itself out. He lay there silent as I pummelled him. His face was expressionless as if he'd surrendered to my fury. When I eventually finished, I sat on the edge of the bed, shaking, and turned my back on him, overcome with embarrassment at myself and bone-deep anger with him at making me lose control.

I felt the movement through the mattress as he sat up and pulled me to him. I stiffened and resisted for a moment, but his warm body and earthy masculine smell were overwhelming. He circled me with his arms, cradling me, as if to absorb my hurt.

A little later, when it was dark outside, he laid me gently down and left the bed. I shivered and stared at the ceiling; being alone was unnatural. After a few minutes, the smell of coffee, warm bread and cheese spread from the kitchen. The emptiness inside me wasn't merely upset; I was starving. As he returned, he glanced at me, hesitated and set the tray down on the table by the bed.

'Here, for energy,' he said, and pushed an oval pastry into my hand. It resembled a *panis focacius* that the Italians called focaccia. It burst in my mouth at the first bite, herbs and cheese delighting my senses.

'Gods, what's this?' I said, almost forgetting my anger.

'*Pogača*. Easy to bake in the fire and eat on the move.'

I stared at him. I could see him hiding up in some remote wood, biting through the crusts, the crumbs irrelevant as he flung himself on his horse and galloped off to avoid border guards or police. The horse was ideal; no engine noise, no reliance on finding petrol or diesel, warm to sleep against and perfect for navigating woods, open plain and even towns. He sipped his coffee and looked directly at me.

'You're a good shot, Aurelia. It hurt like hell. I had to hole up for weeks. I know you were doing your job, but I swore at you long and hard once I'd come through the fever. The old man in the mountain hut who took me in thought I was going to croak. Nobody has ever touched me before. I swore at myself and then I cursed you to destruction. I was determined to find you and have my revenge.'

His look was so hard, fear curled through me. I was here, naked in every sense and nobody knew where I was. This man was strong and fuelled by desire for retribution.

'I *did* find you,' he continued, 'in Roma Nova and discovered your name, but two days later you came here. Bátor and I rode fast to follow you. I've watched you from your first beer sitting by the Spree. You Praetorians are good. I was impressed by how responsive they were when Grosschenk tried to kidnap you and the silver woman. And you are very much one of them.'

He took the coffee cup from my hand that was trembling by now.

'But when I rode in front of Grosschenk's car and saw you trapped there, it hit me. I couldn't carry on. The last thing I wanted to do was hurt you.'

I stared up at him, caught between fright and surprise.

He laughed. That same rich, deep and frankly sexy laugh I'd heard even through the blizzard. The same one as when Joachim and I went to interview Grosschenk's injured heavy after the kidnap attempt. It broke the crust of my fear.

'It was you in the hospital, wasn't it?' I said.

'Yes. You nearly had me there.'

'What were you doing there, anyway?'

'Trying to visit a friend.' He shrugged. 'Well, somebody who'd done some work for me.'

'Another smuggler?'

'What a thing to say about somebody you don't know!' His

indignation was coated with mockery. Then he grinned. 'No, he isn't, but something must have been wrong – there was a police guard by the nurses' desk, so I left it. I was joking with one of the nurses about being in the wrong corridor and laughed at her reply.'

'You're a slippery bastard, you know.'

'Probably,' he chuckled, and touched my nose with the tip of his finger. He bent over and kissed my lips. 'But a lovable one.'

I woke with the daylight, sensing I was being watched. Miklós was staring at my face, as if trying to imprint it. There was no smile.

'What is it?'

'Whatever happens, I will always remember this,' he said. 'Well after you've forgotten.'

'No, I don't want to forget. I want you with me. Come back with me to Roma Nova.'

He laughed. 'What would I do there? I can't live in a city.'

'We'll live at the farm – it's beautiful, open, near the mountains.'

'I left the farm when I was a boy. No more.'

I didn't know what to say. He couldn't slip away from me like this. I sat up and turned my back on him.

'So is that all this means for you?' I said, looking at the wall. 'A quick shag?'

He grabbed my shoulders and pulled me down onto the bed. I tried to keep my back to him, but he turned me over to face him.

'Never use such a stupid word to describe the precious thing we've shared.' He shook me. 'I'm not your pet at your beck and call, and you're no spoilt brat. So stop acting like one.'

I gasped at his hard tone, but he was right.

'Miklós, I can't leave you now.'

'I have no right to ask you to come with me. You know what I do. If I'm caught, I may be years in some Russian gulag or a Western prison.'

'Then come back with me after the trial. You'll have everything you need. You won't have to take such risks.'

'No. After a few months we'll be so sick of each other, and start resenting the smallest things. You'll be immersed in your work and family, I'll get restless and start trading again. Imagine the horror of meeting across that line. Again. We'd never be so lucky as we have been. You'd have to track me down and you'd die inside doing it. But I know you're Roman enough to do it even if your heart was breaking.'

Without looking at me, he left the bed, and pulled on shirt and trousers. I watched every stretch of his arm and bend of his back. Then he left the room.

Numbed by the truth of what he had said, I stumbled out of bed. Shaking with effort and emotion, I dressed in silence and without bothering how anything looked.

Outside, he half walked, half pushed me towards my car.

'Miklós, I—'

'Shush, just go. And don't look back.'

I swallowed hard, fell into the seat and started the engine. His eyes were liquid. He bent down, and with one graceful movement stretched and kissed me softly on the lips.

I gulped.

'Go.' He turned away and walked back to his makeshift house. He stopped halfway, hesitated, then braced his shoulders and carried on. I watched until he'd closed the door. How I made it back to Berlin, I didn't know. A grey lump of misery grew inside me. I didn't cry. I couldn't. I was beyond tears.

'Where in Hades have you been?' Plico shouted at me over the videolink. 'Do you have any idea how much budget I've spent getting them to try and find you? You're a vital witness in the case against a criminal trying to sabotage the economy of your country, let alone attempting to murder you, and you swan off on a jolly.'

He ranted on and on. I hit the mute button, until he held up a note in uneven capital letters, 'TURN THE BLOODY MUTE OFF'.

I poked the button on the console and sat back.

'What were you doing anyway?'

I shrugged but said nothing. He was irrelevant, an angry hornet trapped inside the video tube that couldn't get free or sting anybody.

'The imperial purse won't fund tourist trips, you know.'

'I'll pay it back at the hire car rate,' I said, in order to shut him up.

He flicked his hand impatiently. 'That's not the point.' He paused and frowned at me. 'Are you all right? You look a bit peaky.'

I nodded, wriggled in my chair and sat up in an effort to look attentive.

'Nothing I can't handle. I wanted a break,' I said. Broken was the ideal word for my heart at the moment; the rest of me was merely numb.

'Well, no more cowboy trips. You stay put in the legation until Caius Tellus's trial is over and he's behind bars. If you have an overwhelming desire for fresh air, stay within the city limits and take a Praetorian with you. I've advised the military commander.'

In contrast to the high drama before it, Caius's trial for smuggling was procedural, and over in a week; he was jailed for six years. Plico snorted when we spoke on the vidphone.

'Bastard will get out in four. Then we'll have to deal with him all over again. Shame he hasn't done something worse where they could nail him up forever.'

Most of the legation staff took little notice of me after that. I was a transient, now without authority, influence or purpose. They were courteous of my rank but the military gave me brief nods, the civilians hurried by, intent on their files and tasks. That was perfect; I was delighted to be miserable by myself.

I was packing to catch the morning flight home, thank the gods. I'd finished with Berlin. Marina was waiting for me at home. But the passion had gone out of my life. I would never know that intensity of feeling ever again that I'd experienced in those hours with Miklós. I would need to gather every bit of willpower into my core to carry on in a rational way.

Fabia stuck her head around the corner of the little office I'd used.

'The car's ready for you, major.'

I smiled. Whatever I said, I couldn't get her to stop calling me that. After all, that's how I still thought of myself.

I hesitated by the legation car. Although I was sheltered under the portico, it didn't protect me entirely from the rain blown in by a brisk wind. I shivered. I looked at the hands on my watch. We had plenty of time before the flight.

'Drive east out of the city on the Frankfurter Chaussee.'

'But—'

'Do as I say.'

We crawled through the eastern suburbs; the main dual carriageway was clogged up at this time in the morning, vehicles moving in short spurts of speed between traffic lights. Greasy spray from the vehicles in front and to the side washed over the windscreen. I glanced again at my watch. We were on the wrong side of the city from the airport and my plane was due to take off in ninety minutes. I covered my mouth with my hand. Gods. But I couldn't leave without seeing and touching the doorway where we had kissed, the bed where we had lain together. After another five minutes, before the turning onto the *Landstraße* leading to the woods sheltering Miklós's barn, Fabia twisted her head round.

'We must turn back now.'

'No,' my voice cracked.

'I'm sorry, major, but I must respectfully refuse. You'll miss your flight and I'll be on a disciplinary.'

Three kilometres away.

Hades.

Fabia turned round in her front seat next to the driver with a puzzled expression on her face, but I was too proud to let her see me cry.

# 14

We swung through the entrance to Tempelhof. Fabia had come with me into the terminal building and waited as I queued to check in. Perhaps she was being friendly, or perhaps she had orders to make sure I got on the plane. I handed my passport and ticket booklet over to the check-in agent. He flipped through the carbon copies of the vouchers, frowned at my diplomatic passport and consulted a clipboard he pulled out from below the counter. He lifted a telephone handset, gave his name and the words, '*Sie ist angekommen*.' I glanced at Fabia. They were expecting me. Why? I had elected to go through general passenger processing and not stand out in the VIP route. All I wanted to do was go home, without any fuss. The agent picked up my passport and ticket, clicked his service light off and beckoned an armed border policeman forward.

'If you please, follow me.'

'Why, what is it?' I asked.

Fabia stepped forward. 'The countess is an accredited diplomat. You may not detain her.'

'I don't know who you are, young woman, but please stand out of our way.' He didn't quite sneer at her.

'No, I will not. I am Optio Fabia, part of the Roma Nova diplomatic protection detail. Please state your reason for detaining Countess Mitela.'

'The head of airport security has asked me to bring her to him. If you obstruct us, I will have you arrested.'

'That would be an unwise decision,' Fabia stepped forward and stared at him with half-closed but fully menacing eyes. Her body leant into his so she was barely a centimetre away from him. He swallowed and stumbled back. Even the policeman didn't move, but glanced around as if looking for help.

I cleared my throat. 'This official thinks we have sufficient time, Fabia. No doubt he'll hold the plane for us.'

'Very well, *domina*,' she said, still staring into the agent's eyes, but shifting her weight back, releasing him from the threatening closeness.

I followed him across to the other side of the booking hall, Fabia marching barely a step behind me. The agent knocked at a door with no nameplate, but a camera above it, and on hearing the buzz of a door release, ushered us in. He gave a furtive glance at Fabia and left.

A man sitting behind a desk was jabbing a sheet of paper on a clipboard that a uniformed border policeman was holding out to him. Both looked up as we entered.

'Yes?'

I signalled Fabia back. She was in too bad a mood.

'You have asked to see me? I'm Aurelia Mitela.'

'This was delivered for you by the police with instructions to prevent you boarding the plane, if necessary.'

It was a plain buff envelope with 'Landeskriminalamt Berlin' at the top left and marked 'Urgent. Highly confidential for Aurelia Countess Mitela' written in ink in the middle.

'A car is waiting outside to take you back to the city.'

Pluto himself wasn't going to drag me back there, let alone the local police. I was going home. 'No, I'm on my way back to Roma Nova. My mission is finished.'

'Please,' he said.

I glared at him but I tore open the envelope. Inside was another from the legation with the 'Eyes Only' marking. GROSSCHENK FOUND. RETURN STAT LEGATION. LIAISE SCHOLZ GDKA/OK. T. PLICO

I was so furious I was calm. Perhaps it was the training, or my

Germanic blood. I was saving my anger for Grosschenk. I didn't bother with the legation; we went straight to the police station.

'So where is he?' I shot at Scholz.

He stared at me.

'What?'

'Haven't they told you?'

'Stop play-acting, Scholz. Just take me to him.'

'I can't,' he said to his desk. He looked up at me. 'He's dead.'

Scholz poured me a cup of strong coffee before he settled in the chair behind what had been Joachim's desk. His stubble hair was even shorter, if that was possible, and his shoulders were curled forward, making him into a ball of tension.

'We were taking Grosschenk's house apart. There's some nice stuff in there so we had to wait for those snotty bastards from the arts and antiques recovery service with their nice little cotton gloves and tight smiles.'

'Well, if they find a gold and sapphire earring, it's mine,' I said, trying to lighten the atmosphere. I knew Scholz didn't like me – I didn't think he approved of women in management positions – but he was professional enough.

'In the meantime, we've been clearing the staff area and outbuildings,' he continued. 'Nothing. But Hahn's been running a background check on Grosschenk's assets just to make sure we haven't missed anything. We already knew about the house in the Helvetian Federation. Grosschenk turns out to have had flats in London and in Hamburg as well.'

'Quite the property tycoon,' I said. 'So, any good?'

'Not a thing. The police in London and Zurich were quick off the mark, but those bastards in the Hanseatic Police up north took their time.' He glanced away, then looked at me. 'But that's irrelevant now.'

'What do you mean?' I wriggled in my seat. I didn't know whether Scholz was being cagey or just plain awkward.

'Hahn discovered the woodland at the back of Grosschenk's house belonged to the property. We'd assumed it was part of public land because it was the other side of the garden wall. Anyway, Hahn told them to let the dogs run through just as a precaution.'

'And?'

'One of the dog handlers thought his animal was acting a bit strange, but he smelled something funny himself and called Hahn over.' He pushed half a dozen black and white photographs across the desk.

I'd seen gunshot and knife wounds and tended a few, but this made me want to retch. I swallowed hard and fought to control my stomach muscles as they spasmed. Grosschenk had been decapitated and his remaining body partially burnt.

'The post-mortem's scheduled for later today, but we've confirmed the ID from the tattoo inside his elbow. It's a large version of the ones his lot have.' He snorted. 'Little man trying to look big.'

'That little man nearly killed me.'

Scholz drove me out to Grosschenk's house. I shivered as we went through the gates and wriggled my toes in a ghost of memory of that horrendous night. Although I had full use back, my foot sometimes stiffened from cramp. This damp day was one of them.

In the courtyard, two green police cars were parked by the north wing, near the tower where Grosschenk had tried to kill me. Scholz told me to wait in his car and crossed over to the nearest one. He bent over and talked to the uniformed *Schupo* inside, then both of them looked over at me and stopped speaking. What was going on?

Scholz said nothing as he drove us back out of the main gates. About fifty metres further along, we turned left onto an unmade road, with recent wheel marks pressed into the cinder surface – a goods vehicle or wide trailer. At the end, three figures in yellow oilskins and wellingtons huddled round the open rear door of a van marked 'FORENSIK'. One turned towards us as Scholz parked in perfect parallel; it was Hahn. He waddled over with a yellow jacket and a pair of boots. His face had lost its cheery schoolboy look.

'Here,' he virtually thrust the boots at me, 'or you'll ruin your fancy shoes.'

Scholz and Hahn led me in silence down a track between tall conifers. Perhaps it was the dark green shutting out the sunlight and the still forest absorbing even the sound of our feet on the needle-strewn path, but I shivered. I was dressed in a light cotton coat for travelling, not for hiking through damp, cold woodland. Now and again, luggage tags tied to branches flapped as we passed. I couldn't read the numbers and black writing on them as Hahn marched on and Scholz was almost treading on my heels.

About three hundred, perhaps three hundred and fifty, metres up the path, it crossed with another. Set back a few metres stood a stone-built shingle-roofed hut with a brick chimney at the far end and a shuttered window facing us. Patches of milky green lichen patterned the stone and moss grew all over the roof, vibrant green except in a circle around the chimney area where it had turned dark brown.

A uniformed policeman stood guard outside the open door. Scholz nodded to him and we entered the hut. Inside, it was freezing cold. Two yellow-clad figures with 'FORENSIK' on the back of their jackets crouched down, their work lit by a portable floodlight. At their sides were toolboxes with instruments, plastic bottles, bags and envelopes. One of them was scraping an area of the floor near the chimney with a tiny trowel. His short, precise movements stopped and he tipped black flakes into a plastic bag and sealed it.

'Human tissue,' he said without turning to look at us, 'burnt to a nice crisp.' His breath plumed in the cold.

I staggered outside. Gods. Grosschenk was a murderous little shit, but this? In my mind, there was only one person who could be responsible.

A uniformed *Schupo* approached and held out a radio set to Scholz. He listened, nodding twice, glanced at me and said, '*Ja, sofort*.' He handed the set back to the policeman and took my arm. 'The medical examiner wants to talk to you. So does the boss.'

'So you see, *Frau Gräfin* Mitela, we are at a loss as to why this body's head was cut off and the meaning of this note we found in its mouth.' We stood in the chill mortuary room, the doctor standing back as if not wishing to be involved. Under an intense overhead light, the corpse on the steel examining table was thankfully covered up, apart from its separated head. An acrid sickly smell hung in the air. The police director reached across and handed me a piece of paper, crinkled but intact. He looked over his gold wire-frame spectacles, first at me, then at Scholz with what was supposed to be an intimidating frown; Scholz said nothing.

I stared at the lined paper. It was a small sheet, about ten by fifteen centimetres and torn at the short edge as if from a spiral notebook. I rubbed the note between my thumb and forefinger.

'It's all-weather paper, resistant to body fluids,' I said. Then I read the words.

MIT FECIT

*Merda.*

'Would you care to translate it for us?'

I swallowed and tried to keep my voice neutral. 'Well, it's Latin. "FECIT" means "made" or "did" with an implied "it", and "MIT"… MIT doesn't mean anything in particular.' I waved my hand as if in embarrassment. 'I sometimes use it as a short form of my name.' I was being less than completely truthful. I used it all the time on documents under my signature – it was the Roma Novan custom – but I didn't like the way this conversation was developing. Not one tiny bit.

'I see,' the police director said. 'I think we should continue in one of our interview rooms upstairs.'

Scholz sat straight in his chair on the other side of the table from me, his arms crossed. Hahn fidgeted by his side. A green-uniformed woman *Schupo* stood by the door. Hahn had switched the tape recorder off when it became obvious I wasn't going to say a word until the legation lawyer arrived. Hahn had the grace to look embarrassed now that he had to view me as a suspect instead of a colleague. Tough. I couldn't believe they'd jumped to the conclusion they obviously had on the strength of one piece of paper. And no doubt written by that bastard Caius. After half an hour trying, they left me alone in the room.

An hour and twenty-seven minutes after my phone call to the legation *consultor*'s department, Sharp Nose strode in followed by Scholz and Hahn. About bloody time. Where in Hades had she been? She nodded to me. Hahn gave her a nervous smile and indicated she should take the empty chair beside me. She gave him such a hard look he retreated.

'First of all,' she said, 'you have no right to detain an accredited diplomat to the Royal Prussian Court. Secondly, if she graciously decides to help you with your investigation you are not entitled to make a recording as her testimony is given on an informal basis.'

'You have that incorrect, *Frau* Rechtsanwältin,' drawled Scholz, waving a sheet of paper at her. 'That used to be the case, but the diplomatic agreement between our two countries changed a year ago, following an incident on the Roma Novan border.' He looked straight at me and didn't quite smirk. 'I believe it was called the Mitela Variation.'

Gods, the irony of it all. I'd fought all the way to abolish the automatic right of protection for so-called diplomats to be brought into law. Now I was trapped by my own persistence.

'That covers espionage, Detective,' Sharp Nose shot back, '"foreigners caught in undiplomatic activity", I believe, is the exact wording. There is no case of that here.'

'Murder is fairly undiplomatic.'

'Oh, has my client been arrested for murder?' She asked with a faux-friendly smile. 'If so, what is the name of the appointed investigating prosecutor?' she cooed.

'No, she hasn't been arrested,' he said, and threw his sheet of paper on the table. 'We're pursuing a murder enquiry and she is a person of interest.'

'Of course, we're perfectly happy to cooperate to the maximum, but there is no question of any interview proceeding at present. If you have "cause of higher level suspicion", tell me now.'

Scholz rubbed his finger on the table in little circles. Hahn cast a worried look at his colleague.

'I thought not.' Sharp Nose was almost smug. 'To cover all eventualities, I have a release order signed by the district judge's office in exercise of the Paris International Diplomatic Protocols.'

Scholz snatched the folded sheet she had thrust at him and scanned it.

'Very well,' he said in a voice like grating steel, 'but once the prosecutor issues the arrest warrant, I look forward to pursuing our conversation.'

Back at the legation, after thanking Sharp Nose and agreeing to meet in an hour to go through everything, I went straight down to the comms room and dialled Plico. His terminal was busy. Asking me to please stop pacing around her office as if I were a wolf stalking prey, the duty signals officer handed me a mug of strong tea and suggested I sat down to wait. Ten minutes later, the terminal pinged and Plico's face appeared.

'I heard.' His voice was leaden. 'Galba's messaged me the short version.'

'Galba?'

'The lawyer you call Sharp Nose. Are you asleep or something?'

'She's never given me her name.'

He looked away for a moment.

'I didn't do it, Plico, if you're wondering.'

'No, I don't see you as a mad axewoman. You're more the pressed windpipe type.'

'Thanks so much.'

'Don't use that snotty tone with me and don't use it in the cooler or you'll get beaten up.'

'Is it that bad?'

'The reason Galba got that temporary release, and so quickly, was because I persuaded our justice minister to telephone her opposite number in the Prussian government. We promised you wouldn't leave the legation and you'd voluntarily surrender if they formally arrested you.'

'What!' I shrieked. 'Mars' balls, Plico, if you hadn't sent me that message at the airport, I would have been on that plane and home by now, safe with my daughter.'

'If you'd gone straight to the legation, you wouldn't be in the shit you're in.'

'Really? It sounds as if I'd be in it anyway.'

'True. They'd only apply for extradition. Which, although it's not technically "undiplomatic", we'd have a hard job defending.' He looked at me steadily.

'You know it's Caius behind this?' I said.

'How can he be? He's in jail.'

'Yes, he is now, but what in Hades was he doing at Grosschenk's house that took so long he got caught? And don't tell me he was only shredding paper. He'd do anything to sink me.'

'Is it that bad between you?'

'Yes.' Plico didn't need to know all the back history, but I was starting to become frightened. 'That police director, he knew. When he asked me to translate that note, he knew exactly what it said.'

'Then they have something else. We'll find out when the public prosecutor discloses the evidence. You'd better pack a toothbrush. They'll be back for you tomorrow.'

# 15

'Is that strictly necessary?' Galba, alias Sharp Nose, asked as Scholz nodded at the uniformed *Schupo* to handcuff me. As the cold metal slipped over my wrists, I shivered.

'She's being arrested for direct murder – it's regulations.'

Scholz and two uniforms had arrived at the legation front entrance at 08.30 that morning, Scholz clutching the arrest warrant. Evidently, they'd been able to convince the public prosecutor there was enough evidence to detain me. Galba and I had been ready since 08.00, sitting in the public area. I'd dressed in practical neutrals and packed some essentials in a small case. Fabia and another Praetorian hovered nearby in fatigues, not their normal indoor service uniform. I sighed mentally; she could look as tough as she pleased, but it wasn't going to change anything.

A green and silver police car waited outside, watched by the two Praetorians patrolling the driveway between the building and street. Parked behind it was a legation car and driver for Galba.

I flicked my fingers at Fabia to press the door release. She looked at me, pleading.

'Steady, Fabia,' I murmured.

We stood and Scholz served the custody order on me which I handed to Galba without taking my gaze off his face. Nor did I look away while he cuffed me until he took me by the arm and led me out to the car.

We drove round to the side of the grey concrete and glass police building. A studded steel gate slid open barely enough to let the vehicle through. One of the uniforms took me through a barred gate to the registration desk. The eyes of the custody sergeant wore exactly the same bored expression as the PGSF one at home. And the smell of instant coffee, sweat and stale air was the same. I nearly smiled, but willed myself to remain detached. For all intents and purposes I was in hostile territory in enemy hands. Preserving my inner core and keeping outer calm were essential.

After being released from the handcuffs, undergoing the most cursory medical examination and the most thorough search I'd ever had, I was allowed to dress, even to keep my watch. I'd left my usual rings and earrings locked in my luggage at the legation.

Juno knew how frightening this cold, detached handling would be for an ordinary person. A policewoman and her male colleague took me to an interview room and pushed me down onto one of the chairs. He left and she took up position by the door, folded her hands behind her and painted a cold expression on her face. On the wall facing me was the expected mirror through which they watched. If they followed standard technique, they'd wait for ten minutes to unsettle me. I folded my hands in my lap and closed my eyes, feigning sleep.

I'd counted to a shade under six minutes when I heard the door open.

Scholz was accompanied by two other men, both in suits, the older one in high quality grey wool, plus beautifully polished English brogues, the younger in chain-store from head to foot, plus sporting a dark brown handlebar moustache and sideburns. While the younger one unpacked recording equipment from a cardboard box and fiddled around with cables and microphones, Scholz and the other man sat down opposite me.

'This is *Herr* Kästner from the Public Prosecutor's Office,' Scholz began. 'You will answer his questions, please.'

The older man looked at me gravely, but said nothing. His silver hair was neat, his face square. He was unremarkable, but solid. He opened a small leather case and perched a pair of gold half-glasses on his nose and opened his file. He started asking routine questions, but I said nothing. After five minutes, he paused.

'Why are you not answering my questions? Your silence could damage your case.'

'I'm sure you'll forgive me, but you know I can't answer any questions without my lawyer present. And I'm equally sure you don't want to waste any more of your time talking to yourself.' I gave him my most charming smile. He glanced at Scholz who glowered at me. What in Hades did he expect? That I'd roll over and play dead?

'These are purely preliminary administrative questions, *Frau* Mitela. I'm sure we don't need to bother counsel for the moment.'

'Oh, I think we do, *Herr* Kästner, or we are going no further.'

'I don't understand. Detective Scholz assured me you had waived the presence of a lawyer for the preliminary session.'

'Oh, really?' I bit back, my voice so cold I nearly froze myself. 'Could I see this waiver?'

Kästner searched through the papers in his file while I took some quiet breaths to calm down. Scholz sat hunched over, stone-still. After a minute of rustling paper, the prosecutor turned his gaze on the detective.

'Well, Scholz, where is it?'

Scholz mumbled something, stomped out and slammed the door behind him. Five minutes later, he came back with the personification of the Furies in the shape of Galba.

Kästner was right, the questions were routine, but Galba fought every one, even insisting they put my title in my name. I'd never said 'No comment' so many times. She demanded a break with sandwiches and coffee, and privacy for a client consultation. Under some papers, she slid a scrambler onto the table.

'Optio Fabia gave me this. I wouldn't trust this lot to walk across the room, let alone not listen in.' She spoke in a very strong southern Castra Lucillan accent, just in case they could. That suited me; I'd been born on our estate there and could talk bucolic along with the rest of them.

'I'll serve notice on them for violation of procedure for a start. That was a stupid trick that cop pulled and it can only help us. Then we'll go for early full disclosure.' She glanced at me. 'There's something going on here and I don't know what. Anybody detained by the police must be brought before a judge and charged within twenty-four hours of the arrest, so we'll be in court tomorrow morning. We should find out more then.'

'Thanks, Galba, I appreciate your help. But try not to wind the prosecution up too far.'

'Well, the misogynistic bastards deserve all they get.' Then she did something miraculous – she grinned.

The prison van that collected me had high windows so I only knew we'd arrived at the remand centre by the jolt that nearly threw me off the metal bench in my tiny cell. A grating of metal on concrete – the gate closing – a short drive, then the van lurched to a stop.

The door was flung back on its hinges and a guard jerked his head at me.

'*Komm.*'

My file was signed and stamped at the reception desk, and again after another search, and yet again by the doctor after another medical examination. None of them looked at me as a person; I was a mere case number to be processed.

'This is a remand prison for women and youths,' the last warder said. 'We also take short sentence prisoners. You are not permitted to mix or speak with them.' She looked down at her precious file. The features on her hard face contracted. 'You are marked down to be held in a separate cell.' She sighed. 'I'll have to put you in the juvenile wing – we don't have any spare singles here in the women's area.'

Curious stares focused on me as I passed through the women's section. Silence fell as they tracked me. I stared straight ahead, clutched my case and a towel they'd given me at reception. Each time the barred gates clanged shut behind me, I felt I had penetrated further into a never-ending lobster pot.

The noise in the juvenile wing was twice the level of that in the women's wing. The warder pulled open a studded metal door and gestured me to enter. At least the door locked behind me cut most of the noise out. It was only when I was alone, lying on the bed that I started trembling. I looked round at the grey-walled room, narrower than a ship's cabin; a small barred window, steel washbasin, lavatory pan, chipped plastic-topped table screwed to the floor and plastic chair were the only other furniture apart from the bed. And then there was the smell of strong disinfectant that didn't quite mask the smell of vomit.

Galba thought she was cheering me up by saying it was only custody, not remand, and would only be for one night. She would work tonight to draw up a watertight surety document that would get me released into the legation's custody, whatever the charges. As an office-based functionary, she'd never slept on frozen ground near the top of a mountain for days with the wind trying to take your face off or been in hostage training which included playing the victim role. This room was luxury in comparison.

No, I was apprehensive about what laid behind this. I'd dismissed Scholz as a pain in the neck; he simply didn't like me. But putting me in the frame for Grosschenk's murder smacked of something far more serious. If convicted, I could be put away for over fifteen, maybe twenty years. I stuffed my hand in my mouth. Marina would be twenty-one when I got out. The tears escaped at last.

Next morning after a surprisingly good sleep, I did what I could with my hair and creased clothes. It was important I looked and felt confident before the judge. But as the warder fastened the handcuffs round my wrists, I noticed stains on one sleeve from the splash of gravy caused when one of the catering orderlies had slammed a bowl of stew down on the table the previous evening. Well, I'd enjoy a long soak in a hot bath and a change of clothes back in the legation tonight, and get rid of the smell and the stains.

# 16

Galba was waiting for me in an interview room in the Moabit criminal court. Her severe black tailoring, sleek hair and immaculate make-up made me feel even more unkempt. She glanced at her watch.

'We've got fifteen minutes. Apart from that stupid note which was obviously mischief-making, I don't know what in Hades they have on you. But somehow Scholz managed to persuade the prosecutor to sign that arrest order.' I stared down at the table, almost numb. If Caius was behind it, he would have been thorough. All my life he'd always been one step ahead of me.

'It's only a preliminary hearing and they'll only take it further if the judge thinks the evidence is good enough to take it to trial. You were incapacitated for most of the time after you escaped from Grosschenk's house. I've got the doctor's report from the *Unfallkrankenhaus* and I'll call him if necessary. Scholz is off the case, so we can slate him for prejudice. We'll be out in thirty minutes. Then they can start looking for the real killer.'

We were three hours. Prosecutor Kästner explained about the note found in the mouth of Grosschenk's severed head, quoting my comments and that the paper was the type used by Roma Nova armed forces. I jerked my head up at that. How in Hades had he found that out? Then, while praising my courage and bravery in escaping from Grosschenk's house, he turned it round, and referring to what he implied was my military record in his hand, made me sound as if I were a trained assassin. Next, he outlined my very understandable motivation – Grosschenk had tried to kill me.

Photos of Grosschenk's bloody head and part-burned body were passed round. One of the assistant judges shot me such a look of contempt and loathing, I shrank under the power of it. How dared he? I hadn't been convicted, but they already had me serving life. Galba sneered in a legal fashion dismissing everything as circumstantial. Then Kästner gave a little smile and held up a small plastic bag with a gold and blue gemstone drop earring.

*Merda.*

'This was found a metre from the body. I have confirmation from the photograph taken at the time by the *Unfallkrankenhaus* that Aurelia *Gräfin* Mitela was wearing an earring of this design when she was admitted. But only one.'

'Objection. How is that relevant? You're implying my client lost the earring in the forest hut on the night of the assault on my client. She was incapacitated by a broken foot, and fully occupied fleeing from two men intent on killing her. The recording, although not then transmitting in real time, tracks her from the house down the drive to the gate where she was recovered by the backup team. If the earring was found in the forest hut, then it was not taken there by my client. I leave you to speculate how it got there.'

'The victim was killed in a particularly savage way,' Kästner panned around the room posturing as if he were a stage actor in his greatest role. 'The perpetrator must have caused severe physical pain and mental anguish to the victim at the time. I would remind the court that decapitation and body burning are traditional Roman forms of execution.'

The bastard! Galba was on her feet the instant I was. Two hands from behind me thrust me back down and one of the prison warders clamped her fingers round my wrist.

It was Caius. I knew beyond doubt then it was Caius who had killed Grosschenk.

Then Kästner produced an axe on which they'd found traces of blood. It was a wood axe, the sort you'd find on any farm; I'd used one myself on occasion at Castra Lucilla.

'This is not a particularly difficult tool to use and certainly not beyond the ability of a trained and physically fit woman like the accused.'

By now, the judge was waving Galba down automatically, but she had her turn after the prosecutor had finished.

'As we have seen, it was impossible for my client to have done anything the night of the attack beyond surviving the murderous assault on her. She was hospitalised and has been convalescing since then. Although the breaks in her foot have healed well and she has regained full use, she is still undergoing physiotherapy. While waiting to testify in the case against Caius Tellus, convicted only recently for criminal conspiracy and smuggling, she has been working in the Roma Nova legation on light desk duties with only short exercise times outside. She has thus had no opportunity to perform such a killing.'

She looked straight into the judge's eyes.

'And I would remind the court that Aurelia *Gräfin* Mitela was not the only Roma Novan in that house that night.'

'But she was the only one at liberty as well as being capable of carrying out that killing,' Kästner interrupted. 'And, of course, there is that hubristic note and her sudden departure after Tellus's trial. Moreover, because of the cold conditions in the forest hut, the victim's time of death has not been established. It could easily have taken place anytime during the weeks after the night she was abducted.'

Galba flicked her hand in the direction of her files. 'We can easily file a statement of Aurelia *Gräfin* Mitela's movements since the day she left hospital which will clear her. If the court pleases,' she added hastily.

Silence dropped and we waited while the judge scribbled notes.

'Obviously, there is still more to discover in this matter,' he said at last. 'I am not convinced there is enough corroborated evidence to go to trial. We will re-examine in four weeks.'

Galba smiled at me and mouthed, 'You're out.'

'However, because of the seriousness of the crime, the skills and abilities of the accused and likelihood of flight,' he continued, 'I am remanding the accused in formal pre-trial custody.'

• • •

After they took a photograph of me holding a number board, they handed me a prisoner uniform in exchange for my clothes and thrust two sheets of typed regulations and a towel into my hand. I followed a warder into the women's wing. She led me across a circular hallway with groups of easy chairs, through a barred gate labelled *Untersuchungshaft* to the end of a short corridor, through another gate into an open space with easy chairs and two plastic-topped tables and metal-legged dining chairs. She stopped outside one of the six half-open doors leading off the area and pointed to the top bunk bed in a shared cell.

'That's yours. Don't mind her on the bottom – she doesn't say much but she's harmless.' A body lying still, curled in sleep and clad in the same dull cotton shirt and trousers I now wore. The warder's keychain clinked as she turned and left.

The afternoon sunlight was still strong and white and now shone through double bars and dusty windows. The whole room was bland; dark grey vinyl floor, pale grey walls, pale wood and metal shelves with half a dozen books, utility table screwed to the wall, two plastic chairs and a bunk bed.

I dropped onto one of the two chairs and wiped my hand across my face. How in Hades had it gone so wrong? I didn't know how long I sat there immobile with my mind numb. On the margin of my senses, I registered a hum of something mechanical and the twin smells of cleaning fluid and body odour. I couldn't rant and rage. What was the point? I'd keep it for Caius. Galba had booked a visit for tomorrow. She'd better have some bloody good answers. I was not going to waste fifteen or twenty years of my life in a damned Prussian prison for something I hadn't done.

A bell rang and the form on the lower bunk stirred. She sat up.

'Who are you?' Her face was blotchy with marks from the folds of the sheet on which she'd been lying. She blinked and looked puzzled. 'Where's Krista? Krista is always here. She looks after me.'

'I don't know any Krista. Did she leave today?'

'Krista said she'd never leave.'

The young woman's face became pinker and her eyes stared. She burst into sobbing. Gods, I was stuck here with a simpleton. That was harsh, but what was I supposed to do? From the half-opened door I heard footsteps outside. What was the time? I looked at my empty wrist. Did they think my watch was dangerous? I opened the door further. Women were assembling in the open area.

'What's going on?' I asked one. She ignored me and walked on. A woman in civilian clothing was working her way around the wall looking into different cells and then glancing at a folder in her hand. She looked at me, blinked and hurried over.

'Are you Aurelia? Aurelia Mitela?' I nodded. 'Charlotte Halversen. I'm your social worker. I'm seeing you tomorrow after your lawyer has visited, but I thought I'd check you knew what to do tonight.'

She handed me a plastic bag with a toothbrush and some toiletries. 'They'll bring your bag to you tomorrow after it's passed through security.' She was almost apologising. 'Supper is being served any minute now and after that the doors will be locked for an hour and half. Then it's free associative time until 20.30 when it's lights out.' She gave me an overly cheerful smile and touched my forearm. 'It'll be a bit strange tonight, but we'll go through everything in the morning.'

I nodded, but said nothing. I felt nothing.

'Well, you'd better go and eat now. Goodnight.' She turned on her heel and left me in the corridor staring after her. The sobbing from the cell pulled me out of my stasis. I crouched down by my cellmate who perched on the edge of her bed, hands each side gripping the edge.

'Come on, show me where we eat.' She looked up at me, her mouth open. She looked down at the hand I was stretching out to her and took it, heaving herself up.

A dozen women hovered outside, some murmuring, most silent. They looked as stunned as I felt. They turned almost as one as the gate was opened by a warder followed by two other prisoners pushing trolleys with steel containers, trays and plastic cutlery. Supper. My stomach growled; I hadn't eaten since the chewy rolls sloshed down with watery coffee that was supposed to have been breakfast.

After the initial jostling by others, I led my cellmate, who was still gripping my hand, to the trolley. The taller server, one of the trusties, snorted.

'See you've found a new friend, Greta.' Greta bobbed her head, glanced fearfully at the other woman, then away and half hid behind me.

'So what's your name, then?' the server said to me.

'Aurelia Mitela. And you are?'

'What sort of a name is that? Are you foreign?' She stopped and stared at me, her ladle suspended in mid-air.

'Get on with it, Eggers,' snapped the warder.

Eggers plonked a ladleful of stew on my plate, along with potatoes and carrots. It smelt of nothing, but I was so hungry I couldn't wait to start. Except Greta was still attached to me. I prised her fingers off but waited politely while she was served. Eggers put tiny portions on Greta's plate and sneered. This was ridiculous. Greta was pitiful but didn't deserve such treatment.

'I think you have forgotten to put the full portion on my cellmate's plate.'

The warder didn't say anything, but gestured Eggers to do it. I looked at Eggers, daring her to refuse. Her face flushed red. She banged her ladle down on Greta's plate, splashing the gravy everywhere, but deposited a full portion.

I gave her a little smile, turned my back on her and went to the table to eat, ignoring the stares of the others. The trouble would come later.

After the door banged shut and the warder locked us in for the night, I went through the motions of brushing my teeth and washing on automatic. I grasped the edge of the washbasin, braced my arms and bowed my head. Gods, this was exactly the same as being in basic training, but locked in. I hoped I could cope with that, but not the fear that had crept in and taken root inside me.

After breakfast the next morning, a warder took me to a small room near the prison reception containing a wooden table, two chairs and Galba. I was so pleased to see her I could have thrown my arms around her. I didn't; she would have thought I'd gone insane. Her cherry red skirt and shoes and multicoloured jacket were such a welcome contrast to the bland world I was now inhabiting.

'*Salve*, Aurelia Mitela.'

Why was she so formal? And she didn't meet my eyes.

'Galba? What's wrong?'

'Everything is in order. I wish to outline your defence with you.'

'If you don't come down off your high horse, Galba, we're not going to be doing anything. Tell me.'

She fiddled with her papers, until I grabbed her hand and shook it.

'I am disappointed you did not see fit to place your complete confidence in me,' she said, her tone sullen. 'It was only when I was going through your case with Tertullius Plico last night on the videolink that I learned about your unexplained thirty-six-hour absence.' She glared at me. 'Why in Hades didn't you tell me? What were you doing in that time?'

'Ah! That was private time and nothing to do with this case.'

'Everything is to do with this case! Where were you and can anybody corroborate it?'

I stuck my chin in the air and shook my head.

'I've lied in court for you,' she said. 'You owe me the truth.'

I felt the warmth rise up my neck. It was mainly embarrassment. It hadn't occurred to me that she would be placed in an awkward professional situation. Stupid wasn't the word.

'I... I met somebody and spent some time with him.'

'Name? Where can I contact him?'

'I can't tell you the first and I don't know the second.'

'You must tell me. This is vital for your defence. The prosecution will home in on it, no question.'

I shook my head.

'Very well.' Her lips couldn't be more pursed. 'I strongly advise you to think about this.' She pushed a sheet of paper towards me. 'Please sign this authorisation for me to act on your behalf in all matters. I realise it's very wide-ranging, but I can't keep running out here every time I need to do something for you.' She paused. 'You'll have to trust me. Unless you want a different legal representative.'

I signed. She knew the system here and would stand up to the Prussians.

'I found out via a contact in the prosecutor's office that they intend to interview Kriminalpolizeikommissar Huber, then Grosschenk's employee, Fischer...'

'Who?'

'The one whose jaw you broke.'

'Oh.'

'... and Caius Tellus.'

'I'm stuffed, then.'

'Why?'

'Caius will spin them such a distorted story. You don't know how manipulative he is, Galba. I'm sure he's behind this.'

'Anything I should look for?'

'It's exactly his style to have put that bloody note in Grosschenk's mouth. I know the police reached Grosschenk's reasonably quickly and they only just got him, but why the hell was Caius still there, unless he'd been busy killing Grosschenk. I know this sounds macabre, but it would be a physically strenuous and tiring task. Maybe it had slowed him down. And he still had to burn all those transaction documents.'

'I'll look at the timings in detail. I presume you're happy for me to bring some help in?'

'Bring Cerberus from the Styx if need be.'

# 17

With her blonde wavy hair gathered behind an Alice band and her well-cut, rather prissy clothes, Charlotte Halversen was a nice lady with a nice face from a nice family. What she was doing as a prison social worker was anybody's guess.

'How did you settle in last night? Any problems?'

'No, nothing significant. I suppose it's a question of getting into the routine.'

'You seem remarkably calm and this worries me. Do you realise how serious the charge is?'

'Yes, I do. The most terrifying thing is that I might not see my five-year-old daughter until she is past twenty.'

'Oh, I'm sure they will arrange visits for you.'

'So you also think I carried out such a brutal murder?'

She looked down at her file and scribbled something.

'Look, Charlotte Halversen, unlike many people who come to prison, I do not need any mental health medications nor do I have substance abuse issues. I have been brought up to be resilient. Apologies if I do not conform to the usual pattern of intake.'

She looked away for a moment, then met my gaze squarely.

'I understand you were a diplomat, a trade delegate. Your file shows you had a privileged, aristocratic background. Such a life would not prepare you for prison. I've seen the self-contained personalities crumble within days. I don't want to see that happen to you.'

'Tell me, what do you know about Roma Nova?'

She shook her head.

'We breed our children tough and expect them to stay resilient throughout their lives. It's a pragmatic question of survival. And we've managed for over fifteen hundred years. I'm a soldier by trade. This place,' I waved my hand around, 'is not dissimilar to a training barracks apart from no kilometres-long forced marches.'

'Perhaps, but be careful with being too cocky. Here we lock you in.'

I looked down and tapped my finger on the table.

'Sorry, you're quite right. It's so frustrating sitting here when I should be out looking for the real killer.'

'That's the police's job and they think they've found her.'

'Them! They've taken the easiest option – foreigner, seemingly obvious motive, opportunity – without thinking it through. Grosschenk was a major organised criminal with connections into the highest level of local government. He was up to his armpits in silver smuggling with Caius Tellus at the minimum and possibly illegal trading. I was merely in his way. Tellus is now in prison where he should be and Grosschenk should be there with him, not dead like a stuck pig.' I slapped my hand on the table. 'I'm an officer of the state working with your federal organised crime office. I'm sworn to uphold the law, not break it. And I've been manoeuvred in here. Doesn't that seem odd?'

'I can't comment on your case, obviously. My job is to help you adjust to life here and prepare you for the next stage of the legal process.'

Damn. I'd made her withdraw into her statutory persona. She scribbled away on her notepad, then looked up.

'The court has requested a psychological evaluation. I hope you have no objection?'

The next morning, I received two letters. Both had been opened and stamped by the court office as 'passed'. I went back to my cell to read them. One was in a Foreign Ministry envelope, a snotty letter from Tertullius Plico's secretary on headed notepaper, telling me I had been suspended from duty pending the outcome of the trial, and all pay and privileges were revoked. Well, stuff him. Then I saw the handwritten note below the signature block. 'Don't take it personally – it's regulations.'

Humph.

The other, whose envelope had the post office box number used by the imperial family as their return address, was from Marina. I ran my fingers over the envelope, hardly daring to look inside.

*Dearest Mama,*

*I hope you are well. Uncle Plico said you couldn't come home yet as you had to stay and do some more work for him. Nonna Justina said it was very important, so I understand.*

*We went to the zoo park yesterday. I love the giraffes. Here is a picture. I have a puppy now. She is so funny and licks my face. I hope you will like her when you come home. We can take her for a walk round the farm.*

*I hope you can finish your work soon. I miss you.*

*Love from Marina*

*xxx*

I stared at the painful writing, the grinning giraffe, laid my face on my arms on the ugly table and sobbed my guts out.

I don't know how much later it was when I realised somebody was shaking my shoulder.

'Relia.'

Greta. Piss off, I thought, but I looked up at her, hoping I wasn't scowling.

'Relia, there are some people looking for you.'

I stuffed Marina's letter under the book on the table, brushed my hand across my face and stood, just in time to see Eggers and another woman push Greta aside as they forced their way in.

'You, Mitela, come with us.'

They stood at close right angles to each other, allowing no escape, and hands ready to grab me. My heart sped up instantly. I automatically shifted my weight onto the balls of my feet and flexed my fingers. Both were heavily built, but running to fat. So not such a problem. But I was sure that the penalties for fighting in prison were severe. I took a breath to calm my response down.

'And why is that?' I contented myself with saying.

Eggers' hand swung up as if to strike my face, but I blocked her, twisted her wrist back and stamped hard on her foot. The other woman moved forward, but found my fingers jabbing her thorax. She bent over and coughed violently. I wanted to smile at the two of them squirming, but kept my face impassive.

'Now, shall we start again?'

'The boss wants to see you,' Eggers muttered.

Eggers limped in front of me. Even in the lightweight plimsolls, I'd given her something to think about. Sadly, I was sure I'd have a bruise on the sole of my own foot later. The warder was impassive as she unlocked the gate leading from our section and gave Eggers the tiniest of nods. It was free associative time, but the warder was a little too compliant, I thought.

The circular hallway was unfurnished apart from two plastic-covered easy chairs with a small table between them. A brunette, around fifty and wearing prisoner uniform, was sitting in the right-hand chair and smoking a cigarette in this non-smoking facility. Behind her chair, two further prisoners hovered in attendance.

Eggers and her companion stepped aside once we reached the seated woman. She looked up at me, a hard expression on her over-made-up face. I stared back, straight into her eyes, and waited. After a full minute, she glanced down, stubbed her cigarette out in the empty jar lid on the table and flicked her fingers at me.

'Sit,' she commanded.

I sat opposite her, leant back and crossed my legs.

'You're a cool bitch, aren't you?' she remarked.

'I see no point in hysterics.'

She snorted. 'You showed a lack of respect for one of my people.'

'No, I taught her some manners. And she's had another lesson today.'

The atmosphere dropped beyond freezing. The other four women stared at me, one with her mouth open.

'You're Roma Novan, aren't you?'

I nodded.

'Tough bastards. What did you do there, then?

'Special forces soldier.'

'Fuck me!'

'I'd rather not.'

She burst out laughing. I smiled.

'No wonder they fingered you for topping Grosschenk.'

I said nothing.

'He was a turd. He slashed two of my girls. They were so terrified they were useless after that. Then you'd see the bastard in the papers sliming all over the bloody council. Good riddance.'

One of the two women supporters nodded her head vigorously. The seated woman frowned at her. The supporter stopped moving instantly.

The seated woman stood up and I came up with her. It would be stupid to ignore the power dynamics in a tense place like this.

'Okay, Roman, I'll leave you alone. But no crossing my boundaries. If you get any trouble you tell them you're under Magda's protection. Oh, and *wilkommen im Knast!*'

## 18

Now the prisoner boss had 'welcomed' me, the other inmates treated me differently. Few started conversations but replied easily enough if I spoke to them. Mealtimes were easier; nobody jostled me and I received extra portions at the table. Magda's intervention guaranteed this easier passage into prison life; I had become a 'client' to her 'patron' in the ancient Roman pattern. Not the most rewarding relationship, but bearable. I didn't realise how I'd slipped into the prison routine until Galba visited a week later.

'Are you sticking it out in here?' She glanced around and screwed up her face as if there were rotting cabbage under her nose.

Somehow I didn't want to tell her about my arrangement with Madga – it belonged to a world Galba knew nothing about. I wasn't sure she'd understand.

'Yes, coping. I'm helping with literacy and keep-fit classes and started reading my way through the library.'

She gave me an incredulous look. 'I thought you'd have arranged a prison break by now – that's what Secretary Plico's been worried about.'

'Oh, for Juno's sake!'

'Now you're becoming the perfect little inmate.'

'And you're forgetting who you're talking to,' I retorted.

We both smouldered for a few moments. Galba coughed and pushed a punched and bound folder across the table.

'This is the prosecutor's office disclosure document. It lists all the evidence against you, including the interviews, even the one with Caius Tellus. You're quite right, he's a smarmy bastard. He pretends to be reluctant and super virtuous. He regrets you are so desperate that you must be trying to frame him for Grosschenk's murder. Grosschenk's man, Fischer, has nothing good to say about you, except he finally admitted that Grosschenk ordered him to take you and Prisca Monticola for a ride to "scare you". Huber's interview is factual and describes your role in the undercover operation – a little more positive than the other two. I've had Monticola's statement in – she's wonderful – and Plico has sent in a good report.'

'But?'

'The court will probably discount the last two on the grounds of "they would say that, wouldn't they?"' She gave me a long, strong look. 'We've tied up all the timings except the thirty-six hours you went off on your private visit. Are you protecting him because he's married or some prominent person?'

I glanced at her, then shook my head once.

'So who is he? Gods, he's not some criminal on the run, is he?'

'No.'

She said nothing more for a minute.

'Look, unless we tie the timings up with fully corroborated evidence, they'll convict you. You'll forgive the crudity, but is a good shag worth fifteen to twenty years of your life wasted in a foreign prison?'

I smacked my palm down on the table and jumped up out of my chair. I leant over the table.

'Enough! We are going round and round this point. You go and insist they pinpoint Grosschenk's time of death. Get Plico to dig out a forensics expert from the Central University at home and fly them to Berlin to help these idiots. It's ridiculous in this day and age they can't get a closer time just because it was cold in that forest hut. If they don't cooperate, get Plico to ask the imperatrix to issue a writ of false imprisonment in the League of Nations Court. For Juno's sake, do something instead of bleating about a completely irrelevant event.'

She stared at me with an open mouth. Her face started to pucker into a withdrawn expression, then she stared down at the table and hunched over. I was surprised by her defeated posture.

'I apologise for shouting at you, Galba, but it's so frustrating. None of this is your fault. It's these damned Prussians refusing to consider any other possibility. They've fingered me, solved their case, so they don't care.'

Her head was still bowed, but she spoke with a low intense voice.

'No, I apologise, *domina,* I… I trespassed on personal concerns. And I forgot who I was dealing with.' She looked up at last and waved her hand in a vague circular motion. 'I'm not a criminal lawyer. This place gives me the creeps. When I walk in here, I see all the inmates as either pitiful or dangerous, threatening normal people's lives. They slouch along the corridor or track you with eyes looking as if they want to eat you. People here are failures or cheats and deserve little respect. And I lumped you in with them.'

'Well, never mind that now.' I patted her shoulder. 'The important thing is to go on the offensive and stop taking what other people are dishing out.'

Two days later, I was summoned to the social worker's office. Unlike the rest of the prison, it was painted in a pastel yellow with walls covered in over-jolly posters with optimistic images about resettlement, social help in the community and medical services outside. But instead of the equally pastel Charlotte, I found a middle-aged man with brown and grey hair, blue eyes and a cheerful smile sitting in her place.

'Please, sit.' His voice was as pleasant as a sunny Sunday afternoon. 'I'm Dr Lenz from the Friedrich-Wilhelms-Institut at the university. *Frau* Halversen has explained why this assessment is being carried out, I think?'

I opened my mouth to say she hadn't explained anything, but decided not to land her in trouble. If I didn't cooperate it would be another black mark against me. And perhaps something positive would emerge from it. So I smiled back as if I didn't have a care in the world and waited.

He put a pair of spectacles on and looked at me over the top of the lenses as if he were a professor addressing a student.

'My evaluation is mainly based on a new psychometric questionnaire designed to measure psychological preferences in how you perceive the world and make decisions,' he continued. 'Then we'll discuss various general topics and how you feel about them.'

'Very well,' I replied. I'd faced much worse in our resistance to interrogation training. We'd been taught to stick to the truth as much as possible; it reduced the strain on your mind trying to concentrate on concealing the important things. It also helped you appear to be a more genuine personality to the interrogator.

'You seem remarkably calm about this,' he said.

'I'm not worried, if that's what you mean. I am what I am and I have no wish to conceal anything from you.'

'Hm. Everybody has something to hide, so you may be surprised.'

'I'm sure they have, including you,' and I smiled knowingly at him and watched a tinge of dark pink appear in his cheeks.

'However, I'm not the one being assessed,' he countered. 'Are you happy to complete it in Germanic or would you prefer Latin, or English?'

'Germanic will be fine, thank you.'

He drew a multicoloured form with tick boxes out of his file, wrote my name and prison number at the top and pushed it across the table. It resembled the standard psychometric test I'd completed in the officer selection process years ago. Unlike the fiendish command test when I'd been selected for promotion to major, which had made me and all the other candidates sweat our brains out, this was fairly basic. But as Charlotte Halversen had said, it never paid to be too cocky, so I focused all my attention on it.

He sat there and read his book, not even glancing once at me. He was an academic, conducting a test in the field in an appropriately neutral way. Perhaps I was being cynical, but I wondered how high the fee was the prison department paid for every prisoner examined.

After twenty-three minutes, I laid down the pen and sat back. He blinked but continued reading, ignoring me. Classic power ploy. I laid my hands in my lap and shut my eyes.

'Oh, you've finished,' he remarked after a minute. I opened my eyes, looked surprised that he had spoken. Easy game for two to play. He pulled the form towards him and glanced up at me. 'Please wait outside. I will call you back in when I am ready. And do not discuss the test contents with anyone.'

Nobody was in the corridor. I sat on one of the three plastic chairs and flicked through a magazine from the stack on the floor. Reading a piece about intra-German squabbling, I noticed Charlotte Halversen approaching me, but pretended to be immersed in the magazine until she was within a few metres of me.

'Hello, Aurelia. How did you get on?'

'It went smoothly, thank you.'

'What did he ask?'

'You can do better than that, Charlotte.'

'What do you mean?' Her voice pitch was a little higher and her face outraged dignity. I looked ahead and gave a little smile. She flounced off into her office. Five minutes later, she put her head round the corner and asked me to come back in. The psychologist gestured me to sit.

'I'm not going to tell you anything new when I say you have a very strong, contained personality,' he started. 'My initial briefing said you were serving as a diplomat, but I understand you come from a military background which puts a completely different light on the results. What was your role?'

'I'm sorry, but I can't give you details.'

'A general idea will be enough – support, nursing, clerical, that sort of thing.'

'You must have a strange conception of Roma Nova, Doctor, if you think all that female military personnel do is type in offices and apply dressings.'

'Why, what else can they do?'

I nearly lost control over my rising irritation.

'We fulfil all combat and support arms roles.'

'And you did?'

'Specialist infantry.'

He raised his eyebrows in the way you would when confronted with a direct lie, but he said nothing.

'Do you have trust issues?'

'Not for my friends and colleagues. Everybody else, I take them as I find them.'

'Do you miss your family? Your colleagues?'

'Yes.'

'What would be the hardest loss for you if convicted?'

'Not seeing my daughter grow up.'

'And would your daughter miss you?'

I took a light breath. 'I think so, but you would have to ask her that.'

Three days later, Galba turned up with a face like funeral ash.

'They've set a date for an interim hearing with the intention of committing you for trial. Seeing your test report, I'm not surprised.'

'Why?' Dread crept over me. Despite letting the psychologist know I'd seen through his little games, I'd been completely honest.

'Here, see for yourself.' She slid a Public Prosecutor Office folder over marked 'Supplementary Evidence'. Three pages into the file was the report summary.

*Subject is highly rational, quick-minded and a natural leader. She sees nothing is impossible given enough time and resources. Subject has the confident personality and willpower to pursue and implement her goals, easily bringing others with her. A dominant personality.*

*Strategic thinker, curious, innovative, able to grasp and deal with problems with determination and precision. Energetic and excellent communication skills, happy to confront and negotiate with others. Intelligent enough to recognise other people's talents, and work with them. Requires challenges and even failures, or the self-confidence could easily turn into arrogance and condescension.*

*Personalities of this type cannot tolerate inefficiency or those whom they perceive as lazy or incompetent. They can be chillingly cold and ruthless when the situation arises, operating purely on logic and rationality.*

*They interact very well with others, often charming them to their cause, and paying attention to other people's feelings – or at least pretending that they do. Most mature and successful personalities of this type are genuine in this aspect to some extent, even though their sensitivity may hide a cold and calculating mind.*

*With the proviso that there may be other factors that have not been apparent in such a short time and without a full forensic examination, I would suggest that the subject is psychologically perfectly able to carry out such a criminal act and unlikely to feel much remorse.*

I read it again. I hunched over the table as if somebody had punched me in the middle, pushing the breath out of me. Numbness spread out from my face to the rest of my body. Was this a true picture of me? If I was this cold, efficient automaton, then maybe I should be locked up. I stared at the stark words on the page and wanted to attack them, tearing the sheet into pieces smaller than the finest cross-cut shredder could achieve.

Through the angry haze surrounding my brain, I heard Galba saying something, but not her exact words.

'… as well as the new forensic report we've carried out.'

'Sorry, Galba, I didn't catch that.'

'I'm not surprised.' She stretched out a paper cup of water, which I drank in one go. 'Not very nice to be called a cold-hearted killer.'

'But that's what I'm trained for,' I whispered.

'Perhaps, but the essential word is "trained". And you are trained only to do it in extreme circumstances. We can emphasise that point and even bring in a military expert to explain that.' She glanced at me. 'Are you okay now?'

'Yes,' I lied.

'Well, you have a second visitor. I have to leave as you can only have one at a time.'

Gods, I hoped it wasn't Joachim come to gloat. I tucked the heel of my hand under my chin and stared down at the table.

'Well, sitting there looking as if Nemesis herself has fallen on you isn't going to get you anywhere.'

I jerked my head up. Plico. My mouth dropped open.

'Look out, you'll catch so many flies you won't need lunch.' He smirked. Gods, the bastard was smirking at me. I was never happier. I jumped up and flung my arms round his neck.

'All right, enough of that,' he said after a moment and disentangled himself. 'Calm down and gather your brain cells together.'

'How on earth did they let you in?' As a spymaster, he wouldn't have been welcome in Prussia.

'Oh, I've got a couple of Prussian babysitters, "for my security", their foreign ministry said. Ha! My Praetorians would see them off, but as day visitors we're playing nice.' His face became serious. 'Imperatrix Justina sends her love and asks you be assured every support will be available to you. She doesn't have much time for the Prussian royals and they couldn't intervene now anyway. If you want a top criminal lawyer from home or your own family lawyer, she'll send them.'

'No, Galba's doing very well and she knows the local system. She's called in others as she needs them.'

'Seems competent enough. She's been chasing that poor sod from the Central University forensics department round since she arrived here, and harrying the police and the prosecutor to give her full access. She's got some interim report for you.'

He tapped the folder Galba had left on the table. 'This psych report is unfair. I grant the first part is correct, but the conclusion is rubbish. Did you piss him off?'

'I told him the truth.'

'So, yes, you pissed him off. They can't take it here, you know, women carrying out what they think are male roles. Perhaps you should have been more circumspect.'

'That's rich from you,' I snorted.

He looked down at his hands. 'We won't let you rot here for the next twenty years, whatever happens.'

'I didn't do it, Plico.'

'So you said before. You wouldn't make such a mess.'

'What are the chances?'

'I'm no expert…'

'Tell me the truth.'

'… but at the moment I'd say it was eighty–twenty against you. And the tabloids are having a field day.'

'What do you mean?'

'You won't have seen the papers in here, but headlines like "Brutal Roman slayer rampages through business community" and in-depth articles on Arminius slaughtering the Roman legions in the Teutoburg Forest are all over the place.' He looked away. 'A load of crap about Germanics uniting to drive the Roma Novans out as they did their ancestors. The Prussian foreign ministry are embarrassed, they say, they don't wish the cordial relations with Roma Nova to be disrupted, blah, blah.'

He stopped and rubbed his thumb and forefinger together.

'Oh, don't stop now, Plico. I'm really enjoying this.'

'Some rubbish about women, guns and bedrooms. The usual *Kinder, Küche, Kirche* nonsense.'

Before I could retort, a discreet knock on the door interrupted my misery and his embarrassment. Galba came back in accompanied by two men in tight suits who moved their muscled frames purposefully. The Prussian foreign ministry heavies.

'I'd better go before they drag me out. When you're back from this jolly, I'll have a really tough assignment for you. So sort this out,' he said gruffly. As he turned, he shot me a glance back that I could only interpret as deep concern.

'Well, thanks for dropping in,' I said. My throat constricted. My next words came out as a croak. 'I'll think about it. See yourself out.'

# 19

'You having a problem, Roman?'

Magda had invited me to drink coffee with her that evening. When Eggers had given me the message at lunchtime along with extra fruit, I'd almost told her to get stuffed. I was too tired and felt sick. But my sense of self-preservation stopped me. You didn't annoy the power that ran the society I was now living in without a very good reason. And apart from my adoring but inarticulate cellmate, Greta, and the nods and nervous smiles of the others on my landing, I had nobody to talk to.

I'd lain on my bunk the afternoon after Plico's visit, not in the mood for my usual afternoon keep-fit session. Galba's optimistic report from our forensic scientist had almost put me out of the time frame, but not quite. Grosschenk had been killed in the forest hut as shown by the quantity of dried blood. His body had been burnt on the floor at the far end, by the primitive hearth, and wrapped in a tarpaulin afterwards – a time-consuming and exhausting thing to do. But excluding air had slowed body decomposition significantly in the cold forest hut. Night frosts had further decreased the usual expected level of fly and beetle activity. By the time I'd read the report for the second time, my stomach was queasy and I couldn't stop scratching myself.

Unfortunately, it was still possible that given the state of the body I could have killed Grosschenk at the beginning of my time out with

Miklós. I had no cover for twelve hours. Walking down the corridor to Magda's cell, it was still swirling round my mind. Halfway along, I stopped. I'd missed something, something significant, but I couldn't put my finger on it. I reran the whole evening at Grosschenk's through my mind, from the pickup at the hotel to half falling down the wall into the ditch outside his gate. What was missing? It was hovering at the front of my mind, but pulled itself out of my reach every time I tried to grasp it.

Eggers poured coffee and left. I wondered what Magda wanted. I'd learned by now she was the practical sort. You fell in with her, you survived. You crossed her, you ended up in the infirmary. The prison warders knew what was going on, but as they were equally practical and wanted an easy life, they ignored it. And both those favoured and those punished under Magda's regime kept to a mutual pact of silence towards the officials.

'You are worried about your hearing?' Magda asked.

'My boss thinks it might go against me. The newspapers are biased and I don't have an alibi for some of the time. And I'm going to miss the next twenty years of my daughter's life. Apart from that, everything's perfect.'

She gave a quick laugh. 'I'll miss you, Roman, when they let you out.'

'I may be here longer than you think.'

She lit a cigarette and inhaled deeply. 'I know where to find Grosschenk's chauffeur.'

I stared at her for a full minute almost forgetting to breathe. The distant clank of a door closing and receding footsteps penetrated my brain and woke it up. The chauffeur could corroborate the time I'd been at Grosschenk's house. That's what I'd been trying to remember. Mars' balls! Maybe I could get out of here. When had he left the house? Would he cooperate?

'My contact says he left Grosschenk's that evening and went into hiding in the Mitte.' She glanced over at me and lowered her voice. 'I'd get my own people to dig him out if it was me. The *Kripo* will bugger it up.' As she reached over to take her coffee cup, a tiny piece of paper, a sugar lump wrapper with a scribble on it, fell out of her hand.

• • •

The next day, Galba came to prepare me for the hearing, the *Zwischenverfahren* scheduled for five days' time. She explained the procedure and shoved a pile of papers at me to sign. Holding on to the last one, I stared at her, willing her to lift her eyes from the file in front of her. She grasped the sheet to take it back from me but I wouldn't let go. She looked up at last.

'Is there something you want to ask? Or have explained?' She shot a glance at her watch.

I kept my eyes steadily on hers, trying to convey a sense of importance. I stretched my arm out and handed the sheet back slowly ensuring she had to take it on the side near my fingers which held Madga's sugar lump wrapper concealed underneath.

'I think you should investigate one last avenue with *all* the resources available to you. Consult Fabia. She'll know exactly what to do.' We spoke in Latin, and this was supposed to be a confidential client meeting but who knew who was listening in. I couldn't afford anything to go wrong. 'Remember the ancients' story about he who drives the chariot holds the key.'

She looked at me as if I was deranged, but she took the sheet and the sliver of paper without comment and slid both in her folder.

'Galba,' I said and touched the back of her hand with my fingers, 'I'm relying on you to deal with this urgently.'

'Of course, *domina*, I will prioritise it.'

Well, that was strange. Galba was never so polite. Had she grasped what I had been trying to convey? She had no training in clandestine matters and I had tried to be as obvious as possible without actually telling her what to do in plain language. She gathered her papers together, stuffed them into her briefcase, stood, nodded to me and left.

Back in the grandiose Moabit courtroom five days later, I stood outwardly impassive by Galba's side as the charges were read out. Fabia and her detail had found no trace of Grosschenk's chauffeur and our forensics expert's best analysis had still left a twelve-hour gap. Galba rehearsed all our depositions, but could enter no new evidence.

'And, so, learned judges,' she concluded her pleading, ' it would be deeply unjust to convict an innocent woman of such a brutal slaying, and condemn her to be locked up in a foreign country, irrevocably disconnected from her young daughter's life without cause and on such flimsy evidence.' She tucked her hand under her skirt as she sat down, her face well schooled with a completely confident expression.

The prosecutor declared it all too coincidental and begged the court to be allowed to introduce a new material witness who had a unique view.

I tugged on Galba's arm. 'I thought they'd disclosed all their evidence,' I whispered. 'Who could it be?'

'Not a clue. It's most unusual. Don't worry. I think they're scraping the barrel. There can't be anybody else significant left.'

'You have something to say, *Frau Rechtsanwältin*?' The chief judge cut through our conversation.

'We are surprised at this late submission, *Herr Vorsitzender,* but will accede,' she said in a clear voice, but I heard a slight tremor.

I was still trying to work out who this witness could be when two prison guards brought in my nemesis.

Caius Tellus looked well; his skin was a healthy pink colour and his eyes gleamed. He moved fluidly and strode into the court as if he owned it. He paused directly in front of the witness stand, turned as if he'd suddenly remembered something and looked at me. For an instant he smirked, then changed it into a fake sympathetic smile. Bastard. If Galba hadn't gripped my arm so hard, I would have leapt over the table and floored him.

'Please state your name and then describe your relationship to the accused,' intoned the prosecutor.

'I am Caius Tellus, Roma Novan citizen, of the senior branch of the Tella family. I have known the accused since we were children together. She chose the military while I helped my family and pursued cultural and charity work.'

I nearly choked at his half-truths. Gambling, partying and conning people were the words I would have used.

'Our families have been allied through intermarriage and friendship for centuries but when I suggested a formal contract with her, she laughed in my face.' He sighed and gave a sad smile. 'I was so disappointed, I was distraught and started drinking. Unfortunately, I was vulnerable and became involved with some shady characters who led me to where I am now.' He raised his cuffed hands, shook them ensuring the metal clinked and sighed heavily. Half fascinated myself, I swallowed hard to push back my disgust.

I heard some 'ah's from the public benches and sympathetic looks. Gods, he was doing it again. His rich, almost hypnotic, voice was drawing them in.

'I deeply regret acting so foolishly at Grosschenk's house and realise I should have helped the accused, however much she had hurt me in the past.' He glanced over at me. 'Naturally, it grieves me that she is in this perilous situation. I know there was extreme provocation, but I do feel she shouldn't have killed Grosschenk in such a manner.'

'Objection!' Galba nearly screamed the word out as she shot to her feet.

'Substantiated,' the judge said. 'Witness, you will confine yourself to the facts and not express opinions.'

Caius smiled meekly, but his words couldn't be unsaid.

Galba walked over to where Caius was sitting. He leant back and looked her up and down slowly as if she were a piece of meat. A pink flush crept into her cheeks, but she stood her ground.

'You've been convicted on solid evidence of silver smuggling, attempted murder and conspiracy to damage the economic interests of Prussia, so I see no reason to believe a word you say.' She turned to the chief judge. 'I would ask for it to be noted in the record that we reject this witness as unreliable.' She shrugged. 'More than that, he's a complete liar.'

She ignored the prosecutor's cry of 'objection' and walked back coolly to our table.

'*Macte*!' I whispered. 'But he'll target you now.'

'So be it,' she replied. The judge signalled that the court was finished with Caius and he was escorted out. As he came level with our table, he stopped and glared down at me, his eyes darkened to agates, and full of hate and anger. I held them with my own, focusing all the contempt I could muster to throw back at him. This time, despite the fear that wound itself around me as I stared back, I didn't look away.

The two guards took his arms and hustled him out. I shuddered and pressed the palm of my hand to my breastbone. I took a deep breath. Tartarus receive and destroy him.

• • •

The prosecutor moved for a full formal trial. Cold crept through me, not only from the frightening encounter with Caius, but when I finally realised that within the hour, I was going to be committed to a trial after which I'd be locked up until I was nearly fifty. I would never see Marina's transformation into a young woman, her emancipation at sixteen. I would miss her grumpy adolescence, her first crush on a boy, her laugh and her soft arms. I blinked hard and looked down at the table, staring at the distorted marks where my tears had fallen on Galba's papers.

Galba and the prosecutor batted the familiar arguments back and forth. It sank into a distant buzz along with my spirits. To distract myself, I glanced around the courtroom. I caught Scholz glowering from public seating. A few chairs away sat some of the legation staff including the military commander.

Then I nearly stopped breathing.

I grasped the sides of my chair seat to stop myself swaying. A tall figure with black curly hair in the back row stared at me and nodded. I blinked and looked again. Nobody there.

'Are you all right?' Galba whispered as she sat down after her final speech. 'You look as if you've seen the *manes*.'

No ghost, but Miklós. It was him. No doubt. My heart sang with joy to see him even for a second. But he hadn't stayed. Anger rushed up through me. Where in Hades had he gone? He could testify and save me. No, he'd pulled another bloody disappearing act. My stomach lurched and I put my hand over my mouth and swallowed hard. I would *not* disgrace myself by throwing up in front of these people. But if he did come forward, they'd seize him for smuggling. He'd run a huge risk coming here at all. His soul would shrivel enclosed in prison. Had he come to see me for a last time before I was locked away? I bit my lip and swallowed my bitterness.

I almost didn't see the figure that was bending her head to Galba's ear. Fabia. Where had she come from? She glanced across at me, then went into intense whispering again to Galba and shoved several sets of stapled sheets at her.

'Are you sure?' Galba asked, her eyebrows drawn together.

Fabia nodded, glanced at me and gave a half-bow.

'Is there something you wish to share with the court, *Frau Rechtsanwältin*?' the chief judge asked. 'It must be very important to keep us all in such suspense. In your own time, of course.'

Galba flushed, but she stood and drew herself up to her full height, a martial look in her eyes. 'I apologise, *Herr Vorsitzender*,' she said in the most unapologetic voice I had heard in a long time, 'but it seems there is new vital evidence that will clear my client completely. A new witness has come forward. I must beg the court's indulgence to present this.'

'Another one. This hearing is turning into a circus,' the chief judge replied and frowned. 'We will need to recess to consider your request.' He shifted in his seat, ready to rise.

'No!' Galba almost shouted. 'I mean, it will take very little time and if I may cite the exceptional presentation rules under paragraph six of the Criminal Proceedings Act, I have copies of this new evidence for you and the public prosecutor, and the witness is waiting outside to testify.'

Juno, not Miklós. No, he mustn't. Unable to speak, I grasped the base of my throat with my hand but waved violently at Galba with my other. Keeping her eyes on the judge, she made a short, sharp sideways jab with her hand in my direction. What in Hades was that meant to mean? How dared she dismiss me like that?

'Very well,' the judge said. 'As you conceded to the public prosecutor's new witness, you have leave to present. But if it is not directly relevant, then it may well damage your client's case as well as your own legal integrity. We will suspend proceedings for ten minutes while we read this new document.'

Before I could say anything further, Galba strode up to the judge, handed him a set of papers and merely dropped a similar set on the table in front of the prosecutor without looking at him.

'What in Hades do you think you're doing?' I hissed at her as she sat down beside me.

She leant into me, almost growling. 'You would be wise to sit still and hold your nerve.'

I was so taken aback by her directness, I couldn't think of anything to say. She exuded calm and focus, her back was straight, neck stretched and head upright. She was readying herself for battle, with the confident air of a winner. I'd seen that many times before in training and live operations as the troops prepared themselves mentally. But she'd be sacrificing my love in the process.

'Galba, if you put him on the stand, they'll arrest him the minute he finishes speaking.'

'Yes, and so they should.'

Gods, she was heartless. 'You can't. I won't let you,' I said. I grabbed her wrist and shook it.

'Don't be dramatic. He deserves everything he gets.'

'Please, Galba, don't do this.' Then I remembered I was paying her bill. 'I order you to stop. Now.'

'Sorry, I have instructions from a higher authority.'

'What do you mean?'

She flashed a look at me and shoved a piece of paper across the table. It was a personal executive order dated two days ago and signed 'Justina Imperatrix'. I scanned it carefully, but there was no doubt. It ordered Galba to draw on every resource required and granted her complete freedom of action to bring to an acquittal even in contradiction of my wishes. Bloody Justina, interfering in my life again.

'When did you get this?'

'Fabia gave it to me ten minutes ago, along with the man's statement.'

'Galba—'

'No, I'm not disobeying the imperatrix even if you want to. I don't have the protection you do as a Mitela.'

'Don't fool yourself, Galba. The Twelve Families are even more vulnerable to sanction than the ordinary citizen.' I rubbed the gold-bordered document between my finger and thumb. 'I'll do as I'm told, but I'm never going to forgive her for this.'

Although I would have shouted and screamed at him if he'd been within reach, Miklós was the only man I'd ever truly loved. Then it fell on me as if the Fates were strangling me with the thread of life itself; if I pleaded guilty, I would never see Marina grow up. Oh, gods, this was horrific. Caius had put me in this hellhole where I had to choose between my love and my child. There was no question it would be Marina, but I would destroy Miklós as a result.

I lifted my eyes up to hers, pleading for her to find a way through this. 'Please, Galba.' To say she looked puzzled was an understatement. She opened her mouth, but the chief judge interrupted by calling for the new witness to be brought in to testify. I dreaded seeing Miklós trapped and under escort. My heart thudded. I bowed my head and covered my face with my hands.

But the walk wasn't right. The footsteps sounded lumpen, not light, and slower than I expected. I opened my eyes and raised my head from behind my hands to see Grosschenk's chauffeur.

'What in Hades is *he* doing here?' I hissed at Galba. 'I thought you couldn't find him.'

'This isn't who you were expecting?' Galba whispered, glancing at the new witness being sworn in.

'No, I thought… never mind.' I waved my hand at her. 'Go and do your job.' I gulped, cleared my throat and tried very hard not to sob with relief.

## 20

I listened to the chauffeur's precise tones, I heard his words, but it was as if I was watching it on a television in the corner of the room.

The man recounted how Caius Tellus had forced Grosschenk out of the back of the house, through the back gate and out through the trees to the forest hut, jabbing his pistol at the stumbling Grosschenk's head every other step to hurry him along. The chauffeur's tight, self-contained voice wavered when he told the court how he'd cowered outside listening to Grosschenk's screams.

'I've heard terror in people's voices before.' He shrugged. '*Herr* Grosschenk sometimes had to persuade people to see his point of view, but this…' he glanced at the judge. 'This was like cries from hell.'

'Why didn't you intervene?' the judge asked.

The chauffeur snorted. 'And get myself killed? That Roman was a vicious bastard. I followed them from behind the trees at the side of the path. Just before we got to the hut, I thought Tellus heard me. He made *Herr* Grosschenk stop while he looked round. I couldn't make up my mind whether to run or stay when I heard that first God-awful scream. Something ran across my foot and I cried out. Only a bloody rabbit or rat, I s'pose, but I nearly shat myself. Then the second scream. Then nothing until I smelt burning and saw smoke coming out of the chimney.

'After a few minutes, I crept up and peered through the window and saw the flames. Then Tellus turned and saw me. I shot into the trees and ran like hell for the main road.' He gripped the edge of the witness box and looked down. 'When I was sure he hadn't come after me, I made my way to the railway. It took hours. My legs were shaking by the time I reached the station. I took the first train of the day, just after four a.m. As I rode back into Berlin, I tried to block out the screams, but I couldn't. I haven't slept for weeks. I knew that Roman bastard would come after me, so I holed up with a friend in the Mitte.'

He looked up at the judge. 'I heard Tellus was convicted for smuggling and abduction, but that sort doesn't stay down. Then that gypsy found me.' He glanced at me. 'The same one who stopped the car when *Herr* Grosschenk was bringing her to the house.'

Miklós.

'And where is this gypsy now?' the judge asked.

I held my breath.

'Dunno. He brought me to a house and handed me over to some Roma Novans. Cops or military. Some of her lot.' He jerked his head again in my direction.

'Objection,' the public prosecutor leapt up. 'This witness is making his statement under duress. The court must rule it out of order.'

'A fair point, *Herr Staatsanwalt,*' the judge said. He turned his gaze back to the chauffeur. 'You have taken an oath to tell the truth. You will be protected by the court if you choose to retract. Has anybody forced you to make this statement?'

Gods, what had Miklós done to make the chauffeur talk? The man wasn't doing this out of the goodness of his heart.

'That gypsy, he found me yesterday at Elsa's bar, in the Mitte. He strolled in as if he owned the place. He got a beer, sat down at my table and said he knew exactly who I was. He was that sort you couldn't help talking to. Somehow, I told him the lot. It was a real relief. He suggested if I wrote down my side of the story, then I'd be free from my nightmares. Sounded like a load of mumbo jumbo, but after I'd done it, I slept for twelve hours straight last night.'

'Where and how did you write your statement?' the judge asked.

'When we reached the house with the Roma Novans, they put me in the dining room and left me to it. One of them brought me something to eat and I gave them what I'd written. They didn't say much, but they were okay.'

When he finished speaking, nobody moved, nobody spoke for a second or two. The chief judge stared at the chauffeur as if he was an exotic creature from the planet Mars.

'Very well, thank you for coming forward. *Herr Staatsanwalt,* any questions?'

'We need corroboration from this gypsy and I want to question the Roma Novans about their methods,' said Kästner. His tight features showed he was unhappy at being balked of his prey.

'The gypsy has disappeared, but the Roma Nova detail commander is here at your disposal,' Galba said, a smug tone in her voice.

In perfect step behind the court clerk, Fabia strode in; neat, precise and straight-backed and wearing her dark purple off-duty suit with silver crowned eagle badge on her lapel. Nobody could mistake her for anything but military. People stared as she made her way to the rostrum where she bowed to the judge, who looked surprised. She took her oath, calmly, folded her hands in her lap and waited.

'Please state your name and occupation.'

'Marcia Fabia, centurion, commanding the Aquila security detail at the Berlin Roma Nova legation.'

Centurion. Her promotion had come through.

'You were really in charge of the men who took the statement from *Herr* Grosschenk's chauffeur?' Kästner sneered at her.

'Yes.' Her gaze was steady, but the muscles around her eyes tightened.

'What pressure did you put on this poor man to make him sign this statement? Did you beat him up, fill him full of drugs? You Roma Novans are not known for your gentle ways.' He panned around the court, smiling as if sharing understanding with the public audience.

'The man you have called a gypsy phoned the legation and asked for me by name,' Fabia replied in a cold voice. 'We arranged to meet at the apartment of one of the legation local employees. The gypsy handed the chauffeur into our care and left without giving any contact details. We gave the chauffeur writing materials and a cup of coffee and sandwiches, and left him alone to write. After an hour, he had finished and I asked him to sign his statement. One of my detail typed it up for the court. The chauffeur slept in one of the bedrooms last night and then we all came here today.'

'I think you terrified him, promising unspeakable consequences if he didn't cooperate. Your colleague here had no hesitation in carrying out such brutal acts.' He pointed his papers at me. The bastard.

'Objection!' Galba threw at him.

'Sustained. Keep your questions neutral, *Herr Staatsanwalt,*' the judge said.

'You may think what you wish, advocate,' Fabia answered, once the murmuring from the public had died down. 'However, that does not change the truth which is as I have told you.'

'Why didn't you hand the witness over to the police?'

'There would not have been time for him to be processed for this morning's hearing, and...' she hesitated. The first time I'd ever heard her do that. She looked straight ahead at neither the judge nor prosecutor.

'And what?'

'The lack of judgement by Officer Huber and the prejudicial behaviour of Officer Scholz did not give us sufficient confidence in your police force to do that.'

'So you kidnapped this man? That is a serious charge punishable by a ten-year prison sentence.' He turned to the judge. 'I would like it entered on the record that this witness has admitted she conspired with others to abduct and falsely imprison a free citizen of Berlin.'

'Objection!' Galba sprang up again.

'Sustained.' The judge directed his gaze to Fabia. 'Please give your answer.'

'Sir, the chauffeur arrived at the door of the apartment without our agency. We invited him in, gave him food and drink and provided him with a bed for the night. All this in a completely safe environment for him. His door was not locked and he could have left, if he had wanted. We did not detain the chauffeur; he stayed with us willingly.'

'You would do anything to save your colleague, no, your superior,' Kästner pursued. 'Has she promised you money or promotion? Come, my dear, you can be honest with the court.'

Fabia tensed. She took a breath and swallowed it. When she looked at the prosecutor, I was surprised to find he didn't disintegrate into a heap of ash.

'Firstly, advocate, I am not your dear. Secondly, I must ask you to give me the respect of my rank. Thirdly, I am dismayed and saddened by your complete ignorance of Roma Novan values and ethics. Fourthly, my answer to your question is no.'

I had to cover my mouth with my hand to hide my smile. The prosecutor's face turned red and his eyes flared. He shook his papers in Fabia's direction, but said nothing more. The judge frowned at Kästner then glanced at his watch.

'If you have no more questions, and *Frau Rechtsanwältin* Galba has none, I will proceed to my direction. Otherwise we are wasting public time and money.'

Galba shook her head and looked prim. Kästner jerked his head sideways once and slumped down in his chair.

'With this new testimony, it is obvious there is insufficient evidence to proceed to full trial on the indictment against Aurelia Mitela,' the judge said. 'This case is dismissed and, subject to administrative details, the accused is at liberty to go.'

Galba turned and hugged me with a triumphant smile on her lips. A lock of hair had escaped from her immaculate coiffure and tickled my face.

She released me and I dropped back into my seat. I brought my hands up to the sides of my face, bowed my head and let out a deep sob.

# 21

Fabia stepped forward, blocking the guards when they approached to take me back to the prison to sign final paperwork and collect my belongings. They exchanged a glance; one even took a step towards her, but her cold stare stopped them.

'You may send papers to the legation,' came Galba's clipped voice. 'One of our representatives will collect the countess's possessions. Please clear the way.'

In the corridor, two others from Fabia's detail fell in behind Galba and me as we crossed the hall to the back door.

'There's a mob of news people outside. We came in the back this morning to avoid them.'

'As you wish.' I was too exhausted to do anything but be led to the waiting car. I wanted to get out of this place as easily and as fast as possible, away from the oppression of too many people. More than anything, I wanted to go somewhere civilized where I could shed my clothes and scrub off the prison smell.

At the legation, the vehicle swung into the service entrance gate thus avoiding most of the news pack. The *nuncia* herself greeted me. It was only the third time I'd met her.

'Welcome back, Aurelia Mitela,' she gushed and took my arm. Hm, that seemed a little too friendly. But she made me sit down in one of the armchairs in her private sitting room and gave me a generous helping of brandy.

'I expect it should be champagne, but you look as if you need a stiff drink.' Her eyes studied my face as if looking for something. 'No doubt you want to speak to your family at home. Let the comms room know when you're ready, no need to book it. They're sending an air force transport for you in three days' time. In the meantime, I suggest you try to rest as much as possible.'

Marina stared out of the vid screen, her eyes large and her shoulders curved inward.

'Are you coming home now, Mama?'

'Yes, darling, I'll be home by the weekend. I've missed you so much. I want to hear all about what you've been doing.' A pair of ears, followed by a face and black nose appeared from the bottom edge of the screen. 'Oh, what did you call him?'

'This is Issa. She's a girl.' She frowned at me while stroking the puppy's head. 'Don't you remember? I told you in my letter.'

The tickle of tears falling down my face, although light as a feather, made me feel such a failure. I couldn't even remember something so important to Marina.

'I think Mama is feeling tired now, Marina.' A hand touched Marina's shoulder, then Justina's face appeared in the screen by my daughter's. 'She'll be much happier when she's had a rest. Say goodbye now.'

Marina blew me a kiss and I watched her retreat from the screen as she disappeared from the room.

'You look peaky, Aurelia,' Justina said.

'I am well enough, thank you, imperatrix,' I said.

'Ha! Still annoyed with me about that instruction to your lawyer? She's a good girl, Plico says, and seems to have brought this off well. His worry was that you'd lose your temper and order her to do something stupid.'

I was too fed up to argue, but I felt a shaft of anger. That was the trouble with working for your mother's friends; they always thought of you as six years old.

'Galba is clever, thorough and tough,' I said. 'She should go far. I recommend her for promotion. That is, if my opinion is worth counting.'

'Gods, Aurelia, don't do that self-pitying routine on me. You're as tough as Hades and a clever clogs as well. Go and get some sleep and talk to me when you're less grumpy.'

I was never more pleased to be sitting in a plain canvas seat in the fuselage of an air force transport. Despite the noise and the vibration, I dozed for part of the way, only waking with the engine noise changing as we climbed to go over the mountains separating Bavaria and New Austria from Roma Nova. I was so tired – drained – that I thought I'd sleep for a week when I got home. Shock and stress could account for part of it. I only hoped I hadn't picked up a virus in prison.

Caius had been formally charged with Grosschenk's murder the day following my release. Galba had submitted my full statement to the Public Prosecutor's Office. She reckoned the trial would take place in the next week or so and be over within a few days. Unlike Roma Nova, the Prussians had given up the death penalty, but Caius would probably get fifteen to twenty years.

When we landed in the military part of Portus Airport, an anonymous dark blue saloon drew up by the steps. Foreign Ministry – not a doubt. An equally anonymous driver jumped out and opened the rear door for me. She handed me a radio handset tuned to a secure channel.

'So glad you found time in your schedule to join us.' Plico's disembodied voice was warm despite his sarcastic words.

'Don't start, Plico,' I retorted. 'My schedule no longer exists. I'm going home.'

'No, it's the palace first. The imperatrix wants to make sure you're in one piece.' His eyes gleamed. 'And, of course, your daughter's there.'

I knew he was playing on my emotions, but I ached to see Marina. I had so nearly been separated from her childhood forever. I pulled myself together.

'Thank you for bringing me back. I really appreciate it. I don't think I could have gone through Tempelhof again.' I looked out of the smoked glass window. 'I've lost any desire to see Berlin ever again.'

All I heard for the next few seconds was background radio noise. Had I lost contact?

'Well,' he said, eventually, 'write up your report, including the prison, then we'll talk about your next assignment.'

'I'm not going anywhere.'

'No, not immediately, of course. You've earned a couple of weeks' leave.'

'Two weeks? You're joking!'

What in Hades was he on about? I knew the regulations. I had about two months' respite. He could whistle for it. I was going to the farm at Castra Lucilla with Marina for a few weeks to catch the soft early autumn weather before it turned.

'You're still on strength,' he snapped, 'and you'll get your back pay.'

For Juno's sake, I wasn't doing it for the peanuts the government paid.

'Besides,' he continued, 'I want to talk to you about something when you come into the office. Out.'

I clutched Marina's slender frame to me and stroked her face with my free hand. Soft as rose petals, her skin shone, her flesh a little plumper than when I'd left her. Pale freckles dotted her nose and forearms. Her smile was pure sunshine.

'How she stays alive on what she eats is a mystery to me, but the nursery staff say she's healthy. She certainly runs around enough.' Justina was attempting to be bracing and old school, but I heard the warmth in her tone.

'Nonna Justina,' Marina smiled up at the older woman. 'May I bring my puppy in here? Please? Just this once?'

We were in Justina's drawing room, all Aubusson carpets and rich purple curtains. 'Well, just this once. If she disgraces herself, then she's banned.' But she smiled as Marina skipped off. I blinked back a tear. If only my mother had lived, she would have had the pleasure of seeing this glorious child bloom.

'Marina is flourishing here, Aurelia. And she is so sweet with Julian. Stay here with her while you recover.'

'I'm thinking of taking her to the farm with me. The Castra Lucillan air will do us both good.'

She looked away, so I couldn't read her expression. Unusually, she looked as if she didn't know what to say next.

'Very well, take your two weeks there, but Plico wants you back in the city by a week next Monday. I'll send the nursery maid that Marina's fond of along to do the donkey work.'

As we drove south, I attempted to work out what Plico and Justina had meant. As one of her imperial secretaries, he was in her total confidence, but neither had let any hint out. To be honest, I was too tired to care.

Justina had insisted on us taking one of her new Range Rovers, complete with a driver. Apart from Aemilia, the nursery maid, eighteen years old and excited about seeing the southern countryside, Justina had also sent a factotum who looked suspiciously military in his bearing and self-sufficiency. Did she think I was so vulnerable? Or maybe it was friendship for my late mother or even a twinge of guilt. Or was I being guarded?

After five days, I'd caught up on my sleep and knew exactly which part of the puppy's tummy to tickle. Marina and I played chase, swam, and walked in the woods. The dull ache in my heart for Miklós eased, but had not disappeared. He could have written, even sent a postcard. He knew I would have come home. Maybe there was something waiting for me at Domus Mitelarum in the city. I burned at the idea he'd seen me only as a passing fancy. I pressed my fist to my lips. Was that all it had meant for him and he didn't want any further contact? Gods, I sounded as if I were an adolescent struggling to recover from her first crush.

I left the details of my personal time with Miklós out of the report for Plico and sent it back to the city by one of the farmhands. As I watched the truck set off north, I closed the whole damned nightmare out of my mind. I needed to have a calm, boring life now behind a desk. Better, I'd press Plico, or rather Justina, for my release from state service.

The sixth afternoon, Marina and I got thoroughly messy making honey cakes. The steward wasn't best pleased with the devastation in the old-fashioned kitchen, but Marina and I flopped on the sofa together in front of the open fire and devoured the results. Lazily content and too full of cake to get up, I half closed my eyes and stroked her soft hair. She folded her honey-sticky little paw inside my hand.

Then I heard a buzz outside. It became strident, urgent. Gently disengaging myself from Marina, I crossed over to the window and looked out.

No. They couldn't. It was only Friday. But dropping out of the sky and with a purple and gold livery was a bloody air force helicopter. It thumped above the old barn at ear-splitting level, then landed in the pasture to the side, causing all the cows to scatter as if they were demons released from Tartarus.

'I was going to leave talking to you about your attitude to Caius Tellus until you came back next Monday, but something's happened.' Plico's face was hard, the lines sloping away each side of his nose rigid; no sign of his usual cynical, relaxed expression.

'He's escaped,' he said in an equally hard voice.

A cold stab hit me squarely in my gut.

'How in Hades' name could that have happened?' I croaked. 'Tell me. Now.'

'He's been a model prisoner, but complaining about stomach pains. A classic. The prison medic gave him the usual antacids, but nothing seemed to stop it. He was taken to the hospital for tests in a police car and under armed escort, but they never arrived.' He looked up at me. 'Your friend Scholz found the abandoned police car, two uniforms bundled in the back and an unconscious prison guard with his hand hacked off to release the handcuff.'

I turned away, grabbed his waste-paper bin barely in time to be violently sick into it. I trembled as I wiped my mouth with the tissues he offered and gratefully accepted the glass of water. What the hell was the matter with me? It was gruesome, but nowhere near what he'd done to Grosschenk. All the good of my days at the farm fled.

'Here, take a slug of this.' Plico thrust his spirit flask at me. I drew back, but he put the neck of the flask to my lips. The brandy woke me up and drowned the sour taste in my mouth.

'Surely Caius should have been convicted by now,' I said. 'Safely locked up in a maximum security prison.'

'His trial was scheduled to start today.' Plico's face was grim.

'Oh, gods, it's going to start again. He's haunted me since I was a child.' I swallowed hard and took a second, smaller sip of the brandy. The light-headedness and trembling receded.

'I've sent a recce team to Berlin to do the preliminaries, whatever the local scarabs think. He obviously had help – he's got enough money to buy it. Or his great-aunt has.'

'Countess Tella would never condone such an action.'

'Of course she wouldn't, but you know what a devious bugger he is. He'd have charmed it out of her.'

He passed the Brandenburg police telex to me and waited in silence until I'd read it through. I itched to get back to Berlin, much as I disliked it now.

'What plane am I on?'

'I've got one standing by but you're obviously not fit, so I'll have to send somebody else. Pity. You'd have been perfect.'

'Nothing wrong with me. It was the shock, and I think I've got a minor bug. I'll get some antibiotics to settle it.'

'Nothing doing. In fact, I'm sending you for a full physical. You look terrible.'

The medic probed, poked and took samples. She flitted around, packaging up tubes of my blood, pee and saliva swab, labelled it all with quick fingers then sat at her desk to scribble notes. She had dark brown hair, and hazel eyes not unlike Caius's, but with none of the mockery or hatred.

Despite what Plico said, I was going after Caius. After I'd refused him in Roma Nova and banned him from coming near any of my family, he'd tried to kill me in Berlin, then nearly had me convicted for murder. His debt account was over the limit and I was going to settle it once and for all.

# 22

'How in Hades can somebody not know they're pregnant?' Plico threw the pen on his desk. It landed right in the middle of the doctor's report. 'All that puking and you must have noticed you'd missed your period. You're not some dim-witted adolescent out of a Septarium tenament.'

'I thought it was stress and a stomach bug.' I studied my twitching fingers. I felt stupid enough without him going on about it. Recovering from my broken foot and waiting for Caius's trial, let alone my lack of emotional life, the last thing I'd thought about was contraception. Besides, Roma Novans rarely used it; we loved having children and we loved them, unlike most of our fellow Europeans who thought having a child without a husband was somehow shameful. Ridiculous. Roma Nova would have sunk centuries ago with such a paternalistic restriction.

Then Miklós came into my life. Inside I glowed. Miklós's child, and mine. A child made from love. I closed my eyes and savoured the thought. Then a roll of anger when I thought of Miklós's desertion. My child. Not his. Entirely mine. Miklós didn't want to be part of my life. This child would never be part of his. She would be raised as a true Roma Novan.

'Well, that's you off operations for several months.' Plico's flat voice dragged me back into the real world. He reached for a file on his rack. 'There's an opening in Vienna, desk-based, as part of the political staff. Your experience and fluent Germanic make you ideal for it.'

'No, I'm going after Caius.'

'Not a prayer. I'm not explaining to the imperatrix that I've sent her pregnant adopted daughter into the field to pursue the most dangerous and vicious bastard alive. She'd have my balls.'

An idea not without merit.

'And you could take Marina with you if you accept the Vienna posting. It would be a good experience for her to see a bit of the world. In perfect time for their Winter Fair with all that tinsel and lights. She'll be in heaven.'

'With Caius still at large? You're joking. None of us is secure until he's brought down. At least here she's well guarded.'

'Maybe, but you're still not going after him.' He gave me a sly look. 'At least we know now what you were doing in that missing thirty-six hours.' Before I could respond, he added, 'And I won't report you for misusing the intelligence database in Berlin to look up Hungarian smugglers for very personal reasons.'

I drove to the palace, still fuming at Plico. I thought about writing a curse tablet and sticking it in the boot of his car. The logical part of my mind said he was right. But ever since I had stared Caius down in that Berlin courthouse, I knew he had lost his dominance over me. And I was eager to prove it. But my first duty and pleasure, no, my joy, was to care for my growing baby. Nothing showed, it was only six weeks, but I stroked my stomach with my hand, keeping the other firmly on the steering wheel. My basic fitness was still good and would protect the baby as long as I was careful with my diet. If I wanted to catch Caius, I had a six-to-eight-week window before I became too slow or endangered the baby.

Justina greeted me with a big smile pinned on her face. Juno. Plico had copied the report to her. Was nothing private?

'My dear Aurelia, come, sit down and rest. Your mother would have been absolutely delighted at the news. You must be careful, especially after the worry of the trial. My gynaecologist will care for you, naturally, and supervise your diet and exercise herself.'

'Imperatrix, Aunt Justina, I'm not ill. Thank you, but I'd prefer my own doctor and I'm not giving up work for the next seven months.'

'Let's be clear, Aurelia. Marina isn't a strong child and House Mitela needs a second heir. The medical report says your blood counts are low, so you need rest, a proper diet and supplements.'

Hades. She'd trained as a doctor as a young woman, and worked in the refugee camps full of malnourished Austrians and Germanics immediately after the Great War finished in 1935 so I couldn't argue with her prescription. And she was right about another heir.

'I promise I'll take it carefully, but I won't be cocooned either.'

Waiting in the meeting room at the Foreign Ministry made a change from Plico's dull, paper-strewn office. The foundations of the building were original, dating back to the fifth century. The archaeologists had exposed an ornate mosaic hunting scene now protected by glass in one corner of this grandiose room. A tall man, with grey-red hair to his shoulders and a torc round his neck, wielding a spear and about to stick a wild boar, was reckoned to be Prince Bacausus, the father-in-law of founder Apulius. His square face with its jutting chin certainly reminded me of his descendant, Justina, in one of her determined moods.

The door opened and Plico entered, talking to Senior Centurion Numerus, whom I hadn't seen since we'd arrested those Prussians in the snowstorm nearly two years ago.

'Major!' He saluted and we clasped forearms.

'Fantastic to see you again, Numerus. You look well.'

He shrugged, then tilted his head. 'I gather you've been up to your own adventures in the north from what Secretary Plico tells me.'

'Not ones I wish to repeat. How's the search going?'

Numerus had led the recce team to Berlin, four of them altogether. Liaising with Fabia, now second in command of the entire legation detachment, they'd found no sign of Caius.

'He's vanished completely. Fabia's used every informant she could think of and piled the pressure on the local police. I had the pleasure of hearing her, er, conversation with some dickhead called Scholz.' He glanced at me. 'Doesn't like you, does he?'

'Understatement. Bastard nearly got me locked up for Mars knows how long.' I turned to Plico. 'So what's next?'

He shrugged. 'He's the Prussian police's problem really. We have no jurisdiction, but—'

'That's never stopped you before. Or any other secretary.'

'As I was going to say before you jumped on me, we're not leaving it to them. Numerus here is assembling a second team which will start a parallel but covert search for Caius. Your report was good, but what Numerus needs from you is detail of everything you saw, heard or even smelled in connection with Caius in Berlin. The answer is there. We just need to dig it out.'

After a full day with Numerus and two of his team, my brain was as shredded as mincemeat. I hadn't expected anything less. He might be going grey on top but underneath he was as sharp and tough as he'd been in my anti-smuggling unit. He was especially interested in interviewing Grosschenk's chauffeur, and the informer, Ernst Beck, who I'd packed off to Bavaria.

'But they were Grosschenk's men – hard nuts,' I said.

'Yes, but they would have seen Caius Tellus and possibly overheard conversations between him and Grosschenk. You know yourself how all the tiny things that seem insignificant at the time slot into place when you look at them under different circumstances.' He pulled a page out of his folder. 'That tough that kidnapped you and Prisca Monticola, Fischer, is inside for the next few years, but this might be interesting.' His voice was slightly raised and his eyes gleamed. The sheet was headed 'Königlich-Preußische Polizei' and marked *'Streng geheim'* – a copy of a top secret Prussian police document.

'Where did you get that?'

He grinned. 'The quartermaster asked us to trial some experimental scanning equipment in the field. It's the only positive thing we brought back.'

The chauffeur had been put into witness protection; no real surprise, perhaps a sign of thoroughness by the Prussian police. But Numerus was right to be excited; this document showed his new name and address – in Vienna.

'Well, Fussy-Pants Plico won't let me out in the field, but if I take up his offer of the Vienna posting, I'll be inside the German Federation. I have a few contacts via my business interests there. Best of all, we'll be able to have a private word with the chauffeur on neutral ground.'

'Of course, Marina can come back here. What a ridiculous question.' Justina was as no-nonsense as usual. 'She's had a lovely holiday with you but now she needs to get back into her routine here.' I cringed at the irony of it. But I was in no different a place than many others working for the Roma Nova government, or indeed members of the Twelve Families. My own mother, Felicia, had been fostered at the palace as a girl and grown as close as a sister to Justina, which was why she now treated me as if I was a wayward daughter. Perhaps her grandson, Julian, and Marina would bond in the same way; Mitela and Apulia had always been close since the foundation of Roma Nova fifteen hundred years ago. It never hurt to look to the future.

'Severina's pregnant again,' Justina broke into my thoughts, 'so you'll have company when your baby is born.' The idea of sharing baby chit-chat with Justina's dippy daughter made my heart sink. Severina was my friend, with a kind heart but a shallow brain. Her ability to connect with every member of every Roma Novan family of equestrian rank upwards and to remember everything about them was an impressive talent and left me a social inadequate standing in a corner by myself. But she couldn't string a political or strategic thought together and sat silent in the imperial council meetings, bored to tears, and tried to avoid the policy sessions Justina held every week on top of that.

But no ruler, or ruler-in-waiting, could indulge in a politically idle life. Severina would have to face that uncomfortable fact and remember her duty to her country. Of course, I'd be there to advise and help, but she'd have to step up to the bar herself.

'Aurelia?'

'I apologise, imperatrix. I was a million miles away, thinking about the things I must do before I leave next week,' I lied.

• • •

I caught up with Prisca Monticola who had been elected onto the Silver Guild council as international relations specialist. We sat in the atrium by the tall windows as the last glimmer of light disappeared, she with a glass of Castra Lucillan white from last year's vintage, me with an unexciting fruit juice.

'They think I'm the very devil of an adventurer after that business in Berlin.' She grinned, then sipped her wine. 'But it gets me some good trips abroad.' Not that she couldn't afford to jet off anywhere she pleased.

'Heard anything more about anomalies in the silver trade?' I asked.

'Meaning?' She raised an eyebrow, but her expression was neutral rather than hostile.

'Meaning has it settled down after Caius's smuggling activities stopped? And what about the Prussians and Rammelsberg?'

She set her glass down carefully on the coffee table between us.

'When Caius Tellus was convicted, the price rose slightly, both spot and consumer, and stabilised. The effect spread and calmed the whole European market. There are still some minor blips from time to time in the Germanic centres – the big one in Frankfurt, plus Munich and, strangely, Vienna. Nothing so serious to cause me to call the Oversight Commission but—' She shrugged. 'Maybe I'm over-sensitised, but I can't help feeling something's unsettling it at the moment.'

'How long has it been doing this?'

'Only a week or two.' She fished out a notebook from her handbag and leafed through the pages. 'Here. Ten days ago exactly.'

The columns of figures, dates and squiggles made no sense to me.

'Sorry, it's coded.' She gave a quick smile and pointed a purple-lacquered fingernail at the top of a half-completed page. 'The price fell for a day, picked up again, but not at the same level, then it fell even further and picked up again, but not even to the level of the first fall. And it's been slowly ratcheting down. It recovered a little the day before yesterday. With Rammelsberg production carefully controlled, I'd expect to see prices continuing to rise steadily. I checked with colleagues on the London Metal Exchange but they hadn't recorded anything special there. It's the centre of the physical silver trade in the world, so they'd notice. Although one said they'd been hearing funny rumours about the purity of Roma Nova silver.'

'Speculators?'

'Well, *investors,*' she frowned at me, 'have been paying higher premiums on physical silver as demand has been outstripping supply. But that should force the price up, not down.'

I said nothing, but Caius escaping and this very recent instability clicked together in my mind.

# 23

Vienna was a strange place, in one way similar to Byzantium – a city too big for its surroundings; dozens of palaces, cathedrals, wide carriageways and esplanades, museums and opera houses to serve an empire. Both cities once had empires that had stretched from mountains, plains, rich pastures and fields to great rivers and dominion over strategic seaports and included multiple ethnic groups. Before the Great War, the Austrian Empire had been one of the world's great powers, the second largest country in Europe after the Russian Empire and an industrial and cultural powerhouse. Vienna was known as the city of dreams and music, but was now the city of conferences, town planners and tourists.

We'd traded with Austria for centuries since before the Habsburgs had taken over from the Babenburgs; one of Justina's ancestors had been the brother of Theodora Comnena, the Byzantine princess who'd become the first Duchess of Austria in the 1100s. We had history. But the Great War removed the last Habsburg as effective ruler, although his daughter, Maria Amalia, played a token part now as a state figurehead in New Austria. I was scheduled to meet her sometime in the next few weeks when the *nuncia* presented me.

At Wien-Maria-Theresia Airport I shrugged my coat on and waited by the luggage carousel as it squeaked and groaned, tumbling cases round in front of tense passengers trying to spot theirs from the sea of black bags.

'*Frau Gräfin* Mitela?'

A neat dark-suited man with a solemn look on his face had materialised next to me. Behind him was an airport service employee resting his arm on a trolley and looking bored.

'My name is *Herr* Peters, I'm the deputy service manager. Please follow me.'

Not again.

'I'd rather wait for my luggage first.'

'If you give him the tags, Karl will see to that and deliver it to your legation's car which is waiting outside.' His face relaxed a centimetre. 'I will escort you through immigration.'

I was whisked past the queues full of people shuffling tired feet, grasping passports and staring at me with resentful faces as I went ahead of them. We emerged into a semi-circular arrivals hall, edged with shops, a sprinkling of chairs and tables and the smell of coffee. A dark-purple-suited woman with a gold eagle badge on her jacket lapel moved towards me and flipped open a small leather wallet and showed me the familiar crowned eagle Praetorian ID badge.

'Captain Licinia, head of the legation security detail. Welcome to Vienna, Countess.' She relieved me of my cabin bag. Following the service manager, she ushered me towards the front entrance where a black Mercedes with tinted windows waited.

Riding along the grey concrete of the Ost Autobahn towards the centre of Vienna, and looking over at the far hills through the rain, I was struck how ordinary and quiet it looked. What would it have been like for the Roman legionaries shivering in the cold seventeen hundred years ago in this frontier town of Vindobona with the threat of Mars knew how many hundreds of wild Germanic tribespeople across the Danube wanting to tear you apart? I shuddered, but the idea of the havoc Caius could wreak was to me no less terrifying.

Plico had told me this was a proper job with 'no cloak and dagger stuff', but it looked like an intelligence job to me. As the legation's political officer, my duties included researching and reporting on internal New Austrian political and Europe-wide issues, building a network of contacts with the government, think tanks, academic and business communities and, here was the crux of it, engaging with them to gather information and lobby on behalf of Roma Nova. I was supposed to concentrate on security policy, defence policy and justice/home affairs. And what would I do in my spare time?

I'd been allocated an office on the first floor of the legation on Marc-Aurel-Straße. The Austrians had been so grateful for Roma Nova's legions' support at the Battle of Vienna in 1683 to halt the Ottoman advance into Europe, that they offered the imperatrix at the time the pick of locations for the rebuilt legation. In a moment of hubris, she'd sent surveyors to Vienna to find the site of the *principia,* the heart of the ancient Roman Vindobona camp, and chosen the site shown in their survey. Unfortunately, it proved to be inaccurate, but was still within the original *castra* limits. Her descendant in the late 1800s had lobbied the city to change the legation street name to Marc-Aurel-Straße, so honour was felt to be satisfied.

It had left me with a floor-to-ceiling sash window overlooking the old town. All I did for the first day was read briefings and find out where everything was. Two days later, Captain Licinia, who'd met me at the airport, was ushered into my new office by my new assistant. This time, Licinia wore her beige and black barrack uniform, her dark brown hair gathered in the same tight chignon. And in her wake was Numerus, his civvy coat dark with spots from the sleet that had started this morning. He propped his umbrella up in the base of the coat stand and came forward as I stood up. We grasped arms and exchanged a brief smile.

'Please, sit,' I waved them to the visitors' chairs and waited.

'I'm here to interview Grosschenk's chauffeur,' he said, 'well, ex-chauffeur. Captain Licinia here said she'll assist, but I wondered if you wanted to be involved?'

He looked at me steadily, but I couldn't read him.

'Will it help if I'm present?' I said. I still hadn't got to the bottom of why the chauffeur had been willing to testify at my Berlin trial and I wasn't sure he'd open up about it if I was standing in front of him. 'No, you do it and I'll observe,' I said.

Numerus blinked. 'I think that's best.' He sounded relieved. 'He's Germanic, and even more, a Prussian, so he might respond better to a man questioning him.'

I chuckled. 'Were you *so* worried about offending me?'

• • •

The chauffeur was taller than I remembered, and even watching on a small screen, I could see he still wore the same deadpan expression. But his eyes were wary and I noticed he scratched the side of his neck several times even before Numerus asked him the first question.

Licinia's troops had picked the chauffeur up as he sat in a café eating his 'second breakfast'. Well, he was getting a third cup of coffee and another pastry now as he sat with Numerus in the commercial section's meeting room. I hunched in front of the videolink monitor with Licinia in the neighbouring room. The technicians had installed a temporary camera and audio feed overnight much to the displeasure of the legation steward. He was still grumbling about possible damage to his decorative plasterwork when I'd inspected it with Numerus first thing this morning. Neither of us could see where the installation technicians had been, nor any damage.

'Thank you for agreeing to this interview,' Numerus started, his disembodied voice clear through the feed.

'Did I really have any choice?'

Numerus smiled. 'Please believe me when I say I don't mean you any harm. All I need is to clear up a few details from your testimony in the Berlin court.'

'The police said nobody could find me.'

'Well, we're a little more sophisticated than the Royal Prussian Police. We'll get you back to your apartment completely discreetly.'

'Oh, I'll be moving now.'

'As you wish. I'm particularly interested in the time when you first came across Caius Tellus. Do you know how Grosschenk and he met?'

'I only met him when I went to pick him up at Tempelhof on *Herr* Grosschenk's orders. Tellus seemed friendly enough, but he was the sort who expected you to open his door, act deferential and do what he asked. Once, later, he asked me to do something I wasn't sure about and I said I had to check with *Herr* Grosschenk. Tellus got dead snotty with me and his eyes turned hard as stone. But in the next second he smiled and said "of course". I had to fetch some technician from the airport a few days after he moved in to *Herr* Grosschenk's house. A load of electronic stuff and a telex terminal had arrived and this guy had to fit it. He was Roma Novan as well.'

'Did they ever argue?'

'Not that I heard, but Tellus was the dominant one. *Herr*

Grosschenk wanted to please him like a little boy in the playground sucking up to the class bully.' The chauffeur shook his head. 'I'd never seen him like that before.'

'Do you know if Tellus had any other connections in Berlin?'

'Creep like that was bound to have, but I didn't know of any. He received post most days, though.'

'And here in Vienna?'

'*Himmel!* Don't tell me he's here!' The chauffeur blenched.

'Caius Tellus was sentenced in the Berlin court for silver smuggling and sent to prison for six years, and he was remanded in custody for Grosschenk's murder. ' Numerus said, looking the chauffeur straight in the eye. 'He's hardly likely to be here, is he?'

'You didn't ask him about his motivation for testifying at my trial,' I said. Numerus, Licinia and I sat around the table analysing the interview. Numerus had pushed and prodded for another twenty minutes but the chauffeur hadn't had anything else concrete to say.

'I didn't think it relevant to our current operation. He said at the time he wanted to get it out of his mind. It seems the gypsy Farkas somehow convinced him talking it out would be cathartic. Anything to stop the Furies chasing around in your head would be a relief, I'd think.' He shot me a wondering look.

I shook my head. I'd kept the details of my relationship with Miklós out of all the reports, but Numerus wasn't stupid.

'Interesting about the electronic and telex equipment, though,' I said. 'After a lot of arguing, the federal police made the Prussians hand it over to us after Caius's trial for smuggling. That included one of the new portable computing machines. Remarkable, really – a complete computer with large memories, a full colour display, and a tape drive, all packed into a machine that small. It must have set him back a fortune. I'd bet their boffins took it apart to have a look first.'

'What did you expect?' Numerus said. 'We'd have done the same.'

'True.' I grinned at him. 'So was Caius using this stuff to process the information and calculations quickly enough to manipulate the market?'

'Perhaps, but the Berlin police and the GDKA/OK police found that all the individual transactions they could trace were legal as far as they were concerned.'

I finished my coffee in silence while the other two carried on studying the transcript as if the answer was going to spring out magically.

'Do you want us to track this chauffeur?' Licinia asked Numerus.

'I don't think he can give us anything else, so no, thank you, ma'am.'

'We're not really any further forward, are we?' I was stating the obvious, I knew, but it was so frustrating. How could an escapee hunted by the supposedly dogged Prussian police, as well as our own Praetorians, still be at large?

'Are we looking at insider information, bribery, or is Caius terrorising people into helping him? My contact in the silver world said there'd been some funny movements on the silver market in the last week or so. Could Caius be manipulating trading to raise funds?'

'Hm, unlikely to be the latter,' Numerus said. 'It takes time to set it up and he's only been on the loose for fifteen days, but I'll look into it.' He stood up. 'Thank you, ladies, for your time. I'd best get back to Berlin.'

# 24

I set off for the Argentaria Prima Vienna office after lunch. Although not a national bank as such, and subject to the same regulatory framework as the other banks, it was our leading institution and the most influential one amongst its peers. The Vienna office was important, not least for its location inside the German Federation, but it had connections into the east. I convinced myself meeting the local AP manager was part of my official role, but deep inside, I knew it was a lead in my hunt for Caius.

I dismissed the offer of a car; I'd been inside all morning and the sun was strong enough to lift the temperature into double figures. Vienna was a city, but somehow the air was fresh and clear. I drank it in and felt energised.

Three blocks later, a smiling doorman bowed and swung the glass door open for me. The banking hall resembled an atrium in a private house, but the grey-veined columns rising from the marble floor were much grander than any home could boast. I crossed the inlaid silver and white floor logo of a diademed Juno Moneta, protectress of funds, carefully avoiding her unseeing grey eyes; I didn't want any bad luck from treading on her face. I was ushered into the office of Valeria Festa, the Vienna branch manager. After we'd settled ourselves in soft leather easy chairs, drunk coffee from tiny gold-rimmed cups and exchanged pleasantries, I came to the point.

'I'm looking into possible irregular acts in trading strategic assets, namely, silver.' I smiled at her. She smiled back. Festa's slim figure in its loden-green suit and silk embroidered blouse made her look the perfect New Austrian resident. Her precisely made-up face contrasted with her wildly curling brown hair pushed back with tortoiseshell side combs. Despite that homely tone, she held herself confidently and looked directly at me out of dark brown eyes.

'I know you liaise with the Oversight Commission at the Trade Ministry,' I continued, 'but has your branch seen any signs of unusual trading or dealing in silver in the last fortnight?'

'Nothing comes to mind, but why do you ask, Countess?' Her expression didn't change, but the skin round her eyes tightened. According to Festa's CV in the latest Argentaria Prima annual report, she was an experienced manager with a solid banking and investment background.

'Well, with recent events in Berlin, we're checking every avenue for political and economic fallout,' I said. She would, inevitably, have heard about my unpleasant time in Berlin; the bankers and traders had an information network second only to the state one, and probably better sometimes.

'I'm afraid all transactions are confidential, so I can't help you.'

She gave me a 'close of conversation' smile and half rose out of her seat.

'Sorry, but that's unacceptable,' I replied. 'We're talking about a national strategic asset. A crack team of Praetorians is pursuing enquiries in Berlin as it's regarded as a threat to the state. This is why I'm here talking to you now.'

She looked down at her desk for a few moments. 'Very well. Let me call for the recent accounts.' She lifted the handset on her desk telephone.

'Oh, and while you're looking, can you confirm whether you operate any Tella accounts here?'

'I'm afraid that's also confidential information. I can't release that without a written order,' she shot back a little too quickly.

'Very well. Do you employ any of the Tella family here?'

'That, too, is confidential.' She gave me another bland, but tight smile.

• • •

'She's lying,' Prisca Monticola's voice was flat and hard.

'I'm no accountant,' I said. 'But I've run estate accounts and I know enough to follow an audit trail through a set of books with my steward. The four accounts sheets her assistant brought up looked in good order. But I found no trace of any silver transactions, either metal or futures.'

'It would be bizarre for the trades I showed you the other week not to go through the Argentaria. They're the local accredited registration agent for the Commission. You need to nail this, Aurelia. Something's definitely off. I'm going to dig around here. I'll get back to you.'

I'd scarcely cut the call when the oscillating tone identifying an incoming call sounded and Plico's face appeared on the screen.

'I've had the secretary of the Argentaria Prima whingeing at me about privacy, state interference, *ultra vires* action and all kinds of crap. What are you stirring up there?'

'You won't let me out in the field, so I'm doing some local research.'

'Can't leave it alone, can you? I thought the political job would keep you more than busy. And you're not on case strength.'

'Be realistic, Plico. I have the contacts and the motivation. And I gather from Numerus that you're not getting anywhere.'

He said nothing for a second or two.

'All right, what have you got?' he grumped.

While I gave him my verbal report and Monticola's comments, he scribbled notes, his uncombed hair falling over his forehead. Finished, he pushed the strands back with his fingers as if they were tines on a rake.

'It's circumstantial at best. You obviously ruffled the manager's plumage.'

'I was sweetness and light. And House Mitela is a significant customer. I expected a friendly welcome, not a blank. Can you have a deeper look at Festa's background?'

'Surely you don't expect her to be on the take?'

'Money is one of the strongest motivators of human behaviour, Plico, closely linked to security and power. You know that. We're talking serious temptation here.'

'I'll send the enabling paperwork through, but if you're wrong, you're finished.'

• • •

Festa was stiff in face and stiff in manner – in full Argentaria Prima manager mode. Tensed up like a disapproving spring, her face was tighter than it had been at my meeting with her the day before yesterday. On the boardroom table, a centimetre away from her hand, were a dozen or so standard files tied with buckled cloth straps, and a box file in front of them that had sprung open due to bulging contents.

I sat opposite her with Licinia standing behind me and a member of the legation financial staff who was a qualified accountant lounging in the seat next to me. He'd taken a paper pad and ballpoint pen out of his zipped folder and after writing the date, laid his pen down and waited, occasionally clicking his fingers. Irritated enough, I frowned at him and he stopped and sat straighter. After a few moments, a balding middle-aged man with a discreet AP logo on his briefcase was shown in along with another younger man and woman, and Licinia's *optio* from the legation.

'Drusus, compliance officer from the Argentaria Prima Head Office,' the older man said. 'I apologise, the flight from Roma Nova was delayed.' He nodded to me and went to sit next to Festa, his colleague. The younger man and woman were from our Trade Department; they'd been made late by picking Drusus up at the airport, and frowned at him as they sat opposite him to my left.

'Very well,' I said, and distributed copies of the Interior Ministry search order Plico had faxed through. 'I am disappointed at the lack of cooperation the Argentaria Prima Vienna office and its staff have shown. This meeting is taking up valuable time and taxpayer money. Should the fault lie with the Argentaria, the state will expect reimbursement of those costs.'

'I must protest—'

'As you wish, Drusus,' I interrupted. 'But these are the rules and you know them. And we're wasting more time discussing them.' I passed him a sheet of paper. 'This list is in confirmation of the fax sent to you yesterday. To reiterate, please produce immediately the following items: records of all deposits or credits made in the past twenty days, all silver trade transactions, and full details of all accounts held or operated here by the principal members of the Tella family. Moreover, you must provide a full staff list for this office and have the details of each employee to hand, should we wish to see their individual files.'

Festa slid the bound folders and the box file slowly across the polished surface as if she was handing over her newborn to Pluto himself.

'You may retire to your office, Valeria Festa,' I said. 'I will call you when I need you again.'

She stood and grasped the upper curve of the dark wood chairback and hesitated. After a glance at Drusus, she fixed me with her eyes for several seconds. I refused to break contact. Eventually, she looked away and stalked out of the room. Drusus raised his eyebrows but said nothing. Licinia signalled the *optio* to follow the manager. I didn't want Festa running out of the front door.

After another ten minutes' silence as the accountant and two trade officials worked on the files and the four accounts sheets I'd been given previously, Drusus gave up fiddling with his glasses case and left. Not quite forty minutes later, the accountant slid the four sheets in front of me. Columns were carefully marked up with tiny squiggles and cryptic numbered notes. The senior trade officer nodded at the accountant who cleared his throat.

'Every transaction that has been recorded appears to have been carefully entered. There is no fault in the methodology.' He laid a sheet of graph paper on the table in front of me. 'However, when the transactions for the week before, the two weeks in question and the five days since are plotted, we can see something very interesting.'

I couldn't see anything special, only three fluctuating lines with highs and lows marked by little circles. I was the dunce in the room.

'What does this signify?' I said.

'This line,' he said pointing to the blue one, 'shows the general activity of all non-retail transactions – personal deposits, transfers and withdrawals by the general public are excluded. This green one is intra- and inter-government payments executed by the Quaestor's and Censor's departments, but this red one…' His eyes lit up. 'This one is the commercial trading by Roma Novan businesses and sole traders. And my colleagues here have identified seven anomalies.'

'Anomalies?'

'These movements…' He tapped several places on the graph with his pen. 'Although extremely important to us, the global silver market is smaller and more vulnerable to speculation than gold. Even so, these events are unexpected. We'd expect one or two now and again in a month, but not seven in a fortnight.'

I unclipped the clasp on my handbag and pulled out a folded paper. 'Do any of these points match up with these dates?'

The senior trade officer gasped when she saw the copy of Monticola's coded record. 'Where did you get this?' she shot at me, grabbing it.

Licinia, frowning, took a half-step towards the official, but I signalled her back.

'Answer my question, if you please.'

The poor woman's face went bright red. 'I apologise, Countess.' She stared at Monticola's columns. 'I've never seen an extract from a silver trader's book. I only learnt about their existence during my training.' She glanced at me. 'A privilege.'

'Well, this is only lent to me as a special dispensation. You know what a secretive lot the silver traders are!'

The official's expression relaxed and she released a long breath. She snatched up a pen and her hand travelled back and forth through the air from the copy to the accountant's graph.

'Yes! Here and here.' The three financial experts forgot my existence as they nodded and whispered amongst themselves. Not my area, but they seemed genuinely excited by their paper hunt. Eventually, they looked up remembering I was there. The senior official's face shone as she turned to face me.

'They're a perfect match. Unbelievable! The transactions haven't been recorded.'

I nodded to Licinia and she left the room. Two minutes later she came back in with Festa in front of her, the manager's arm held by the *optio* and Drusus following them. The *optio* laid her hand on Festa's shoulder and pressed her down into the chair opposite me and went to stand barely two centimetres behind it. Festa rubbed the side of her neck, then dropped her hands to her lap. I nodded to the senior trade officer who related briefly, thank Juno, the findings of the expert group.

Two patches of deep pink bloomed on Festa's cheekbones as she listened. The atmosphere in the room grew tense as I deliberately stayed silent for a few minutes. The only sound was the soft swish of the heating switching on, making the warm room even warmer. Festa glanced at Drusus who looked away, then at each of the legation staff who stared down at their files. Finally, her eyes settled back on me.

'You will kindly explain these anomalies,' I said at last.

She looked straight at me but said nothing. Perhaps she'd had time to think about it while we were analysing the financial data, but she must have realised she was guilty of financial mismanagement at a minimum.

'Well?' I injected as much ice as I could into my voice, mirroring the temperature outside.

'I have nothing to say,' she said. 'I refuse to answer any questions without my lawyer present.'

'I see,' I replied. Her tight face radiated defiance. Her non-cooperation was starting to annoy me, but she was our only lead. My instinct said she was up to her neck in illegal dealing. However, we had to prove it.

We'd found only two Tellae employed by the bank branch and they were relatively junior; one was only eighteen and the other was a very distant cousin of the main branch. According to their records, neither of them had been anywhere near trading; one was an archivist close to retirement and the other had recently passed apprentice clerk stage so had very restricted access. Their records were impeccable with no trading activity of any kind. And there were apparently no Tellae accounts held at this branch apart from the staff accounts by these two employees. So it came back to Festa.

'Well, Drusus, as compliance officer perhaps *you* can enlighten us about these trades.'

He had the grace to look away. After a moment he recovered himself. 'I don't know what to say, Countess. Of course, there will be a thorough internal inspection.'

'I'm afraid that's not good enough. This is silver we're talking about, our chief strategic asset. Your manager will return to Roma Nova under escort to be questioned by the authorities.'

'Is that really necessary?'

'Yes, and you know it is,' I replied.

'You can't force me to go back,' Festa said. 'The Argentaria Prima is a private company and we're outside Roma Nova.' She smiled almost in triumph.

'You seem to forget your basic law,' I replied. 'The Argentaria Prima is indeed a privately constituted organisation, but in the case of the silver trade the branch manager is also an official agent of the state. You signed an agreement when you were appointed. That gave you the status and protection of a state servant and, of course, the honorarium that goes with it. But you also carry the obligation of *fides* which you appear to have broken.'

Her expression froze. 'But—'

I held up my hand. 'Valeria Festa, I am arresting you on suspicion of contravening the silver trading laws. As you must know, this constitutes an offence against the state. You will be escorted to your apartment to collect some personal things and then accompanied onto the next flight home.'

'You're sure?' Plico frowned at me out of the black and white screen.

'Completely. The accountant and trade officers are writing up their findings which will be sent to you along with my report in the next couple of hours as soon as I've signed it off. And they'll come back with Festa and explain it in minute detail to you. Prisca Monticola has agreed to release a certified copy of that part of her private trade book to the court.'

'Gods, this is a pile of pig shit.' He grunted. 'Well, I can't say I won't get a certain pleasure out of the AP secretary's face when I tell him what his shining star has been up to.' He paused. 'You went beyond your authority as a legation official saying you were arresting her. Technically, you can't.'

'Oh, really?'

'Yes, really. No doubt there'll be a complaint, but it'll be too late. I'll field it anyway.'

'You won't need to. You're always harping on how I'm still on the government payroll. I know it was you who suggested using me to Justina. If you remember correctly,' I said, pulling in all my sarcasm, 'I still hold my commission. As a Praetorian officer, I hold the power of arrest until the day my resignation is accepted. I've used it. "Deal with it", as our American friends say.'

# PART III

# PURSUIT

## 25

The next day, I had an appointment at Soane's, a branch of a private British bank that had been established in Vienna for nearly two hundred years. My great-grandfather had been English, from London, and following tradition, he'd joined the family firm. He'd frowned on his eldest son, Henry Soane, my grandfather, emigrating to Roma Nova when he'd married my grandmother. Peter John, my grandfather's younger brother, had taken over the business in London, expanding it through Europe as Britain became an industrial powerhouse. He'd based their success on a steadily increasing and highly confidential list of clients, which included royalty, but one of whom had been my mother, his niece, and then me.

The Vienna branch, located in a bland, stone-faced nineteenth-century block just off the Ringstraße, resembled a lawyer's office from the outside, complete with a modest brass plate engraved with the single word 'Soane's'. I glanced up at the camera discreetly perched on the window recess above the glass-panelled front door. Inside, a suited man hovered to one side. Security. The receptionist said nothing apart from murmuring *'Grüß Gott,'* and buzzed my name upstairs. Within two minutes a medium-height man with brown wavy hair and pale eyes entered the lobby from the inside.

'Aurelia,' he said. David Soane took my hands, bent and kissed my cheeks French-fashion. He smelled of citrus. His tailored suit and black polished shoes oozed discretion and money. 'No calls, except my father, if urgent,' he ordered the receptionist.

Upstairs in his oak-panelled office we sat in his very English Queen Anne wing chairs and sipped smooth Viennese coffee. After five minutes exchanging family news, he set his cup down on the table beside his chair and said, 'It's lovely to see you again, Aurelia, but I'm sure you didn't come here to hear about hatches, matches and dispatches. How can I help you?'

'I need some information.

'Always the intelligence officer,' he said, and smiled as if at some inner knowledge. I always had the feeling he saw twice as much as he admitted to. I knew our file on him was thin, mostly information supplied by me. He was the perfect fit for the secretive Austrian banking community.

'It's a delicate matter and the usual channels aren't leading anywhere,' I said.

'Good gracious! Don't tell me the exceedingly efficient Secretary Plico is having a problem?'

'Don't be sarcastic, David. Or play the innocent. I always reckoned the European bankers had an intelligence system as efficient as any state one, better than most.'

His face split into a grin, so unexpected in his usually composed demeanour. 'We try.'

'Silver,' I said. I nearly missed it; it was a mere tightening of muscles, hardly a millimetre of movement, but it was there. 'You must have been following the recent fluctuations,' I added.

'Tell me a little more.'

I passed him copies of my marked-up spreadsheets. Drusus would have had a fit and Licinia wouldn't have been far behind, but I knew that if I didn't make full disclosure of what was classified as a Roma Novan state secret, David wouldn't give me anything. He darted a sharp look at me, but switched back to studying the lines and columns. Eventually he looked up.

'We've been following it, obviously, but as observers. Interesting. What do you want to know?'

'The Argentaria Prima is investigating how it was possible to bypass the office here and effect the trades that led to these movements. I'll leave that to them. I want to know what you think of Valeria Festa. Not her public CV, but the person and her reputation.'

'You want me to dish the dirt on one of your own financial officers? Really, Aurelia!'

'Don't quote ethics at me, please. Is there dirt, then?'

'Totally off the record?'

'Of course.'

'She lives in an exclusive apartment, eats in smart restaurants and is always at the opera or theatre with an equally smart escort.' He glanced at me. 'But then she's paid well by the AP, and as the silver agent of your government.'

I waved my hand at him to continue, disturbed at his knowledge of Festa's confidential pay structure.

'She's known to, er, enjoy gambling, which is possibly a concern.'

Romans lived and breathed gambling; hardly unusual in a high-earner, but I didn't comment.

'But I've heard rumours she's overstretched herself. At the last reception of the Viennese Bankers' Association, she introduced a couple of unlikely business people to me and to representatives of several other niche finance houses. I asked myself why she was doing this and if she had some kind of obligation to them.'

'Why?'

'It didn't seem in character. She's almost more Viennese than a Viennese.'

'Meaning?'

'Apart from fine living, she mixes with only the most exclusive, both in business and socially. These two were a little on the shady side. Now you've shown me these,' he touched the sheets, 'it seems to be making a pattern. Perhaps the silver trading has been giving her a chance to "rectify" her situation.'

'Is she capable of doing this?'

'Oh, yes, she's certainly knowledgeable and experienced enough. Unless somebody came sniffing around and had the expertise to spot it, she'd get away with it.' That almost private smile again. 'But if there was a suspicion, any decent analyst could deconstruct it.'

'But why? Surely there were other ways to accumulate capital. Stocks and shares and so on.'

'Yes, but silver's highly profitable, often traded very quickly. She needed money fast, it seems.'

'Perhaps, but she must have known where it would lead, I mean, pushing the price down like that and devaluing a state asset.'

'It does start to sound calculated, doesn't it?'

I faxed a report to Plico, quoting 'sources in the Viennese banking community' and under an 'Eyes Only' flag. Thirty minutes later, I wasn't surprised when one of the comms office staff put his head around my door saying Plico was on the videolink and wanted to speak to me, stat.

'For once, the *vigiles* have managed to get off their backsides. They found that Festa had been cautioned for debt when she was a student,' Plico said. 'Not something she thought to mention when she applied for a job at the AP,' he added drily. She wouldn't have reached the interview stage if they'd known, despite her first-class degree. 'And the other thing is that she doesn't have much in the way of personal savings, despite her good salary.'

'What about her family?'

'Both parents are dead, but she's got a grandmother in Aquae Caesaris.' He looked at the file on his desk. 'And a younger brother who runs a land agency there. Festus junior seems to enjoy being obnoxious in the local *caupona* and has had a couple of public drunkenness fines. He fancies himself as a politician with a yen for the old Roman Republic, "when men were men".'

'For the gods' sake! What rubbish.'

'Yes, it doesn't exactly add to his sister's credit. He's visited her twice since she's been posted to Vienna, once three weeks ago. I'm going to get somebody to have a closer look at him.'

'Call me paranoid, but I still think Caius is linked to it somehow.'

'You're paranoid. Satisfied?' He smirked. 'Or are your hormones playing up?'

'Do you know how offensive that is?' I glared at him, but the screen flickered and I couldn't see his expression.

'Well, don't overdo it or go off on any silly adventures.'

'I'm perfectly well, thank you, full of energy,' I lied, ignoring the tiredness that pulled me down like a personal gravitational force. 'Tell me,' I said in the most acid voice I could produce, 'how are *you* doing in the search for Caius?'

# 26

If I had to go to another diplomatic reception, I'd scream. This was the third one in two weeks; forced to smile and make small talk at the same time while trying to catch snippets of information about the other sharks in the water.

'You're starting to cultivate a very good poker face, Aurelia,' the *nuncia* had remarked as we drove from our legation in Marc-Aurel-Straße north-west to Boltzmanngasse, where the Eastern United States Embassy was located. 'But be particularly careful of their public affairs and commercial services people.' She'd glanced at me. 'You've read Captain Licinia's briefing?'

By the end of the evening, I'd realised how accurate Licinia's briefing had been. A smarty-pants called White, officially one of their foreign commercial officers, had tried to pump me for my opinion of Severina's ability to succeed her mother as imperatrix. Damn cheek! When I'd fudged the issue, he suggested forming this opinion was beyond my competence and perhaps he'd better ask the senior political secretary – a man. Only his measuring look had stopped me; I realised he'd wanted to provoke me. According to Licinia, this White was one of the resident American spooks in Vienna.

I pulled my shoes off my aching feet, but couldn't get rid of the aching nag in my mind. White had mentioned some of the leading Roma Novan families – he'd been very well informed, or briefed. When he came to the Tellae, my antennae leapt into full receive mode.

White understood that Caius Tellus was 'absent'. I hadn't commented, but moved on to ask him about his home town and family. But he'd come back to the Tellae. I fobbed him off with some history, including about how formidable old Countess Tella had been in her younger days as a senator. Perhaps he was gathering general information, but I sensed something else.

Juno, I was starting to see bloody Caius everywhere. Perhaps Plico was right and I was losing my sense of perspective. He'd given me a simple clipped 'no progress' last night from the vid screen. Caius had been on the run for over three weeks now – surely somebody had heard or seen something. Numerus was efficient and persistent; Plico was no slouch, but he was concentrating on the silver business. The Prussians were smarting from the barefaced effrontery of Caius's escape and the frontier police in Bavaria, New Austria and the North Italian and Helvetian Confederations were on alert. Even the *vigiles* were making an effort back home. I itched to get out there and hunt him down myself, but where in Hades would I start?

'This "Eyes Only" secure fax came for you ten minutes ago.' Licinia strode into my office the next morning. 'The comms sergeant called me as soon as she saw the confidential imperial header code.' She paused and glanced at me. 'I handled it myself. I'm the only one who's seen the contents.'

I read Plico's message: he'd scribbled, *Call me as soon as you've read this. But don't panic.* Attached to the cover sheet were a grainy copy of a letter and an even grainier black and white photograph. Despite the poor quality of the picture, Marina's hesitant smile and confused look were obvious. It looked as if it had been taken in the old palace pleasure garden, now a public park. What was she doing there? The private palace grounds were generous enough for any child to run around. Where was Aemilia, the nursery maid? I glanced at the copy of the letter and an iron hand gripped my heart.

*Your child has developed very well into a charming little girl. She didn't seem to remember me very well, but she still enjoys honey cake. I thought you'd like this photograph to remind you of how she looked before she changes.*

I clamped my left hand over my mouth. The sheet of coated paper fluttered in my other hand then dropped onto the table as my fingers lost their grip.

Oh, gods, gods.

That bastard had my child.

I shot out of my office along the corridor. Anybody in my way was pushed aside. Grabbing the handle of the service stairway to the basement, I swore as it wouldn't open.

*Don't panic,* Plico said.

Pluto take him and smash him into the depths of Tartarus.

A hand came over my shoulder and pressed the keypad. Licinia. She ran down the stairs barely a pace behind me into the comms office. She jerked her head at the operator in front of the terminal who jumped up immediately. Licinia slid into the chair and punched in the number for the Foreign Ministry and the eight-figure passcode – my fingers were trembling too much to have done it even if I'd known the code sequence for the day. She gave me the seat the instant we got through. After two clerks, Plico's face appeared.

'It's all right. She's safe,' he said, before I could get the first word out. I flopped back in the chair and closed my eyes to shut out the spinning world. My heart was thudding at twice its usual rate, but I released my breath and became aware of Plico's harsh tones.

'Mitela! Pull yourself together. The child is safe. Listen to me.'

I stared at him, my eyes nearly crossing. I took a deep breath to feed some oxygen to my brain, but my heart still pumped on.

'Tell me,' I croaked.

'The nursery maid had taken the two children—'

'Two?' My hand touched my stomach.

'The imperatrix's grandson, Julian, of course.' Plico frowned at me. 'He and Marina are inseparable. There was a children's fair with games, something vaguely connected with last fruits festival, or some nonsense. Anyway, the children went with the maid, Aemilia, and two Praetorians.' He snorted. 'Busy and noisy down there, surely, but not exactly a dangerous situation. The organiser smarmed around them for a bit, gave both children an ice cream then left them to get on with it. They were under guard all the time, but the sensation seekers wanted to see them, have their photo taken with them and so on, but the Praetorians kept most of them away.

'The maid was concentrating on holding the children's hands, but apparently Julian threw up with all the excitement. The girl turned away to clean him up and we think that's when the note writer took that bloody photo. The Praetorians were on Marina within instants. The *optio* is mortified they didn't catch the person who took the photo, but they prioritised getting the children away. A witness at the fair has given a description of an older man limping away, but not enough for a positive ID.'

'It's Caius, obviously, in disguise.'

'We don't know that. You're so fixated on him you think he's behind everything.'

'Don't be so damned stupid. Of course it's him. Who in Hades else hates me so much to write a threat like that?'

'You tell me. I expect there's a list we could put together.'

I scowled at him.

'Caius is a manipulative bastard. He tried to use Marina before to get to me when my mother was alive. Something about a families' alliance. I told him to get lost.'

'So he's the spurned lover?'

'Don't talk rubbish.'

'Well, he seems to be taking it to the personal level.'

'He aches for power, Plico. Whether he does it by alliance, or by removing people in his way or plain grabbing it, that's what he craves.'

I fretted as I waited for the call for the gate. How long did it take to get a plane ready? Licinia had driven me out to Wien-Maria-Theresia and stood with me now, her eyes glancing round continuously. As the gate number flipped up on the display board, she nodded to the *optio* to follow us. The latter would be travelling back to Roma Nova with me. I'd protested, but Plico had overruled me.

I fidgeted as I waited at the gate itself, too unsettled to take much notice of anything. My gaze flittered around, but not in the calm, professional way Licinia's did. I spotted a child, a boy about nine or ten, dark haired, darker skin than even most Roma Novans. He walked along the other side of the woven ropes strung to separate us from people not flying. He searched faces, then his eyes widened when he saw me. He broke into a trot, heading for me. Licinia ducked under the rope and intercepted him, grabbing hold of his arm. He struggled, but she held him in her grip.

*'Nee, Die Dame. Der Dame muß ich dies geben,'* he insisted, his voice rising. He thrust out a flower with his other hand, a red rose. Tied round its stem with a thin velvet ribbon was a card. *'Weidmannsheil. M.'*

Juno.

My stomach fluttered and I dropped my hand to my middle, but grasped the rose with the other. I snapped my head up and searched round the departure hall. Was Miklós watching me? At this precise moment? The boy's sudden movement caught my eye, then the sound of his grunting as he struggled to get away from Licinia's grasp.

'Relax, Licinia. Let the boy speak.' I knelt down beside him. Wet patches shone below his eyes and he sniffed. 'Who gave you this flower to give to me?' I said, in Germanic.

'A cousin.' That could be any relation in Miklós's world.

'Tell me what he looks like.'

'Big, and he wears dusty boots.'

'And what is his hair like?'

'Black and funny, like he hasn't combed it.'

'Well done, you've described him well. Thank you.' I found my purse in my handbag and gave him a twenty mark note. 'Look after this and spend it carefully.' I nodded at Licinia to release the boy. He ran as if the devil was after him, but as he reached the door he turned round and gave me a cheeky wave.

A two-tone chime interrupted us. We were boarding.

'Goodbye, Licinia. Thank you for all your help.' I held my hand out, but she pulled my arm into a military clasp, forearm to forearm.

'Come back soon, major. Tell me to mind my own business, but what did the message on the card mean?'

I looked at her steadily. 'It's a country expression meaning "good hunting".'

On the way to the gate, I stopped by a bin. I fiddled with the rose, almost crushing the bud, and caused a few petals to drop. I couldn't understand my feelings for Miklós. I'd tried to dismiss him from my mind; I knew I would never manage to erase him from my heart. He was watching over me, yet didn't contact me direct. Perhaps he thought it was too dangerous. But the Austrians weren't seeking him and he was afraid of nothing. Gods, I didn't know what to think. I dropped the rose in the bin.

Back in Roma Nova the usual dark limousine met me at Portus Airport and barrelled its way through the falling snow up the hill to the palace. The driver slowed down once inside the palace gates, but even though he jumped out to open my door as soon as he'd stopped, I was already halfway out.

Luckily, the vestibule guard recognised me and opened the door barrier as I ran up the steps. The click-clack from my shoes echoed across the marble floor of the silent atrium. At the far side, a steward bowed and opened the door into the family quarters and I hurried up the stairs to the nursery. At the top, I ran into two Praetorians, armed. I gasped. Although carrying side arms in the rest of the palace, the guards in the children's area never carried firearms, only a concealed knife or a short nightstick attached to the back of their belts. They blocked the corridor, coolly assessing me, but not giving a centimetre of ground.

'Let me pass. I am Marina's mother.'

'If you say so, *domina*,' the female guard said. 'But I don't know you. And there are no further visits scheduled today. Please wait.' She raised the handheld radio to her mouth and asked for ID information. Well, I didn't know her, or the man. I thought I knew almost every guard; there were only around five hundred in the entire force. Another bitter reminder that now I'd been out a few years, I supposed there would be faces I wouldn't recognise. I folded my arms, frowned at them both, tapping my fingers of my right hand on my left arm. The corridor light was dim. I glanced at my watch. The children would be in bed, but I had to see Marina. While she waited, the female guard watched me, glancing at my hands, my face and the space behind. The man stood stock-still, overpoweringly tall.

A wave of tiredness rolled through me and I longed for a chair. I glanced around, half turning, and the man shifted as if to cut me off.

'For Juno's sake, I'm looking for somewhere to sit down,' I snapped at him. 'Where's the little sofa that used to be opposite the day room?' I waved at the door five metres down the corridor behind him. 'And the two chairs?'

'They've been moved to provide a better sight line,' the man said. The woman glared at him, but was distracted by her radio cackling into life. A voice pierced the distorted sound made by the radio.

'Guard commander. Go ahead.'

The guard stared at the radio in disbelief. I'd give money that she hadn't expected the commander herself to reply to her query on the internal radio circuit.

'Am I wasting my time or is anybody there?' The voice crackled out again.

'No, no, sorry, ma'am,' the guard stuttered. 'I didn't expect you.'

'Report!' the disembodied voice barked.

Glancing once more at me, the guard described me and that she needed to identify me.

'Get off the line, you donkey, and give your radio to Countess Mitela. And look sharp.'

The young guard thrust the handset into my hand as if it was a live tarantula. I pressed the rocker button for transmit.

'Who is this and why am I being prevented from seeing my daughter?'

'Lieutenant Volusenia, Countess. We're on double alert at the palace.' Her voice sounded a little breathy. I heard footsteps running up the stairs behind me. A medium figure in beige and black uniform, curling brown hair pulled back at the neck and a frown on a face with pronounced features strode onto the landing. The two guards snapped to attention and looked directly at the opposite wall, not daring to look at this cross woman.

'Volusenia, I presume?' When she nodded, I snapped. 'I've been travelling most of the day, I'm expecting, and I need to sit down and have some food. Now can you please let me in to see my daughter?' Being truthful, I was exhausted and wanted my bed. Despite the fiasco in the park, I knew Marina would be safe behind such a security barrier – they'd be ten times more vigilant – but I was irritated at being stopped in this way. I'd had free run of the palace since I was a child.

'Please come with me,' Volusenia said. The two guards pressed themselves against the walls to let us through. Once out of earshot, she apologised. 'They're good soldiers, but a little over-eager.' She glanced at me. 'Not a bad way to be in these circumstances.'

'Is it then so bad?'

'The imperatrix has commanded a round-the-clock guard on the children. She thought it best for both to be guarded at the same level so that Marina didn't take fright at being picked out for extra attention. The imperatrix has asked that you be taken to her as soon as you arrive, but I'm sure we can divert to the nursery first.'

We stopped and she entered a code on a keypad I hadn't seen there before. I pushed the door open gently. Volusenia followed me in and I winced as the lock clicked shut loudly. I crept through the day room and to the interior landing leading to the children's bedrooms. I gently turned the silver chased doorknob of Marina's room and slipped in. Her wan face on the pillow was relaxed, her lips slightly open and a baby snore, more a loud breath, escaped her nose.

'She's got a cold, so they've given her a weak sedative to help her sleep,' Volusenia whispered.

I leant over her and kissed her warm forehead, my heart filled with love for my fragile child. How was she going to fight a simple virus, let alone the threat of a brutal bastard wanting to destroy her to get to me?

## 27

'There's no question of you returning to Vienna,' Justina growled. 'Plico reckons Caius Tellus has hopped back to the German Federation or even over the border to Russia. The Reds are welcome to him. With any luck, their paranoia will automatically lead them to throw him in one of their delightful gulags.' She sipped a brandy and gazed at the flames leaping in the stone fireplace. 'As for you, Aurelia, if Plico can't find you something suitable, you can keep Severina company. She may possibly learn something from you.'

Juno save me. I'd rather scrub floors at the Foreign Ministry than spend my days listening to her daughter wittering on about shopping and celebrities. I nursed my warm honey drink and waited.

'You'll let Plico's people and the *vigiles* investigate this, won't you, Aurelia?' She gave me a sharp look. 'I think you're taking this too personally. You're not to get involved. Do you understand?'

'I understand what you are saying, imperatrix.' I tried to keep my voice neutral, but I resented the way she thought I was being obsessive. From my childhood and all through my adult life, Caius had been there, sniping and mocking me. Even at my emancipation ceremony at sixteen, he'd thrown up, causing a disgusting interruption during one of the most solemn moments of my life. He'd laughed it off, joking with his cronies afterwards. He sneered at me as he'd said the words of apology, but his eyes were gleaming with malice and pleasure at spoiling my special day.

Ignoring all the other opportunities he'd taken or made to try and humiliate me or twist opinions against me, he'd tried to manipulate Grosschenk into killing me and then have me convicted for murder in Berlin.

Yes, it was personal.

I swallowed hard. 'I have complete faith in the *vigiles*, of course,' I lied, smoothing my hand over my skirt and looking down as I did it. Since my mother's so-called accident I'd lost what faith I had previously had in them. When I looked up again, I smiled at her. 'Since I'm back, I thought I'd visit a few of the other families, out of courtesy, if for nothing else.' I couldn't remember when the last families' council had been convened; in the meantime, it would make political sense to renew links. The gods knew I hadn't seen many of them since my mother's funeral. And I'd include old Countess Tella on my list, whatever Justina said.

'Very commendable,' Justina said and stood. I placed my cup on the side table and rose, knowing I was dismissed.

'But you don't need to bother with Domitia Tella. I had the old dear in here last week, trying to find out if she'd heard from her great-nephew. She waved aside my question about Caius in a few seconds flat. Then she went on for the next twenty-nine minutes about crooked accountants and servants' pilfering. Apparently, a quarter of the Tella family treasure account seems to have disappeared. She's not the woman she was in her fiery days, but she's sufficiently *compos mentis* to check her accounts.'

Hades. That family asset was meant to be left untouched, grown and passed on to succeeding generations. It didn't take a genius to work out who had taken it.

I was up at half past five the following morning, anxious to see Marina as soon as she woke. Somebody had unpacked my suitcase and hung my clothes in the wardrobe, the gods knew when. Justina's staff were rarely seen, and ran the palace almost by stealth.

In the corridor outside the day room, I nodded to the two new guards on duty and went in. A startled face greeted me – Aemilia, the nursery maid who had cared for Marina since my daughter had first lived at the palace. Her eyes widened. She dropped the cutlery she'd been laying on the table and grasped the base of her neck with her right hand. She opened her mouth, but any words she wanted to say died in her mouth.

'Calm yourself,' I said. She didn't move. 'Here, sit down.' I took her arm and gently pushed her down on the child-level bench at the side. I searched around and found a jug of water. I waited until she'd drunk half a glass.

'*Domina,* I… I can only apologise. I meant no neglect, Julian was ill, he—'

'Shush,' I said and took her hand. 'Don't upset yourself. I don't blame you.' I pressed her fingers and smiled at her. There was no point being angry. She'd been duped by a master. She looked up at me with red-rimmed tired eyes, searched my face and burst into tears. Poor child. She was only eighteen herself. She would never, ever let anything like that happen again. I only hoped it didn't make her nervous of every other human on the planet. I handed her my handkerchief. She sniffed and gave me a watery smile back.

'Very well, Aemilia, let's set this table before the children wake up and you can tell me all about it.'

I didn't have to prompt her. She poured it all out, then went back over and over every minute detail. Ten seconds of horror had been spinning around her head for over twenty-four hours. She fidgeted about, moving bowls and plates a few millimetres here and there, swapping the position of mugs and spoons. She paused for a second and said, 'One funny thing about him… it's just struck me. I mean, he looked like anybody's granddad, but his eyes, they weren't wrinkly. My dad's only forty-eight and he's got funny little lines coming down from the edges of his eyes. This man had greeny-brown eyes but no wrinkles.' She looked at me. 'That's not very helpful, is it?'

'Yes, it is, it's very good,' I patted her shoulder. Out in the corridor I commandeered a secure radio from one of the guards. After some crackling and patching through, Plico's voice grumped at me.

'I know it's early, Plico, but listen. Can you send somebody over with a retouched photo showing how Caius might look as an older man, say mid-sixties, but don't alter the area around his eyes.'

'Why?'

'I think the maid's positively identified him.'

I slid back into the day room to check Aemilia. Shoulders hunched, she was sitting at the children's table, staring at the floor. I poured myself a glass of juice and waited a few moments to let her recover. As I was about to say a comforting word to her, the door from the inner corridor opened and a little girl entered.

'Milia? Nobody's come to wake me up. Where are you?' She sniffed a wet sniff, rubbed her eye socket with her tiny hand, then dropped it and stared at me.

'Mama?'

I managed to set my glass safely on the table before running across the room and folding Marina into my arms before she could take breath for another word.

Whatever Justina's steward's staff procedures were, I would insist Aemilia be retained as Marina's attendant. Marina trusted the girl and was affectionate towards her, something I realised with a lump in my throat as I watched the two of them during the morning. I was shut out of their universe as they sang learning songs, worked on letters and coloured in drawings.

I read Marina a story with her sitting on my knee, but she ran to Aemilia afterwards. I remembered my own nurse with great affection and running to her crying when my strict English tutor had punished me. Her arms had always been a comfort and refuge.

After lunch, I kissed Marina on the top of her soft hair and left quietly, promising to be back for bedtime. I was pulled abruptly back into the hard practical world when I walked into Plico's scruffy office. It looked as if he hadn't touched any of the files since I was last there.

'No news of that bastard Tellus, but the bank manager you bounced, Valeria Festa, seems to be unbending. Maybe she's realised what a pile of shit she's in. She's finished with the Argentaria Prima whatever happens. I think you'll find the report on the brother interesting. Read it in the car on the way over to the PGSF.'

'Oh?'

'I've had a request from them for you to go and help interrogating her "at your earliest convenience" as you were the arresting officer. And don't forget to sign the damned paperwork.' As I drew breath to retort, he said, 'You're looking better. I'm glad.' He bent his head and resumed studying his file. I took that as my exit cue.

The PGSF headquarters had a bland exterior; the front public entrance resembled a standard government office with a small reception area. Separated by five metres further along the street was the vehicle entrance, closed by solid metal gates with a pedestrian service door in the left one. You had to pass through a short tunnel which opened onto a courtyard parade ground strewn with sand. Access was controlled by photo and X-ray systems plus a battle-ready guard detail, so unless you passed all the checks plus the human one, you stayed out. If the guards were suspicious, not only did they sound the alarm, but shutters would crash down either end of the tunnel trapping the offending vehicle and releasing paralysing gas. When you recovered consciousness, you would wake in the cells with a thumping head, if you hadn't been shot by an annoyed security detail.

I opted for the safe choice and walked back to the public entrance.

I gave my name to the clerk and two minutes later, a slim young woman almost too petite for her beige uniform, her black undershirt barely showing at the neck, came through the door at the back of the reception office. She strode up to the counter in a purposeful way and easily hefted the hinged part back.

'Major,' she exclaimed and saluted. Something stirred in my memory; I'd last seen this girl on the top of a freezing mountain, her uniform sleeve slashed open and blood dribbling from her arm onto the snow.

'Mercuria?' I spotted the gold eagle badge on her pocket and the double *hastae* collar badges. 'Oh, I beg your pardon, Lieutenant Mercuria. Congratulations! How's the scar from the knife wound?'

Her eyes widened. 'You remember that?'

I touched my ear and smiled. 'I never forget whenever somebody tries to injure me or mine.'

'I was careless, but I know better now.' She grinned. 'Numerus gave me an imperial bollocking when I was back on strength and sent me off on a refresher personal combat course. Then he suggested I apply for officer training. I almost fell off my chair with surprise.'

Numerus was a good judge of character. Mercuria must have become one of his protégées. I'd missed so much.

'I'm hoping you can help us with this woman you arrested in Vienna, ma'am,' she said. 'She's been carrying on as if she's being brutalised in a Russian gulag, instead of a detention room with a comfortable bed and three meals a day. But she seems to want to talk.'

Festa glanced up as I entered the interview room. A quick blink of her eyes and a minute head jerk were the only signs of reaction, then she settled back into her chair and folded her hands. Her appearance wasn't as polished as it had been in her Vienna office – she was wearing the standard yellow prison tunic – but her hair seemed neater, brushed back into submission. She sat up straight.

'Good afternoon, Festa,' I began.

'Have you come to gloat?'

'Gloat? Tell me why I would want to do that.'

She didn't reply.

I set my buff file down on the table between us.

'To be honest, I find it rather sad that somebody of your obvious competence and excellent record should have fallen to the criminal level. No doubt we'll come to that.'

'You can't make me say anything.'

'I wouldn't dream of forcing you to say anything against your will, but I understand from the case officer you wished to say something.'

She gave a brief, almost unwilling nod.

'I'm puzzled by your motivation. But let's look at some history.' I took a photocopied sheet out of the file and showed her. 'This wasn't a very good start to your financial career was it?'

She looked at the twenty-year-old caution sheet, her expression aghast.

'Where did you get this? It was cleared from my record years ago.'

'Yes, from your personal civic record, but all criminal records, even the spent ones, are microfilmed and stored confidentially, in case we need to refer to them. It may not have come up when you were appointed the state silver agent two years ago for the Vienna job, but I think the Argentaria Prima would have been very interested in this when you applied to them as a graduate. I was under the impression they vetted all applicants very carefully. I would like to know how you hid it from them.'

She looked away. The harsh white neon light accentuated the pink tinge below her cheekbones. She swallowed but said nothing.

'Your brother seems to have had an, er, chequered career, faking school reports for other pupils to take home to their parents and passing dud bank drafts. Dear me, it must run in the family.' I smirked at her. Her mouth tightened into a grim little line. 'Interesting that his girlfriend worked in the *vigiles* records office in Aquae Caesaris at the time of your application to the AP, isn't it? And even more interesting that her father was a member of the Tella family.'

She shrugged. I stared at her for a long five minutes. After a minute, she fidgeted, shifting the weight of her upper body from one buttock to the other. After three minutes, she was twisting her fingers together. She looked everywhere and anywhere but at me. In the silence, I poured water into a paper cup and took a good swallow and then another, keeping my gaze on her. She glanced at the cup when I'd set it back on the table, at the ribbed plastic jug and the spare cup on the tray, then at my face. She looked at the water again with longing, then down at her hands.

I waited.

'I'm thirsty,' she said.

'That's unfortunate.'

'Can I have some water?'

'I think you'll have to give me something first. Fair exchange, you know.'

She wiped her hand across her forehead.

'What do you want to know?'

I pushed the empty paper cup across the table. 'I want to know when you first met Caius Tellus.'

'I can't talk with a dry throat,' she said with a spark of temper or was it truculence? I poured her a quarter of a cupful. She grabbed it and drank greedily.

'Now you can talk.'

'It was my brother. He was trying to raise money for me. I had some gambling losses and need to make a payment.'

'You didn't think to apply for a loan at your own bank? The staff discounts would be generous.'

'Are you mad?'

I frowned at her. 'Don't forget where you are, Festa, and why.'

She shrugged. I signalled for her to continue.

'It would have been flagged up straight away at the bank's head office as my second loan. They would have required me to make full disclosure of the reasons for it. How long do you think I'd have lasted after that?'

'And?'

'My brother said he had a connection who could help me, no questions asked, he said, in return for a couple of favours. Anyway, my brother turned up the following day in Vienna at my flat. I'd barely stepped out of the lift when he jumped out of nowhere and grabbed my arm. My heart went into overdrive. I laid into him and told him never to frighten me like that again. He just laughed. Idiot. As soon as I'd found my key and opened my door, he pushed me through and a stranger followed him in.'

'A stranger?'

'I asked him who the hell this was and my brother said he was the one who could help me. The stranger was tall and stood very close to me while he shook my hand. So close, I could almost smell his confidence. He held on to my hand and bent over me, staring down with his weird eyes.

'At first, he scared me. I tried not to let him see it. He was quite scruffy, as if he'd borrowed the clothes he was wearing, but there was no doubt he was the one in charge. He ordered my brother to make some sandwiches and coffee and somehow I was sitting at my dining room table as if I were a guest in my own flat, receiving instructions on what trades to make.' She gave a short laugh, but without a drop of humour. 'Ridiculous, now, but he had such a natural air of authority.'

'Is this the man?' I pushed a photo of Caius Tellus across the table.

'Yes,' she muttered and looked down at the table.

'His name?'

'He called himself Caius Pius.'

Pius? Caius the conscientious, righteous, the good? The gods give me strength!

I filled her cup from the plastic jug. She drank in silence, but didn't look any more at ease at having told me what I'd wanted to know. Most people who'd never been in custody before were first frightened, then relieved once they'd got their story out. Of course, the *vigiles* had hardened criminals to deal with and it was different, but our cases were more espionage, political and national security. I could understand Festa was embarrassed, but an educated young woman in a white-collar job, despite her shady brother and the early caution, should have shown considerable relief at this stage.

She held on to the empty paper cup, tracing the rim with her index finger round and round. Her shoulders were curved inwards and her eyes darted all over the place. There was more.

'What happened after that?'

She looked at the opposite wall.

'Festa?'

'Nothing,' she muttered.

'I think there was, Festa. Now we've got so far, you'd better tell me everything.'

Silence.

'Did he come back another day?' I prompted.

Her fingers closed around the paper cup and tightened until the paper sides buckled. Her hand released the crushed remains which dropped onto the floor. She stared down at the table.

Then it hit me. Caius had pulled his usual trick.

'You slept with him, didn't you?' I said.

She hunched over. 'He didn't have anywhere to stay, he said. And he was quite good,' she added, the defiance in her voice plain.

'How long did he stay?'

'Ten days.' She looked up, tears on her cheeks. 'Ten days and then he buggered off. My phone bill went through the roof, I'd waited on him hand and foot. He said he'd come back for me but I haven't heard a squeak. He left a pile of notes on the bedside table as if all I'd been was a whore.'

Still fuming at how easily Festa had been duped, I sat in Mercuria's tidy office and wrote up my notes. Of course, she'd taped the interview, but notes added another dimension. Mercuria glanced through them before taking them to the typist.

'Sad, really,' she said. 'But stupid. How in Hades did she think she was going to get away with it? Now she's got sheltering an escaped murder suspect on her charge sheet. The Prussians may even want to extradite her for that.'

'You've never met Caius Tellus, have you?' I said and leant back in my chair and crossed my arms. 'He's charming, manipulative and a complete bastard. He has natural sexual charm and the instincts of a predator. Unfortunately, he's intelligent with it, but somehow, the Fates forgot to give him the least sense of good and evil when he was born. They also forgot to tell him how to think beyond himself.' I half closed my eyes for a moment. 'His younger brother, Quintus, has drive and intelligence, too, but is a loyal and honest servant of the state. How those two had the same mother and share the same genes is a total mystery.'

'At least we know where he disappeared to for ten days of the four weeks since he escaped,' Mercuria replied.

'Can you ask Licinia at the Vienna legation to request a record of long-distance phone calls from the New Austrian post office? And tell them it's extremely urgent. We need to know who Caius was phoning during those ten days.'

Mercuria handed me a sheet. 'We've compiled a list of all known movements and possible sightings. Senior Centurion Numerus telexed me two additions last night. It looks as if Caius Tellus has been making his way south from Berlin via Vienna. Now the nursery maid at the palace has ID'd him as the man in the park who disturbed your daughter, we know he's arrived here in Roma Nova.'

'Anything from the public CCTV?'

'Not yet. I have a team looking through the tapes. Some cameras in the city centre have updated resolution, but none in the other towns. We've checked his family's villa out near Brancadorum, but the steward swears he hasn't seen him for a year.'

'No, Caius is an urban creature,' I said. 'He hated the countryside even as a child.' I stood up and shook Mercuria's hand. 'I know you'll send a copy of Festa's interview and my notes back to Secretary Plico, but let me know the instant you have even a hint of a sighting of Caius.'

I shivered as I made my way back to the reception lobby despite the perfectly adequate heating. As I sat on the plastic-covered bench waiting for my car, safe behind the glass entrance door, I watched the snow outside. The dancing flakes reflected the yellow light from the building. But beyond the first few centimetres, I could see nothing but swirling darkness.

But I knew Caius was out there, nearby and he was coming after me.

# 28

Reluctant to disturb Marina's routine as well as take her out of her circle of protection, I moved back home by myself. Some inner instinct told me I needed to reconnect with my own household, my *familia*. The porter opened the side gate almost as soon as I'd rung the bell and welcomed me back with a smile. I hoped he'd checked the screen in his lodge first. I'd had one of the new twin CCTV systems with high resolution cameras each side of the gate area installed before I'd left for Vienna.

As soon as I walked in I saw everything was running smoothly; every surface sparkling, windows clear, a smell of polish and fresh flowers. Perhaps the servant mafia at the palace had forewarned the one at Domus Mitelarum. But towards lunchtime I noticed little glances of anxiety from one or two of the younger servants and on one young man's shoulder a faintly pink weal showed when his sleeve slipped back.

Milo had been my mother's steward, and like her was old school. He'd known me since I was a child. Then, I'd been a little afraid of him. When he said 'jump', he considered the most appropriate reply was 'how high, sir?'

Now, his upright figure stood straight and stiff in front of my desk. He never forgot he'd been a centurion before he came to work for the family. Perhaps it was time to remind him this was a civilian establishment.

'Please, Milo, sit,' I began. His hard face didn't relax, nor did his spine touch the back of the chair when he sat. 'I don't need a detailed report,' I continued, 'more of a catch-up.'

'Of course, *domina*.' He passed a dozen sheets across the desk. 'I've prepared this for you detailing expenses, stocks, percentage of home produced and other food, cellar, repairs and renewals, security and staff.'

'Thank you. I'm sure it will be comprehensive. But tell me in your own words. How are the staff? Any new partnering or children? Are the pensioners all well?'

'One of the assistant cooks is expecting a child, and my under-steward has left to marry a hotelkeeper in Brancadorum.' He sniffed. 'Good luck to him – she's a tough one. He'll be her third.' He glanced away. 'Apart from that, two juniors have gone, but we've replaced them.'

'I see.' I took a deep breath. 'Well, I sensed some tension in the air, and nervousness when the staff are around me. Yet they're all ones who know me. What's happened?'

'Some became lax when you first went away to Berlin, but I tightened up the discipline and everything is now in order.'

I wondered what in Hades he meant by 'tightened up the discipline'. Discipline in the military was tough – that was normal – but it shouldn't be hard in a civilian household. There hadn't been a problem when I left. I picked up my pen and let it see-saw between my first and second fingers.

'I presume you haven't reverted to any form of corporal punishment?' I said after a few moments. 'Or has there been fighting? I would be extremely unhappy about that. Any form of physical abuse would be grounds for instant dismissal, of course.'

He looked at me, his eyes balls of granite, but didn't say anything. Slapping lazy female servants or whipping disobedient boys had persisted into this century. My mother had said there were worse things in the world when I'd noticed it as a child. She'd slapped me on occasion. But those times were finished in my house.

He said nothing and continued staring at me. After a minute, I ended it.

'Thank you for the report,' I said at my driest. 'I'll read it and come back to you if I have any questions.'

His dignity obviously offended, Milo gave me his most formal bow, turned and strode off.

Damn.

I flinched at the cold jelly on my stomach. But as the nurse spread it, it warmed up. He concentrated on the black and white screen lost in a maze of wires, but relaxed as the image cleared.

'This is the last test,' he said and smiled.

Thank Juno. I'd given liquids, been prodded, had cloth-covered bands and sensors on my limbs, breathed and stretched for the past hour and a half. Now the sickness had stopped, I felt completely well, only tired in the evenings. I hadn't started thickening either.

When I was dressed, Justina's obstetrician frowned at me. I was sure she was a very competent specialist, but I preferred my own doctor. I'd only agreed to see this woman to stop Justina nagging me.

'You're in good health, Countess, but your blood pressure is elevated significantly above the normal level. I must prescribe complete rest for at least two weeks. If the placenta doesn't get enough blood, your baby will receive less oxygen and fewer nutrients. This can mean slow growth, low birth weight or premature birth which, of course, can lead to breathing problems for the baby.'

She had no idea how complicated my life was at present, nor the stress of it. Two weeks off was completely out of the question. I was about to say as much, but stopped, realising she would report back to Justina.

'Is there any medication you recommend?' I asked, and smiled like a good little patient. She scribbled a prescription which I filed in my handbag.

Back in my car, I rested my forehead on the steering wheel and took a deep breath. Then I swore; at the snotty obstetrician, Justina, Plico, bloody Caius. All of them interfered with my life. All of them thought they could control me. I had my duty to my family, and to Roma Nova – that I took as read – but I was nobody's poodle. The only person I wanted to intervene in my life had slid out of my reach. Oh, Miklós.

I placed my palm over my middle. I wanted this baby. I couldn't endanger it, but abandoning the hunt for Caius was impossible.

• • •

'So you see, Plico, I've been told to rest quietly which is why I'm phoning you from home. I'm sure you can survive without me for a few weeks.'

'I could do with your desk space. We don't have anywhere to base the new data entry clerks. They're as pale and silent as a crowd of mushrooms and sit there feeding information into this new mainframe system we bought last month.'

'That's the future. You'll be tapping away at a keyboard one day.'

'The gods forbid! That's what we have typists for. What in Hades would we do with all the spare young men who sit in the typing pool? Anyway, don't change the subject. Tell me exactly what the doctor said.'

After I'd finished, he said, 'You're taking it very coolly. I thought you'd be flouncing around spitting nails.'

'Well, I have to admit, I do get tired, and I want to make sure this baby has the best possible future.'

One without Caius.

As I replaced the handset after Plico's gruff instruction to take care of myself, I went through my conversation with him. While I had skirted round some of the questions, I hadn't told an actual untruth.

Mercuria raised an eyebrow at my appearance in combat trousers and shirt, then looked at me for a few seconds without saying a word.

'Are you absolutely sure, ma'am?' she said eventually.

'A hundred per cent. I can't practise with a firearm – the noise and shockwaves could damage the baby, but some physical exercise would merely enhance my fitness. And I need to test my reactions at a professional level.'

She led me from her office downstairs to the gym and through to the small arena. The smells of wood polish, stale sweat and leather hit me. Twin neon strip lights along each side of a square frame above shone down on the sand circle. Along one side, protective leather body armour hung on pegs. I selected a medium and shrugged it on. I zipped the side and fastened the shoulder buckles. Mercuria's must have been a cadet size; she looked about twelve in it.

I picked up a wooden shield for each of us, the small circular ones. She twisted the combination lock on the grey steel cabinet and swung the door open. Inside were racks of short swords, fifty-centimetre blades modelled on the so-called Pompeii *gladius* pattern. While some late Roman armies used the longer *spatha* towards the end of the Western Empire, we'd kept the shorter *gladius*. Now only the military or licensed gyms used them for training. But they were unrivalled for learning the sheer physicality of close-quarter combat. If you were careless and let your opponent cut you, then more fool you. This evening, I was sure I was going to be that fool.

We circled, she trying a few experimental jabs, me trying to keep my feet moving as fast as hers. Despite the fitness training I was doing each morning, I didn't have the stamina by this time of the day. But I took some deep breaths for oxygen, pulled the training shield up to my chest, brought the sword up to high line and launched myself at her.

She looked surprised, but dodged down at my first thrust. The tip of my sword speared the empty air above her shoulder. She went to attack from at a forty-five-degree angle, but I swung down hard. My arm jarred as I met her shield, but I quickly regrouped to parry her next thrust aimed at my neck. I struck it down and barely avoided her return aimed at my midriff. I drew back.

'No!' I shouted in her face. 'Oh, gods, that was pathetic.' I dropped the *gladius* and held my hand up. 'Sorry, Mercuria. I can't do this.'

She shook her head. 'Thank Mars for that. To be honest, I didn't feel comfortable fighting a pregnant woman, however skilled she may be.'

'Skilled? Ha! More like one of Hannibal's bloody elephants.'

'No,' she said, her eyes studying my face. 'You may be a little slower than before, but the skill and strength are still there. Forgive me if I'm poking my nose in where I shouldn't, but why don't you leave it until the baby's born? I'd be glad to take a few turns with you then.'

By then it would be too late. Either Caius would be dead or I would.

Mercuria agreed to some wooden sword practice the next few afternoons, but no more bladed weapons.

I arrived home exhausted, but more confident, each day. As I lay in bed four evenings later, I fought sleep while I assessed my readiness.

Morning lie-ins, exercise, vitamins and my self-imposed ban on coffee as well as alcohol were getting my body ready, but was my mind there?

# 29

Milo, the steward, sat the other side of my desk the following morning, no less stiff in attitude than at our confrontation the previous week. He was meticulous going through the domestic programme for the next fortnight, almost to the point of boredom. Perhaps it was because working out how to track Caius down was occupying most of my waking moments that I found water leaks, torn linen and adolescent servant upsets irrelevant at present. But I pushed my resentment back. It would be not only undignified to show impatience but wrong. Whatever his or her personality, the steward was key in the *familia*, the household, and I'd do well to pay attention.

'... and the new security cameras on the exterior walls are performing very well.'

I blinked. Had I really heard the austere Milo praise something?

'Have you seen anything of interest? Some of the younger servants canoodling?' I chuckled.

'No, *domina*. I do not allow such exhibitionism.'

'No, of course not,' I replied quickly.

'If you are at all interested,' he said in a voice reproving and sarcastic at the same time, 'there were two occurrences yesterday which I find disturbing.'

Probably somebody dropping a piece of paper on the pavement, knowing Milo.

'In what way?' I asked dutifully.

'Perhaps you would accompany me to the porter's lodge and I'll show you the films?'

To the side of the tall gates a stone kiosk with three large windows was built against the high wall surrounding the outside of the whole property. The little building's two walls set at ninety degrees to each other met at a corner which had been shaved off to form a diagonal where the largest window was set. As we approached, the porter jumped off his chair inside and stood at the window looking nervous.

'Porter,' Milo said by way of greeting. 'We need to see the tape from yesterday. Please prepare the screen.'

Hampered by his trembling hands, the old man searched a wooden rack at the side of the screen and found the cartridge. He tried to insert it into the player slot but it wouldn't go in.

'Take the current one out, you old fool,' Milo shouted at him. I laid my hand on Milo's arm and shook my head. He shrugged, but said nothing. I smiled in thanks at the porter when he'd managed to start the video replay. He stepped back into the corner, putting the furthest distance he could between himself and Milo.

'There are two machines for each of the two cameras with a control box,' Milo began. 'One is on time lapse, so it records a frame every four minutes. But if either of the cameras detects any movement in the area it's covering, it triggers the second recorder in hi-res mode.'

'What's that?'

'You will appreciate, *domina,* that complete twenty-four-hour surveillance would be impossible to run all the time. They'd be changing the tapes every six hours.' His voice carried that semi-exasperation of an expert explaining to a pupil. 'The higher quality machine only starts if there's any movement and keeps recording until the movement stops.' He waved at the bank of machinery. 'The feeds from both cameras and the recorders are all controlled centrally and the hi-res recordings are time-stamped.'

'That's all very good, Milo, but what does all this wonderful new technology show us?'

He pressed a button from the bank of machinery. 'This.' The black and white picture was sharp and showed a man, walking energetically, arms swinging naturally, nothing out of the ordinary. He wore a coat, hat, scarf and gloves against the cold. I estimated him to be in his thirties from his build and gait.

Pedestrians weren't as common as in other parts of the town. Domus Mitelarum was in the outskirts; the houses were spaced out and most people drove here. The original Mitelae had built their first stone house and run their original farm from the countryside when it had been a mile or two outside the original *colonia* walls in the fifth century. But the city had expanded over the centuries and the house, rebuilt several times, was now within the city proper.

'Pity we can't see his face,' I remarked.

'Ah, but we can.' He pressed another switch and a new film started with the date and time stamp a few minutes later. The same man walking at the same pace approached from the opposite direction. His face was clear. He even looked up at the camera and tipped his hat .

The bastard.

Back in the house, I grabbed the handset from the telephone on the vestibule side table and dialled Plico's personal number. For the first time in two weeks I felt queasy, not the morning sickness of two months ago, but an oily, lumpy feeling in my gut. I wanted to go after Caius, but was unnerved by how easily he was stalking me in my own house. When Plico came on the line, I explained what had happened.

'What time was this?' he growled.

'15.35 and 16.05 yesterday, according to the time and date stamps,' I said, glancing at Milo, who nodded. 'My steward can give you the exact technical details if you need them.'

'Why in Hades didn't he report this earlier?'

'I don't know why my steward didn't mention it to me before,' I said, fixing my eyes on Milo, who looked away.

'I'll get a twenty-four-hour *vigiles* guard on your place as of now and I'll see if the imperatrix will agree to Praetorians as well. Stay put inside the house.'

'We have security here. My steward is ex-military and so are a number of my household. And with the new CCTV—'

'No amount of fancy electronics will protect you if Caius gets inside.' He coughed. 'Your steward is now, what, fifty-six, fifty-seven? And those two ex-infantrywomen are the same age.'

'And tell me exactly how you know that?' Even I was startled by the ice in my voice.

'I... er, had them checked.'

'You did what? How dare you!' I slammed the handset down. Milo raised an eyebrow. I stalked back into the atrium, jerking my head for Milo to follow me. Who in Hades did Plico think he was, ferreting around in my private household affairs? I crossed my arms and took a very deep breath.

'Well, Milo, why didn't you tell me about this before?'

He looked away, then brought his gaze back to me. 'I wasn't completely sure it was Tellus. And I gained the impression, now I see the wrong impression, that you were too busy with your investigation, your medical appointments and meeting your former colleagues to be interested.' He coughed. 'I apologise.'

'We'll discuss this further, have no doubt. If we can't work together without rubbing each other up the wrong way, then—'

The phone cut across the rest of what I was going to say and Milo went to answer it. I stared out at the new roses I'd had planted a month ago in the inner courtyard; bare and forlorn, little wax-tipped sticks that a child could have pushed in the ground.

Milo appeared, face impassive.

'Secretary Plico for you.'

'Tell him to get lost.'

'He says he'll send Senior Centurion Numerus round to talk sense into you if you don't come to the phone.'

'Numerus is back?'

'Apparently so.'

I took my time approaching the vestibule table and picking up the handset. I fiddled with the telephone cord with my other hand.

'Plico. I apologise for my rudeness, but you had no right. None whatsoever.'

'Yes, I know, but—'

'However, I realise you were doing it for my protection.'

'The gods be praised, your brain is working again.'

'If you ever pull another trick like that—'

'I know, I'll be thrown into Tartarus, never to re-emerge. Now can we get back to the matter in hand, please?'

A PGSF short wheelbase appeared at the front gate an hour later and once in the courtyard with the gates shut behind it, Numerus stepped out and pulled a kitbag and briefcase out of the back.

'Secretary Plico has instructed me to work from here to coordinate the operation. Three more of my team will arrive this evening so that we can maintain a proper watch and try to catch the bastard. The psychologist says Caius is fixated on you, so it's extremely likely he'll come back here.'

'You're very welcome, Numerus. We have plenty of room. The porter's quite old and a little deaf. He's finding it a bit much especially with Milo breathing down his neck. The old chap's worked for the Mitelae since he was fourteen and his mother before him. If your people are going to be in the lodge watching the screens, then I'll send him to the farm out at Castra Lucilla.'

I wasn't unhappy to send the porter back with the farm truck that had made the weekly run with meat, fruit and vegetables. Milo was pleased the farm manager had included two large hams and a tub of honey, remarking that we had all these additional hungry mouths to fill. Sometimes, Milo out-grumped himself.

Numerus went through his observation strategy; there'd be two guards on, two off at all times. One guard per shift would be watching the screen in the former porter's lodge and the other in the courtyard ready to run out of the gate if anybody suspicious turned up.

'I don't want to post a guard outside and put Caius Tellus off from making his move,' Numerus said. 'And I've told the *vigiles* to keep their drive-by to twice a day only. They have to be seen to have increased their presence in some way. Caius isn't stupid – he'd expect some reaction from his smart-arse little walk-by.'

'I bet the *vigiles* love being told what to do by the Praetorians,' I said.

'Well, Secretary Plico's cleared it with their prefect, apparently.' Numerus looked sceptical.

'Quite,' I replied, and grinned at him.

'Secretary Plico gave me this for you.' Numerus handed me an envelope. Inside were photocopies of six pages of Festa's Vienna phone bill. And all six pages were double-sided. Juno! Neat annotations and an analysis were attached. Plico had added a scribbled note of his own. 'Some of them are press, some are silver/metal trade or bankers. Get your silver friend to comment, please.'

• • •

'I'm deeply sorry to ask you this, Prisca, but I would deem it an enormous personal favour if you have a few minutes. I can send photocopies round within the hour.'

'Gods, Aurelia, stop pussyfooting around.' Monticola's crisp tone reassured me I wasn't trespassing on our friendship. 'I told you I'd help in any way. Besides, if something's going on that affects the silver market, I need to know. I appreciate being consulted.'

'Well, Plico ordered me to ask you and I was about to tell him where to put his request when I thought about it. If there's a link in the timing of those phone calls and the anomalous trades, it might be enough evidence to nail those responsible.'

Justina's steward sent a car for me later the next morning so I could spend part of the day with Marina. I would not be permitted to travel unescorted and unguarded until Caius was caught.

After three days of being a prisoner in my own house, I rebelled.

'Look, Numerus, he's after me. Let me go and be the bait. I can wear a tracker and a wire. We're never going to catch him unless we go on the offensive.'

'Not a chance, Secretary Plico would have my balls in a sling and fire them over the city wall.'

'Then how long do we wait?'

'As long as it takes.'

Bundled up in my tracksuit, I went for a run around the park that stretched out behind Domus Mitelus to disperse my frustration. It was nearly five, so I'd be quick. Dusk would fall suddenly and the air would freeze shortly afterwards.

A pretty garden with walkways gave way to lawns which sloped gradually down to the stream. Tall cedars and oaks provided welcome shade in summer over part of the parkland; the result of my great-grandmother's time in England as a diplomat. She must have been impressed by the stately homes over there and fallen in love with the Capability Brown style.

Now the trees were stark black against the grey November sky. The sickle moon rising gave little light. The land we owned beyond the river was still farmed, but by a tenant these days. She had access to the water for her cattle, via a gate, but the fields would be deserted now, her animals in barns for the winter.

On our side, about five metres before the river, a deep sloping trench faced with a stone wall about three metres high, apparently called a ha-ha by the English, stopped the cattle wandering into our parkland if they crossed the river. But it wouldn't stop even an unfit human being.

The ancient hedge interspersed with trees along the top of the far bank gave the tenant and us privacy, but now I saw them as a possible place to conceal the menace against me. I'd talk to Milo in the morning about some additional security. Damn Caius for making me turn my home into a fortress.

I was tired, exhausted by the anxiety of not knowing where he was. If only he'd make his move and get on with it. I shivered in the chill November wind and looked back at the house which suddenly seemed a long way away. A hot bath and a warm drink before bed would settle me.

As I turned to jog back, I registered a slight movement from the corner of my eye. As I turned, a body slammed into me and I fell to the ground. I rolled and sprang up, crouching. My arms and legs tingled, my heart pounded, ready for action.

# 30

'Always the comic warrior, Aurelia. Such an exhibitionist.'

Caius.

Of course.

'Better than a murderer.'

'An exaggeration.'

In the falling light I saw his eyes gleaming, the rising moon reflected in them. In one movement, I leapt from crouch to full length, the fingers of my right hand curved for a throat grip, and found a gun barrel in my face. A double-action service revolver. I froze. My head would explode and scatter into formless cells at this range. And his finger was ready on the trigger. He blew on my face as if I was an irritating insect. I flexed the fingers of my left hand and tensed my legs.

'I wouldn't, if I were you,' he said. 'Really, I wouldn't.'

He was right. The instant I moved against him, he'd fire. At three centimetres, he'd hardly miss. I dropped my right hand slowly. I was still so close to him that I could feel his body heat rising from his open shirt neck as well as his warm breath on my face. I swallowed hard.

'What do you want, Caius?'

'You know, irritating as you are, Aurelia, I never took you for a simpleton.' His voice hadn't lost any of its inbuilt mockery. He stared at me intently. 'You, of course.'

Keeping the revolver against my forehead, he pulled the hem of my tracksuit top up, exposing my skin to the cold air. He shoved his hand underneath. I shivered as his hand found my breast and pinched the nipple through the soft material of my brassiere.

I pulled back, loathing instinctively taking over, but not far or fast enough. He smashed the revolver butt down on my temple. I staggered backwards several steps out of the range of his fists, my head spinning. I shook it to clear my vision. Too many seconds wasted. He brought his revolver up and I saw death in the barrel.

'Goodbye, Aurelia.'

No.

With nothing to lose, I leapt towards him, swinging my arm upwards and smashing the underside of his wrist with my fist. The gun arced through the air. A thud as it landed several metres away.

'You bitch, I'll have you,' Caius shouted as he shook his bruised wrist.

Run. I had to run.

I could hardly see for my thumping head. I cleared the first tree, and zigzagged towards the next one. A dribble of blood in my eye. Gods, I was slow. I needed to take deep breaths to feed my body oxygen, but gasped instead. Oh, Mercury, give me your legs now, I prayed.

Two shots rang out, instants apart. Hades, he'd found his gun. A stab on my left upper arm like a hot poker slowly drawn across the flesh. I stumbled and skidded onto the icy ground. Must get up and keep running or the next one would kill me. Breathe. I grasped the wound with my other hand and forced myself on. The house lights became bigger and brighter. The garden wall – only another two hundred metres. I might make it.

An iron grab on my legs and they were yanked back. He brought me down on my face so hard I passed out for an instant. As I came round, he was kicking me, one blow after another. Everywhere.

I was too winded to do anything but grunt at each kick. Gaining more breath, I rolled from side to side, trying to escape his feet. Then I saw what was in his hand. Juno, that bloody gun. He brought it round and aimed at me. I grabbed his ankle as it came to stamp down on my face, jerked my head away as I wrenched his foot to the side as hard as I could. He screamed and fell back. A clatter of metal on stone.

Panting, my throat dry and throbbing with the effort of breathing the freezing air, I struggled to my knees. The pain in my arm nearly made me faint. I swayed, but as I got to my feet, agony flowed through my middle. My head roared. I collapsed, and went out.

A hand on my head. Sore. The smell of antiseptic. A beep. I opened my eyes to a very bright light, then shut them again. I was in a hospital. Again. I swallowed. My throat prickled. I tried to raise my right hand, but another hand grasped it and placed it back on the bed. The other one was trapped. I wriggled my shoulders and pain shot through them. I cried out and felt wetness on my cheeks. Then I took a deep breath and pain exploded through my body.

'Gently, gently. Try not to move,' a woman's voice said. 'Take shallow breaths as slowly as you can.'

A moist cloth on my face. A straw with a drink. Bliss.

'You've been badly beaten, and shot in the upper arm. You have a couple of broken ribs, but you're safe now here in the Central Valetudinarium.'

I looked around slowly, warily, but it was a standard white-walled hospital room with a wide window, the blind half closed not completely shutting out the pink and lemon dawn. A drip line ran from my hand upwards. I was lying half propped up. The nurse, also all white apart from her black hair and brown eyes, held my hand and looked at me. Her face was solemn as if the world weighed on her. She chewed her lips then took a deep breath.

'I'm very sorry, but you've lost the baby,' she said.

I stared at the white ceiling not hearing what she said next, only the noise of her voice. A hum grew into a buzz which pierced my head. Somebody was screaming, then sobbing. My gut clenched and a huge spasm in my chest sent waves of pain through me. Then I realised I was the one screaming.

The doctor glanced down at her clipboard, looked over her silver-framed glasses, then sat down by my bed. I saw her, but couldn't focus. My head was full of fog. I blinked at the bright light. It must be afternoon – the sun was halfway to the horizon. Juno, I ached. My body felt like a lump of cold, set concrete. Then I remembered.

'You've been sedated for most of the day,' she said. 'You'll be with us for a week while we check there are no internal complications. You're doing well physically and we'll start electrotherapy tomorrow morning to stimulate bone repair and reduce the bruising.' She paused. 'You'll probably feel very upset about losing the baby. Not just your hormones playing silly devils, but loss and anger.' She laid her hand on mine. 'It's a dreadful business. Give yourself time to grieve.'

I knew she meant well, but I wanted her to go away and let me die in peace. I closed my eyes and sobbed myself to sleep. When I woke next, it was dark, but I smelled something, somebody. I flinched. Last time it was dark Caius was beating me up. Paper rustled. Somebody was sitting by my bed.

'Steady. It's all right, it's me.'

Plico.

'What are you doing here?' I croaked.

'I came to see if you were faking it.' He leant over with a beaker of water which he held carefully as I drank. 'Apparently not. The doctors tell me you'll live.'

'Plico, I lost… I lost my baby.'

'I know. You must feel like shit about that.' He patted my hand, but didn't look at me. He laid his file on my bed, patted his pockets, pulled out a packet of cigarettes, then stuffed it back.

'Do you want me to try and find your Hungarian friend? I presume he was the father. I'll get that Praetorian captain in Vienna, Licinia, to start a search for him.'

'No!'

'Surely you want to tell him?'

'I said no.'

I'd excised Miklós out of my life before I'd taken up the post in Vienna. I stared at Plico, daring him to contradict me. But I bit my lip at the memory of Miklós nodding at me in the Berlin courtroom. And that red rose at the airport. I gasped as a jab of pain shot through my chest. Maybe the strapping around my ribs was too tight. Would I ever get out of the mess my life had become?

Plico cleared his throat.

'I could kick myself we didn't think of the far perimeter of your place.'

'Kick is not a word I want to hear.'

'No, sorry.' He glanced at me. 'We found the revolver at the foot of the wall, about ten metres away from you, but we haven't caught the bastard. Sorry, again.'

'Look for a man with a limp. I certainly twisted his ankle, if not broke it.'

A female nurse came in, checked my line, frowned at Plico, and pointedly gave him back his papers and smoothed the top cover where the contaminating file had been.

'Your steward's a good man,' Plico said, talking to the window. 'I take back what I said before. You were out for the count. He insisted on riding with you in the ambulance. He was the one who raised the alarm after he heard the gunshots.'

'Thank him for me, will you?'

'I think he'll want to come and see you himself.'

'I don't want to see anybody, Plico. I'm too tired.'

'Tough. The man saved your skin. Do him the courtesy of a few minutes.'

'Leave me alone,' I croaked.

'No, you'll go maudlin. Seeing others will help you out of this.'

'You don't understand.'

'Yes, I do.' He coughed and looked away. 'My sister miscarried twice. Believe me, I've seen what happens. And I know you. You'll look back later and be so embarrassed at yourself.'

'Do whatever you want. I don't care.' I shivered and pulled the sheet up to my chin.

'Milo will be here tomorrow morning,' he ploughed on. 'I'll make sure the guards let him through.'

'Guards?'

'The *vigiles* have stepped up patrols. There's a patrol car back and front of the hospital and we've checked out the personnel coming near you. When a nurse or doctor isn't in your room, a Praetorian will be. All the time. Oh, and the imperatrix will be visiting tomorrow.'

I groaned.

'Count yourself lucky. It was touch and go fending her off for today.' He glanced at the wall clock. 'I have to go. Somebody has to keep the country running.' He stood, bent over and patted my uninjured arm. 'Try not to irritate the nurses too much.'

The evening nurse spooned some soup into me and persuaded me to eat a sandwich, but my stomach protested at the effort of receiving food. He checked all my vital signs, gave me a syrupy drink and a couple of coloured tablets and settled my pillows. He turned down the main lights and settled down with his book slanted towards the light from a shaded desk lamp.

I watched him for a while from under half-closed eyes. He was probably only a few years younger than me but he seemed barely out of his teens, his mother's treasure with that smooth skin and curling brown hair. When he was a young child, she would have run her fingers through it, then hugged his soft body to her chest. She would have watched his first steps and heard his first words. She would have nursed him when he was born and held him close, a living part of her flesh.

I turned my face away and wept.

'No.'

My stomach and head had woken up spinning and I was not going to move out of my bed.

'You'll feel it's worth the effort. Try a few steps.' The young nurse had taken the drip line out a minute ago. Fumes from the antiseptic swab made my nose tickle. He was smiling at me and holding his hand out.

'Not today,' I snapped. 'Now, please go away leave me to rest.' My left arm was trussed up, my ribs tight with the strapping and my insides wobbled like jelly. If the gods ripped open Tartarus, and Pluto was gunning for me personally, I wouldn't have had the energy to move. The nurse looked at me steadily for a few moments, then left the room.

Ten minutes later, the door was pushed open, a beige-and-black-uniformed figure scanned the room, then gave way to a crowd; the hospital director, the doctor with the silver glasses and clipboard, the young nurse and Justina.

Gods.

Justina bent down and kissed my cheek, then stood back and scrutinised me. She nodded to the nurse as he placed a chair beside the bed for her. She laid her palm on my forehead, then her fingers on the base of my throat and glanced at her watch. Once a doctor, always a doctor.

'You're a little warm, but nothing to worry about.' She held her hand out and the doctor hurriedly proffered the clipboard.

'Hm,' she said, then read aloud, 'Deep graze to upper arm from gunshot, no humeral fracture, no damage to nerves or arteries, two fractured ribs, multiple contusions, loss of conception. Antibiotics, electric therapy, painkillers and physiotherapy prescribed. Nowhere does it mention bed rest.'

I squirmed and a sore pain jabbed my arm. I looked at the other faces which remained totally passive, but I could guess what they thought of me. Justina looked at me from half-closed eyes.

'Well, I expect you've done enough for now. You're obviously feeling too weak.'

'Imperatrix, it's only thirty-six hours since…' I couldn't say it. 'I need to catch my breath.' I braced myself for her reply. She'd tell me to make an effort and not be so pathetic. I wasn't the first person who'd lost a baby, been beaten half to death or shot, she'd say.

'I can see you're not really up to it, Aurelia. Don't push yourself.'

I couldn't believe I'd heard her correctly. Where was the 'pull yourself together' speech?

'I'll send Severina to visit you. She'll be able to bring you up to date on all the latest gossip without taxing you.'

Oh, Juno, no.

She stood and the white coats took a pace back. 'I'm sorry to see you so diminished and I'm sure Felicia would have felt the same. Obviously, Marina will stay with us for now. She certainly doesn't need to see you in this poor state. Goodbye, my dear.' Her voice was light, almost bland. Not a hint of her usual decisive tone. What was going on?

Then I twigged. She thought I'd given up.

# 31

Bloody Justina. It was only when I'd struggled out of bed and used the lavatory by myself unaided to prove to them all I wasn't a complete loss, that I realised how she'd finessed me. Waving the Praetorian away, I stood in the middle of the room, balancing myself by gripping the end of the bed, sweat running down my face. I was so angry, I couldn't move. When I'd calmed down, I realised she was right. I'd lost my direction, my grip.

Not any longer.

When Milo came to visit me that afternoon, I was sitting up in a chair.

'*Domina.*' He stopped when he saw the Praetorian. I nodded at her to leave, but she hesitated.

'This is my steward, the man who recovered me after the attack,' I said. 'I think we can take it he's safe.' She left, but I could see her the other side of the glass observation panel in the door, watching us.

'Please sit, Milo. I can't hold my head cranked up looking at you.'

He bowed and pulled up a chair, but kept a respectful distance away. He would never unbend that much.

'Before you say anything else, I want to thank you,' I began. 'I'll never be able to repay you for my life. If you ever need or want anything, you know I'll grant it, don't you?'

'I did my duty.'

'No, Milo, you didn't. You exceeded it. Thank you.'

'I wish to offer my formal condolences for the loss of your child, *domina*. Your mother would have mourned with you as the whole household does now.'

'That's very kind. Please thank everybody. Will you arrange a date for the *pontifex* to conduct the proper ceremonies?'

The idea of receiving the tiny urn made me scream inside my head. I would have to face it, but not yet. Plico had said his sister went through this hell twice. How had she coped?

The sun shed horizontal pale yellow light of a winter afternoon and it struck Milo's face. In amongst the harsh features, I thought I saw a relaxation of his face muscles as he nodded.

'I don't suppose you saw anything, did you?' I said.

'The *vigiles* have been through all that with me, and then Secretary Plico.'

'Yes, but you haven't answered my question.'

'No, I didn't,' he added, 'but as I told them, I heard the sound of a boat engine, so I suppose he escaped that way.'

I took a deep breath, which was intensely painful. 'He must have hired or stolen that from somewhere. I wonder—'

'You must not worry, *domina*. Leave it to the *vigiles*.'

'They couldn't trace a boat theft if it was taken from a mooring under their noses.'

I left hospital five days later with the doctor tutting at me, and escorted by a Praetorian. Milo had brought me warm clothes, my Loden coat and fur hat, but it was snowing with a vengeance outside. I shivered as I left the over-warm hospital and crossed the short distance to the car. A slicing wind caught my neck and I pulled the folds of my scarf up to my ears.

Numerus greeted me at my own house as if he were the new porter.

'Nothing to report, I'm afraid, major. One walk-by that interested us for a few minutes, in walking boots and a felt hat. Some Swiss or Austrian tourist, I suspect. He didn't come back the same way.'

'I hope he was wearing more than a hat and boots in this weather.'

'Ha! Usual walking outfit, complete with cape.' He glanced at me. 'He was short and he wasn't limping.'

I lay on the sofa for the rest of the day, only interrupted by a home visit from the physiotherapist. She checked I was doing the infernal deep breathing exercises which hurt like Hades. At least the strapping had been taken off before I left the Central Valetudinarium. The jagged groove in my arm caused by Caius's bullet had scabbed and itched as if a whole hive of bees had stung it, but it wasn't infected. The therapist brought me a different cocktail of pills from the doctor which helped with pain and swelling. It would be past Saturnalia before I healed physically, but my mind was clear now; *glasklar,* as my cousin Achim would have said.

I forced Numerus to show me the whole file on Caius, but I couldn't see anything new. No blinding insight fell from the gods either.

'They have a proper incident board at headquarters, but I doubt Lieutenant Mercuria would let me have that.' He smiled as if joking.

'Then we'll go to her.'

Bundled up in the car with rugs by Milo at 08.30 the following morning, I resembled a mobile pile of blankets. At the PGSF building, Mercuria was tactful enough not to greet me as if I was a walking wreck, but as we rode up to her office I appreciated the new lift they'd installed. She gave me a coffee in the military standard issue earthenware mug. I cupped my hands round it, absorbing the heat, the steam of the hot drink and memories of my past life.

'Are you up to a briefing session in the operations room, ma'am?'

'Of course, that's why I'm here. Lead on.'

The bullring hadn't changed. Three rows of desks, buff files bursting with paper, cardboard boxes stacked in the corners and beige figures bent over desks, with the occasional one in combats. Down one side of the vast room were smaller private offices. We carried on through to an open area round the corner that served as an operations room.

Weak winter light shone through the side windows and highlighted the three hinged display boards, the middle one with a large photo of Caius Tellus. Sightings and known associates ran down one side and what Mercuria had headed 'speculations' on the other side. My photo and Plico's were pinned above them.

I sat slightly to one side and watched the tactical group members file in, some uniformed, most not. I counted seventeen altogether. Mercuria gave a rundown so far; nothing I didn't know.

'Our problem is that while Caius Tellus has left a trail of damage in his wake after escaping – the Prussian prison guard, the Argentaria Prima manager and Countess Mitela – we're still no further forward. Berlin says a bag was pulled over the guard's head before he was attacked so he saw nothing. Nor do they have any forensic evidence that Caius Tellus was anywhere near the maimed guard. Unless somebody turns state's evidence, they can't prove it was him. He'd say he took advantage of circumstances. We know what a slippery bugger he is.

'We know he's here in Roma Nova, and specifically in the city. The attack on Countess Mitela is the only charge we can arrest him on domestically, once we catch him, of course. Extra *vigiles* patrols are out, all informants are being pressured, they say, yet they have nothing.' She looked round the room. 'I know you have all been working hard, but the unhappy truth is that we, too, have a blank. This in itself is remarkable.'

She paused to take a sip from a glass of water.

'I'm prepared to listen to any ideas, however simple or unorthodox, at this point.'

'Somebody must be sheltering him, as the bank manager did in Vienna,' an older centurion observed. 'He's holed up in a private residence, maybe even holding some poor householder at gunpoint.'

'That's not as easy as the films make it look,' chimed in one of the younger ones. 'Especially if you have nosy neighbours.' Somebody chuckled.

'Ref his foot,' Mercuria continued, without reacting to the laugh. 'We've drawn a blank at the hospitals and doctors' practices. We've even checked the three Asclepius temples. The priests there are at least paramedics – one's a doctor. Nothing.'

I put my hand up. 'May I ask, lieutenant, who you have questioned from the Tella family?'

'Quintus Tellus has been very helpful with background information. My impression is that there's very little love lost between the two of them. But he says he has no idea of his brother's whereabouts. He's given us a list of Caius Tellus's associates. Well, the ones he knows about.' She handed me a report sheet. I smiled as I read it. I could almost hear Quintus's cultured and concise tones. If he continued to climb the career ladder, the *cursus honorum*, as quickly as he had already, he'd end up as the chief secretary one day. Unless, of course, Caius pulled him off.

'Another question,' I said. 'Has Domus Tellarum been submitted to a full search? It's a very old building with a lot of odd rooms and cellars.'

'I suggested it earlier, when the images of Caius Tellus were caught on your video surveillance system, but the legate said we didn't have any evidence or sufficient legal grounds.' She paused and I suddenly remembered the current legate was some sort of cousin of Domitia Tella's, but on her father's side. That was the one aspect I hated about the families' system which counterbalanced all the positive ones; some of them closed ranks rather than do the right thing.

'I went with the *vigiles* prefect myself to see Countess Tella while you were in hospital,' Mercuria continued. 'She refused point blank to let us even inspect it informally. Her words were, ah, unambiguous. The prefect refused to push it further. He said her word of honour that Caius Tellus was not living in her house was sufficient for him.' She coughed, then looked straight at me. 'I am reluctant to doubt the word of the head of the second oldest of the Twelve Families.'

The room fell silent; not a rustle of paper, a sniffle or creak of a chair. She hadn't said it, but I could feel her frustration at being blocked by ancient privilege. At that moment, with eighteen pairs of eyes looking at me, I felt responsible for the poor behaviour of the whole patrician class. Well, abusing privilege would be the head item at the next Twelve Families' council. I had to arrange one as soon as we'd finished with Caius, and the agenda would be full.

'Regrettably, lieutenant, there are members of the Twelve who forget their primary duty is to the imperatrix and the state,' I said. 'Fortunately, they are very few. I can assure you that I will do everything within my power and influence to ensure the two we are discussing will be submitted to the full vigour of the law and treated no differently from any other citizen.'

'Of course, ma'am. I don't doubt it.'

'If you can show me to the nearest secure telephone, I will consult Secretary Plico now and request he issue a full search order for immediate execution. And, if you don't mind, lieutenant, I'll come with you.' I let a deep breath out. 'If nothing else, I can keep Countess Tella talking while you take the place apart.'

Domus Tellarum was even older than Domus Mitelarum, some parts dating back over a thousand years. The tall main gates were wooden, flaking in places, but solid enough with long studded hinges and black metal straps across. Numerus tugged on the old-fashioned bell pull by the service gate. The observation panel opened to reveal a cross, rather young, face.

'Who are you?'

'Senior Centurion Numerus of the Praetorian Guard. Please open the door.'

'But—'

'Open the door, son, or you'll be in so much trouble you won't work the fine off until you retire. Let's be sensible, shall we?'

The porter gave in and Numerus and two other troops stepped through the service door and opened the tall gates.

We parked the three long wheelbases on the gravel area just inside the wall gates. No security cameras anywhere, only the porter's lodge and an open-sided shelter with two storage bins.

Built on more traditional lines and resembling a country villa dropped into the city, the main house was only two storeys high on the surface, but I knew there were two more levels underground.

As we walked between the immaculately clipped cypresses and elegant statues lining the slab pathway, I drew a long breath, but slowly. I'd need it to confront Domitia Tella.

The strong sunlight reflected off the polished marble-faced portico columns as we waited for somebody to answer. Mercuria flicked her fingers and a section of six guards set off past a dry fountain towards the back of the house. The troops carried only personal side arms and nightsticks – enough to contain most urban situations – but I was relieved she sent a whole section.

Mercuria frowned when there was no answer at the door and she signalled the *optio* to ring again. He thudded on the door as well, but it was solid oak. He probably damaged his hand more than made any impact.

'If that door isn't opened in the next ten seconds, we'll ram it,'

Mercuria said and fixed her eyes on her watch. At eight seconds, the three-hundred-year-old door was saved. The steward's face appeared in the gap as he opened it.

'Where's the revolution?' he grumped.

'It'll be here now if you stand in my way,' Mercuria shot back as she thrust a trifold document into his hand. 'I am Lieutenant Mercuria of the Praetorian Guard and this is an official search order signed by Imperatrix Justina. Please stand aside.'

'You can't come in now. The countess is taking her nap.'

'Then we'll wake her up.'

'She won't have it.' He stood, arms crossed and face cross. He was a big man, although his jowls suggested he'd run to fat.

'There is no choice.' She nodded to Numerus who grabbed the steward's shirt collar and barrelled forward, pushing the steward off balance by sheer momentum. Numerus lowered him to the ground before the servant had time to take the next breath. He retrieved the search order for Mercuria and left two guards with the truculent steward. Revolver in hand at chest level, Numerus stepped through into the hallway, two more guards close behind him. Four more followed, splitting off in different directions.

We heard 'clear', so Mercuria and I followed. The vestibule was lined both sides with marble and plaster busts, the *imagines,* but the ancestors' faces were poorly lit. Numerus waited for us by the half-open atrium door. Two guards took up position at the foot of the stairs to the left.

'Let's see if there's anybody in the atrium,' I whispered to Mercuria. She signalled Numerus in and drew her own revolver, gesturing me to wait. A scream, followed by a crash. I pushed in. Both guards were pointing their weapons at a young woman, a pile of porcelain shards at her feet and her hands over her mouth. Her eyes were round and terrified.

'Okay, relax.' Mercuria holstered her revolver. 'Who are you?'

The girl, she could only have been sixteen or seventeen, shook her head. She had frozen. I walked over to her and touched her arm. She flinched.

'It's all right. Nobody is going to hurt you. All we want to know is where Countess Tella is.'

The girl glanced from Mercuria to Numerus and took a breath.

Then her eyes widened and she stared over my shoulder. I heard the sound of light steps and a walking stick and turned to see a tall, sturdy figure in traditional dress – navy *stola* over sky blue undertunic, a silver belt cinching the folds in and a magnificent, almost barbaric, silver pendant with a sparkling amethyst the size of a baby's fist. Her grey hair was swept up into a severe bun at the back of her neck with the traditional *nodus* roll at the front. She resembled the most fearsome of the statues of the ancient empress Livia.

'I'm here,' her clipped voice rang through the atrium. 'And before I have you thrown out, tell me who it is I am going to drag through the court for trespass and criminal damage.'

# 32

I took a half-step forward but Mercuria beat me to it.

'Countess Tella, I am Lieutenant Mercuria of the Praetorian Guard ordered by Imperatrix Justina to conduct a search of this house.' She proffered the search order, but Domitia Tella ignored it. 'I am also commanded to advise you that you are required to produce all members of your household, both family and servant, for questioning. Please assemble them immediately.'

'I'll do no such thing, young woman. You can take yourself off and be glad I'm inclined to ignore this impertinence.' She gathered up the folds of her floor-length *stola* and started walking away.

'One moment, Domitia Tella.' I raised my voice so she couldn't claim she hadn't heard. 'You cannot disobey the imperatrix's command.' The older woman stopped and turned to face me.

'And who do you think you are, Aurelia, to speak to me like that? You're not much further on from a snotty schoolgirl who keeps going off her head when the mood takes her. I have nothing to say to you.'

I heard a gasp from Mercuria. Numerus came up beside me and stared at Tella with contempt. Before he could do anything, I stalked over to the older woman. My ribs were hurting, my arm aching and my tiredness was making me irritable. But more than anything, fury raced through me at her unreasonable attitude. She'd made a career out of being obnoxious but it was going to stop here. I halted within centimetres of her, almost touching her clothing.

'You will take that back, Tella,' I spoke in a low voice, struggling to keep the anger out of it. 'Remember who you are speaking to. I may be younger in years, but I am the head of the Twelve Families and you will be wise to respect that.'

'Are you threatening me?'

'No. Threats are bluster and so useless.' I stared her direct in the eyes, those strange hazel eyes the twins of Caius's. 'This is what will happen. Firstly, you will stand aside and permit the search as instructed by Lieutenant Mercuria. Secondly, you will summon your household members immediately. And thirdly, for having shown disrespect to the head of the senior family in front of strangers, I will be issuing a sanction against you through the Families' Court.'

As I turned my back on her, I was trembling, but I walked away in what I hoped was a dignified way. I nodded at Mercuria who then issued orders to send the troops on their search. I spotted a small table and two chairs at the side and flopped down on one. Tella remained where she was, a pillar of frustration. I wondered when the last time was when somebody had crossed her and won.

After five long minutes of the two of us alone in the atrium, she marched over to me, jabbing the marble floor with her stick at each step.

'I don't know what you hope to achieve by ransacking my house. I spoke to Justina last week and explained that my great-nephew was being a little unruly and she assured me the matter was closed.'

I looked up at her.

'Unruly?' I retorted. 'That's what you call murder, smuggling silver, and causing a run on the market, attacking our state interests, terrifying my child, twice attempting to murder me and having me falsely imprisoned.' I snorted. 'Let's add suborning a senior state employee and maiming a Prussian prison guard.'

'The Prussian doesn't count.'

'For the gods' sake, Domitia, how can you be so blind? Of course, the guard counts. The poor man's disabled for life. He will have lost his job and his livelihood. Your precious boy is a nasty piece of work who won't stop at anything to take what he wants in order to gain power. Look at the way he stole part of your family treasure account.'

'That's private information.' She scowled. 'And he could have had it if he'd asked, so it comes to the same thing.'

'No, it doesn't. It's a trust from previous generations to the next. You're only the steward.'

I wiped my hand across my face. Where could I start?

'Sit down. Please,' I said.

'I will stand.'

'As you wish.'

'Between you, you and your niece spoiled Caius, not correcting his antisocial tendencies when he was younger.'

'You know nothing of it.' A pink flush spread over Tella's cheeks.

'On the contrary, I've been Caius's target since I was a child. Oh, he was clever, no doubt about it. You will have seen only his smiles, not the frightened faces of the other children. He would have told you he was puzzled why the others didn't want to play with him, that they were excluding him, that he didn't understand why.'

She looked away.

'Children are adept at hiding things from their family,' I added. 'We naturally take the part of our own child. And he's played on it all his life.'

'You've never liked him, Aurelia. You were always such a stuck-up little miss. Nobody was ever good enough for you.'

'That's beside the point.' I stood, but grasped the chair back for support. 'Where is he, Domitia?'

'I don't know.' She shook her head, daring me to contradict her. Her face had turned dark pink and her eyes glittered, but she stood ramrod straight in her dignity. Before I could say another word, I saw Mercuria come back. She stopped behind Domitia Tella and hesitated.

'Yes, Mercuria?' I said, keeping my gaze fixed on Domitia Tella.

'I think you should come and see what we've found, maj—, er, countess.'

'Very well. Please send two of your troops in here to ensure Countess Tella stays here and does not attempt to contact anybody. Your troops are authorised to use restraint if necessary.' Tella shot me a venomous look, but I turned my back on her for the second time.

Mercuria led me down three stone steps into the domestic corridor. I knew this area well; Quintus and I had sat at the long kitchen table drinking milk and eating biscuits when we were children. The cook had often slipped us some of her cakes and pastries warm from the oven. But one day Caius had come in and sat by me. Then he'd spat on my cinnamon tart. I'd burst into tears, not believing anybody could do anything so disgusting. After that, I only went back there as a child when I thought he wouldn't be there.

Mercuria's boots clattered on the worn red tile floor as we passed by the doors to the kitchen, pantry, linen room, boiler room, equipment room and conveniences. Further along the stone corridor were the staff dormitories and bathrooms. At the end, the door was open to a flight of steps down to the cellars. The first level was really a half-basement with windows along the tops of the walls, and used mostly for food storerooms and wine cellar. Racks of files and cabinets lined the documents room, now unlocked. A male household servant fidgeted nervously with the bunch of keys in his hand, closely watched by Numerus. Two guards were inside, sifting through cabinets. I shivered instinctively at this invasion of the family's personal papers, but finding Caius was the priority.

'Leave the safe for the moment, Numerus,' I said.

He raised an eyebrow, but said nothing. I knew what would be inside: the Tella *insigniae*, and some of their most ancient documents, jewellery and artefacts. And the family treasure, both physical objects and documents. Well, the three-quarters Caius had left of it.

Mercuria beckoned me on to a second set of steps leading down from a gaping rectangular opening in the floor of the next room. I saw moving lights below us and heard voices.

'It's our people,' she said and switched on her own torch. We started down. I pulled my coat around me, and my scarf up to my ears, but it wasn't as cold as I feared. I missed my step and scraped my shot arm against the wall. I grunted with the pain blooming from the wound site and my jarred ribs. Mercuria took my other arm and guided me down the rest of the flight.

At the bottom was a rough-hewn corridor with rooms without doors. As I glanced in each one, I saw pressed earth floors and stone benches each side big enough for a single person to sleep on. In the corner of one were a couple of amphorae, chipped but recognisable. In the middle room a rickety set of empty shelves. Other pottery shards littered the other rooms. These were ancient refuge rooms used during barbarian invasions a thousand years ago, and during later wars. The people sheltering here would have been terrified, but safe.

The doorway of the last room had a thick curtain hung across it. As

Mercuria raised her hand to pull it aside, I tensed. She shook her head. Inside, a survival sleeping bag and several blankets were bunched up on a camp bed. On the stone ledge were candles, a tin, now with its lid off, containing matches, cutlery, a small first aid kit, and a roll of banknotes. A knapsack in the corner and a metal box held changes of clothes and a pair of boots. A faint smell of stale smoke hung in the air.

Mercuria dropped the curtain. 'I'll get one of the *vigiles* forensic teams in to go through it all.' She smiled at me. 'Apparently, when Secretary Plico tore the prefect to shreds for not helping us before, he insisted they share their technical services with us. Now at least we can use their science people direct.'

'Gods, I was working on a proposal for *vigiles* reform ages ago, before I went to Berlin, and that sharing proposal was one of the top items. But it was blocked.' I flicked my hand at the closed curtain. 'Anyway, let's get on. Anything else?'

She shook her head. Then her eyes narrowed.

'You know, apart from in that little room, the air's remarkably fresh,' she said.

'There'll be concealed shafts for passive ventilation,' I replied. 'It was a standard feature when they built these shelters. Engineers, you know.' We grinned at each other. 'Most of them have been filled in by now or they're clogged up with leaves and earth.'

'But he couldn't get out that way, could he?'

'No, far too narrow. Wait. Of course. Why didn't I think of it before?' The painkillers must have been suppressing my brain functions more than I thought. 'There would have been an escape tunnel. Otherwise they'd have been trapped like rats if the barbarians had got in.'

She assigned pairs of guards to knock on the walls in each room and check for a different sound. She and I tackled the corridor wall. I had no expectation of finding Caius, but we had blocked off his refuge.

I was tapping away when I realised what I'd missed. I stumbled back to the middle room and seized the shelving against the back wall. My ribs protested as I pulled. I caught my breath and stood back as the two guards took over.

'Mercuria,' I called.

The back of the shelving unit had been fitted with two grab handles. A rope had been looped through them. A rope leading up through a hole in the wall.

'Mars' balls,' Mercuria said. 'You two,' she nodded at the two guards, 'go and see where that goes. Extreme caution – there may be armed resistance.'

Even though Caius could be up there waiting ready to blast the head off anybody who approached, I wanted to be the one squirming through that tunnel. As the two soldiers disappeared, the sound of cloth brushing against rock slowly vanished, as did the flashes from their torches. Mercuria sent a runner up to the section on the surface to alert them for anybody surfacing.

'The plot is about a hundred and fifty metres long from the front to back wall,' I said, running my finger against the wall in an invisible horizontal line. 'From here they have at least a hundred metres to crawl if they want to get out the other side of the back wall.'

'Surely they'd go for the shorter route to the side?' Mercuria said. 'That's, what, fifty or sixty at most. I'll send Numerus and his section outside to scout around.'

After ten minutes I couldn't bear the waiting and went upstairs. I walked up to the atrium, ignored Domitia Tella and made my way to the back of the house and out through the French windows. I stood on the flagged terrace watching the figures in combats searching amongst the trees and shrubs. At the far end, behind the tall oaks, there was no back gate entrance in the wall. It wasn't the original wall, but was built on the same line of the previous one. The tunnel had to end on the other side or the escapees would be caught. I'd have to check an old map, but I was reasonably sure that until the twelfth or even thirteenth century, there would have only been woodland at the back of Domus Tellarum, not another street of houses as now.

Where was bloody Caius? Was he hiding in the tunnel ready to murder the young soldiers?

The *optio*'s radio crackled and I heard Numerus's disembodied voice, but not his words. I stumbled after the *optio* who had broken into a run. I cursed my short, painful breathing and waved her on. As I turned the corner from the main street I saw, two-thirds of the way down the side wall, Numerus, radio in hand and a grim expression on his face. Another two guards pointed their weapons down at the pavement. Gods, had we got Caius? My heart thudded as we approached them.

Numerus looked up and put his finger to his lips. He pointed at the manhole cover with its familiar SPQRN stamp and parallel grid like two combs laid spine to spine. I heard a fluttering noise, then a deeper, rasping sound. Somebody was in the drain below the manhole. A flash of light followed by an obscenity which made the *optio* draw her head back and the others smile. They shifted their feet and relaxed their aggressive stance; they'd recognised the voice.

'That you, Sergius?' One of the guards dropped to one knee.

'Who the fuck do you think it is?' came a voice from the grille. 'Hades come to shag Proserpine? Get me out of here!'

The grille came away easily, and a grinning face emerged, followed by his shoulders and arms. He pulled himself out and sat on the edge.

'Language, young man,' Numerus said and tried to frown. But I'd seen his little smile.

'Sir?'

Numerus nodded in my direction. The poor kid, all of nineteen or twenty, opened his mouth, shut it again and swallowed. 'I apologise, *domina*,' he mumbled, his face pink.

'Relax, soldier,' I said, and laughed. 'I've heard worse, but Proserpine may have an argument with you.' I looked down the tunnel entrance. 'Where's your oppo?'

'We came to a fork in the tunnel and she took the other one.' He glanced at Numerus. 'Is she all right? I mean, I didn't want to separate, but—'

'That's enough, Sergius, we'll take it from here,' Numerus cut him off.

Numerus and I walked a few steps away leaving the young soldier to be ribbed by his comrades.

'Well, now we know how he was getting in and out, but where does the other tunnel come out?'

He pressed the rocker switch on his radio. 'Aquila One. Report.'

'Aquila Two. Nothing in the garden. Continuing to search.'

'Aquila Three. Nothing on the perimeter. Continuing to observe.'

'Aquila Zero.' Mercuria. 'Inactive here. Aquila One, RV in thirty, ground floor previous location. Out.'

Numerus looked at his watch. 'Going on Sergius's performance, we have at least another eight to ten minutes before the other one hits the surface and she's fitter than him. The outside rear perimeter is fully covered, so we'll spot any movement.'

Fifteen minutes later I was back in the underground refuge room with a worried Mercuria. Ten more minutes went by before an exhausted guard tumbled back out of the entrance in the refuge room. She lay gasping on the floor for a few moments, then sat up. Mercuria handed her a water flask.

'Report,' Mercuria said, after the guard had taken a few gulps.

'I went up the second tunnel for another ten minutes after we split up, ma'am, but it was blocked. I had to back up feet first to the fork.'

No wonder she was exhausted.

She took another gulp of water and a deep breath. When she looked up, her eyes were gleaming in her dirt-caked face. She fished into her jacket pocket and pulled out a small oblong object. Her wrist flexed as her hand dropped down with the weight.

'But I found a load of these at the end.'

# 33

'We've recovered five hundred and thirty-two ingots of one thousand grams each overnight,' Mercuria said to the briefing meeting the next morning. 'All shapes and markings, worth over two hundred thousand *solidi,* the woman from the Oversight Commission reckons. They're sending somebody in this morning to assess and document it.'

She strode over to the incident board and pointed to new photos of the silver hoard *in situ* before they started taking it away. 'It's obvious from the dirt on some of the bars that this stash has been accumulated over a period, but a hundred and forty of them were cleaner, some still wrapped in acid-free paper.' She looked round the room. 'But no clue of Caius Tellus's whereabouts. The surface end of the side tunnel has now been filled with rocks and the grille soldered closed. Domus Tellarum is closed and guarded, so he can't go back there.'

'What's happened to the old lady?'

Mercuria frowned at the guard who'd asked the question and glanced at me.

'Countess Tella has been persuaded to accept the gracious invitation issued by the imperatrix to stay at the palace for the foreseeable future,' I said in my driest voice. While she'd been uncooperative, we had no proof Tella had actively supported Caius. That was something for the lawyers to argue about.

'The *vigiles* are continuing to question people at his previous haunts and his known friends' Mercuria continued. 'They're also stepping up inspection of hotels and guest houses and even the *mansio* hostels on the roads out of the city. Our troops are assisting the *vigiles* in watching and analysing the public CCTV. We will have him.'

I wasn't surprised to see Prisca Monticola tripping in with the Oversight Commission inspector. Almost bouncing with energy and her eyes glinting with excitement, she threw me a grin.

'The Silver Guild has a significant interest in this. Besides, you may want to refer to our records.' She gestured to the young man behind her, his bony shoulders weighed down with two enormous file bags. He could only have been twenty and still had remnants of teenage acne.

Mercuria led them downstairs to the custody suite. As we walked behind her, Prisca dropped back and handed me an envelope.

'I think you'll find it interesting reading.' She gave me a smug little smile as if she'd found something we'd missed.

'Thank you, Prisca – really appreciated. The next meal's on me.'

As we went through the barred gate and it clanged shut behind us, Prisca started at the harsh metal on metal sound. She sniffed; the air was slightly stale and smelled of human sweat and cleaning fluid. When one of the guards instructed Prisca's assistant to put his bags on the security scanner belt, she stepped between them.

'Is that strictly necessary?'

'Yes, it is,' he said in a dour tone. 'And put your handbag through after the bags. Please.'

She looked at me, her eyebrows raised. I shrugged but gave her a smile of sympathy. Difficult for civilians to understand the level of physical security we needed. The bag disappeared behind the rubber flaps. The next second the alarm screeched. One guard pushed the young assistant to the wall, another trained his weapon on Monticola. The Oversight inspector froze. Mercuria strode up to Prisca, a grim look on her face. I stepped between them.

'What in Hades have you got in those bags, Prisca?' I said.

'Technical equipment.'

'Such as?'

'For testing.' She glanced at the Oversight inspector who nodded.

'We need to know if what you've found is genuine,' she said with an impatient note in her voice.

'I think you misunderstand the situation, Prisca Monticola,' Mercuria said. 'We invited the Oversight Commission inspector here as a consultant. You are here by your request as an observer and out of courtesy only. If I wish you to test anything, then I will ask you. You will submit your bags to physical search or you will be escorted outside and take no further part in the proceedings.'

Prisca stuck her chin out. As the owner of one of the largest silver extraction companies, she probably wasn't used to being denied. Her whole appearance in designer suit, pearls, sleek hair and make-up exuded an indefinable air of confidence and command. Mercuria stood there, arms crossed, legs braced, the archetypal Praetorian in beige and black, refusing to compromise.

Prisca broke first under the tense atmosphere.

Without looking at Mercuria, she opened the offending bag the scanner had regurgitated and took out a small polished wooden box with a folded scrolled metal handle in the centre of the lid. With a theatrical gesture and a sharp look in Mercuria's direction she snapped open the lid. Inside were a row of bottles of coloured liquids and a small flat stone. From a velvet drawstring bag she drew out a brick-shaped metal box about twenty-five by ten centimetres and five centimetres deep. There was a small green screen on the front face and a window with a transparent screen on the back.

'What is this?' Mercuria picked it up and twisted it around.

'A very sensitive prototype analyser used to detect metal content.' Prisca hovered close, watching Mercuria with anxious eyes. She didn't quite put her hands underneath the gadget to catch it in case Mercuria dropped it, but damn near.

'XRF?' Mercuria said. 'I thought spectrometry was still lab-based. The portable ones were considered very unreliable when I was completing my doctorate in the physics faculty. I was in pure spectroscopy, so what do I know about technological applications?' She smiled blandly at Monticola who looked uncomfortable. 'Shall we get on?'

Prisca meekly followed the inspector through the metal detector arch and along the corridor to the interview room. Inside stood three tables and half a dozen plywood and metal chairs. Silver bars had been laid out, grouped in types and shapes. Monticola's assistant glanced at the two armed guards and swallowed hard.

'We'll leave you to get on with your work,' Mercuria said. 'I'll have coffee brought to you in an hour. If you need anything, ask either of the guards.'

'She's a hard nut, your silver friend, isn't she?'

'You're not bad at dishing out the superiority yourself, Doctor Mercuria,' I said.

'Sorry, ma'am, she was beginning to irritate me.'

'That analyser was obviously precious to her. You know many civilians see us as insensitive squaddies without half a brain between us.'

Us. I was slipping back, automatically aligning myself on Mercuria's, the Praetorian, side.

She shrugged.

Sitting on the other side of her desk upstairs, I opened the flap of the envelope Monticola had handed me and found the copies of Festa's phone bills, now covered with neat annotations. On top were two pages of typescript. I read it through in silence, laid it on the desk, sat back for a few moments. I reached for Mercuria's phone.

'May I?'

She gestured with her hand, palm upwards. I pressed the red encrypt button and dialled Plico's number.

'Our fugitive made some very interesting calls while he was shacked up with Festa in Vienna. Have you got a few minutes?'

'Let me get this straight,' Plico said. 'Caius was sitting there, talking the market down but using Festa to buy in silver at the lower price when it was on a run down.'

'Yes, that's what the little ratchets up are – the anomalies. When somebody starts buying again, the quantity available is diminished and the price goes up. You know, supply and demand.'

'Yes, yes,' Plico said testily. 'I do know the basics of price elasticity, thank you.' He looked up, his face frowning. 'Can we prove any of this?'

'You'll have to ask the lawyers, but to get anywhere we'll have to request the New Austrian police to interview every one of the people Caius talked to – general press, trade press, silver factors, market makers, metal merchants and futures dealers.'

'That'll take forever.'

'Yes, and there's another problem. They're a secretive lot and will scream client confidentiality. My cousin, David, is a member of the Vienna Chamber as well as the bankers' association. I'll have a word, but don't hold your breath.'

'Keep your conversation general – I don't want to start a panic.'

I hated to think what his comments would have been about my previous disclosure to David. Probably throw me in the Transulium and swallow the key.

'And if you connect it to all that computer and telex equipment he had installed when he was at Grosschenk's in Berlin,' I said, 'he might well have started then. But the German federal cops said all the trades were legal.'

Plico threw the phone report on his desk. 'This doesn't get us any nearer finding him, though.'

'No, but the *vigiles* and Praetorians are stepping up their investigation and patrols. It may have to be a hard slog.'

'Are you happy with your own security?'

'Now the garden and park perimeter is secured, my house is an armed camp. And you won't let me go anywhere without Numerus and his troops.'

'Let's hope we catch the bastard soon. The budget won't stand it for much longer.'

Prisca and the inspector weren't expected to finish cataloguing until later that afternoon so I went to see Marina. The servants everywhere with armfuls of greenery, propping ladders against the columns and reaching up to fix gauze drapery, brought it home to me it was nearly the start of Saturnalia. Juno, I hadn't thought about presents, the household feast, theatricals, visits or games. What sort of festival would it be for us?

As I slipped into the children's day room at the palace, Aemilia looked up. She stared at me, her eyes tensing, but I gave her what I hoped was a reassuring smile. Marina, neglecting the chicken and vegetables in front of her, was cutting up the food on Julian's plate with precise determination. Her face wore a serious expression as she talked to him; she was clearly instructing him on something. He looked up at her, adoringly, taking in every word she said. The perfect older sister and younger brother. My throat clenched at the thought of what might have been. I swallowed hard to release it.

Aemilia stood and broke the moment. Marina looked up.

'Mama?'

'Hello, darling,' I bent down to kiss her and caught my breath, not only from a jab of pain from my ribs.

'Have you had another accident?' she said and pointed at my left arm still supported in a sling.

'Yes, I'm helping the Praetorians to catch a bad man and he attacked me.'

'Why? You're not a soldier now.'

Should I tell her? She wasn't even six. But how could she protect herself if she didn't know the danger?

'You remember Caius Tellus?'

She nodded, her little mouth closed into a tight line.

'He's the one we're trying to stop. He's done some very bad things.'

'If he hurt you, Mama, then I hate him.' She looked down at her plate. 'I was scared of him in the park. He made me feel hot and uncomfortable. I thought he'd gone away.'

Her voice couldn't have accused me more.

'So did I, darling. He's escaped from prison and wants to hurt us.' I stroked her hand and she looked up at me without blinking. 'You're safe here, Marina. You have to be brave and try to keep Nonna Justina cheerful. You can do that, can't you?'

Driving home through the blizzard, the soft thump-thump of the windscreen wipers and the warmth from the car heater were soporific. I closed my eyes for a few seconds. How comforting to reach home, slide into a warm bed and rest my aching body. No Caius, no silver smuggling, but no child inside me.

The scrape of wall gates opening across icy ground jolted me awake. I fought through the snow and up the steps to the door. Milo wore his usual dour expression, but gave me a half-smile when I returned his greeting. The soft light in the vestibule was welcoming, mitigating the stern look of the *imagines*. I hurried through as a cold draught had followed me in. Milo opened the double doors with a flourish. What in Hades was he up to?

I caught my breath. The atrium blazed with light. Everywhere was covered in ferns, spruce and pine. And in the centre was a large square table covered with linen, silverware, glasses and the best china. I smelt roast pork, lemons and spices. The housekeeper gave me a glass of champagne and a smile.

'Io Saturnalia!'

I blinked at the hearty shout from the household gathered around. Numerus and one other guard stood to the side. He raised his glass in my direction.

Milo led me to the table and whispered, 'I thought we'd bring it forward by a day. We all need some relief from recent events.'

Io Saturnalia, indeed.

# 34

Driving away from the Central Valetudinarium after my outpatient discharge examination five days later, my mood was sombre. Perhaps my mind was finally reacting to the loss of my baby, Caius's brutal attack and the frustration of always being two steps behind him. He'd spoiled my life whenever he'd touched it; as a child, a young soldier, a family head and mother. And he'd threatened the country's economy by attacking the silver trade. As a Foreign Ministry employee as well as a Praetorian in my heart, it was my duty to protect the state and I was failing. Would I ever be free of him?

The car crawled along the Dec Max, stopping and starting intermittently. The engine coughed and revved under the strain. Why in Hades this high street hadn't been made one-way defeated me. They could easily loop it with the parallel street taking the eastbound traffic. I rubbed the window to wipe away the condensation. People were huddled up against the still frosty late morning, youngsters with hands in their pockets, older citizens swathed in hats, deep scarves and thick gloves.

Then I saw him.

The little runt who'd followed me in Berlin. Last time I'd seen him was at the Anhalter station when I packed him off on the train to Bavaria. Now he was ambling along the Dec Max as if he were a summer tourist. Far too casually.

I almost ordered the driver to stop, but remembered I was in no fit shape to go chasing anybody.

'Give me your handset,' I said. I waited five agonising seconds waiting to be patched through.

'Plico.'

'Get a Praetorian detail out now to pick up a small man, brown hair, pinched nose, light grey coat, no hat, walking slowly west along the Dec Max. He's just passed the *macellum* north entrance.'

'Why?'

'Do it,' I hissed down the microphone. 'Please. He's one of Caius's Prussian runners, Ernst Beck.'

The interview room we used for Beck was the 'comfortable' one with two plastic covered green sofas and a chocolate box mountain print on the wall. Numerus and I watched him for a few minutes through the two-way mirror. Now with overcoat removed by the custody guards, the little man sat on the edge of one of the sofas and twitched. He picked up the glass of water, took a gulp and placed it back on the table, then repeated it every twenty seconds. He glanced around anxiously in between. Under the harsh light from the overhead twin neon lights a faint sheen of sweat reflected from his forehead just below his receding hairline.

'Okay, Numerus, do you want to soften him up for a few minutes?' I said.

'And I was looking forward to playing bad cop,' he replied, with a quick grin. He picked up the clipboard with the standard detainment form and a pen from the table and left. In the interview room, he sat at right angles to Beck, asking him standard ID questions, reasons for travel, length of stay. Incredibly, Beck was using his own name, but travelling on a Bavarian passport. Mercuria's staff had already asked the *vigiles* to fax it through to the Bavarian National Police.

Numerus asked his questions in a pleasant, soothing tone, nodding his head and smiling all the time. Gradually, Beck relaxed, his back became straighter.

'Now, *Herr* Beck,' Numerus said at his most reassuring, 'a colleague is going to ask you a few more questions and then if everything's satisfactory, you'll be on your way to enjoy the rest of your stay in Roma Nova.'

'I haven't got anything else to tell you – I'm a simple tourist. I don't understand why you've picked me up. You're military, not the police.' His tone had become petulant.

'Well, it's a routine matter of state security, and that's what we do in support of the *vigiles*.'

I chuckled to myself. The only support Numerus would want to give the *vigiles* was a crutch to walk with after he'd kicked them.

'You can't hold me – I demand a lawyer.' Beck was becoming confident, or at least showing bravado.

'I'm sure everything will be sorted out shortly, *Herr* Beck. A few more minutes should do it.'

'Well, hurry up, then.'

Numerus stretched over for Beck to sign and date the form. Beck hesitated. Numerus smiled again at him and nodded. Giving Beck a last bland smile, Numerus picked up the signed form and left the room. He reappeared in the observation room two seconds later.

'Obnoxious little git,' Numerus said almost matter of factly. 'I'm going to enjoy watching you take him apart, major.'

I'd borrowed a dark purple Praetorian civvy suit, partly to get myself into the mental framework, but mainly to look more formal than the slacks and jumper I'd arrived in on the way back from my hospital appointment. I closed the door quietly behind me.

'Hello, Ernst,' I said in Germanic. 'I didn't expect to see you again.'

His jaw dropped open, revealing his uneven yellow-stained teeth.

'Now, you remember the last time we had a little chat. Today, we're going to take it a little further.'

He squirmed on the sofa.

'What are you doing here in Roma Nova? Please don't spin me the one about being a tourist.' I bent over and looked direct into his eyes, staring at him until he looked away.

'I… I'm looking for work.'

I glanced down at the form Numerus had completed.

'Really? You've given your occupation on the immigration form as commercial agent. Do explain exactly what you do in this occupation.'

'This and that. It's confidential.'

I sighed. 'Look here, Ernst, I haven't got the time to go through the "I don't know what you mean" routine. I simply want to know what you're doing for Caius Tellus.'

He hesitated. His mistake.

'I don't know who you're talking about.'

I waved at the mirror and a minute later, two guards, one carrying a medical pack, entered the room. One walked up to Ernst and stood within millimetres of him. The little man flinched. The other sat next to me and pulled on a pair of surgical gloves. She opened a tin to reveal swabs in sealed paper packets, a bottle of pale yellow liquid, a syringe and three ampoules. She snapped the neck off one of the ampoules, the crack breaking the silence, and filled the syringe chamber. Ernst retreated as far back on the sofa as he could.

The second guard swooped down, grabbed his wrist and shoved the shirtsleeve up his arm. She clamped her other arm above his elbow and nodded at her colleague.

'Last chance, Ernst,' I said, and yawned.

He hesitated, then shook his head. More sweat broke out above his top lip and he tried to arch away from the vice-like grip on his arm.

I nodded to the medic and she swabbed his inner forearm skin, inserted the needle and pressed the plunger down slowly but firmly to the top exterior lip of the barrel. She withdrew the needle, pressed a clean swab on Ernst's skin for a few seconds then packed her kit up and waited; the other guard released Ernst's arm and withdrew to the wall. Ernst flopped back, holding his arm above the puncture site, staring at the tiny droplet of blood that was clotting.

Once the medic had done two sets of checks separated by five minutes, I looked up from the paperwork I was pretending to read.

'Well, Ernst, feeling talkative now, are you?'

'You caando thiss.'

'We just have. If you'd been more cooperative, as you were in Berlin, there would have been no need.'

'Not saying anything 'bout Tellus. Says nothing… jus' gives me orders.'

I glanced at the mirror. Numerus would be taping this as well as taking notes.

'What does he order you to do?'

Ernst Beck trembled with the effort of trying not to answer, but failed. He hunched over and talked to the floor.

'Sends me out to buy stuff.'

'What have you bought for him?'

'He kill me, or worse,' he croaked.

'He won't if what you say helps us to catch him.'

'You don' know him. Hard, a real hard bastard.'

'Believe me, Ernst, I know exactly what he is.' I softened my voice. 'Why are you working again for him?'

Beck shuddered. 'Made me. Threatened to cut me if I didn't. You know, where it hurts.' He swallowed hard. 'He looks at you weird. Like he's looking right inside you. Bloody frightenin'.'

'Tell me what you've bought for him.'

'Yesserday, he give me a list for TV workshop.' I waited. 'Bloke there gave me a bag of coils and metal bits. Wire. Said I had to carry it carefully, 'specially box of transistors.'

'And where were you going today when we picked you up?'

He glanced up at me. 'Goin' back to hostel after delivering stuff to him. Trousers 'n' shirt.'

'What sort of clothes?'

'Beige-y,' he gurgled. He pointed to the guard in her Praetorian barrack uniform. 'Like hers. Trousers 'n' shirt.'

'Anything else?'

'Black T-shirt.'

Mars' eyeballs.

'And where did you have to take them?'

'Back to his gaff.'

'Which is where?'

'Down by station.'

'Address?'

'I dunno. Via somethin'. Can't follow the weird names here. Know what it looks like.' He looked up and grasped my hand. 'Don' let him get me, will you?' His fingers pinched the skin on mine. 'Will you?'

'No, Ernst, I won't.'

He shuddered, and gave a huge sob.

One of Numerus's troops was showing Beck photos of the streets near the station. The medic had given him a vitamin shot and water. The stimulant would be out of his system within twelve hours.

I balled my hand and held it to my mouth. Using the clothes Beck had brought him, Caius could pass as a Praetorian. He had enough brass neck to carry it off. As guardians of the state, they had access to everything, everywhere. The palace was the obvious target.

'I've already alerted the palace guard to look out for a possible imposter,' Numerus said. 'Lieutenant Volusenia is on shift up there tonight.' He let a heavy breath out. 'Jupiter, she nearly bit my head off when I asked her to ensure each guard wanting access was to be verified by two others already verified.'

'Ha! She's formidable,' I replied, 'but very efficient.'

'Personally, I'd pity Caius Tellus if she caught him.'

'Enough, Numerus. Get a signal out to all the Praetorian commanders down to junior *optio* level.'

'You know those components Beck described could make a radio, or even a crude jammer?' he said.

'What unit did Caius do his national service in?' I asked. 'Please don't tell me it was signals.'

'I'd have to look in his file which will take time, but let's assume the worst.'

'The range would be very limited. He'd need a reasonable-sized battery if he was going mobile, something as big as a motorcycle one.'

'A fit man could carry that without too much difficulty,' Numerus remarked.

But we'd alerted Volusenia and she'd confirmed comms were running at full strength and clear.

Oh gods.

It hit me like a fist blow to my heart. It wasn't the palace he was targeting. Marina was coming home this afternoon to celebrate the children's Saturnalia feast with the household juniors and children of the staff. She would be escorted by Aemilia and a Praetorian driver, but once in our house, they would assume the detail there would take over security.

I grabbed the telephone handset and punched in the numbers for Domus Mitelarum on the keypad.

Unobtainable.

Pluto in Tartarus.

'Numerus! Contact the house detail, stat,' I shrieked.

He talked calmly, but in a staccato rhythm, into the transceiver in his hand.

Only the crackle of static answered.

# 35

The rotating blue dome light clamped to the top of the window frame parted the lines of cars before us as if we were slicing through jelly. Numerus drove the long wheelbase through the traffic along the Dec Max without mercy. During the frustrating moments waiting for the vehicle to be brought round, Numerus had confirmed with Volusenia that Marina, Aemilia and a Praetorian had left the palace fifteen minutes ago.

'You think he's definitely at Domus Mitelarum?' Numerus asked.

'Yes. I'm sorry, but your troops may no longer be alive.'

Thank the gods the other children weren't due there for another hour. If only I had been there when Caius had tricked his way into my house, Marina would not now be in danger. I shrank at the horror of losing a second child to Caius.

My hand trembled as I gave Numerus the keys to the back service entrance. 'Secure that area and deploy another detail on the perimeter wall. I'm going in through the front door.'

'I'll come in with you,' he said.

'Denied. If Caius is in there, and armed, all you'll do is add to the body count.' He went to say something, but I held my hand up. 'I want you to come in at the first floor level. There's a maintenance shaft, at the far corner of the domestic service yard opposite the back service gate. Take the metal hatch cover off. It's heavy, but two people can manage it reasonably quietly. Inside there's an old metal ladder.

Find Marina and get her away. That is your primary task. Leave Caius to me.'

'Lieutenant Mercuria was adamant that I shouldn't let you out of my sight.'

'Then the sooner you get up that shaft the better. You'll be able to observe from behind the first floor balustrade.'

'I'm bringing a marksman.'

'Disabling shot only, Numerus.'

'Of course.'

'I mean it. He has to stand his trial.'

Numerus didn't reply.

My hand trembled as I inserted the key in the narrow service door in the big gates at the front of Domus Mitelarum. I knew Numerus had to get into position, but I couldn't wait any longer. I took a deep breath to calm myself, but only received sore pain in reply. Juno, I was a wreck. I'd refused Numerus's offer of a service revolver. If Marina was anywhere near Caius, I couldn't risk her being caught in crossfire or by a ricochet. I'd kept it simple; a knife in a back waist holster along with a set of handcuffs. I clipped *caesti* around my hands. Unlike the ancient clumsy boxing gloves, these were chain-link mittens designed to protect your hands as well as deepen any blow.

The ice crackled beneath my feet as I crossed the courtyard. No lights in the porter's lodge where Numerus's guard team should have been. I put my shivering down to the cold; it was minus five and dropping and I was only wearing a light jacket over a jumper with slacks and soft boots. Somehow the shallow flight of steps seemed twice as high today as I trudged up them.

The front door was unlocked.

I heard nothing; no hum of machinery, no murmur of voices, no footsteps. No Milo to greet me. I walked carefully through the vestibule, drawing imaginary strength from the *imagines* of the ancestors staring blindly at me as I passed them. Behind them hung a tapestry woven after the Battle of Vienna in 1683 when a Mitela had led legions to support Sobieski defeating the invaders. The gods give me the same courage she'd had.

The atrium double doors were half open. The last of the winter light falling at an angle through the *oculus*, the glazed bull's eye in the roof, settled on the wall opposite the row of floor-to-ceiling windows. In the centre, ten metres away and directly underneath the *oculus*, and in my mother's favourite carved oak chair, sat Caius Tellus. My blood boiled to see him in the fake PGSF uniform he hadn't earned, and having invaded my home. But worse, so much worse, he held Marina on his lap.

I closed my eyes for an instant. A cold wave of despair coursed through me. Not again. Marina cried 'Mama' and struggled to climb down, her arms flailing against Caius's tight grip around her waist. He grabbed her wrist, pinioned it with the hand around her waist and slapped her face. I hurtled towards her, but he had his hand around her throat before I could get near them and was squeezing. Her sobs diminished into gurgles.

I froze.

'Let her go, you bastard.'

'I don't think so,' he said and held her throat tighter. She closed her eyes and became still.

I fell on my knees. 'Please.'

'Dear me, always the dramatic turn.'

He released Marina who slid onto the floor. She looked as if she was sleeping. She couldn't be dead. He rested his foot on her neck.

'You may stand, but one false move, Aurelia, and I'll stamp on her neck and break it. Understand?'

I nodded. My throat was parched with terror, but I refused to let him see how frightened I was. I stared at the slumped form of Marina. Pale skin, her eyelashes resting on her cheeks, immobile, a recumbent marble statue. Then I saw a slight rise of her shoulder. Then another. She was breathing. I looked up at my nemesis.

'What do you want, Caius?'

'You. You've always denied me. Since you were sixteen.'

'What! Because I refused to have sex with you at Aquileia's party?'

'You refused me again when your mother was alive. She wanted our families to be allied.'

'You should have married her, then.'

'I knew you'd need me when she was gone, but you still said no.'

'Why would I need you?'

'All women need somebody.'

I stared at him. 'What century are you living in, Caius? This is Roma *Nova.* People are independent. That includes men as well as women.'

'What are you afraid of, Aurelia?'

'Afraid?' I snorted. 'You don't get it, Caius, do you? I said no because I didn't like you. I wasn't attracted to you. I despised the way you lived your life. And I haven't changed my mind since. Is that enough for you?'

'You will consent, for your daughter's sake.'

'You can only kill her once.' Gravel ground in my stomach at the thought, but I had to stand up to him.

'Oh, I wouldn't kill her. I'd change her, corrupt her and put such a distance between you, you'd never bridge it. And you'll be watching day by day, powerless to do anything about it.'

A sharp stab of pain ran through my chest.

'You won't be able to – you'll be locked up in a Prussian prison while she's growing up. She'll be safe.'

He laughed. 'Please credit me with some intelligence. I have no more intention of rotting in the northern wastes of Germania than of becoming that old bag Justina's lover.'

'How dare you speak of her like that!'

'Touched a nerve, eh? On second thoughts, maybe I'll cosy up to her daughter Severina. She'll do as I say and give me a full pardon for anything I do. I might even contract marriage with her if she asks nicely.'

Juno, he could do it as well. He had the good looks and film star charm that Severina would fall for. He'd keep her pregnant and compliant while he pursued power for himself. And the country would go to the wolves.

'Tellus and Apulius have been allied since the founding,' he continued.

'Tella and Apulia,' I snapped back.

'Don't give me that feminist crap.' He pressed his foot down on Marina's thin neck. I swallowed my retort.

We stayed like that for several minutes, he lounging in my mother's chair, me standing, petrified to make a move.

'You forget who I am, Aurelia. You might technically be senior, but once you and your pathetic little daughter are gone, Tellus will take over as senior of the Twelve Families.'

He was going to kill us.

'No, it won't happen,' I replied. 'You're a convicted criminal, and a murderer. You killed Grosschenk and you'll get sent down for that as well as the smuggling. Whatever happens to us, you'll be sent back to the Prussians.' I'd had enough of this. I drew myself up. 'You've got it completely wrong, Caius. The Twelve Families are the servants of the state and the imperatrix, not their exploiters. There are plenty of Mitelae to take over and serve Roma Nova. One of them is married to Severina, if you remember. You're finished.'

He sighed. 'You are so remarkably stubborn, Aurelia. If you'd contracted with me, I would have made sure you wouldn't run around causing me such trouble. You've sabotaged my business career—'

'Your smuggling career and attempt to wreck the Roma Novan economy!'

'How you exaggerate. Merely a demonstration of my indispensable talents. You're blocking my social and political prospects and you won't even acknowledge how attracted you are to me. What a little hypocrite you are.'

If I opened my mouth I'd be sick. I swallowed the sourness down and took a deep breath. He sat back and smiled. A smug smile.

'What happens now?' I said.

'You watch me leave with your little girl. If you try to stop me, I'll snap her neck in front of you.'

'Don't do this, Caius. She's a fragile child. Leave her. Your quarrel's with me. I'll be your hostage.'

'Certainly not. You'll be far more compliant if you think I'll hurt your little princess.'

The gods knew that was true. And he was going to walk out with her, right in front of me.

# 36

I had to delay him, so my brain could think what to do next. 'What have you done with my people and Marina's nursemaid?' I babbled.

'They're all cosy in the basement. The two Praetorians, too. They're unconscious, of course. That old retainer of yours is a tough nut, I'll grant you.' He stood, stepped back and grabbed the top of the carved chair. In the changed light, I saw a large bruise blooming on his face, and also the revolver at his waist. 'But a gun usually makes even people like that see reason.'

Gods, he'd held Marina on his lap with a loaded revolver inches from her.

'Please don't try any heroics, Aurelia. You'd never forgive yourself if you caused your only child's death.'

'I can't let you walk out of here.' I took a step forward. He planted his foot on Marina's neck, pushing her head back with the toe of his boot so her mouth fell open. She stirred, but didn't wake. As he raised his foot, he didn't flex it, but the raised trouser hem exposed strapping round his ankle. And his boot was tied at its widest.

I dropped my head and let my shoulders slump as if submitting in defeat. But I watched him through my eyelashes. He was standing straight and confident but his skin was pale with a sheen of sweat covering his forehead, nose and upper lip. If I approached him in a curved run, I might just be able to able to push him away from Marina. If his reflexes were dulled by the pain in his foot and the awkward bandage, I'd gain another second. But if I misjudged it, either his foot, or mine, could break Marina's jaw or kick her head in.

Caius drew the revolver out of his waistband with his right hand and pointed it in my direction.

Hades.

Watching me, he bent down to scoop Marina up with his other hand. He faltered, unable to balance properly with his injured foot, and the barrel tilted upwards.

In that second, I launched myself at him. My legs pumping, I covered the ten-metre arc in three seconds. I dipped, then jabbed my right elbow upward into his stomach, following through, slamming my whole body weight behind the movement. His feet left the ground clear of Marina's body as he flipped backwards and landed on his back.

The gun skittered across the floor. Before he could recover his wind, I kicked his injured foot. He screamed, but I felt no remorse as I watched him writhing in agony. I heaved him over onto his front, face down and dropped hard onto his lower spine. While he was still catching his breath, I seized his left wrist, grabbed the handcuffs from the back of my belt and snapped them on both his wrists.

He grunted, and strained to lift his foot off the floor. I knelt back, allowing him to turn over. He struggled up to a sitting position. His eyes boiled like molten onyx.

'You cow,' he gasped. 'I'll have you and when I do, you'll wish I killed you and your feeble child tonight.'

He spat in my face.

I wiped it deliberately with my sleeve then smacked him hard in the mouth. The *caestus* ripped his lips open and broke at least two teeth.

'That's the last time you spit at me or mine, Caius Tellus,' I shouted in his face and raised my fist to smash him again, but it was caught in a vice-like grip in mid-air.

'We'll take over now, major.'

Numerus.

As they led Caius away, I watched, but felt absolutely nothing inside. Then I gathered my child up in my arms and held her to me and bent down and kissed her hair.

• • •

'She'll sleep for a good twelve hours,' the doctor said, and tucked Marina's hand back under the sheet. She was in her soft bed, in her lemon yellow room, her stuffed toy wolf cub peeping out of the sheet fold beside her. Aemilia, now freed from the basement and sitting by Marina's bed, glanced up at me. I smiled at her, but she didn't look reassured.

'I'm sorry you've had a rough time, Aemilia,' I said, 'but everything should be a lot calmer now. I hope you'll stay with us – Marina is very fond of you.'

'Oh, yes, *domina,* I want to stay with her. Thank you. She needs me.'

Having been put firmly in my place by the young servant, I bent over and kissed Marina's forehead, then left.

I let the doctor check me for any further damage, and was relieved he found nothing more than bruising on my right shoulder from the impact with Caius. I peeled off the rest of my clothes, showered and took the painkillers he'd prescribed. Lying in my bed seemed so normal but my mind was numb while my body trembled with delayed reaction. After five minutes, I drifted off, but felt the dribble of tears running from the corners of my eyes down the sides of my face.

'He's on his way back to Berlin, manacled and under guard,' Plico said two days later. We were sitting in his scruffy office. 'The cheeky bastard's filed a complaint of brutality against you. I suppose you had to kick him to pacify him.' He glanced up from the file.

'No, I did it because I wanted him to experience intense pain.'

'Are you being sarcastic?'

'Take it as you want.'

'Well, Caius Tellus won't be bothering us for quite a while.' He closed the dark red file and tied the binder string. 'Do you have any thoughts about what job you want next? I think a nice restful posting might suit you.'

'Restful like Berlin or Vienna?'

'Very funny. Speaking of Vienna, that banker woman, Festa, has been chucked out of the Argentaria Prima, but she's been sentenced to community work with a charity as a financial manager. Waste not, want not, and all that.'

'Ha! She'll have it in profit within months.'

'Now, how would London as political officer suit you? It would start in May. Good schools there as well for Marina.'

Marina and I returned from the farm in the third week of February, rested and healed. I hadn't done anything special for my birthday earlier in the month; I was content to be in the quiet countryside with my daughter. Milo greeted us and early spring sunshine flooded the atrium through the tall windows. The roses I'd planted last year in the atrium garden were starting to break leaf.

At the end of the nine days of the Parentalia, the week of honouring the dead, we drove out to the Mitela family tombs and took offerings of flower garlands, wheat, salt, wine-soaked bread and violets to honour our ancestors. I smiled at and greeted cousins and hangers-on, all of whom would be keen to come back to the house for the free Caristia banquet, but I didn't mind.

I'd laid my formal flowers for my mother, then a tiny bunch of violets and primulae for my lost baby. Holding Marina's hand, and watching the priest go about her ceremonies, I bent down and whispered, 'Do you remember Nonna Felicia, how she was poorly after her accident?'

Marina screwed her face up. 'Sort of. She had a funny smile, all crooked, but she liked the drawings I did for her.'

'Would you like to put your snowdrops in the niche in front of her plaque?'

She nodded, and ignoring all the cousins, she trotted over to the carving of my mother and laid her flowers on the tiny shelf. She looked at the portrait with its sad eyes, wiped her own eyes once and ran back to my arms.

I'd finished my English refresher course and briefing for my new post and was enjoying a quiet round of social visits and tying up household details with Milo. I emphasised a lighter touch with the household during this absence. I wasn't entirely sure he'd comply, though.

One afternoon a week before I was due to depart, I was surprised he brought me my afternoon tea himself. When he placed the tray on the low table, I saw there was an envelope with a Foreign Ministry logo and Plico's personal seal, plus a long, slim cardboard box.

I opened the envelope first. A visiting order for Berlin. The Prussian judiciary had expedited Caius's trial and he'd been convicted as expected. Disappointingly, his sentences for smuggling, Grosschenk's murder and his attempted murder of me in Berlin would run concurrently. I didn't particularly want to gloat, but I hadn't seen them take Caius back to prison. I wanted to see him there, contained, securely locked up, unable to touch us.

Then I picked up the box. It was overprinted with *Blumenversand* and stamped with a Prussian postmark. Inside was a single red rose and a small envelope. The card inside read: 'I'm back in Berlin. Please come to me. M.'

I stared at the rose. Did I want to see him? Wasn't that part of my life closed? Warmth crept up my throat into my face at the memory of his long, tanned fingers on my body, at his warm, eyes and—.

The card fluttered from my fingers.

Galba, the lawyer, met me at Berlin-Tempelhof the next evening. Efficient and elegant as usual, she nevertheless gave me a broad smile of genuine pleasure to see me.

'When Secretary Plico advised me you were coming, I dropped everything else. The appointment is made. We go first thing tomorrow morning. It should only last about thirty minutes.' She glanced at me, her eyes betraying deep curiosity. 'As per your instructions,' she continued, 'your flight back to Roma Nova has been booked for three days' time.'

I said nothing in reply, just smiled.

In the morning, Galba had a legation car and driver take us to the stark nineteenth-century building. Originally built as a military barracks, it now housed the men's maximum security prison and work camp. Galba fiddled in her leather briefcase.

'I have to deliver the extradition order to the prison governor. He'll hold it until the day Caius Tellus finishes his sentence.'

I shivered as the heavy door slammed behind us. The guards' faces were stripped of any expression, but they tracked our every movement as we went through security. They searched our bags and coats as well as patting us both down.

We entered a small room with a grille that straddled a long continuous table running the whole width of the room and reached up to the ceiling. A guard stood by the door on our side. Galba and I sat down on the two orange moulded plastic chairs and waited.

Caius, supported by a guard, entered through a door on the other side of the grille. He limped and his lips were puckered and chin scarred from when I'd hit him with the *caestus*.

He took one look at me and spat on the floor. The guard shoved him down on the plastic chair opposite us. Caius stared at me with an intensity stemming only from hatred. He didn't blink once.

Neither did I.

Galba squirmed in her seat. She outlined details of the annual consular visit and read out the extradition order. She asked Caius if he'd heard and understood everything she'd said. He ignored her.

He and I stared each other out for a few more minutes. As far as both of us were concerned, we were the only ones in that dismal room.

Galba coughed, then rose, scraping her chair. I stood up slowly, still holding Caius's gaze. When the lawyer coughed again, I turned my back to Caius, nodded to the guard and stepped towards the door.

'You know I'll come after you, Aurelia,' Caius called out. 'You've dumped me here, but I'm going to spend the next fifteen years working out exactly how I'm going to tear you apart. No, I think I'll start with Marina. You can watch.'

It took every gram of my strength to hold myself together. I turned around and marched back to the grille. He stood and grasped the grille with both hands so his fingers poked through.

'You can try, Caius. But you know I'll be ready for you. If you touch anybody nearly or remotely connected with me, I'll destroy you.'

In the corridor outside, I put my hand out and touched the wall. I took several deep breaths before I walked on.

Galba glanced at me. Her assured air had vanished. 'Juno, Countess, he really hates you.'

'No, what Caius hates is that I stand in his way. He hungers and thirsts after power. He wants to control people's lives and doesn't care what or who he breaks on the way. Don't get me wrong, he's not stupid or lazy. Our biggest problem will be when the Prussians let him out and he lands back in Roma Nova in fifteen years' time.'

Outside the prison, I shook my head to dispel the negativity. The sharp air contained a hint of spring freshness and I took several breaths.

A saloon car drew up and a young man stepped out and handed me the keys and a wallet of papers. I turned to Galba and smiled.

'Can you give this man a lift back to the city?'

She frowned for a brief moment. 'Will you come back to the legation before you return to Roma Nova?'

'Of course.'

I waited until the legation car had disappeared and the dust from its tyres had settled. Turning my back on the prison, I started the hire car and drove towards the east of Berlin. I turned off the Frankfurter Chaussee down a minor road, then a narrow unmade track through the trees. In the farmyard, I cut the engine, but this time I didn't need to look round. He was sitting there on a wooden bench, reading a book, utterly relaxed. His dark curly hair fell forward almost over his eyes. He looked up, smiled a lazy smile, laid the book down and walked towards the car. I was out already, meeting him halfway. He stretched out his hand, took mine and raised it to his lips.

***

*You can read the terrifying events that unfold when Caius Tellus returns to Roma Nova twelve years later…*
*INSURRECTIO*

# WOULD YOU LEAVE A REVIEW?

I hope you enjoyed AURELIA and its adventures and passions.

If you did, I'd really appreciate it if you would write a few words of review on the site where you purchased this book.

Reviews help AURELIA feature more prominently on retailer sites and let more people into the world of Roma Nova.

Very many thanks!

# HISTORICAL NOTE

What if Julius Caesar had taken notice of the warning that assassins wanted to murder him on the Ides of March? Suppose Elizabeth I had married and had children? If plague hadn't rampaged through Europe in the $14^{th}$ century? Or if Christianity had remained a Middle Eastern minor cult?

Alternative history stories, which allow us to explore the 'what if', are underpinned by three things: the point of divergence when the alternate timeline split from our timeline; how that world looks and works; and how things changed after the split.

While the whole idea of a society with Roman values surviving fifteen centuries is intriguing, I have dropped background history about Roma Nova into AURELIA only where it impacts on the story. Nobody likes a straight history lesson in the middle of a thriller! But if you are interested in finding more about the mysterious Roma Nova, read on...

**What happened in our timeline**

Of course, our timeline may turn out to be somebody else's alternative one as shown in Philip K Dick's *The Grasshopper Lies Heavy*, the story within the story in *The Man in the High Castle.* Nothing is fixed. But for the sake of convenience I will take ours as the default.

The Western Roman Empire didn't 'fall' in a cataclysmic event as often portrayed in film and television; it localised and eventually dissolved like chain mail fragmenting into separate links, giving way to rump provinces, local city states and petty kingdoms. The Eastern Roman Empire survived until the Fall of Constantinople in 1453 to the Muslim Ottoman Empire.

Some scholars think that Christianity fatally weakened the traditional Roman way of life and was a significant factor in the collapse. Emperor Constantine's personal conversion to Christianity in AD 313 was a turning point for the new religion.

By AD 394, his several times successor, Theodosius, banned all traditional Roman religious practice, closed and destroyed temples and dismissed all priests. The sacred flame that had burned for over a thousand years in the College of Vestals was extinguished and the Vestal Virgins expelled. The Altar of Victory, said to guard the fortune of Rome, was hauled away from the Senate building and disappeared from history.

The Roman senatorial families pleaded for religious tolerance, but Theodosius made any pagan practice, even dropping a pinch of incense on a family altar in a private home, into a capital offence. And his 'religious police' driven by the austere and ambitious bishop Ambrosius of Milan, became increasingly active in pursuing pagans...

**The alternate Roma Nova timeline**

In AD 395, three months after Theodosius's final decree banning all pagan religious activity, over four hundred Romans loyal to the old gods, and so in danger of execution, trekked north out of Italy to a semi-mountainous area similar to modern Slovenia. Led by Senator Apulius at the head of twelve prominent families, they established a colony based initially on land owned by Apulius's Celtic father-in-law. By purchase, alliance and conquest, this grew into Roma Nova.

Norman Davies in *Vanished Kingdoms: The History of Half-Forgotten Europe* reminds us that:

> *...in order to survive, newborn states need to possess a set of viable internal organs, including a functioning executive, a defence force, a*

*revenue system and a diplomatic force. If they possess none of these things, they lack the means to sustain an autonomous existence and they perish before they can breathe and flourish.*

I would add history, willpower and adaptability as essential factors. Roma Nova survived by changing its social structure; as men constantly fought to defend the new colony, women took over the social, political and economic roles, weaving new power and influence networks based on family structures. Eventually, given the unstable, dangerous times in Roma Nova's first few hundred years, daughters as well as sons had to put on armour and carry weapons to defend their homeland and their way of life. Fighting danger side by side with brothers and fathers reinforced women's roles.

The Roma Novans never allowed the incursion of monotheistic, paternalistic religions; they'd learnt that lesson from old Rome. Service to the state was valued higher than personal advantage, echoing Roman Republican virtues, and the women heading the families guarded and enhanced these values to provide a core philosophy throughout the centuries. Inheritance passed from these powerful women to their daughters and granddaughters.

**And more modern times?**

Roma Nova's continued existence has been favoured by three factors: the discovery and exploitation of high-grade silver in their mountains, their efficient technology, and their robust response to any threat. Under pressure from the Eastern Romans, they sent an envoy to stop the Norman invasion of England. Remembering the Fall of Constantinople, Roma Novan troops assisted the western nations at the Battle of Vienna in 1683 to halt the Ottoman advance into Europe. Nearly two hundred years later, they used their diplomatic skills to forge an alliance to push Napoleon IV back across the Rhine as he attempted to expand his grandfather's empire.

Prioritising survival, Roma Nova remained neutral in the Great War of the 20th century which lasted from 1925 to 1935. The Greater German Empire, stretching from Jutland in the north, Alsace in the west, Tyrol in the south and Bulgaria in the east, was broken up afterwards into its former small kingdoms, duchies and counties. Some became republics. There was no sign of an Austrian-born corporal with a short, square moustache.

AURELIA goes back to the late 1960s – a time of social change in the Roma Novan world as well as in our time line. The small but tough country of Roma Nova has endured since the break-up of the Roman Empire but a malignant criminal is determined to stop its life-blood – silver.

This book begins the second Roma Nova trilogy and tells the story of the young Aurelia Mitela, the grandmother of Carina, the heroine of the first three Roma Nova thrillers.

https://alison-morton.com

## THE ROMA NOVA THRILLER SERIES

*The Carina Mitela adventures*

### INCEPTIO

Early 21st century. Terrified after a kidnap attempt, New Yorker Karen Brown, has a harsh choice – being terminated by government enforcer Renschman or fleeing to Roma Nova, her dead mother's homeland in Europe. Founded sixteen hundred years ago by Roman exiles and ruled by women, it gives Karen safety, at a price. But Renschman follows and sets a trap she has no option but to enter.

### CARINA – *A novella*

Carina Mitela is still an inexperienced officer in the Praetorian Guard Special Forces of Roma Nova. Disgraced for a disciplinary offence, she is sent out of everybody's way to bring back a traitor from the Republic of Quebec. But when she discovers a conspiracy reaching into the highest levels of Roma Nova, what price is personal danger against fulfilling the mission?

### PERFIDITAS

Falsely accused of conspiracy, 21st century Praetorian Carina Mitela flees into the criminal underworld. Hunted by the security services and traitors alike, she struggles to save her beloved Roma Nova as well as her own life.

But the ultimate betrayal is waiting for her…

### SUCCESSIO

21st century Praetorian Carina Mitela's attempt to resolve a past family indiscretion is spiralling into a nightmare. Convinced her beloved husband has deserted her, and with her enemy holding a gun to the imperial heir's head, Carina has to make the hardest decision of her life.

*The Aurelia Mitela adventures*

### AURELIA

Late 1960s. Sent to Berlin to investigate silver smuggling, former Praetorian Aurelia Mitela barely escapes a near-lethal trap. Her old enemy is at the heart of all her troubles and she pursues him back home to Roma Nova but he strikes at her most vulnerable point – her young daughter.

## INSURRECTIO

Early 1980s. Caius Tellus, the charismatic leader of a rising nationalist movement, threatens to destroy Roma Nova.

Aurelia Mitela, ex-Praetorian and imperial councillor, attempts to counter the growing fear and instability. But it may be too late to save Roma Nova from meltdown and herself from destruction by her lifelong enemy....

## RETALIO

Early 1980s Vienna. Aurelia Mitela chafes at her enforced exile. She barely escaped from a near fatal shooting by her nemesis, Caius Tellus, who grabbed power in Roma Nova.

Aurelia is determined to liberate her homeland. But Caius's manipulations have ensured that she is ostracised by her fellow exiles. Powerless and vulnerable, Aurelia fears she will never see Roma Nova again.

---

## ROMA NOVA EXTRA

*A collection of short stories*

*Four historical and four present day and a little beyond*

A young tribune sent to a backwater in 370 AD for practising the wrong religion, his lonely sixty-fifth descendant labours in the 1980s to reconstruct her country. A Roma Novan imperial councillor attempting to stop the Norman invasion of England in 1066, her 21st century Praetorian descendant flounders as she searches for her own happiness.

Some are love stories, some are lessons learned, some resolve tensions and unrealistic visions, some are plain adventures, but above all, they are stories of people in dilemmas and conflict, and their courage and effort to resolve them.

Printed in Great Britain
by Amazon